THE EGYPTIAN CROSS
MYSTERY

ELLERY QUEEN was a pen name created and shared by two cousins, Frederic Dannay (1905-1982) and Manfred B. Lee (1905-1971), as well as the name of their most famous detective. Born in Brooklyn, they spent forty two years writing the greatest puzzle mysteries of their time, gaining the duo a reputation as the foremost American authors of the Golden Age "fair play" mystery.

Besides co-writing the Queen novels, Dannay founded *Ellery Queen's Mystery Magazine*, one of the most influential crime publications of all time. Although Dannay outlived his cousin by nine years, he retired the fictional Queen upon Lee's death.

OTTO PENZLER, the creator of American Mystery Classics, is also the founder of the Mysterious Press (1975), a literary crime imprint; MysteriousPress.com (2011), an electronic-book publishing company; and New York City's Mysterious Bookshop (1979). He has won a Raven, the Ellery Queen Award, two Edgars (for the *Encyclopedia of Mystery and Detection*, 1977, and *The Lineup*, 2010), and lifetime achievement awards from NoirCon and *The Strand Magazine*. He has edited more than 70 anthologies and written extensively about mystery fiction.

THE EGYPTIAN CROSS MYSTERY

ELLERY
QUEEN

Introduction by
OTTO
PENZLER

AMERICAN
MYSTERY
CLASSICS

Penzler Publishers
·*New York*

Published in 2020 by Penzler Publishers
58 Warren Street, New York, NY 10007
penzlerpublishers.com

Distributed by W. W. Norton.

Cover image: Andy Ross
Cover design: Mauricio Diaz

Paperback ISBN 978-1-61316-178-4
Hardcover ISBN 978-1-61316-177-7
eBook ISBN 978-1-45328-938-9

Library of Congress Control Number: 2020915160

Printed in the United States of America.

9 8 7 6 5 4 3 2 1

INTRODUCTION

OFTEN CALLED the Golden Age of the detective novel, the years between the two World Wars produced some of the most iconic names in the history of mystery. In England, the names Agatha Christie and Dorothy L. Sayers continue to resonate to the present day. In America, there is one name that towers above the rest, and that is Ellery Queen.

That famous name was the brainchild of two Brooklyn-born cousins, Frederic Dannay (born Daniel Nathan, he changed his name to Frederic as a tribute to Chopin, with Dannay merely a combination of the first two syllables of his birth name) and Manfred B. Lee (born Manford Lepofsky). They wanted a simple nom de plume and had the brilliant stroke of inspiration to employ Ellery Queen as both their byline and as the name of their protagonist, reckoning that readers might forget one or the other but not both.

Dannay was a copywriter and art director for an advertising agency while Lee was writing publicity and advertising material for a motion picture company when they were attracted by a $7,500 prize offered by *McClure's* magazine in 1928; they were twenty-three years old.

They were informed that their submission, *The Roman Hat Mystery*, had won the contest but, before the book could be published or the prize money handed over, *McClure's* went bankrupt. Its assets were assumed by *Smart Set* magazine, which gave the prize to a different novel that it thought would have greater appeal to women. Frederick A. Stokes decided to publish *The Roman Hat Mystery* anyway, thus beginning one of the most successful mystery series in the history of the genre. Since the contest had required that books be submitted under pseudonyms, the simple but memorable Ellery Queen name, born out of necessity, became an icon.

The success of the novels got them Hollywood offers and they went to write for Columbia, Paramount, and MGM, though they never received any screen credits. The popular medium of radio also called to them and they wrote all the scripts for the successful *Ellery Queen* radio series for nine years from 1939 to 1948. In an innovative approach, they interrupted the narration so that Ellery could ask his guests—well-known personalities—to solve the case as they now had all the necessary clues. The theories almost invariably in vain, the program would then proceed, revealing the correct solution. The Queen character was also translated into a comic strip character and several television series starring Richard Hart, Lee Bowman, Hugh Marlowe, George Nader, Lee Philips, and, finally, Jim Hutton.

While Lee had no particular affection for mystery fiction, always hoping to become the Shakespeare of the twentieth century, Dannay had been interested in detective stories since his boyhood. He wanted to produce a magazine of quality mystery stories in all sub-genres and founded *Mystery* in 1933 but it failed after four issues when the publisher went bankrupt. However, after Dannay's long convalescence from a 1940 automobile accident that nearly took his life, he created *Ellery Queen's Mystery Magazine*; the first issue appeared in 1941 and remains the leading mystery fiction magazine in the world to the present day.

Although Dannay and Lee were lifelong collaborators on their novels and short stories, they had very different personalities and frequently disagreed, often vehemently, in what Lee once described as "a marriage made in hell." Dannay was a quiet, scholarly introvert, noted as a perfectionist. Lee was impulsive and assertive, given to explosiveness and earthy language. They remained steadfast in their refusal to divulge their working methodology, claiming that over their many years together they had tried every possible combination of their skills and talent to produce the best work they could. However, upon close examination of their letters and conversations with their friends and family, it eventually became clear that, in almost all instances, it was Dannay who created the extraordinary plots and Lee who brought them to life.

Each resented the other's ability, with Dannay once writing that he was aware that Lee regarded him as nothing more than "a clever contriver." Dannay's ingenious plots, fiendishly detailed with strict adherence to the notion of playing fair with readers, remain unrivalled by any mystery American author. Yet he did not have the literary skill to make characters plausible, settings visual, or dialogue resonant. Lee, on the other hand, with his dreams of writing important fiction, had no ability to invent stories, although he could improve his cousin's creations to make the characters come to life and the plots suspenseful and compelling.

The combined skills of the collaborators produced the memorable Ellery Queen figure, though in the early books he was clearly based on the best-selling Philo Vance character created by S.S. Van Dine. The Vance books had taken the country by storm in the 1920s so it was no great leap of imagination for Dannay and Lee to model their detective after him. In all candor, both Vance and the early Queen character were insufferable, showing off their supercilious attitude and pedantry at every possible opportunity.

When Queen made his debut in *The Roman Hat Mystery*, he was ostensibly an author but spends precious little time working at his career. He appears to have unlimited time to collect books and help his father, Inspector Richard Queen, solve cases. Although close to his father, the arrogant young man is often condescending to him as he loves to show off his erudition. As the series progresses (and as the appetite for Philo Vance diminished), Ellery becomes a far more realistic and likable character.

One characteristic of the Queen novels is an opening situation in which a murder is committed that appears so confounding that it may be insoluble. If it weren't, the police would handle it and not have to bring Ellery Queen to the scene to help them figure out what happened, how it was achieved, and who did it.

While one of the defining hallmarks of Golden Age detective stories is that they be cerebral rather than violent, *The Egyptian Cross Mystery* has more violent corpses than most traditional mysteries, and certainly the most of any Queen novel, of the era.

The crime that brings Ellery and his father Richard Queen to the village of Arroyo was the Christmas morning discovery of the body of Andrew Van, a reclusive schoolteacher, who was beheaded, crucified, and nailed to a signpost.

At the inquest, suspicion, not surprisingly, has fallen on Velja Krosac, a foreigner with a heavy limp who had been searching for Van's house on Christmas Eve and then disappeared.

Neither the police nor the Queens solved the murder but after six months pass, another body, this one belonging to a devotee of the game of checkers, turns up—also beheaded and tied to a totem pole. The man who had a limping foreigner as an employee in Arroyo happens to be running a nudist colony in the same neighborhood as the second victim.

This time, Ellery Queen will not be thwarted. Clues to the solution of the mystery include a red checker, the remnants of a checkers game, a pipe filled with the wrong tobacco, and a missing rug. Ellery will be making deductions from these clues—the same clues shown to the careful reader who is challenged to come up with a rational explanation for motivation behind the bloodbath.

"Ellery Queen *is* the American detective story," as Anthony Boucher, the mystery reviewer for the *New York Times*, wrote, and it would be impossible for any reasonable person to disagree.

The tantalizing puzzles created by the Ellery Queen writing team are irresistible to anyone who enjoys fair-play detective stories, no matter how outre or impossible they may seem. We selected *The Chinese Orange Mystery* for the American Mystery Classics series because it features one of the most extraordinary scenes in the history of mystery fiction, followed it with *The Dutch Shoe Mystery*, which some readers have called his masterpiece of observation and deduction, then with *The Siamese Twin Mystery* and its Queen trademark of the dying clue, and now with *The Egyptian Cross Mystery*.

We are confident that you will agree that these have been the right choices—although there still are other Queen novels tempting us. After you have read one or two, you will understand why the London *Times* wrote that "Ellery Queen is the logical successor to Sherlock Holmes."

The American Mystery Classics series plans to bring back into print the greatest authors and books of the Golden Age of the detective novel. Please look at the back of the book to see other distinguished crime novels.

—OTTO PENZLER

CAST OF CHARACTERS

Ellery Queen—The cosmopolitan, pince-nezed special investigator knew his logic could solve anything, but he had trouble making sense out of T squares

Andrew Van—The withdrawn, correct schoolmaster lived a quiet life in Arroyo, hiding more from the town than his money-stuffed mattress

Ol' Pete—The slightly daffy, rag-clad hillman lived behind barbed wire because he liked privacy, but his primed shotgun guarded something else

Harakht—The shaggy-bearded Healer of the Weak led a flock of naked disciples to salvation and kept solvent by selling "elixir of youth"—a possibly lethal brew

Velja Krosac—The "furrin'-looking" vendettist was the No. 1 suspect. The limping man appeared at every murder scene

Professor Yardley—Ellery's old prof joined a country-wide search that led him far from the Halls of Ivy and had him learning lessons from his famous student

Margaret Brad—The well-cushioned but handsome matron couldn't offer any information about her husband—she was more concerned about her future than his past

Helene Brad—Margaret's lovely daughter kept a suitor on land and another at sea, then both came running without an S.O.S.

Jonah Lincoln—The lean, levelheaded New Englander had one eye on Helene and the other on money. He might have won both, but his employers lost their heads

Paul Romaine—The tanned, well-muscled Adonis had a string of women, but the police were more interested in his male associates

Hester Lincoln—Jonah's plain-faced sister with a not-so-plain body left her clothes trailing from Bradwood to the Island nudist colony, but she was conventional about one thing—murder

Victor Temple—The retired army doctor pursued his lady-love during the day and eavesdropped under open windows at night

Stephen Megara—The globe-trotting yachtsman hesitated to reveal his past—it could only shorten his future

FOREWORD

THERE IS ONE MINOR mystery connected with the various major mysteries of *The Egyptian Cross Mystery* and that is a puzzle which has little, if anything, to do with the story itself. It might properly be called "the mystery of a title." It was brought to my attention by the author himself—my friend, Ellery Queen—in a note appended to the manuscript, which he had sent on from his little place in Italy after urgent solicitations by cable from his very devoted servant.

The note said, among other things: "Give 'em hell, J. J. This *isn't* the usual claptrap on *le crime égyptologique*. No pyramids, no Coptic daggers in the midnight dark of a creepy museum, no *fellahin*, no Oriental pooh-bah of any sort . . . in fact, no Egyptology. Why, then, *The Egyptian Cross Mystery*, you ask? With, I admit, justification. Well, the title is provocative, for one thing; it positively magnetizes me. But if there's no Egyptian significance! Ah, there's the beauty of it. Wait and see."

Typical Elleryana, observe; which, as Ellery's readers are apt to know, are always interesting and often cryptic.

The investigation of these appalling murders was one of my friend's last jobs. It is the fifth Ellery Queen case to be presented to the public in fiction form. It is composed of extraordinary elements: a peculiar and unbelievable concoction of ancient religious fanaticisms, a nudist colony, a seafarer, a vendettist from the hotbed of Central European superstition and violence, an oddly mad "reincarnated god" of Pharaonic Egypt . . . on the surface a potpourri of impossible and fantastic ingredients; in actuality the background of one of the most cunning and horrible series of crimes in modern police annals.

If you are disappointed at the absence of that rare old codger of a manhunter, Inspector Richard Queen—I always insist that Ellery doesn't half do his father justice—let me reassure you. He will be back. In *The Egyptian Cross Mystery*, however, Ellery played a peculiarly lone hand, due to certain geographical ramifications of the case. I was tempted to request the publisher to recommend an atlas as supplementary reading to this novel, or to issue as the frontispiece a map of the United States. It began in West Virginia. . . .

But there I go. After all, this is Ellery's story. Let him tell it.

J. J. McC.

RYE, N.Y.
August, 1932

PART ONE

Crucifixion of a Schoolmaster

"A working knowledge of psychiatry has been of invaluable assistance to me in my profession of criminology."

—JEAN TURCOT

Chapter One
CHRISTMAS IN ARROYO

It began in West Virginia, at the junction of two roads half a mile out of the little village of Arroyo. One was the main road from New Cumberland to Pughtown, the other a branch leading to Arroyo.

The geography, Ellery Queen saw at once, was important. He saw many other things in that first glance, too, and felt only confusion at the contradictory nature of the evidence. Nothing matched. It was necessary to stand off and think.

How Ellery Queen, a cosmopolite, happened to be standing beside a battered old Duesenberg racing car in the muddy cold of the West Virginia panhandle at two o'clock *post meridiem* of a late December day requires explanation. So many factors contrived to bring about this extraordinary phenomenon! One—the primary one—was a busman's holiday instigated by Inspector Queen, Ellery's father. The old man was knee-deep in what might be termed a policemen's convention; affairs in Chicago as usual were wretched, and the Commissioner had invited prominent police officials from major cities to lament with him the deplorable lawlessness in his bailiwick.

It was while the Inspector, in rare fettle, was scurrying from his hotel to Chicago's police headquarters that Ellery, who had accompanied him, learned of the puzzling crime near Arroyo—a crime which the United Press piquantly dubbed "The T Murder." There were so many elements of the newspaper accounts which titillated Ellery—the fact, for example, that Andrew Van had been beheaded and crucified on Christmas morning!—that he peremptorily yanked his father from the smoky Chicago conferences and headed the Duesenberg—a second-hand relic capable of incredible speed—eastwards.

The Inspector, although a dutiful father, immediately surrendered his good humor, as might have been expected; and all the way from Chicago—through Toledo, through Sandusky, through Cleveland, Ravenna, Lisbon, a host of Illinois and Ohio towns, until they came to Chester, West Virginia—the old man maintained a threatening silence, punctuated by Ellery's sly monologues and the roar of the Duesenberg's exhaust.

They were through Arroyo before they realized they had been in it; a tiny place of some two hundred souls. And . . . the junction.

The signpost with its crossbar at the top was visible in stark silhouette for some distance before the car rolled to a stop. For the Arroyo road ended there, meeting the New Cumberland-Pughtown highway at right angles. The signpost therefore faced the exit of the Arroyo pike, one arm pointing northeast to Pughtown, the other southwest to New Cumberland.

The Inspector growled: "Go on. Make a fool of yourself. Of all the dumb poppycock! Hauling me down here . . . just another crazy murder . . . I won't be—"

Ellery switched off the ignition key and strode forward. The road was deserted. Touching the steel sky above posed the mountains of West Virginia. Underfoot the dirt was cracked and stiff. It was sharply cold, and a keen wind blew the tails of Ellery's overcoat about. And ahead stood the signpost upon which Andrew Van, eccentric schoolmaster of Arroyo, had been crucified.

The signpost had once been white; it was now a filthy gray, and it was streaked with encrusted mud. It stood six feet high—its top was on a level with Ellery's head—and its arms were stout and long. It looked for all the world, as Ellery paused several feet away, like a gigantic letter T. He understood now why the U.P. man had christened the crime "The T Murder"—first this signpost in the form of a T, then the T-shaped crossroads at the head of which the signpost stood, and finally the fantastic T swabbed in blood on the door of the dead man's house, which Ellery's car had passed a few hundred feet from the junction of the roads.

Ellery sighed, and took off his hat. It was not necessarily a gesture of reverence; he was, despite the cold and the wind, perspiring. He wiped his forehead with a handkerchief and wondered what madman had committed this atrocious, illogical, and completely puzzling crime. Even the body . . . He recollected vividly one of the newspaper accounts of the discovery of the corpse, a special piece written by a famous Chicago reporter who was practiced enough in the description of violence:

"The most pitiful Christmas story of the year was revealed today when the beheaded body of Andrew Van, 46-year-old schoolmaster of the little West Virginia hamlet of Arroyo, was discovered crucified to the signpost on a lonely crossroads near the village early Christmas morning.

"Four-inch iron spikes had been driven into the upturned palms of the victim, impaling them to the tips of the signpost's weatherbeaten arms. Two other spikes transfixed the dead man's ankles, which were set close together at the foot of the upright. Under the armpits two more spikes had been driven, supporting the weight of the dead man in such a way that, his head having been hacked off, the corpse resembled nothing so much as a great letter T.

"The signpost formed a T. The crossroads formed a T. On the door of Van's house, not far from the crossroads, the murderer had scrawled a T in his victim's blood. And on the signpost the maniac's conception of a human T . . .

"Why Christmas? Why had the murderer dragged his victim three hundred feet from the house to the signpost and crucified the dead body there? What is the significance of the T's?

"Local police are baffled. Van was an eccentric but quiet and inoffensive figure. He had no enemies—and no friends. His only intimate was a simple soul named Kling, who acted as his servant. Kling is missing, and it is said that District Attorney Crumit of Hancock County believes from suppressed evidence that Kling, too, may have been a victim of the most bloodthirsty madman in the annals of modern American crime. . . .

There had been much more in the same vein, including details of the unfortunate schoolmaster's bucolic life in Arroyo, the meager tidbits of information gleaned by police about the last-known movements of Van and Kling, and the pompous declarations of the District Attorney.

Ellery took off his pince-nez eyeglasses, polished them, put them on again, and let his sharp eyes sweep over the gruesome relic.

In both arms, near the tips of the crossbar, were jagged holes in the wood where the police had torn out the spikes. Each hole was surrounded by a ragged stain of a rusty brown color. Little brown tendrils trickled from the holes, where Andrew Van's blood had dripped from his mutilated hands. Where the arms protruded from the upright were two other holes, unrimmed; the spikes which had been wrenched from these holes had supported the armpits of the corpse. The entire length of the signpost was streaked, smeared, runneled with dried blood, the drippings emanating from the head of the post, where the raw, gaping wound at the base of the victim's neck had rested. Near the bottom of the centerpost there were two holes not more than four inches apart, also ringed in brown blood; and these holes, where Van's ankles had been nailed to the wood, had dribbled blood to the earth in which the signpost was staked.

Ellery walked soberly back to the car, where the Inspector waited in a familiar attitude of dejection and irritation, slumped against the leather next to the driver's seat. The old man was bundled to the neck in an ancient woolen muffler, and his sharp red nose stuck out like a danger signal. "Well," he snapped, "come on. I'm frozen."

"Not the least bit curious?" asked Ellery, slipping into the driver's seat.

"No!"

"You're another." Ellery started the engine. He grinned and the car leaped forward like a greyhound, turned on two wheels, plowed and bumped about in a circle, and shot off the way it had come, toward Arroyo.

The Inspector clutched the edge of his seat in mortal terror.

"Quaint idea," shouted Ellery above the thunder of the motor. "Crucifixion on Christmas Day!"

"Huh," said the Inspector.

"I think," shouted Ellery, "I'm going to like this case!"

"Drive, darn you!" screamed the old man suddenly. The car straightened out. "You'll like nothing," he added with a scowl. "You're coming back to New York with me."

They raced into Arroyo.

"Ye know," muttered the Inspector as Ellery jerked the Duesenberg to a stop before a small frame building, "it's a shame the way they do things down here. Leaving that signpost at the scene of the crime!" He shook his head. "Where you going now?" he demanded, his birdlike little gray head cocked on a side.

"I thought you weren't interested," said Ellery, jumping to the sidewalk. "Hi, there!" he cried to a muffled countryman in blue denim who was sweeping the sidewalk with a tattered old besom, "is this the Law in Arroyo?" The man gaped stupidly. "Superfluous question. There's the sign for all the world to see. . . . Come along, you fraud."

It was a sleepy little settlement, a handful of clustered buildings. The frame structure at which the Duesenberg had stopped looked like one

t mushroom boxes of the old West. Next door there
re, with a single decrepit gasoline pump before it and
garage adjoining. The frame building bore a proudly hand-
lettered sign:

ARROYO MUNICIPAL HALL

They found the gentleman they sought asleep at his desk in
the rear of the building, behind a door which announced him as
CONSTABLE. He was a fat, red-faced countryman with yellow buck
teeth.

The Inspector snorted, and the Constable raised heavy lids. He
scratched his head and said in a rusty bass: "Ef ye're lookin' fer Matt
Hollis, he's out."

Ellery smiled. "We're looking for Constable Luden of Arroyo."

"Oh! I'm him. What d'ye want?"

"Constable," said Ellery impressively, "let me introduce you to
Inspector Richard Queen, head of the Homicide Squad of the New
York Police Department—in the merry flesh."

"Who?" Constable Luden stared. "N'Yawk?"

"As I live and breathe," said Ellery, stepping on his father's toe.
"Now, Constable, we want—"

"Set," said Constable Luden, kicking a chair toward the Inspector,
who sniffed and rather delicately sat down. "This Van business, hey?
Didn't know you N'Yawkers was int'rested. What's eatin' ye?"

Ellery produced his cigarette case and offered it to the Constable,
who grunted and bit a mouthful off a huge plug of tobacco. "Tell us all
about it, Constable."

"Nothin' to tell. Lots o' Chicago an' Pittsburgh men been snoopin'
round town. Sort o' sick of it, m'self."

The Inspector sneered. "Can't say I blame you, Constable."

Ellery took a wallet from his breast pocket, flipped it open, and
stared speculatively at the greenbacks inside. Constable Luden's

drowsy eyes brightened. "Well," he said hastily, "maybe I ain't so sick of it. I can't tell it jest once ag'in."

"Who found the body?"

"Ol' Pete. Ye wouldn't know'm. Got a shack up in th' hills some'eres."

"Yes, I know that. Wasn't a farmer involved, also?"

"Mike Orkins. Got a coupla acres down off th' Pughtown pike. Seems like Orkins was drivin' his Ford into Arroyo—let's see; this is Mond'y—yep, Frid'y mornin', 'twas . . . Christmas mornin', pretty early. Ol' Pete, he was headed fer Arroyo, too—come down offen th' mountain. Orkins give Pete a hitch. Well, sir, they git to th' crossroads where Orkins has to turn in t'wards Arroyo, an' there it was. On th' signpost. Hangin' stiff as a cold-storage yearlin'—Andrew Van's body."

"We saw the post," said Ellery encouragingly.

"Guess most a hundred city people druv out in th' past few days to see it," grumbled Constable Luden. "Reg'lar traffic problem I had. Anyways, Orkins an' Ol' Pete, they was both pretty much scared. Both of 'em like to've fainted. . . ."

"Hmph," said the Inspector.

"They didn't touch the body, of course?" remarked Ellery.

Constable Luden wagged his gray head emphatically. "Not them! They druv into Arroyo like th' devil hisself was after 'em, an' roused me outa bed."

"What time was this, Constable?"

Constable Luden blushed. "Eight o'clock, but I'd had a big night b'fore over to Matt Hollis's house, an' I sorta overslept—"

"You and Mr. Hollis, I think, went immediately to the crossroads?"

"Yep. Matt—he's our Mayor, ye know—Matt an' me, we got four o' th' boys out an' druv down. Some mess, he was—Van, I mean." The Constable shook his head. "Never seen nothin' like it in all my born days. An' on Christmas Day, too. Blasph'my, I calls it. An' Van an atheist, too."

"Eh?" said the Inspector swiftly. His red nose shot out of the folds of the muffler like a dart. "An atheist? What d'ye mean?"

"Well, maybe not an atheist exac'ly," muttered the Constable, looking uncomfortable. "I'm not much of a churchgoer m'self, but Van, he never went. Parson—well, mebbe I better not talk about *that* no more."

"Remarkable," said Ellery, turning to his father. "Really remarkable, Dad. It certainly looks like the work of a religious maniac."

"Yep, that's what they're all sayin'," said Constable Luden. "Me—I dunno. I'm jest a country constable. I don't know nothin', see? Ain't had more'n a tramp in th' lock-up fer three years. But I tell ye, gentlem'n," he said darkly, "there's more to it than jest religion."

"No one in town, I suppose," asserted Ellery, frowning, "is a suspect."

"Nob'dy that loony, mister. I tell ye—it's someb'dy connected with Van's past."

"Have there been strangers in town recently?"

"Nary a one. . . . So Matt an' me an' th' boys, we identified th' body from th' size, gen'ral build, clothin' an' papers an' sech, an' we took 'im down. On th' way back to town we stopped in at Van's house. . . ."

"Yes," said Ellery eagerly. "And what did you find?"

"Hell let loose," said Constable Luden, chewing savagely on his cud. "Signs of a ter'ble struggle, all th' chairs upset, blood on most everythin', that big T in blood on th' front door th' papers been makin' so much about, an' poor ol' Kling gone."

"Ah," said the Inspector. "The servant. Just gone, hey? Take his duds, did he?"

"Well," replied the Constable, scratching his head, "I don't rightly know. Coroner's sort o' taken things out o' my hands. I know they're lookin' fer Kling—an' I think," he closed one eye slowly, "I think fer someb'dy else, too. But I can't say nothin' about that," he added hastily.

"Any trace of Kling yet?" asked Ellery.

"Not's I know of. Gen'ral alarm's out. Body was taken to th' county seat, Weirton—that's eleven-twelve mile away, in charge o' th' Coroner. Coroner sealed up Van's house, too. State police are on th' job, an' the District Attorney o' Hancock County."

Ellery mused, and the Inspector stirred restlessly in his chair. Constable Luden stared with fascination at Ellery's pince-nez.

"And the head was hacked off," murmured Ellery, at last "Queer. By an ax, I believe?"

"Yep, we found th' ax in th' house. Was Kling's. No finger marks."

"And the head itself?"

Constable Luden shook his head. "No sign of it. Guess th' crazy murd'rer jest took it along as a sort o' souvenir. Haw!"

"I think," said Ellery, putting on his hat, "that we'll go, Dad. Thank you, Constable." He offered his hand, and the Constable took it flabbily. A grin came over his face as he felt something pressed into his palm. He was so delighted that he forwent his siesta and walked them to the street.

Chapter Two
NEW YEAR'S IN WEIRTON

THERE WAS NO LOGICAL reason for Ellery Queen's persistent interest in the case of the crucified schoolmaster. He should have been in New York. Word had come to the Inspector that he must cut short his holiday and return to Centre Street; and where the Inspector went, Ellery usually followed. But something in the atmosphere of the West Virginia county seat, a suppressed excitement that filled Weirton's streets with whispered rumors, held him there. The Inspector gave up in disgust and entrained for New York, Ellery driving him to Pittsburgh.

"Just what," demanded the old man, as Ellery tucked him into a Pullman seat, "do you think you'll accomplish? Come on—tell me. I suppose you've got it solved already, hey?"

"Now, Inspector," said Ellery in a soothing voice, "watch your blood pressure. I'm merely interested. I've never run across anything as baldly lunatic as this. I'm going to wait for the inquest. I want to hear that evidence Luden hinted at."

"You'll come back to New York with your tail between your legs," predicted the Inspector darkly.

"Oh, no doubt," grinned Ellery. "At the same time, I've quite run out of fiction ideas, and this thing has so many possibilities . . ."

They let it go at that. The train pulled out and left Ellery standing on the platform of the terminal, free and vaguely uneasy. He drove back to Weirton the same day.

This was Tuesday. He had until Saturday, the day after New Year's Day, to wheedle what information he could from the District Attorney of Hancock County. District Attorney Crumit was a dour old man with shrewd ambitions and an exaggerated opinion of his own importance. Ellery reached the door of his anteroom; and no amount of pleading or cajolery could get him farther. The District Attorney can see no one. The District Attorney is busy. Come back tomorrow. The District Attorney cannot see any one. From New York—Inspector Queen's son? I'm sorry. . . .

Ellery bit his lip, wandered the streets, and listened with tireless ears to the conversation of Weirton's citizenry. Weirton, in the midst of its holly, tinsel, and glittering Christmas trees, was indulging in an orgy of vicarious horror. There were remarkably few women abroad, and no children. Men met hurriedly, stiff-lipped, and discussed ways and means. There was talk of lynching—a worthy purpose which failed because there was no one to lynch. Weirton's police force prowled the streets uneasily. State police dashed in and out of town. Occasionally the peaked face of District Attorney Crumit flashed in steely vindictiveness as his automobile darted by.

In all the hubbub that churned about him, Ellery maintained his peace and an inquiring air. On Wednesday he made an attempt to see Stapleton, the County Coroner. Stapleton was a fat young man in a constant state of perspiration; but he was canny, too, and Ellery learned nothing from him that he did not already know.

So he devoted the remaining three days to ferreting out what he could about Andrew Van, the victim. It was incredible how little was known about the man. Few had seen him in the flesh; he had been a retiring gentleman of solitary habits and had rarely visited Weirton. It was rumored that the villagers of Arroyo had considered him an exemplary teacher: he had been kind, although not lenient, to his pupils; he had rendered satisfactory service, in the opinion of the Arroyo

Town Board. Moreover, although he had not been a churchgoer, he had been a teetotaler; and this, it seemed, had cemented his position in a God-fearing and sober community.

On Thursday the editor of Weirton's leading newspaper turned literary. The morrow was New Year's Day, and it was too fecund an opportunity to let lie barren. The six reverend gentlemen who ministered to Weirton's spiritual heeds preached their sermons on the front page. Andrew Van, they said, had been an ungodly man. He who lives in ungodliness shall die in ungodliness. Yet deeds born of violence. . . . The editor did not stop there. There was an editorial in ten-point bold face. It was fruitily dotted with references to the French Bluebeard, Landru; to the Maniac of Dusseldorf; to the American bogey, Jack-the-Ripper; and to many other monsters of fact and fiction—a dainty tidbit served to the good people of Weirton as dessert for their New Year's dinners.

The County Court House, where the Coroner's inquest was to be held on Saturday morning, was crowded to the doors long before the appointed hour. Ellery sagely had been one of the earliest comers, and his seat was in the first row, behind the railing. When, at a few moments before nine o'clock, Coroner Stapleton himself appeared, Ellery sought him out, exhibited a telegram signed by the Police Commissioner of New York City, and with this sesame secured entrance to the anteroom in which Andrew Van's body was laid out.

"Corpse is in something of a mess," wheezed the Coroner. "After all, we couldn't hold the inquest during Christmas Week, and it's a good eight days. . . . Body's been kept in our local undertaker's parlor."

Ellery steeled himself and removed the cloth which covered the corpse. It was a sickening sight, and he replaced the cloth quickly. The corpse was that of a large man. Where the head had been was nothing . . . a gaping hole.

On a table nearby lay a man's garments: a sober dark gray suit, black shoes, a shirt, socks, underclothes—all stiff with faded blood. Articles taken from the dead man's clothing—a pencil, a fountain pen, a wallet, a bunch of keys, a crumpled packet of cigarettes, some coins, a cheap watch, an old letter—proved, as far as Ellery could see, utterly uninteresting. Except for the fact that several of the objects were initialed *A V* and the letter—from a Pittsburgh bookstore—was addressed to *Andrew Van, Esq.*, there was nothing in them likely to be of importance to the inquest.

Stapleton turned to introduce a tall, bitten old man who had just entered and was staring at Ellery suspiciously. "Mr. Queen—District Attorney Crumit."

"Who?" said Crumit sharply.

Ellery smiled, nodded, and returned to the inquest room.

Five minutes later Coroner Stapleton rapped with his gavel and the packed courtroom stilled. The customary preliminaries were hastily disposed of, and the Coroner summoned Michael Orkins to the witness stand.

Orkins lumbered down the aisle followed by whispers and eyes. He was a gnarled, bent old farmer burnt mahogany by the sun. He sat down nervously and folded his big hands.

"Mr. Orkins," wheezed the Coroner, "tell us how you came to find the body of the deceased."

The farmer licked his lips. "Yes, sir. Was comin' into Arroyo Frid'y mornin' last in my Ford. Jest b'fore I got t' th' Arroyo pike I seen Ol' Pete, from up th' mountain, trampin' in th' road. Give'm a lift. We come to th' turnin' o' the road, an'—an' there was th' body, hangin' on th' signpost. Nailed, it was, by th' hands, an' feet." Orkins's voice broke. "We—we beat it lickety-split fer town."

Someone tittered in the audience, and the Coroner rapped for silence. "Did you touch the body?"

"No, sir! We didn't even git out o' th' car."

"All right, Mr. Orkins."

The farmer sighed gustily and pottered back up the aisle, mopping his brow with a large red kerchief.

"Er—Old Pete?"

There was a stir, and in the rear of the courtroom a queer figure rose. It was that of an erect old man with a bushy gray beard and over-hanging eyebrows. He was dressed in tatterdemalion garments—a conglomeration of ancient clothing, torn, dirty, and patched. He shambled down the aisle, hesitated, then wagged his head and sat down in the witness chair.

The Coroner seemed nettled. "What's your full name?"

"Hey?" The old man stared sidewise out of bright unseeing eyes.

"Your name! What is it—Peter what?"

Old Pete shook his head. "Got no name," he declared. "Old Pete, that's me. I'm dead, I am. Been dead twenty years."

There was a horrified silence, and Stapleton looked about in be-wilderment. A small alert-looking man of middle age, sitting near the Coroner's dais, got to his feet. "It's all right, Mr. Coroner."

"Well, Mr. Hollis?"

"It's all right," repeated the speaker in a loud voice. "He's daffy, Old Pete is. Been that way for years—ever since he popped up in the hills. He's got a shack somewhere above Arroyo, and comes in ev-ery couple of months or so. Does a little trappin', I guess. Got pretty much the run of Arroyo. A regular character, Mr. Coroner."

"I see. Thanks, Mr. Hollis."

The Coroner swabbed his fat face, and the Mayor of Arroyo sat down in a murmur of approval. Old Pete beamed, and waved a dirty hand at Matt Hollis. . . . The Coroner continued brusquely. The man's replies were vague, but enough was elicited to make formal confirma-tion of Michael Orkins's story, and the hillman was excused. He shuf-fled back to his seat, blinking.

Mayor Hollis and Constable Luden recited their stories—how they had been roused out of bed by Orkins and Old Pete, how they had gone to the crossroads, identified the corpse, removed the spikes, carted the body off, stopped in at Van's house, viewed the shambles there and the bloody T on the door. . . .

A fat, ruddy old German was called. "Luther Bernheim."

He smiled, showed gold teeth, shook his belly, and sat down.

"You own the general store in Arroyo?"

"Yes, sir."

"Did you know Andrew Van?"

"Yes, sir. He bought in my store."

"How long were you acquainted with him?"

"*Ach!* Many years. He was a good customer. He always paid in cash."

"Did he purchase his groceries himself?"

"Sometimes. Mostly it was that Kling, his helper. But always he came himself to pay bills."

"Was he friendly?"

Bernheim screwed up his eyes. "Well . . . yes, and no."

"You mean he never got personal, was just pleasant?"

"Ja, ja."

"Would you say Van was a peculiar man?"

"Hah? Oh, yes, yes. F'rinstance, always he ordered caviar."

"Caviar?"

"*Ja.* He was my only customer for it. I used to order special for him. All kinds—Beluga, red, but mostly the black, the best kind."

"Mr. Bernheim, will you, Mayor Hollis, and Constable Luden step into the next room for a formal identification of the body."

The Coroner left the stand, followed by the three Arroyo citizens, and there was a buzzing interlude until they returned. The good storekeeper's red face was tinged with gray, and there was horror in his eyes.

Ellery Queen sighed. A schoolmaster in a village of two hundred souls ordering caviar! Perhaps Constable Luden was shrewder than he appeared; Van had evidently had a more lustrous past than his employment and environment indicated.

The tall spare figure of District Attorney Crumit strutted up to the stand. A little thrill ran through the audience. What had gone before was trifling; this was the beginning of revelations.

"Mr. District Attorney," said Coroner Stapleton, leaning forward tensely, "have you investigated the background of the deceased?"

"Yes!"

Ellery slumped lower in his seat; he disliked the District Attorney with vigor, but there were bodings in Crumit's frosty eye.

"Please relate what you have discovered."

The District Attorney of Hancock County gripped the arm of the witness chair. "Andrew Van appeared in Arroyo nine years ago in answer to an advertisement for a village schoolteacher. His references and preparation were satisfactory, and he was hired by the Town Board. He came with the man Kling, his servant, and rented the house on Arroyo Road in which he lived until the time of his death. He performed his teaching duties satisfactorily. His conduct during his residence in Arroyo was above reproach." Crumit paused impressively. "My investigators attempted to trace the man before his appearance in Arroyo. We have discovered that he had been a public-school teacher in Pittsburgh before coming to Arroyo."

"And before that?"

"No trace. But he was a naturalized citizen of the United States, having been admitted to citizenship in Pittsburgh thirteen years ago. His papers, on file in Pittsburgh, give his nationality before naturalization as Armenian, born in 1885."

Armenian! thought Ellery, nursing his chin behind the railing. Not far from Galilee . . . Peculiar thoughts raced through his head, and he dismissed them impatiently.

"You also investigated Kling, Van's servant, Mr. District Attorney?"

"Yes. He had been a foundling, cared for by the St. Vincent's Orphanage of Pittsburgh, and on reaching maturity he was employed by the orphanage in a man-of-all-work capacity. He lived there all his life. When Andrew Van resigned from the Pittsburgh public-school system and accepted the Arroyo appointment, he visited the orphanage and signified his desire to employ a man. Kling had been agreeable, it seems, Van investigated him scrupulously, expressed himself as satisfied, and the two men went to Arroyo, where they remained until the time of Van's death."

Ellery wondered lazily what motives might impel a man to resign a berth in a metropolis like Pittsburgh to accept one in a hamlet like Arroyo. A criminal record, desire to hide from the police? Improbable; concealment came in large cities, not in hamlets. No, it was something deeper and more obscure, he felt certain; perhaps rooted in the brain of the dead man irremovably. Some men sought solitude after thwarted lives; this might very well have been the case with Andrew Van, caviar-eating schoolmaster of the Arroyoites.

"What sort of man was Kling?" asked Stapleton.

The District Attorney looked bored. "The orphanage reports him as rather a simple-minded man—psychologically a moron, I believe they rated him. A harmless fellow."

"Did he ever show homicidal tendencies, Mr. Crumit?"

"No. He is considered at St. Vincent's to have been a mild-tempered, rather stolid and stupid man. He was kind to the children of the orphanage. He was humble, content, and respectful to his superiors at the Home."

The District Attorney moistened his lips afresh and appeared about to launch into the promised revelations; but Coroner Stapleton hastily excused him and recalled the Arroyo storekeeper.

"You knew Kling, Mr. Bernheim?"

"Yes, sir."

"What sort of man was he?"

"Quiet. Of good nature. Dumb, like an ox." Someone laughed, and Stapleton looked annoyed. He leaned forward.

"Is it true, Mr. Bernheim, that this Kling was well-known in Arroyo for his *physical strength*?"

Ellery chuckled to himself. The Coroner was a simple soul.

Bernheim clucked. *"Ach,* yes. Very strong, that Kling. He could lift a barrel of sugar! But he wouldn't hurt a fly, Mr. Coroner. I remember once—"

"That's all," said Stapleton irritably. "Mayor Hollis, please take the stand again."

Matt Hollis beamed. He was an oily little man, Ellery decided.

"You are head of the Town Board, Mayor Hollis?"

"Yep!"

"Tell the jury what you know about Andrew Van."

"Always gave satisfaction. Had nothin' to do with anyone. Sort of studious feller. He kept to the fine house I rented him outside of school hours, off by himself. Some thought him stuck up, and others a furriner, but not me." The Mayor looked sententious. "Just quiet, that's all. Not neighborly? Well, that was his business. If he didn't want to join me and Constable Luden on a fishin' trip, that was his business, too." Hollis smiled and nodded. "And he spoke perfect English, like you or me, Mr. Coroner."

"Did he ever have visitors, as far as you know?"

"No. But of course I can't say for sure. Funny feller, though," continued the Mayor thoughtfully. "Couple of times when I was goin' to Pittsburgh on business he asked me to buy books for him—queer books, they were, highfalutin' stuff. Philosophy, hist'ry, about the stars and such."

"Yes, yes, very interesting, Mr. Hollis. Now, you're the Arroyo banker, aren't you?"

"Yes, I am that." Mayor Hollis blushed, and looked modestly down at his small feet. Ellery gathered, from the Mayor's expression, that he was just about everything in the town of Arroyo.

"Did Andrew Van have an account in your bank?"

"He did not. He used to collect his salary regular, in cash, but I don't think he ever banked it anywhere because I asked him a couple of times—you know how it is; business is business—and he said he kept his money in the house." Hollis shrugged. "Didn't trust banks, he said. Well, every man to his taste. I'm not one to argue—"

"Was this generally known in Arroyo?"

Hollis hesitated. "We-ell maybe I did mention it around some. I guess most everybody in town knew of this queer kink of the schoolteacher's."

The Mayor was waved off the stand, and Constable Luden was recalled. The Constable came up stiffly, as one who has his own ideas about how such things should be conducted.

"You searched Andrew Van's house, Constable, the morning of Friday, December the twenty-fifth?"

"Right."

"Did you find any money?"

"Nope."

Gasps broke out through the room. Robbery! Ellery frowned. There was no rhyme or reason to any of it. First a crime with all the earmarks of religious mania, and then a theft of money. The two did not blend. He leaned forward. . . . A man was carrying something to the dais. It was a cheap battered green tin box. Its hasp was badly twisted, and the puny lock hung limply. The Coroner took it from the attendant, opened it, held it upside down. It was empty.

"Constable, do you recognize this green tin box?"

Luden sniffed. "I'll say," he said in his rusty bass. "Found it jest like that in Van's house. It's his money box, all right."

The Coroner held it up to the jury of countrymen who were craning at it. "The Coroner's jury will please observe this article of evidence. . . . All right, Constable. Will the Postmaster of Arroyo please take the stand?"

A wizened little old man hopped up to the witness chair.

"Did Andrew Van receive much mail?"

"Nope," shrilled the Postmaster. "'Ceptin' advertisin' lit'rachoor, hardly ever."

"Was there any letter or package during the week preceding his death?"

"Nope!"

"Did he send letters often?"

"Nope. Jest a couple once in a while. None fer three-four months now."

Dr. Strang, the Coroner's physician, was summoned. At mention of his name the spectators whispered frantically. He was a seedy man with a mournful look, and he slouched down the aisle as if he had all the time in the world.

When he was seated, the Coroner asked: "Dr. Strang, when did you first examine the body of the deceased?"

"Two hours after its discovery."

"Can you fix for the jury the approximate time of death?"

"Yes. I should say the man had been dead between six and eight hours when he was found at the crossroads."

"That would set the murder at some time around midnight of Christmas Eve?"

"That's right."

"Can you give the jury further details about the condition of the corpse which might be pertinent to this inquiry?"

Ellery smiled. Coroner Stapleton had worked himself into a fine fettle; his language was sublimely official, and the spectators, to judge from their open mouths, were properly impressed.

Dr. Strang crossed his legs and said in a bored voice: "No marks on the body other than the raw wound at the neck where the head had been severed, and the nail holes in hands and feet."

The Coroner half-rose and plumped his belly over the edge of the desk. "Dr. Strang," he asked hoarsely, "what is your conclusion from this fact?"

"That the deceased was probably struck over the head, or shot in the head, since there are no other marks of violence on his body."

Ellery nodded; this sad-looking country doctor had a head on his shoulders.

"It's my opinion," continued the Coroner's physician, "that the victim was already dead when the head was cut off. From the nature of the wound left at the base of the neck, a very sharp instrument must have been wielded."

The Coroner picked up a carefully bedded object on the desk before him and held it up. It was a long-handled, wicked-looking ax, its blade winking where there was no blood. "Would you say that this weapon, Dr. Strang, could have severed the victim's head from his body?"

"Yes."

The Coroner turned to the jury. "This exhibit was found in the back kitchen of Andrew Van's house, on the floor, where the murder was committed. Let me call to your attention, gentlemen, that there are no fingerprints on the weapon, showing that the murderer had either worn gloves or wiped the ax clean of prints after using. This ax has been established as the property of the deceased, and was habitually kept in the kitchen, normally being used by the missing Kling to chop firewood. . . . That's all, Dr. Strang. Colonel Pickett, will you please come to the stand?"

The head of the West Virginia State Police complied—a tall, soldierly-looking man. "Colonel Pickett, what have you to report?"

"Thorough search of the vicinity of Arroyo," said the Colonel in a machine-gun voice, "fails to turn up the head of the murdered man. No trace of the missing servant Kling has been found. A description of Kling has been sent to all neighboring states and he is being watched for."

"I believe you have been in charge of the investigation relative to the last-known movements of both the deceased and the missing man, Colonel. What have you discovered?"

"Andrew Van was last seen at four o'clock on the afternoon of

Thursday, December twenty-fourth. He visited the house of Mrs. Rebecca Traub, a resident of Arroyo, to warn her that her son William, a pupil in his school, was falling behind in his studies. Then he went away and no one, as far as we can find, saw him alive again."

"And Kling?"

"Kling was last seen by Timothy Traynor, a farmer between Arroyo and Pughtown, the same afternoon at a little past four. He bought a bushel of potatoes, paid for it in cash, and lugged it away on his shoulder."

"Was the bushel of potatoes found on Van's premises? This might be important, Colonel, in determining whether Kling ever reached the house."

"Yes. Untouched, and identified by Traynor as the one bought from him that afternoon."

"Have you anything else to report?"

Colonel Pickett looked around at the courtroom before replying. His mouth was like a trap as he said grimly: "I certainly have!"

The courtroom became still as death. Ellery smiled wearily; the revelations had arrived. Colonel Pickett leaned over to whisper something into the Coroner's ear; Stapleton blinked, smiled, wiped his fat cheeks, and nodded. The spectators, too, sensed the coming event, and twisted in their seats. Pickett signaled quietly to someone at the rear of the room.

A tall trooper appeared, grasping the arm of an amazing individual: a little old man with unkempt long brown hair and a shaggy brown beard. He had small glittering eyes, the eyes of a fanatic. His skin was the color of dirty bronze, wrinkled and battered by sun and wind as if he had lived out doors all his life. He was dressed—Ellery's eyes narrowed—in mud-encrusted khaki shorts and an old gray turtle-neck sweater. On his bare brown feet ropy with gray veins he wore a curious pair of sandals. And in his hand he carried a remarkable object—a wandlike rod topped by a crude representation of a snake, apparently handmade by a poor craftsman.

There was instant hubbub, a burst of laughter, and the Coroner rapped like a madman for order.

Behind the trooper and his fantastic charge shuffled a white-faced young man in oil-spattered overalls. That he was well-known to most of the spectators was evident, for hands furtively reached out as he passed and patted him encouragingly, while spectators throughout the room pointed openly at his shrinking figure.

The three passed through the gateway of the railing and sat down. The brown-bearded old man was plainly in the grip of terrible fear; his eyes rolled, and his thin brown hands clenched and unclenched convulsively about the odd baton he carried.

"Caspar Croker to the stand!"

The white-faced young man in the oily overalls gulped, rose, and took the stand.

"You operate a garage and gas station on Main Street, Weirton?" demanded the Coroner.

"Why, sure. You know me, Mr.—"

"Answer my question, please," said Stapleton sternly. "Relate to the jury what occurred about eleven o'clock at night of Christmas Eve."

Croker drew a deep breath, looked around as if for a last friendly eye, and said: "I closed my garage Christmas Eve—wanted to celebrate. I live in a house right back of my garage. Eleven that night, while I was sittin' in my front room with the wife, I heard an awful poundin' and racket outside somewhere. Seemed like it was comin' from my garage, so I ran out. Dark as old fury it was, too." He gulped again, and resumed quickly. "Well, it was a man out there hammering on my garage door. When he saw me—"

"Just a minute, Mr. Croker. How was he dressed?"

The garageman shrugged. "Dark, an' I couldn't make out. Didn't have no reason to take particular notice, anyways."

"Did you get a good look at the man's face?"

"Yes, sir. He was standin' under my night light. Bundled up, he was—pretty cold at that—but it seemed to me like he didn't want to be recognized. Anyways, I seen he was clean-shaved, dark, and kind of furrin-lookin', though he talked good old American."

"How old would you say he was?"

"Oh, in his middle thirties, maybe more, maybe less. Hard to say."

"What did he want?"

"He wanted to hire a car to take him to Arroyo."

Ellery could hear the asthmatic breathing of a stout man in the row behind him, it was so still in the courtroom. They were tense, sitting on the edges of their seats.

"What happened?" asked the Coroner.

"Well," replied Croker, with more assurance, "I didn't like the idea much—here it was eleven o'clock Christmas Eve, an' my wife was alone an' all. But he pulls out a wallet an' he says: 'I'll give you ten dollars to drive me over.' Well, sir, that's a lot o' money to a poor man like me an' I says: 'Okay, stranger, you're on.'"

"You drove him down?"

"Yes, sir, I did. I went back to get my coat, told the wife I'd be away a half-hour or so, came back, took out my old bus, and he climbed in an' off we went. I asked him where he wanted to go in Arroyo, an' he said: 'Isn't there a place where the Arroyo road meets the New Cumberland-Pughtown road?' I says, yes, there is. He says: 'Well, that's where I want to go.' I drove him down there, he got out, give me the ten-spot, an' I turned the car around and beat it for home. Felt kind of shivery an' scary anyways."

"Did you see what he did as you left?"

Croker nodded emphatically. "I was watchin' over my shoulder. Damn near run into a ditch. He took the fork t'wards Arroyo, on foot. He limped pretty bad, sir."

There was a gasp from the brown-bearded eccentric seated by the trooper; his eyes roved wildly as if seeking an avenue of escape.

"Which foot, Mr. Croker?"

"Well, he sort o' favored his left leg. Put all his weight on the right."

"That's the last you saw of him?"

"Yes, sir. An' the first. Never did see him before that night."

"That's all."

Gratefully, Croker left the witness chair and hurried up the aisle toward the door.

"Now," said Coroner Stapleton, transfixing the brown-bearded little man, who was cowering in the chair, with his beady eye. "You, there. Come to the stand."

The trooper rose and hauled Brown-Beard to his feet, prodding him forward. The little man went unresistingly, but there was panic in his mad eyes and he kept shrinking back. The trooper plumped him unceremoniously in the witness chair and returned to his own seat.

"What's your name?" demanded Coroner Stapleton.

A shout of laughter went up from the spectators as the full oddity of the man's dress and appearance burst upon them from the vantage point of the witness chair. It was a long time before order was restored, during which the witness licked his lips and swayed from side to side, mumbling to himself. Ellery got the startling feeling that the man was praying; praying—it was shocking—to the wooden snake on the tip of the wand.

Stapleton nervously repeated the question. The man held the rod at arm's length, threw back his skinny shoulders, seeming to summon a reserve of strength and dignity from the posture, looked directly into Stapleton's eyes and said, in a clear shrill voice: "I am he who is called Harakht, god of the midday sun. Ra-Harakht, the falcon!"

There was a stunned silence. Coroner Stapleton blinked and recoiled as if someone had suddenly uttered gibberish threats in his presence. The audience gaped, and then burst into hysterical laughter—animated not by derision this time, but by a nameless fear. There was something dreadful and eerie about this man; he emanated an earnestness too maniacal to be assumed.

"Who?" asked the Coroner weakly.

The man who called himself Harakht folded his arms across his scrawny chest, the wand clutched firmly before him, and did not deign to reply.

Stapleton swabbed his cheeks and seemed at a loss how to continue. "Er—what is your business, Mr.—Mr. Harakht?"

Ellery sank lower into his seat and blushed for the Coroner. The scene grew painful.

Harakht said from stiff stern lips: "I am the Healer of the Weak. I make ill bodies well and strong. I am he who sails *Manzet,* the Bark of the Dawn. I am he who sails *Mesenktet,* the Bark of the Dusk. Some call me Horus, god of the horizons. I am son of Nut, goddess of the sky, wife of Qeb, mother of Isis and Osiris. I am the supreme god of Memphis. I am one with Etōm—"

"Stop!" cried the Coroner. "Colonel Pickett, for God's sake, what is this? I thought you said this lunatic had something of importance to contribute to the inquest! I—"

The chief of the state police rose hurriedly. The man who called himself Harakht waited calmly, his first terror completely gone, as if in the recesses of his twisted brain he realized that he was master of the situation.

"Sorry, Mr. Coroner," said the Colonel quickly. "I should have warned you. This man isn't all there. I think I'd better tell you and the jury what he does, and then you can ask more direct questions. He runs a sort of medicine show—nutty sort of thing, all painted up with suns and stars and moons and queer drawings of Egyptian pharaohs. Seems he believes he's the sun, or something. He's harmless. Travels around in an old horse and wagon, like a gypsy, from town to town. He's been going through Illinois, Indiana, Ohio, and West Virginia preaching and selling a medicinal cure-all that puts hair—"

"It is the elixir of youth," said Harakht gravely. "Bottled light of the sun. I am the appointed, and I preach the gospel of solarity. I am Menu, and Attu, and—"

"It's just plain cod-liver oil, as far as I can tell," explained Colonel Pickett with a grin. "Nobody knows his real name; I think he's forgotten it himself."

"Thank you, Colonel," said the Coroner with dignity. . . .

Ellery sat in his hard seat thrilled to the marrow by a sudden discovery. He had recognized the poorly made emblem in the madman's hand. It was the uraeus, serpent scepter of the chief divinity of the ancient Egyptians and of their god-descended kings. At first he had been inclined to think it a makeshift caduceus, from the snake design; but the emblem of Mercury always included wings, and this, as he saw by straining his eyes, had a crude solar disc surmounting the serpent or serpents. . . . Pharaonic Egypt! Some of the names which had fallen from the mouth of this engaging little madman had been familiar: Horus, Nut, Isis, Osiris. The others, while strange, had an Egyptian flavor. . . . Ellery sat up very straight.

"Er—Harakht, or whatever you call yourself," the Coroner was saying, "have you heard the testimony of Caspar Croker concerning a dark, clean-shaven man with a limp?"

A more rational look came into the bearded man's eyes, and with it a return of that lurking fear. "The—the man with a limp," he faltered. "Yes."

"Do you recognize any one by this description?"

Hesitation. Then—"Yes."

"Ah!" said the Coroner, sighing. "Now, Harakht, we're getting somewhere." His tone was gay and friendly. "Who is this man and how do you know him?"

"He is my priest."

"Priest!" little mutters went up from the throng, and Ellery heard the stout man behind him say: "Damn blasph'my, by God!"

"You mean he's your—assistant?"

"He is my disciple. My priest. High priest of Horus."

"Yes, yes," said Stapleton hastily. "What's his name?"

"Velja Krosac."

"Hmm," said the Coroner with a frown. "Foreign name, eh? *Armenian?*" he shot at the brown-bearded little man.

"There is no nation but Egypt," said Harakht quietly.

"Well!" Stapleton glared. "How do you spell that name?"

Colonel Pickett said: "We've got all that, Mr. Stapleton. It's V-e-l-j-a K-r-o-s-a-c-. We found it on some papers in this man's caboose."

"Where is this Vel—Velja Krosac?" demanded the Coroner.

Harakht shrugged. "He has gone away." But Ellery saw the glint of panic in the staring little eyes.

"When?"

He shrugged again.

Colonel Pickett stepped into the breach once more. "Maybe I'd better tell it, Mr. Stapleton, and expedite the business of the inquest. Krosac's always kept himself under cover, as far as we could find out. Couple of years now that he's been with this man. Mysterious sort of fellow. Acted as business manager and advertising agent, sort of, letting Harakht here take care of the hokum. Harakht picked him up out West somewhere. The last time Krosac was with Harakht was Christmas Eve. They'd been camped up near Holliday's Cove"—a few miles from Weirton; Ellery remembered certain signposts. "Krosac went off around ten o'clock or so, and that's the last What's-His-Name claims to have seen of him. The times match, all right."

"You've found no trace of this Krosac?"

The Colonel looked irritated. "Not yet," he snapped. "Disappeared as if the earth swallowed him. But we'll find him. He can't get away. We've sent out descriptions of him and Kling."

"Harakht," said the Coroner, "have you ever been in Arroyo?"

"Arroyo? No."

"They never got that far north in West Virginia," explained the Colonel.

"What do you know about Krosac?"

"He is a true believer," asserted Harakht deliberately. "He worships at the altar with reverence. He partakes of *kuphi* and hears the holy writings with high spirit. He is the pride and the glory—"

"Oh, all right," said the Coroner wearily. "Take him away, Trooper."

The trooper grinned, rose, grasped Brown-Beard's skinny arm, and hauled him off the stand. The Coroner heaved a sigh of relief as the two disappeared in the crowd.

Ellery echoed the sigh. His father had been right. It looked very much as if he were due to return to New York, if not precisely with his tail between his legs, at least with a hangdog look about him. The entire proceeding was so insane, the affair so incomprehensible, so impervious to logic, that it hinged on farce. And yet—there was that brutally mutilated body, crucified to . . .

Crucified! He started, almost with an audible gasp. Crucifixion—ancient Egypt. Where had he run across that odd fact?

The inquest procceded swiftly. Colonel Pickett produced a number of articles which he had found in Harakht's wagon and which Harakht had said belonged to Krosac. They were inconsequential, of no value either intrinsically or as possible clues to the man's background or identity. There had been no photograph of Krosac, as the Coroner pointed out to the jury—a fact which made the apprehension of the man even more difficult. To augment the difficulties, there were no samples available of the man's handwriting.

Other witnesses were called. Small points were brought out. No one could be found who had had Andrew Van's house under observation on Christmas Eve, or who saw Krosac after Croker the garagemen left him at the crossroads. Van's house was the only dwelling in the vicinity of the crossroads, and no one had passed by that night. . . . The spikes found in Van's crucified body had come from his own tool box, usually kept in his kitchen-pantry. They had been purchased by Kling from storekeeper Bernheim long before, it was revealed; many of them having been used in the construction of a woodshed.

Ellery came to a consciousness of his surroundings just as Coroner

Stapleton was rising to his feet. "Gentlemen of the Jury," the Coroner was saying, "you have heard the proceedings of this inqu—"

Ellery leaped to his feet. Stapleton stopped to look around, annoyed at the interruption. "Yes, Mr. Queen? You're interfering with the business of the—"

"One moment, Mr. Stapleton," said Ellery quickly, "before you address the Coroner's jury. There is in my possession a fact which it seems to me is pertinent to your inquiry."

"What's that?" cried District Attorney Crumit, starting from his seat. "A new fact?"

"Not a new fact, Mr. District Attorney," replied Ellery, smiling. "A very old one. More ancient than the Christian religion."

"Here," said Coroner Stapleton—the audience was craning and whispering, and the jury had risen from their seats to stare at this unexpected witness—"what are you getting at, Mr. Queen? What's the Christian religion got to do with it?"

"Nothing—I hope." Ellery leveled his pince-nez at the Coroner. "The most significant feature of this horrible crime," he said severely, "if I may be permitted to say so, has not been touched upon at all in this inquest. I refer to the fact that the murderer, whoever he was, deliberately went out of his way to plaster the letter or symbol T around the scene of his crime. The T shape of the crossroads. The T shape of the signpost. The T shape of the corpse. The T scrawled in blood on the victim's front door. All these things have been commented upon in the press—and rightly so."

"Yes, yes," interrupted District Attorney Crumit with a sneer, "we know all that. Where's your fact, though?"

"Here." Ellery stared at him hard, and Crumit flushed and sat down. "I fail to see the connection—I confess to complete bewilderment—but do you know that the symbol T may quite possibly not refer to the alphabet at all?"

"What do you mean, Mr. Queen?" asked Coroner Stapleton anxiously.

"I mean that the symbol T has a religious significance."

"Religious significance?" repeated Stapleton.

A portly old gentleman wearing a clerical collar rose from the thick of the audience. "If I may make so bold," he said sharply, "to interrupt the learned speaker—I am a minister of the gospel, and *I* have never heard of a religious significance embodied in the symbol T!"

Someone cried: "That's tellin' him, Parson!" and the minister blushed and sat down.

Ellery smiled. "If I may contradict the learned dominie, its significance is this: There is one cross among the many religious symbols which takes the shape of a T. It is called the *tau* cross, or *crux commissa.*"

The minister started from his seat. "Yes," he cried, "That's true. But it isn't originally a Christian cross, sir. It was a *pagan* sign!"

Ellery chuckled. "Exactly, sir. And wasn't the Greek cross in use by pre-Christian peoples for centuries before the Christian era? The *tau* antedates the familiar Greek cross by many hundreds of years. It's thought by some to have been a phallic symbol in origin. . . . But the point is this."

They waited in bated silence as he paused and drew a breath. Then he leveled his pince-nez at the Coroner again and said crisply: "The *tau*, or T, cross is not its only name. It is sometimes called"—he paused, and concluded quietly—"the *Egyptian* cross!"

PART TWO

Crucifixion of a Millionaire

"When a crime is committed by a nonhabitual criminal, that is the time for the policeman to watch out. None of the rules he has learned will apply, and the information he has amassed through years of studying the underworld becomes so much dead wood."

—DANILO RIEKA

Chapter Three

PROFESSOR YARDLEY

AND THAT WAS ALL. Extraordinary, incredible—but it died there. The cryptic connection which Ellery Queen pointed out to the Weirton populace deepened rather than lightened the mystery. As for himself, he could see no solution. He consoled himself with the thought that one could scarcely apply logic to the divagations of a madman.

If the problem was too much for him, it was certainly too much for Coroner Stapleton, District Attorney Crumit, Colonel Pickett, the Coroner's jury, the citizens of Arroyo and Weirton, and the scores of newspapermen who had flocked to town on the day of the inquest. Directed by the Coroner, who sternly resisted the temptation to leap to the obvious but unsupported solution, the jury scratched its collective head and brought in a verdict of "death at the hands of person or persons unknown." The newspapermen prowled about for a day or so, Colonel Pickett and District Attorney Crumit went about in ever slowing circles, and finally the case died in the press—a death warrant indeed.

Ellery returned to New York with a philosophic shrug. He was inclined to believe, the longer he mulled over the problem, that the explanation was after all simple. There was no reason, he felt, to doubt the overwhelming indications of the evidence. Circumstantial, to be sure, but positive in their implications. There was a man by the name of Velja Krosac, an English-speaking foreigner, something of a charlatan, who for dark reasons of his own had planned, sought, and finally taken the life of a country schoolmaster, also foreign-born. The method, while interesting from the criminological standpoint, was not necessarily important. It was the horrible but comprehensible expression of a mind buckled by the strange fires of manic psychology. What lay behind—what sordid story of fancied wrong or religious fanaticism or blood-demanding vengeance—would probably never be known. Krosac, his gruesome mission accomplished, would naturally vanish, and perhaps even now was on the high seas, bound for his native country. Kling, the manservant? Undoubtedly the innocent victim, caught between two fires, done away with by the executioner because he had witnessed the crime or caught a glimpse of the murderer's face. Kling represented in all likelihood a bridge that Krosac felt compelled to burn behind him. After all, a man who did not shrink from severing a human head merely to illustrate in broken flesh the symbol of his revenge would hardly turn squeamish at the necessity of killing an unexpected danger to his own safety.

And so Ellery returned to New York to accept the shrewd twigging of the Inspector.

"I'm not going to say 'I told you so,'" chuckled the old man over the dinner table on the night of Ellery's return, "but I want to point out a moral."

"Do," murmured Ellery, attacking a chop.

"The moral is: Murder is murder, and ninety-nine and nine-tenths per cent of the murders committed anywhere on the face of the globe, you young idiot, are as easy as pie to explain. Nothing fancy, you understand." The Inspector beamed. "I don't know what in time you expected to accomplish down in that God-forsaken country, but any flatfoot pounding a beat could have told you the answer."

Ellery laid down his fork. "But logic—"

"Mumbo-jumbo!" snorted the Inspector. "Go on and get some sleep."

Six months passed, during which Ellery completely forgot the bizarre events of the Arroyo murder. There were things to do. New York, unlike its kin in Pennsylvania, was not exactly a city of brotherly love; homicides were plentiful; the Inspector dashed about in an ecstasy of investigation, and Ellery trailed along, contributing his peculiar faculties to those cases which piqued his interest.

It was not until June, six months after the crucifixion of Andrew Van in West Virginia, that the Arroyo murder was forcibly brought back to his mind.

It was on Wednesday, the twenty-second of the month, that the spark was touched off. Ellery and Inspector Queen were at breakfast when the doorbell rang, and Djuna, the Queens' boy-of-all-work, answered the door to find a messenger there with a telegram for Ellery.

"Queer," said Ellery, tearing open the yellow envelope. "Who the deuce could be wiring me this early in the morning?"

"Who's it from?" mumbled the old man out of a mouthful of toast.

"It's from—" Ellery unfolded the message and glanced down at the typed signature. "From Yardley!" he cried, in vast surprise. He grinned at his father. "Professor Yardley. You remember, Dad. One of my profs at the University."

"Sure I do. The Ancient History feller, hey? Stayed with us one weekend when he came into New York. Ugly chap with chin whiskers, as I recall."

"One of the best. They don't make 'em that way any more," said Ellery. "God, it's years since I've heard from him! Why on earth should he—"

"I'd suggest," said the old man mildly, "That you read the message. That's generally the way to find out why a person writes to you. In some ways, my son, you're thicker than mud."

The twinkle in his eye disappeared as he watched Ellery's face. That gentleman's jaw had dropped perceptibly.

"What's the matter?" asked the Inspector in haste. "Somebody die?" He still preserved the middle-class superstition that telegrams boded no good.

Ellery tossed the yellow slip across the table, jumped from his chair, hurled his napkin at Djuna, and dashed into the bedroom, flinging off his dressing gown as he went.

The Inspector read:

THOUGHT AFTER ALL THESE YEARS YOU MIGHT LIKE TO COMBINE BUSINESS WITH PLEASURE STOP WHY NOT PAY ME THAT LONG DEFERRED VISIT STOP YOU WILL FIND NICE JUICY MURDER ACROSS THE ROAD FROM MY SHACK STOP HAPPENED THIS VERY MORNING AND LOCAL GENDARMES STILL ARRIVING STOP VERY INTERESTING STOP MY NEIGHBOR FOUND CRUCIFIED TO HIS TOTEM POST WITH HEAD MISSING STOP I SHALL EXPECT YOU TODAY

YARDLEY

Chapter Four

BRADWOOD

THAT SOMETHING EXTRAORDINARY WAS going on was apparent miles before the old Duesenberg arrived at its destination. The Long Island highway it was following at Ellery's customary reckless speed was thick with country troopers, who for once seemed uninterested in the spectacle of a tall earnest young man traveling at the rate of fifty-five miles per hour. Ellery, with the egotism of the specially favored speedster, was half hoping that some one would stop him. He would then have the opportunity of hurling "Police special!" in the teeth of his motorcycled antagonist; for he had cajoled the Inspector into telephoning the scene of the crime and explaining to Inspector Vaughn of the Nassau County police that "my famous son," as the Inspector subtly said, was on his way, and would Vaughn accord the young hero every courtesy? Especially since, as the old man put it, this famous son had information which should prove of remarkable interest to Vaughn and the District Attorney. Then another call to District Attorney Isham of Nassau County, with a repetition of the encomia and the promise. Isham, a much harassed man that morning, mumbled something about "any news will be good news, Inspector; send him along," and promised that nothing would be removed from the scene of the crime until Ellery arrived.

It was noon when the Duesenberg swung into one of Long Island's immaculate private roads and was challenged by a trooper on a motorcycle.

"Bradwood this way?" yelled Ellery.

"Yeah, but you ain't goin' there," replied the trooper grimly. "Turn around, mister, and step on it."

"Inspector Vaughn and District Attorney Isham are expecting me," said Ellery with a grin.

"Oh! You're Mr. Queen? Sorry, sir. Go ahead."

Vindicated and triumphant, Ellery shot forward and five minutes later drew up in the highway between two estates—one, from the cluster of official cars in its driveway, obviously Bradwood, where the murder had been committed; the other, by inference, since it was across the road, the dwelling of his friend and former instructor, Professor Yardley.

The Professor himself, a tall, rangy, ugly man bearing a striking resemblance to Abraham Lincoln, hurried forward and grasped Ellery's hand as he jumped out of the Duesenberg.

"Queen! It's good seeing you again."

"And you, Professor. Lord, it's been years! What are you doing here on Long Island? Last I heard of you, you were still living on the campus, torturing sophomores."

The Professor grinned in his short black beard. "I rented that Taj Mahal across the road"—Ellery turned and saw spires and a Byzantine dome peeping above the trees where Professor Yardley's thumb pointed—"from a crazy friend of mine. He built that atrocity himself when he was bitten by the Oriental bug. He's gone on a prowl through Asia Minor, and I'm working here this summer. I wanted a little quiet to do my long-deferred opus on Sources of the Atlantean Legend. You recall the Platonic references?"

"I recall," smiled Ellery, "Bacon's *New Atlantis*, but then my interests were always literary rather than scientific."

Yardley grunted. "The same fresh youngster, I see. . . . Quiet! Well, this is what I ran into."

"How on earth did you happen to think of me?"

They strode along the cluttered driveway of Bradwood toward a large colonial house, its vast pillars gleaming in the noon sun.

"The long arm of coincidence," said the Professor dryly. "I've followed your career with interest, naturally. And since I'm always fascinated by your exploits, I read quite avidly the accounts five or six months ago of that extraordinary murder in West Virginia."

Ellery took in the scene before replying. Bradwood was meticulously landscaped, the estate of a wealthy man. "I might have known nothing would escape the eyes that have examined thousands of papyri and stelai. So you read that highly romanticized version of my little sojourn in Arroyo?"

"I did. And your highly romanticized lack of accomplishment." The Professor chuckled. "At the same time, I was gratified by your application of the fundamental I tried to drive into your stubborn head—always go to the source. Egyptian cross, my boy? I'm afraid your sense of theater strangled the purely scientific truth. . . . Well, here we are."

"What do you mean?" demanded Ellery with an anxious frown. "The *tau* cross was certainly a primitive Egyptian—"

"I'll discuss it with you later. I suppose you want to meet Isham. He's been kind enough to let me potter around."

District Attorney Isham of Nassau County, a stubby man of middle age with watery blue eyes and a horseshoe fringe of gray on his head, was standing on the steps of the long colonial porch engaged in heated conversation with a tall powerful man in civilian clothes.

"Er—Mr. Isham," said Professor Yardley. "Here's my protégé, Ellery Queen."

The two men turned quickly. "Oh, yes," said Isham, as if he were thinking of other things. "Glad you came, Mr. Queen. I don't know what you can do to help, but—" He shrugged. "Meet Inspector Vaughn of the Nassau County police."

Ellery shook hands with both of them. "You'll permit me to wander about? I promise not to get under your feet."

Inspector Vaughn displayed brown teeth. "We need somebody to get under our feet. We're just standing still, Mr. Queen. Like to see the main exhibit?"

"I suppose it's customary. Come along, Professor."

The four men descended the steps of the porch and began to walk along a gravel path around the eastern ell of the house. Ellery experienced a sense of the vastness of the estate. The main house, he now saw, was situated halfway between the private highway where he had left his Duesenberg and the waters of a cove, whose sun-painted ripples were visible from the elevation of the main house. This body of water, District Attorney Isham explained, was a tributary of Long Island Sound; it was called Ketcham's Cove. Beyond the waters of the Cove could be seen the woody silhouette of a small island. Oyster Island, remarked the Professor; housing as queer a collection of . . .

Ellery looked at him inquiringly, but Isham said: "We'll get to that," testily, and Yardley shrugged and refrained from further interruption.

The gravel walk led gradually away from the house, and massed trees enclosed them not thirty feet from the colonial structure. A hundred feet farther, and they came suddenly upon a clearing, in the center of which stood a grotesque object.

They stopped short, and ceased talking, as people do in the presence of violent death. Around the object were county troopers and detectives, but Ellery had eyes only for the object itself.

It was a thick carved post nine feet high which once, to judge from what remained, had been garishly colored, but now was faded and stained and battered, as if it had gone through centuries of weathering. The carving, a conglomeration of gargoyle masks and hybrid animal symbols, culminated at the top in the crudely hewn figure of an eagle with lowered beak and outstretched wings. The wings were rather flat, and Ellery was struck at once with the fact that the post with its outflung wings at the top was very like a capital T.

The decapitated body of a man hung on the post, arms lashed to the wings with heavy rope, legs similarly lashed to the upright about three feet from the earth. The sharp wooden beak of the eagle hovered an inch above the bloody hole where the man's head had been. There was something pathetic as well as horrible in the hideous sight; the mutilated corpse emanated a helplessness, the pitiful impotence of a beheaded rag doll.

"Well," said Ellery with a shaky giggle, "quite a sight, eh?"

"Shocking," muttered Isham. "I've never seen anything like it. It makes your blood curdle." He shivered. "Come on; let's get this over with."

They drew nearer the post. Ellery noticed that some yards away, in the clearing, there was a small thatched summer-house, in the entrance to which a trooper stood. Then he returned his attention to the corpse. It was that of a middle-aged man; there was a heavy paunch, and the hands were gnarled and old. The body was clothed in gray flannel trousers and a silk shirt open at the neck, white shoes, white socks, and a velveteen smoking jacket. From neck to toes the body was a gory mess, as if it had been washed in a vat of blood.

"A totem pole, isn't it?" Ellery asked Professor Yardley, as they passed beneath the body.

"Totem post," said Yardley severely. "Much the preferred term . . . Yes. I'm not an authority on totemism, but this relic is either very primitive North American, or a clever fake. I've never seen one quite like it. The eagle would signify Eagle Clan."

"I suppose the body has been identified?"

"Sure," said Inspector Vaughn. "You're looking at all that's left of Thomas Brad, owner of Bradwood, millionaire rug importer."

"But the body hasn't been cut down," said Ellery patiently. "So how can you be certain?"

District Attorney Isham looked startled. "Oh, it's Brad's, all right.

Clothing checked up, and you couldn't very well disguise that belly, could you?"

"I suppose not. Who discovered the body?"

Inspector Vaughn told the story. "It was found at half-past seven this morning by one of Brad's servants, a sort of combination chauffeur and gardener, chap by the name of Fox. Fox lives in a hut on the other side of the house, in the woods; and when he came up to the main building this morning as usual to get the car—garage is at the back of the house—for Jonah Lincoln, one of the people who live here, he found that Lincoln wasn't ready and went around this end to look at some of the flowers. Anyway, this is what he ran up against. Gave him quite a turn, he says."

"I imagine it would," remarked Professor Yardley, who betrayed a surprising lack of squeamishness himself; he was examining the totem post and its grisly burden with thoughtful impersonality, as if it were a rare historic object.

"Well," continued Inspector Vaughn, "he took hold of himself and ran back to the house. Usual stuff—roused the household. Nobody touched anything. Lincoln, who's a nervous but levelheaded fellow, took charge until we came."

"And who is Lincoln?" asked Ellery pleasantly.

"General Manager of Brad's business. Brad & Megara, you know," explained Isham, "the big rug importers. Lincoln lives here. Brad liked him a lot, I understand."

"An embryonic rug magnate, eh? And Megara—does he live here, too?"

Isham shrugged. "When he's not traveling. He's off on a cruise somewhere; he's been away for months. Brad was the active partner."

"I take it, then, that Mr. Megara, the traveler, was responsible for the totem pole—or post, in deference to the Professor. Not that it matters."

A cold little man sauntered up the path toward them, carrying a black bag.

"Here's Doc Rumsen," said Isham with a sigh of relief. "Medical Examiner of Nassau County. Hi, Doc, take a look at this!"

"I'm looking," said Dr. Rumsen in a nasty tone. "What is this— the Chicago stockyards?"

Ellery scrutinized the body. It seemed very stiff. Dr. Rumsen looked up at it professionally, sniffed, and said: "Well, get it down, get it down. Do you expect me to climb the pole and examine it up there?"

Inspector Vaughn motioned to two detectives, and they jumped forward unclasping knives. One of them disappeared in the summerhouse, returning a moment later with a rustic chair. He placed it beside the totem post, climbed to the seat, and raised his knife.

"Want me to cut it, Chief?" he asked before bringing the blade down on the lashings of the right arm. "Maybe you'd rather have the rope in one piece. I think I can untie the knot."

"You cut it," said the Inspector sharply. "I want to take a look at that knot. Might be a clue there."

Others came forward, and the depressing business of taking the body down was accomplished in silence.

"By the way," remarked Ellery, as they stood about watching the proceedings, "how did the murderer manage to get the body up there, and then lash the wrist to the wings nine feet above ground?"

"The same way the detective's doing it now," replied the District Attorney dryly. "We found a blood-stained chair, like the one he's using, in the summerhouse. Either there were two of 'em, or the fellow who pulled this job was a husky. Must have been quite a job heaving a dead body up to that position, even with a chair."

"You found the chair where?" asked Ellery thoughtfully. "In the summerhouse?"

"Yes. He must have put it back there after he was through with it. There are plenty of other things in the summerhouse, Mr. Queen, that'll bear looking into."

"There's something else that might interest you," said Inspector

Vaughn, as the body was finally freed from its lashings and deposited on the grass. "This."

He took a small circular red object from his pocket and handed it to Ellery. It was a red wooden checker.

"Hmm," said Ellery. "Prosaic enough. Where did you find this, Inspector?"

"In the gravel of the clearing here," replied Vaughn. "A few feet from the right side of the pole."

"What makes you think it's important?" Ellery turned the piece over in his fingers.

Vaughn smiled. "This is the way we found it. It hasn't lain here very long, for one thing, as you can see by its condition. And on that clean gray gravel a red object would stand out like a sore thumb. These grounds are gone over by Fox with a finecomb each day; it's not likely, then, that it was here in the daytime—Fox says it wasn't, anyway. I'd say offhand that it has something to do with the events of last night; in the darkness it wouldn't be seen."

"Excellent, Inspector!" smiled Ellery. "A man after my own heart." He returned the checker just as Dr. Rumsen ripped out a string of lurid oaths wholly unprofessional.

"What's the matter?" asked Isham, hurrying over. "Did you find something?"

"The queerest damn' thing *I* ever saw," snapped the Medical Examiner. "Look at this."

The corpse of Thomas Brad lay outstretched on the grass a few feet from the totem post like a fallen marble statue. It was so unnaturally rigid that Ellery, out of his own sad but thorough experience, realized that *rigor mortis* had not yet left the body. As it sprawled there, arms still outflung, it bore except for the paunch and clothes a marked resemblance to the body of Andrew Van as Ellery had seen it in Weirton six months before; and both of them, he reflected without satisfaction, were human figures hacked into the shape of a T. . . . He shook his head and stooped with the others to see what had disturbed Dr. Rumsen so.

The physician had raised the right hand of the dead man; he was pointing to the blue dead palm. In the center, neatly printed as if by a die, there was a circular red stain, its outline only faintly irregular.

"Now what on earth d'ye call that?" grumbled Dr. Rumsen. "It isn't blood. Looks more like paint, or dye. But I'll be damned if I can see any reason for it."

"It seems," said Ellery slowly, "that your prediction is coming true, Inspector. The checker—the right side of the pole—the right hand of the dead man. . . ."

"By God, yes!" cried Inspector Vaughn. He produced the checker again and placed it on the stain in the dead palm. It fitted, and he rose with a mingled look of triumph and puzzlement. "But what the devil?"

District Attorney Isham shook his head. "I don't think it's important. You haven't seen Brad's library yet, Vaughn, so you don't know. But there's the remains of a checker game there. You'll find out more about it when we go into the house. Brad for some reason had a checker in his hand at the time he was killed, and the murderer didn't know it. It fell out of his hand about the time he was being strung up, that's all."

"Then the crime was committed in the house?" asked Ellery.

"Oh, no. In the summerhouse here. Plenty of evidence for *that*. No, I think the explanation of the checker is simplicity itself. It looks like a defective piece, and probably the perspiration and heat of Brad's hand made the color run."

They left Dr. Rumsen exploring the inhuman figure on the grass, surrounded by silent officers, and made for the summerhouse. It was only a few steps from the totem post. Ellery looked up and around before stepping through the low entrance.

"No electrical fixtures outside, I see. I wonder—"

"Murderer must have used a flashlight. That is, if this thing really did take place," said the Inspector, "in the dark. Doc Rumsen will clear that up for us when he tells us how long Brad's been dead."

The trooper at the entrance saluted and stood aside. They went in.

It was small and circular, constructed of rough tree boughs and limbs in the artificially rustic manner. It had a peaked thatched roof and half-walls, the upper halves composed of green lattice. Inside were a hewn table and two chairs, one of them smeared with blood.

"Not much doubt of it, I'd say," said District Attorney Isham with a feeble grunt, pointing to the floor.

In the center of the floor there was a large thick stain, brownish-red in hue.

Professor Yardley for the first time showed nervousness. "Why— that isn't human blood—that ghastly large mess of it?"

"It certainly is," replied Vaughn grimly. "And the only thing that will explain why there's so much of it is that Brad's head was cut off right on this floor."

Ellery's sharp eyes were fixed on that portion of the wooden floor which was directly before the rustic table. Scrawled there boldly, in blood, was a capital T.

"Pretty thing," he muttered, and swallowed hard as he tore his gaze from the symbol. "Mr. Isham, have you been able to explain the T on the floor?"

The District Attorney spread his hands. "Now, I ask you, Mr. Queen. I'm an old hand at this game, and from what I know of you, you've had plenty of experience with such things. Could any reasonable man doubt that this is the crime of a maniac?"

"No reasonable man could," said Ellery, "and no reasonable man would. You're perfectly right, Mr. Isham. A totem pole! Felicitous, eh, Professor?"

"Post," said Yardley. "You mean the possible religious significance?" He shrugged. "How anyone could put together symbols of

North American fetishism, Christianity, and primitive phallicism is beyond the imagination of even a maniac."

Vaughn and Isham stared; neither Yardley nor Ellery enlightened them. Ellery stooped to examine something which lay on the floor, near the coagulated blood. It was a long-stemmed brier pipe.

"We've looked that over," said Inspector Vaughn. "Fingerprints on it. Brad's. His pipe, all right; he was smoking in here. We've put it back for you just where we found it."

Ellery nodded. It was an unusual pipe, of striking shape; its bowl was skillfully carved in the semblance of a Neptune's head and trident. It was half full of dead gray ashes, and near the bowl on the floor, as Vaughn pointed out, were tobacco ashes of similar color and texture; as if the pipe had been dropped and some of the ashes had spilled.

Ellery stretched his hand out to take the pipe—and stopped. He looked at the Inspector. "You're positive, Inspector, that this was the victim's pipe? I mean —you've checked up with the residents of the house?"

"As a matter of fact, no," replied Vaughn stiffly. "I don't see why the hell we should doubt it. After all, his prints—"

"And he was wearing a smoking jacket, too," pointed out Isham. "And no other form of tobacco on him—cigarettes or cigars. I can't see, Mr. Queen, why you should think—"

Professor Yardley smothered a smile in his beard, and Ellery remarked almost idly: "But I don't think anything of the sort. It's merely habit with me, Mr. Isham. Perhaps . . ."

He picked up the pipe and carefully knocked the ashes out on the surface of the table. When no more ashes fell, he looked into the bowl and saw that a covering of half-burnt tobacco remained on the bottom. He produced a glassine envelope from his pocket-kit and, scraping the unsmoked tobacco from the bottom, poured it into the envelope. The others watched in silence.

"You see," he said, rising, "I don't believe in taking things for granted. I'm not suggesting that this isn't Brad's pipe. I do say, however, that the tobacco in it may be a definite clue. Suppose this is Brad's pipe, but that he borrowed the *tobacco* from his murderer. Surely a common enough occurrence. Now, you'll notice that this tobacco is cube-cut; not a common cut, as you perhaps know. We examine Brad's humidor; do we find cube-cut tobacco? If we do, then this is his, and he did not borrow it from his murderer. At any rate we have lost nothing; confirmed the previous facts. But if we don't find cube-cut tobacco, there's a fair presumption that the tobacco came from his murderer, and that would be an important clue. . . . Excuse me for babbling."

"Very interesting," said Isham. "I'm sure."

"The minutiae of the detective science," chuckled Professor Yardley.

"Well, how does it stack up to you so far?" demanded Vaughn.

Ellery polished the lenses of his pince-nez thoughtfully; his lean face was absorbed. "It's ridiculous, of course, to make any more concrete statement than this: The murderer was either with Brad when Brad came to the summerhouse, or he was not; there is nothing so far to tell. In any event, when Brad strolled out into his gardens, headed for his summerhouse, he had in his hand a red checker which for some peculiar reason he must have picked up in his house—wherever the remains of the checker game are to be seen. In the summerhouse he was attacked and killed. Perhaps the attack occurred while he was smoking; the pipe dropped from his mouth and fell to the floor. Perhaps, too, his fingers were in his pocket playing with the checker absently. At the time he died the checker was still clutched in his hand, and remained so all the time he was being decapitated, hauled to the totem post and lashed to the wings. Then the checker fell and rolled off in the gravel, unobserved by the murderer. . . . Why he brought the checker with him at all seems to me a most relevant query. It may have a definite bearing on the case. . . . An unilluminating analysis, eh, Professor?"

"Who knows the nature of light?" murmured Yardley.

~

Dr. Rumsen fussed into the summerhouse. "Job's done," he announced.

"What's the verdict, Doc?" asked Isham eagerly.

"No signs of violence on the body," snapped Dr. Rumsen. "From this it's perfectly evident that whatever killed him was directed at his head." Ellery started; it might have been Dr. Strang repeating the testimony he had given in the Weirton courtroom months before.

"Could he have been strangled?" asked Ellery.

"No way of telling now. Autopsy will show, though, by the condition of the lungs. The body's stiffness is a simple *rigor*, which won't wear off for another twelve to twenty-four hours."

"How long has he been dead?" asked Inspector Vaughn.

"Just about fourteen hours."

"Then it was in the dark!" cried Isham. "Crime must have been committed around ten o'clock last night!"

Dr. Rumsen shrugged. "Let me finish, will you? I want to go home. Strawberry birthmark seven inches above the right knee. That's all."

As they left the summerhouse Inspector Vaughn said suddenly: "Say, that reminds me, Mr. Queen. Your father mentioned over the phone that you had some information for us."

Ellery looked at Professor Yardley, and Professor Yardley looked at Ellery. "Yes," said Ellery, "I have. Inspector, does anything about this crime strike you as peculiar?"

"Everything about it strikes me as peculiar," grunted Vaughn. "Just what do you mean?"

Ellery thoughtfully kicked a pebble out of his path. They passed the totem post in silence; the body of Thomas Brad was covered now, and several men were placing it on a stretcher. They headed down the path toward the house.

"Has it occurred to you to ask," continued Ellery, "why a man should be beheaded and crucified to a totem post?"

"Yes, but what good does it do me?" snarled Vaughn. "It's crazy, that's all."

"Do you mean to say," Ellery protested, "that you haven't noticed the multiple T's?"

"The multiple T's?"

"The pole itself—a fantastic T in shape. The pole for the upright, the flatout spread wings for the arms." They blinked. "The body: head cut off, arms outstretched, legs close together." They blinked again. "A T deliberately scrawled in blood on the scene of the crime."

"Well, of course," said Isham doubtfully, "we saw that, but—"

"And to bring it to a farcical conclusion," said Ellery without smiling, "the very word totem begins with a T."

"Oh, stuff and nonsense," said the District Attorney instantly. "Pure coincidence. The pole, too, the position of the body—it just happened that way."

"Coincidence?" Ellery sighed. "Would you call it coincidence if I told you that six months ago a murder was committed in West Virginia in which the victim was crucified to a T-shaped signpost on a T-shaped crossroads, his head cut off, and a T smeared in blood on the door of his house not a hundred yards away?"

Isham and Vaughn stopped short, and the District Attorney turned pale. "You're not joking, Mr. Queen!"

"I'm really astounded at you people," said Professor Yardley with placidity. "After all, this sort of thing is your business. Even I, the veriest layman, knew all about it; it was reported in every newspaper in the country."

"Come to think of it," muttered Isham, "I seem to recall it."

"But, my God, Mr. Queen!" cried Vaughn. "It's impossible! It's— it's not sensible!"

"Not sensible—yes," murmured Ellery, "but impossible—no, for it actually happened. There was a peculiar fellow who called himself Ra-Harakht, or Harakht. . . ."

"I wanted to talk to you about him," began Professor Yardley.

"Harakht!" shouted Inspector Vaughn. "There's a nut by that name running a nudist colony on Oyster Island across the Cove!"

Chapter Five

INTERNAL AFFAIRS

FOR THE MOMENT THE tables were turned, and it was Ellery's astonishment which dominated the scene. The brown-bearded fanatic in the neighborhood of Bradwood! The closest link to Velja Krosac appearing on the scene of a crime the duplicate of the first! It was too good to be true.

"I wonder if any of the others are here," he remarked as they strode up the steps of the porch. "We may be investigating merely a sequel to the first murder, with the identical cast! Harakht . . ."

"I didn't get a chance to tell you," said Yardley sadly. "It seems to me that, with your odd notions about the Egyptian business, Queen, you should already have arrived at my conclusion."

"So soon?" drawled Ellery. "And what is your conclusion?"

Yardley grinned all over his pleasantly ugly face. "That Harakht, much as I dislike accusing people indiscriminately, is . . . Well, certainly crucifixions and T's seem to follow the gentleman about, do they not?"

"You forget Krosac," remarked Ellery.

"My dear chap," retorted the Professor tartly, "surely you know me well enough by this time . . . I don't forget anything of the sort. Why does the existence of Krosac invalidate what I've just timidly suggested? After all, there are such things as

57

confederates, I understand, in crime. And there's a huge primitive sort of fellow—"

Inspector Vaughn came running back to meet them on the porch, interrupting what promised to be an interesting conversation.

"I've just had Oyster Island put under guard," he panted. "No sense in taking chances. We'll investigate that bunch as soon as we finish here."

The District Attorney seemed bewildered by the rapidity of events. "You mean to tell me that it was this Harakht's business manager who was suspected of the crime? What the devil did he look like?" He had listened to Ellery's recital of the Arroyo affair with feverish attention.

"There was a superficial description. Not enough, really, to work on, except for the fact that the man limped. No, Mr. Isham, the problem isn't simple. You see, so far as I know, this man who calls himself Harakht is the only person capable of identifying the mysterious Krosac. And if our friend the sun-god proves stubborn . . ."

"Let's go in," said Inspector Vaughn abruptly. "This is getting too much for me. I want to talk to people and hear things."

In the drawing room of the colonial mansion they found a tragic group awaiting them. The three people who creaked to their feet on the entrance of Ellery and the others were red-eyed, drawn of face, and so nervous that their movements were a series of jerks.

"Uh-hello," said the man in a dry, cracked voice. "We've been waiting." He was a tall, lean and vigorous man in his mid-thirties; a New Englander, to judge from his choppy features and the faint twang in his voice.

"Hullo," said Isham glumly. "Mrs. Brad, this is Mr. Ellery Queen, who's come down from New York to help us."

Ellery murmured the conventional condolences; they did not shake hands. Margaret Brad moved and walked as if she were gliding through the horrors of a nightmare. She was a woman of forty-five, but well set up and handsome in a mature well-cushioned way. She said out of stiff lips: "So glad . . . Thank you, Mr. Queen. I—" She turned away and sat down without finishing, as if she had forgotten what she meant to say.

"And this is the—is Mr. Brad's stepdaughter," continued the District Attorney. "Miss Brad—Mr. Queen."

Helene Brad smiled grimly at Ellery, nodded to Professor Yardley, and went to her mother's side without a word. She was a young girl with wise, rather lovely eyes, honest features, and faintly red hair.

"Well?" demanded the tall man. His voice was still cracked.

"We're getting along," muttered Vaughn. "Mr. Queen—Mr. Lincoln . . . We want to set Mr. Queen straight on certain things, and our own confab here an hour ago wasn't any too complete." They all nodded, gravely, like characters in a play. "You want to handle this, Mr. Queen? Shoot."

"No, indeed," said Ellery. "I'll interrupt when I think of something. Pay no attention to me at all."

Inspector Vaughn stood powerful and tall by the fireplace, hands clasped loosely behind his back; his eyes were fixed on Lincoln. Isham sat down, mopping his bald spot. The Professor sighed and walked quietly to a window, where he stood looking out upon the front gardens and the drive. The house was quiet, as after a noisy party, or after a funeral. There was no bustle, no crying, no hysteria. With the exception of Mrs. Brad, her daughter, and Jonah Lincoln, none of the other members of the household—servants—had appeared.

"Well, the first thing, I guess," began Isham wearily, "is to get that business of last night's theater tickets straight, Mr. Lincoln. Suppose you tell us the whole story."

"Theater tickets . . . Oh, yes." Lincoln glared at the wall above Isham's head with the glassy eyes of a shell-shocked soldier. "Yesterday Tom Brad telephoned Mrs. Brad from the office that he'd secured tickets for a Broadway play for her, Helene, and myself. Mrs. Brad and Helene were to meet me in the city. He, Brad, was going on home. He told me about it a few minutes later. He seemed rather keen on my taking the ladies. I couldn't refuse."

"Why should you want to refuse?" asked the Inspector quickly.

Lincoln's fixed expression did not change. "It struck me as a peculiar request to make at the time. We've been having some trouble at the office; a matter of accounts. I had been intending to remain late yesterday, working with our auditor. I reminded Tom about this, but he said never mind."

"I can't understand it," said Mrs. Brad tonelessly. "Almost as if he wanted to be rid of us." She shivered suddenly, and Helene patted her shoulder.

"Mrs. Brad and Helene met me at Longchamps for dinner," continued Lincoln in the same strained voice. "After dinner I took them to the theater—"

"Which theater?" asked Isham.

"The Park Theater. I left them there—"

"Oh," said Inspector Vaughn. "Decided to do that work, anyway, eh?"

"Yes. I excused myself, promised to meet them after the performance, and returned to the office."

"And you worked with your auditor, Mr. Lincoln?" asked Vaughn softly.

Lincoln stared. "Yes . . . God." He tossed his head and gasped, like a man drowning. No one said a word. When he resumed, it was quietly, as if nothing had happened. "I finished late, and went back to the thea—"

"The auditor remained with you all evening?" asked the Inspector in the same soft voice.

Lincoln started. "Why—" He shook his head dazedly. "What do you mean? No. He left about eight o'clock. I continued to work alone."

Inspector Vaughn cleared his throat; his eyes were glittering. "What time did you meet the ladies at the theater?"

"Eleven-forty-five," said Helene Brad suddenly in a composed voice that nevertheless made her mother dart a glance up at her. "My dear Inspector Vaughn, your tactics aren't too fair. You suspect Jonah of something, goodness knows what, and you're trying to make him out a liar and—and other things, I suppose."

"The truth never hurt anybody," said Vaughn coldly. "Go on, Mr. Lincoln."

Lincoln blinked twice. "I met Mrs. Brad and Helene in the lobby. We went home. . . ."

"By car?" asked Isham.

"No, by the Long Island. When we got off the train Fox wasn't there with the car and we took a taxi home."

"Taxi?" muttered Vaughn. He stood thinking, then without a word left the room. The Brad women and Lincoln stared after him with fright in their eyes.

"Go on," said Isham impatiently. "See anything wrong when you got home? What time was it?"

"I don't really know. About one o'clock, I suppose." Lincoln's shoulders drooped.

"After one," said Helene. "You don't remember, Jonah."

"Yes. We saw nothing out of the way. The path to the summer-house . . ." Lincoln shivered. "We didn't think of looking there. We couldn't have seen anything, anyway—it was too dark. We went to bed."

Inspector Vaughn came back quietly.

"How is it, Mrs. Brad," asked Isham, "that you didn't know your husband was missing until this morning, as you told me before?"

"We sleep—we slept in adjoining bedrooms," explained the woman from pale lips. "So I wouldn't know, you see. Helene and I retired . . . The first we knew of what—happened to Thomas was when Fox got us out of bed this morning."

Inspector Vaughn stepped over and bent to whisper something into Isham's ear. The District Attorney nodded vaguely.

"How long have you been living in this house, Mr. Lincoln?" asked Vaughn.

"A long time. How many years is it, Helene?" The tall New Englander turned to look at Helene; their eyes met and flashed in sympathy. The man braced his shoulders, drew a deep breath, and the glassiness in his eyes vanished.

"Eight, I think, Jonah." Her voice trembled, and for the first time tears clouded her eyes. "I—I was just a kid when you and Hester came."

"Hester?" repeated Vaughn and Isham together. "Who's she?"

"My sister," replied Lincoln in a calmer voice. "She and I were left orphans early in life. I've—well, she goes with me as naturally as my name."

"Where is she? Why haven't we seen her?"

Lincoln said quietly: "She's on the Island."

"Oyster Island?" drawled Ellery. "How interesting. She hasn't become a sun worshiper by any chance, Mr. Lincoln?"

"Why, how did you know?" exclaimed Helene. "Jonah, you haven't—"

"My sister," explained Lincoln with difficulty, "is something of a faddist. Goes in for things like that. This lunatic who calls himself Harakht rented the Island from the Ketchams—old-timers who live on the Island; own it, in fact—and started a cult. Sun cult and—well, nudism . . ." He strangled over something in his throat. "Hester—well, Hester became interested in—the people over there, and we had a quarrel over it. She's headstrong, and left Bradwood to join the cult. The damned fakers!" he said savagely. "I shouldn't be surprised if they had something to do with this ghastly business."

"Shrewd, Mr. Lincoln," murmured Professor Yardley.

Ellery coughed gently and addressed the rigid figure of Mrs. Brad. "I'm sure you won't mind answering a few personal questions?" She looked up, and down at the hands in her lap. "I understand that Miss Brad is your daughter and was your husband's stepdaughter. A second husband, Mrs. Brad?"

The handsome woman said: "Yes."

"Mr. Brad had been previously married as well?"

She bit her lips. "We—we were married twelve years. Tom—I don't know much about his first—his first wife. I think he was married in Europe, and his first wife died very young."

"Tch-tch," said Ellery with a sympathetic frown. "What part of Europe, Mrs. Brad?"

She looked at him and a slow flush filled her cheeks. "I don't really know. Thomas was Roumanian. I suppose it happened—there."

Helene Brad tossed her head and said indignantly: "Really, you people are being absurd. What difference does it make where people come from, or whom they were married to years and years ago? Why don't you try to find out who *killed* him?"

"Something tells me with insistence, Miss Brad," replied Ellery, smiling sadly, "that the matter of geography may become extremely important . . . Is Mr. Megara Roumanian, too?"

Mrs. Brad looked blank. Lincoln said curtly: "Greek."

"What in the world—?" began the District Attorney helplessly.

Inspector Vaughn smiled. "Greek, eh? You people are all native Americans, I suppose?"

They nodded. Helene's eyes were flashing angrily; even the fiery glints in her hair seemed to glow brighter, and she looked at Jonah Lincoln as if she expected him to remonstrate. But he said nothing, merely looking down at the tips of his shoes.

"Where is Megara?" went on Isham. "Somebody said he was on a cruise. What kind of cruise—round-the-world?"

"No," said Lincoln slowly. "Nothing like that. Mr. Megara is something of a globe-trotter and amateur explorer. He has his own yacht and keeps sailing about in it. He just goes off and stays away for three and four months at a time."

"How long's he been away on this trip?" demanded Vaughn.

"Almost a year."

"Where is he?"

Lincoln shrugged. "I don't know. He never writes—just pops in without warning. I can't understand why he's stayed away so long this time."

"I think," said Helene, wrinkling her forehead, "that he went to the South Seas." Her eyes were luminous and her lips quivered; Ellery regarded her curiously and wondered why.

"What's the name of his yacht?"

Helene flushed. "The *Helene*."

"Steam yacht?" asked Ellery.

"Yes."

"Has he a radio—wireless sending outfit?" demanded Vaughn.

"Yes."

The Inspector scribbled in his notebook and looked pleased. "Sail it himself, does he?" he asked as he wrote.

"Of course not! He has a regular captain and crew—Captain Swift, who's been with him for years."

Ellery sat down suddenly and stretched his long legs. "I do believe . . . What's Megara's first name?"

"Stephen."

Isham growled deep in his throat. "Oh, Lord. Why can't we stick to essentials? How long have Brad and Megara been partners in this rug-importing business?"

"Sixteen years," replied Jonah. "Went into business together."

"Successful business, is it? No financial troubles?"

Lincoln shook his head. "Both Mr. Brad and Mr. Megara founded very substantial fortunes. They were hit by the depression, like everyone else; but the business is sound." He paused and an odd look changed the expression of his lean healthy face. "I don't believe you'll find money troubles at the bottom of this thing."

"Well," grunted Isham, "what *do* you think is at the bottom of it?"

Lincoln closed his mouth with a little snap.

"You don't by any chance," drawled Ellery, "think there's *religion* behind it, Mr. Lincoln?"

Lincoln blinked. "Why—I didn't say so. But the crime itself—the crucifixion . . ."

Ellery smiled pleasantly. "By the way, what was Mr. Brad's creed?"

Mrs. Brad, still sitting with her ample back arched, chest out, chin up, murmured: "He once told me he had been raised in the Orthodox Greek Church. But he wasn't devout, to fact, he was a non-believer in ritual; some people considered him an atheist."

"And Megara?"

"Oh, he doesn't believe in anything at all." There was something in her tone which caused all of them to look at her sharply; but her face was expressionless.

"Orthodox Greek," said Professor Yardley thoughtfully. "That's consistent enough with Roumania. . . ."

"You're looking for inconsistencies?" murmured Ellery.

Inspector Vaughn coughed, and Mrs. Brad regarded him tensely. She seemed to sense what was coming. "Did your husband have any identifying marks on his body, Mrs. Brad?"

Helene looked faintly nauseated, and turned her head aside. Mrs. Brad muttered: "A strawberry birthmark on his right thigh."

The Inspector sighed with relief. "So that's that. Now, folks, let's get down to bedrock. How about enemies? Who might have wanted to do Mr. Brad in?"

"Forget this business of the crucifixion and everything else for the moment," added the District Attorney. "Who had a motive for murder?"

Mother and daughter turned to regard each other; they looked away almost at once. Lincoln kept staring steadfastly at the rug—a magnificent Oriental, Ellery noted, with a beautifully woven Tree of Life design; an unhappy juxtaposition of symbol and reality, considering the fact he reflected, that its owner . . .

"No," said Mrs. Brad. "Thomas was a happy man. He had no enemies."

"Were you in the habit of entertaining comparative strangers?"

"Oh, no. We lead a secluded life here, Mr. Isham." There was something again in her tone that made them look keenly at her.

Ellery sighed. "Do any of you recall the presence here—guest or otherwise—of a limping man?" They shook their heads instantly. "Mr. Brad knew no one with a limp?" Another concerted negative.

Mrs. Brad said again: "Thomas had no enemies," with dull emphasis, as if she felt it important to impress this fact upon them.

"You're forgetting something, Margaret," said Jonah Lincoln slowly. "Romaine."

He looked at her with burning eyes. Helene flashed a glance of horrified condemnation at his clean profile; then she bit her lip and tears came to her eyes. The four men looked on with growing interest and a sense of underflowing byplay; there was something unhealthy here, a sore on the Brad body domestic.

"Yes, Romaine," said Mrs. Brad, licking her lips; the position of her figure had not changed for ten minutes. "I forgot. They had a quarrel."

"Who the devil's Romaine?" demanded Vaughn.

Lincoln said in a low quick voice: "Paul Romaine. Harakht, that lunatic on Oyster Island, calls him the 'chief disciple.'"

"Ah," said Ellery, and looked at Professor Yardley. The ugly man raised his shoulders expressively, and smiled.

"They've built up a nudist colony on the Island. Nudists!" cried Lincoln bitterly. "Harakht is a nut—he's probably sincere; but Romaine is a faker, the worst kind of confidence man. He trades on his body, which is only the cloak of a rotten soul!"

"And yet," murmured Ellery, "didn't Holmes recommend: 'Build thee more stately mansions, O my soul'?"

"Sure," said Inspector Vaughn, intent on soothing this strange witness. "We understand. But about that quarrel, Mr. Lincoln?"

Lean face worked fiercely. "Romaine's responsible for the 'guests' on the Island—works up the business. He's hooked a bunch of poor fools who either think he's some kind of tin god, or else are so damn repressed that the very thought of running around naked . . ." He stopped abruptly. "Excuse me, Helene—Margaret. I shouldn't talk. Hester . . . They haven't been bothering any of the residents here, I'll admit. But Tom and Dr. Temple feel the same way I do about it."

"Hmm," said Professor Yardley. "Nobody consulted *me.*"

"Dr. Temple?"

"Our neighbor to the east. They were seen capering around Oyster Island absolutely nude, like human goats, and well—we're a decent community." Ah, thought Ellery; thus spake the Puritan. "Tom owns all this property fronting the Cove, and he felt that it was his duty to interfere. He had some sort of run-in with Romaine and Harakht. I think he was intending to take legal measures to oust them from the Island, and he told them so."

Vaughn and Isham looked at each other, and then at Ellery. The Brads, mother and daughter, were very still; and Lincoln, now that he had rid himself of his accumulated bile, looked uneasy and ashamed.

"Well, we'll look into that a little later," said Vaughn lightly. "You say this Dr. Temple owns the estate adjoining on the east?"

"He doesn't own it; he just rents it—rented it from Thomas." Mrs. Brad's eyes were relieved. "He's been here for a long time. A retired army doctor. He and Thomas were good friends."

"Who lives on that piece of property to the west?"

"Oh! An English couple named Lynn—Percy and Elizabeth," replied Mrs. Brad.

Helene murmured: "I met them in Rome last fall and we became very friendly. They said they were thinking of paying a visit to the States and so I suggested that they come back with me and be my guests for the duration of their stay."

"Just when did you return, Miss Brad?" asked Ellery.

"About Thanksgiving. The Lynns crossed with me, but we separated in New York and they traveled about a bit seeing the country. Then in January they came up here. They were wild about the place—" Lincoln grunted, and Helene flushed. "They were, Jonah! So much so that, not wanting to impose on our hospitality—it was silly, of course, but you know how stuffy the English can be sometimes—they insisted on leasing the house to the west, which is—was father's property. They've been here ever since."

"Well, we'll talk to them, too," said Isham. "This Dr. Temple, now. You said, Mrs. Brad, that he and your husband were good friends. Best of terms, eh?"

"There's nothing in that direction," said Mrs. Brad stiffly, "if you're insinuating, Mr. Isham. I've never been overfond of Dr. Temple myself, but he's an upright man and Thomas, a wonderful judge of character, liked him tremendously. They often played checkers together in the evening."

Professor Yardley sighed, as if slightly bored with this recital of the neighbors' vices and virtues when he himself could provide a more penetrating analysis.

"Checkers!" exclaimed Inspector Vaughn. "Now, that's something. Who else played with Mr. Brad, or was this Dr. Temple his only opponent?"

"No, indeed! We all played with Thomas on occasion."

Vaughn looked disappointed. Professor Yardley rubbed his black Lincolnian beard and said: "I'm afraid you're on barren ground there, Inspector. Brad was a fiendishly clever checker player, and tackled everyone who came here for a bout. If they didn't know how to play, he insisted—with patience, to be sure—on teaching them. I think," he chuckled, "that I was the only visitor here who successfully resisted his blandishments." Then he became grave and fell silent.

"He was a remarkable player," said Mrs. Brad with a faint sad pride. "I was told that by the National Checker Champion himself."

"Oh, you're a good player yourself, then?" asked Isham quickly.

"No, no, Mr. Isham. But we entertained the champion last Christmas Eve, and Thomas and he played incessantly. The champion said that Thomas held him quite even."

Ellery jumped to his feet, his keen face intent. "I believe we're wearing these good people out. A few questions, and we'll not bother you again, Mrs. Brad. Have you ever heard the name Velja Krosac?"

Mrs. Brad looked genuinely puzzled. "Vel—what a queer name! No, Mr. Queen, I never have."

"You, Miss Brad?"

"No."

"You, Mr. Lincoln?"

"No."

"Have you ever heard the name Kling?"

They all shook their heads.

"Andrew Van?"

Another blank.

"Arroyo, West Virginia?"

Lincoln muttered: "What is this, anyway? A game?"

"In a way," smiled Ellery. "You haven't, any of you?"

"No."

"Well, then, here's one you certainly can answer. Exactly when did this fanatic who calls himself Harakht come to Oyster Island?"

"Oh, that!" said Lincoln. "In March."

"Was this man Paul Romaine with him?"

Lincoln's face darkened. "Yes."

Ellery scrubbed his pince-nez, perched it on the bridge of his straight nose, and leaned forward. "Does the letter T mean anything to any of you?"

They stared at him. "T?" repeated Helene. "Whatever are you talking about?"

"Evidently it doesn't," remarked Ellery, as Professor Yardley chuckled and whispered something in his ear. "Very well, then, Mrs. Brad, did your husband often refer to his Roumanian history?"

"No, he never did. All I know is that he came to the United States from Roumania eighteen years ago, with Stephen Megara. It seems they were friends or business partners in the old country."

"How do you know this?"

"Why—why, Thomas told me so."

Ellery's eyes sparkled. "Pardon my curiosity, but it may be important. . . . Was your husband a wealthy man as an immigrant?"

Mrs. Brad flushed. "I don't know. When we married, he was."

Ellery looked thoughtful. He said "Hmm" several times, shook his head in a pleased way, and finally turned to the District Attorney. "And now, Mr. Isham, if I may have an atlas, I shan't bother you for some time."

"An atlas!" The District Attorney gaped, and even Professor Yardley seemed disturbed. Inspector Vaughn scowled.

"There's one in the library," said Lincoln dully. He left the drawing room.

Ellery strolled up and down, an abstracted smile on his lips. Their eyes followed him without comprehension. "Mrs. Brad," he said, pausing, "do you speak Greek or Roumanian?"

She shook her head bewilderedly. Lincoln returned, carrying a large blue-covered book. "You, Mr. Lincoln," said Ellery. "You're in a business which is largely European and Asian in its contacts. Do you understand and speak either Greek or Roumanian?"

"No. We haven't occasion to use foreign languages. Our offices in Europe and Asia correspond in English, and our distributors do the same in this country."

"I see." Ellery hefted the atlas thoughtfully. "That's all from me, Mr. Isham."

The District Attorney waved a weary hand. "All right, Mrs. Brad. We'll do our best, although frankly it looks like an insoluble mess. Just stick around, Mr. Lincoln, and you, Miss Brad; don't leave the premises for a while, anyway."

The Brads and Jonah hesitated, looked at each other, then rose and left the room without speaking.

The instant the door closed after them Ellery hurled himself into an armchair and opened the blue atlas. Professor Yardley was frowning. Isham and Vaughn exchanged helpless glances. But Ellery was occupied with the atlas for five full minutes, during which he returned to three different maps and the index, and consulted each page minutely. As he searched, his face brightened.

He placed the book with studied care on the arm of the chair and rose. They looked at him expectantly.

"I thought, by thunder," he said, "that it would be so." He turned to the Professor. "An amazing coincidence, if it is a coincidence. I leave you to judge. . . . Professor, hasn't something about the names of our peculiar cast of characters struck you?"

"The names, Queen?" Yardley was frankly confounded.

"Yes. Brad—Megara. Brad—Roumanian. Megara—Greek. Does it strike a responsive chord in you?"

Yardley shook his head, and Vaughn and Isham shrugged.

"You know," said Ellery, taking out his cigarette case and lighting one up with quick puffs, "it's little things like this that make life interesting. I've a friend who is a lunatic on one subject—that inane and juvenile game called Geography. Why he's attracted to it the Unknowable only knows, but he plays it at every conceivable opportunity. With Brad it was checkers, with many it's golf—well, with this friend of mine it's Geography. He's developed it to the point where he knows thousands of little geographic names. Something that came up not long ago . . ."

"You're being provocative," snapped Professor Yardley. "Proceed."

Ellery grinned. "Thomas Brad was a Roumanian—there is a city in Roumania named Brad. Does that mean anything to you?"

"Not a damned thing," growled Vaughn.

"Stephen Megara is a Greek. There is a city in Greece named Megara!"

"Well," muttered Isham, "what of it?"

Ellery tapped Isham's arm lightly. "And suppose I tell you that the man who seemingly has no connection with either our millionaire rug importer or our millionaire yachtsman, the poor Arroyo schoolmaster who was murdered six months ago—in a word, that Andrew *Van* . . ."

"You don't mean to say—" spluttered Vaughn.

"Van's naturalization papers gave his native country as Armenia. There's a *city* in Armenia called Van—and a lake, too, for that matter." He relaxed, and smiled. "And if in three cases, two related on the surface, the other related to one of the two by method of murder, the same phenomenon occurs—" Ellery shrugged. "If that's coincidence, then I'm the Queen of Sheba."

"Certainly peculiar," muttered Professor Yardley. "On the surface a deliberate attempt to authenticate nationalities."

"As if all the names are assumed, were picked from an atlas." Ellery blew a smoke ring. "Interesting, eh? Three gentlemen, obviously of foreign extraction, very desirous indeed of concealing their real names, and, judging from the care they employed to authenticate their nationalities, as you say, of concealing their true birthplaces as well."

"Good God," groaned Isham. "What next?"

"An even more significant fact," said Ellery cheerfully. "One would suppose that Van, Brad, and Megara having changed their names, the fourth foreign actor in the tragedy, the elusive Krosac, also picked his moniker from Rand McNally. But he didn't—at least, there's no city anywhere in Europe or in the Near East named Krosac. No city, lake, mountain, anything. The inference?"

"Three aliases," said the Professor slowly, "and one apparently genuine name. With the owner of the apparently genuine name indubitably involved in the murder of one of the aliases. Perhaps . . . I should say, Queen, my boy, that we're beginning to grasp the key to the hieroglyphs."

"You agree, then," said Ellery with eagerness, "that there's an Egyptian aroma in the atmosphere?"

Yardley started. "Oh, that! My dear chap, can't a pedagogue use a simple figure of speech without being taken literally?"

Chapter Six
CHECKERS AND PIPES

Tiiey were all thoughtful as they left the drawing room and Isham led the way to the right wing of the house, where the late Thomas Brad's study was situated. A detective paraded the hall in front of the closed library door. As they paused before it, a stout motherly-looking woman in rustling black appeared from somewhere in the rear.

"I'm Mrs. Baxter," she announced anxiously. "Can I offer you gentlemen some luncheon?"

Inspector Vaughn's eyes grew brighter. "An angel in disguise! I forgot all about chow. You're the housekeeper, aren't you?"

"Yes, sir. Will the other gentlemen eat, too?"

Professor Yardley shook his head. "I've really no right to impose this way. My own place is just across the road, and I know Old Nanny is furious at my absence. Vittles gettin' cold, as she says. I think I'll leave now. . . . Queen, you're my guest, remember."

"Must you go?" asked Ellery. "I've been looking forward to a long talk. . . ."

"See you tonight." The Professor waved his arm. "I'll take your bags out of that old wreck of yours and park your car in my own garage."

He smiled at the two officials and walked off.

Luncheon was a solemn affair. It was served in a cheery dining room to the three men—no one else in the house seemed inclined toward food—and for the most part they ate in silence. Mrs. Baxter served them herself.

Ellery munched doggedly; his brain was spinning like a planet and hurling off some extraordinary thoughts. But he kept them to himself. Isham complained once, with fervor, about his sciatica. The house was quiet.

It was two o'clock when they left the dining room and returned to the right wing. The library proved a spacious affair, the study of a cultured man. It was square, and its immaculate hardwood floor was covered except for a three-foot border by a thick Chinese rug. There were built-in shelves filled with books on two walls, from floor to beamed ceiling. In an alcove chiseled out of the angle of two walls stood a small grand piano with mellow keys, open, its top propped up—evidently as Thomas Brad had left it the night before. A low round reading table in the center of the room was covered with magazines and smoking accessories. A divan stood before one of the walls, its front legs resting on the rug; on the opposite wall a secretary, its dropleaf down. Ellery noticed that on the dropleaf, in plain view, stood two bottles of ink, red and black; both, he observed mechanically, were nearly full.

"I went through that secretary with a magnifying glass," said Isham, flinging himself upon the divan. "First thing we did, naturally. It stood to reason that if that was Brad's personal writing desk it might contain papers of value to us in the investigation." He shrugged. "Nothing doing. Everything is as innocent as a nun's diary. As for the rest of the room—well, you can see for yourself. Nothing else here of a personal nature, and besides the murder was committed in the summerhouse. It's just those checkers, now."

"Now," added Inspector Vaughn, "that we've found the red checker near the totem pole."

"You've gone through the rest of the house, I suppose?" remarked Ellery, strolling about.

"Oh, yes, in a routine way. Brad's bedroom, and so on. Absolutely nothing of interest."

Ellery turned his attention to the circular reading table. Taking from his pocket the glassine envelope of tobacco fragments from the pipe found on the summerhouse floor, he unscrewed the cap of a large humidor lying on the table and dug his hand into it. It emerged with a fistful of tobacco identical in color and cut—the uncommon cube-cut—with the tobacco from the pipe.

He laughed. "Well, no question about the filthy weed, at any rate. Another clue gone up the chimney. It was Brad's, if this humidor was Brad's."

"And it was," said Isham.

Experimentally, Ellery opened a tiny drawer whose outline was visible beneath the table's circular top. It was, he found, cluttered with a veritable collection of pipes, all of them of excellent quality, all well-used, but all in the conventional shapes—the usual bowls with straight or curved stems. There were Meerschaums, briers, and bakelites; two were thin and very long—old English clay churchwardens.

"Hmm," he said. "Mr. Brad belonged to the inner shrine. Checkers and pipes—they invariably go together. I'm surprised that there's no dog before the hearth. Well, nothing here."

"Any like this one?" demanded Vaughn, producing the Neptune-and-trident pipe.

Ellery shook his head. "You'd scarcely expect to find another, would you? A man wouldn't have two like that. No case, either. I should think he'd get lockjaw just holding that monstrosity in his mouth. It must have been a gift."

Ellery turned his attention to the main exhibit—the object which stood to the left of the open secretary on the same wall, across the room from the divan.

It was an ingenious device: a collapsible checker table which, it was evident, could be folded and swung back into a shallow niche in the wall directly behind it, to which it was attached by hinges. A sliding shutter, now resting above the niche, could be lowered to conceal the entire contrivance. In addition, there were two wall chairs, one at each side of the table, which could be similarly swung back into the wall.

"Brad must have been an addict indeed," remarked Ellery, "to have installed built-in apparatus. Hmm . . . I suppose this is as he left it. It hasn't been touched?"

"Not by us, anyway," said Isham indifferently. "See what you can make of it."

The top of the table, a glittering piece of craftsmanship, was inlaid in the usual design of sixty-four alternating white and black squares, all surrounded by a rich mother-of-pearl border. There was a wide margin at each player's side for the stacking of pieces not in play. In the margin, on the side nearer the secretary, nine red checkers lay scattered—red pieces captured by the Black side. In the opposite margin were three black pieces, captured by Red. On the board itself, in position of play, lay three black "kings" (made by placing one black piece above another), and three single black pieces; also two single red pieces, one of which was situated on Black's first, or starting, row of squares.

Ellery studied the board and the margins thoughtfully. "Where's the box these came from?"

Isham kicked in the direction of the secretary. On the open dropleaf lay a cheap cardboard rectangular box, empty.

"Eleven red pieces," said Ellery, gazing at the wall. "There should be twelve, of course. One red piece of the identical description found near the totem post."

"Right," sighed Isham. "Checked over with the rest of the household; there aren't any other checker sets in the house. So that red piece we found must have come from here."

"Quite so," said Ellery. "This is interesting, most interesting." He looked down at the pieces again.

"You think so?" said Isham sourly. "You won't in a minute. I know what you've got in mind. It isn't so. Wait till I get Brad's butler in here."

He went to the door and said to the detective: "Get that Stallings fellow in here again. The butler."

Ellery raised eyebrows that spoke eloquently, but he said nothing. He went to the secretary and idly picked up the empty cardboard checker box. Isham watched him with a little snarling grin.

"And that, too," said Isham unexpectedly.

Ellery looked up. "Yes, I wondered about that the moment I came in here. Why an inveterate player who goes to the trouble and expense of installing an elaborate checker outfit should use cheap wooden pieces."

"You'll find out in a minute. Nothing startling, I can promise you that."

The detective opened the door from the hall, and a tall thin man with sallow cheeks and bland eyes entered. He was dressed simply in black. There was something obsequious about him.

"Stallings," said Isham without preliminary, "I want you to repeat for the benefit of these gentlemen some of the information you gave me this morning."

"I'll be glad to, sir," said the butler. He had a soft, pleasant voice.

"First, how do you explain the fact that Mr. Brad played with these cheap checkers?"

"Very simple, sir, as I told you before. Mr. Brad"—Stallings sighed and rolled his eyes ceilingward—"always used only the best. He had this table and the chairs made to order, and the wall was hollowed out for them to fit into. At the same time he purchased a very expensive set of ivory checkers, all very intricately carved, you might say, and he has used them for years. Then not long ago Dr. Temple admired the set so much that Mr. Brad, as he said to me one day"—Stallings sighed again—"meant to surprise him by giving him a set just like it. Only two weeks ago he sent his set to some private carver in Brooklyn to have the twenty-four pieces duplicated, and they haven't come back yet. He couldn't get anything but these cheap ones at the moment, so he used them in the meantime."

"And, Stallings," said the District Attorney, "now tell us about what happened yesterday evening."

"Yes, sir," Stallings ran the tip of a red tongue along his lips. "Just before leaving the house last night, as Mr. Brad had ordered—"

"Hold on," said Ellery sharply. "You were instructed to leave the house last night?"

"Yes, sir. When Mr. Brad got home from the city yesterday, he called Fox, Mrs. Baxter, and myself into this very room." Stallings swallowed hard at some tender memory. "Mrs. Brad and Miss Helene had already left—they were going to the theater, I believe; Mr. Lincoln didn't come home for dinner at all. . . . Mr. Brad looked very tired. He took out a ten-dollar bill and gave it to me, and told Fox, Mrs. Baxter, and me to take the evening off after dinner. He said he wanted to be alone for the entire evening, and told Fox he might take the small car. So we went."

"I see," muttered Ellery.

"What's the story about the checkers, Stallings?" prompted Isham.

Stallings bobbed his long head. "Just before I left the house—Fox and Mrs. Baxter were already in the car in the driveway outside—I went into the library to see if there was anything I could do for Mr. Brad before we left. I asked him, and he said no, and he told me, rather nervously, I thought, to go out with the others."

"An observant chap, aren't you?" said Ellery, smiling.

Stallings looked gratified. "I try to be, sir. Anyway, as I told Mr. Isham this morning, when I came in here last evening Mr. Brad was sitting at the checker table playing with himself, so to speak."

"Then he wasn't playing with somebody," muttered Inspector Vaughn. "Why the devil didn't you tell me, Isham?"

The District Attorney spread his hands, and Ellery said: "Just what do you mean, Stallings?"

"Well, sir, he had all the pieces spread out, blacks and reds, and he was playing both sides. It was the beginning of a game. First he moved a piece from the side where he was sitting, then he thought a while and moved a piece from the opposite side. I saw only two moves."

"So," said Ellery, with pursed lips. "In which chair was he sitting?"

"In that one, near the secretary. But when he made the red move he got up and sat in the opposite chair, studying the board as he always does." Stallings smacked his lips. "A very good player, Mr. Brad was, very careful. He used to practice alone that way very often."

"And there you are," said Isham wearily. "The checker business doesn't mean a curse." He sighed. "Now about yourselves, Stallings."

"Yes, sir," replied the butler. "We all drove to the city. Fox dropped Mrs. Baxter and me off at the Roxy Theater, and said he'd come back for us after the picture let out. I don't know where he went."

"And did he come back for you?" asked Inspector Vaughn, suddenly alert.

"No, sir, he did not. We waited a full half-hour for him, but we thought he must have had an accident or something, so we took the train back and cabbed from the station."

"Cabbed, hey?" The Inspector looked pleased. "Boys at the station did a rushing business last night. What time was it you got back?"

"Around midnight, sir, maybe a little after. I'm not sure."

"Was Fox back when you got here?"

Stallings looked prim. "I'm afraid I can't say, sir. I don't know. He lives in the little cabin in the woods near the Cove, and even if there was a light we couldn't see it because of the trees."

"Well, we'll attend to that. You haven't had much of a talk with Fox, have you, Isham?"

"I haven't had the opportunity."

"One moment," said Ellery. "Stallings, did Mr. Brad say anything to you last night about expecting a visitor?"

"No, sir. He just said he wanted to be alone for the evening."

"Did he often send you, Fox, and Mrs. Baxter off that way?"

"No, sir. It was the first time."

"One thing more." Ellery went to the circular reading table and tapped the humidor with the tips of his fingers. "Know what's in this jar?"

Stallings looked astonished. "Certainly, sir! Mr. Brad's tobacco."

"Very good! Is this the only pipe tobacco in the house?"

"Yes, sir. Mr. Brad was fussy about his tobacco, and that's a special blend he had made up and imported from England. He never smoked anything else. In fact," said Stallings in a burst of confidence, "Mr. Brad often said there wasn't an American pipe tobacco worth its salt."

For no reason at all an incongruous thought flashed into Ellery's mind. Andrew Van and his caviar; Thomas Brad and his imported tobacco. . . . He shook his head. "There's another thing, Stallings. Inspector, would you mind showing that Neptune's-head pipe to Stallings?"

Vaughn produced the carved pipe again. Stallings looked at it for a moment, and then nodded. "Yes, sir, I've seen that pipe around."

The three men sighed in concert. Luck seemed to be working in the interests of crime rather than punishment. "Yes, that's the way it goes. . . . It was Brad's, eh?" grunted Isham.

"Oh, I'm sure of it, sir," said the butler. "Not that he'd smoke any one pipe for very long. He always said that a pipe, like a human being, needs a vacation every once in a while. His drawer is full of very good pipes, sir. But I recognize that one, sir. I've seen it many times before. Although not lately, come to think of it."

"All right, all right," said Isham irritably. "Beat it, now," and Stallings, with a stiff little bow, became the butler again and marched out of the study.

"That settles the checker business," said the Inspector grimly, "and the pipe business, and the tobacco business. Just a lot of wasted time. Gives us an interesting lead on Fox, though." He rubbed his hands. "Not so bad. And with that Oyster Island bunch to look over, we're going to have a busy day."

"Days, don't you think?" smiled Ellery. "This is quite like old times!"

Someone tapped on the door, and Inspector Vaughn crossed the room to open it. A man with a saturnine face stood there. He whispered for some minutes to Vaughn, and Vaughn nodded repeatedly. Finally, the Inspector closed the door and returned.

"What's up?" demanded Isham.

"Nothing much. A lot of blanks, I'm afraid. My men report that they haven't found a damned thing on the grounds. Not a thing. Cripes, it's unbelievable!"

"What were you looking for?" asked Ellery.

"The head, man, the head!"

No one said anything for a long time, and the chill wind of tragedy crept into the room. It was hard to believe, looking out into the sunny gardens, that the master of all this peace and beauty and luxury lay, a stiff headless corpse, in the County Morgue, like any nameless vagrant fished out of Long Island Sound.

"Anything else?" said Isham at last. He was growling to himself.

"The boys have had the railroad station people over the coals," said Vaughn quietly. "And every resident within five miles. Been looking, Mr. Queen, for possible visitors last night. From Lincoln's and Stallings's stories it's pretty obvious that Brad expected somebody last night. A man doesn't ship his wife, his stepdaughter, his business associate, and his servants off unless there's something queer in the wind and he wants privacy. Never did it before, either, see?"

"I see only too clearly," retorted Ellery. "No, you're perfectly justified in that assumption, Inspector. Brad expected someone last night, there's no doubt about it."

"Well, we didn't strike one person who could give us a lead. Even the conductors on the trains and the station people don't remember a stranger coming by rail around nine o'clock or so last night. Neighbors?" The Inspector shrugged. "Couldn't expect anything there, I suppose. Anyone might have come and gone without leaving a trail."

"As a matter of fact," said the District Attorney, "I think you're attempting the impossible, Vaughn. No visitor coming here last night with criminal intent would be such a damned fool as to get off at the nearest railroad station. He'd get off a station or two before or after and walk the rest of the way."

"How about the possibility of the visitor's having come by automobile?" asked Ellery.

Vaughn shook his head. "We looked for that early this morning. But in the grounds themselves the roads are gravel, which aren't any help; the highways are macadam, and it didn't rain or anything—no go, Mr. Queen. It's possible, of course."

Ellery mused deeply. "There's still another possibility, Inspector. The Sound!"

The Inspector stared out of the window. "And haven't we thought of *that*," he said with an ugly little laugh. "What a cinch it would have been! Hire a boat from the New York or Connecticut shore—a motorboat. . . . I've got a couple of men following that lead up now."

Ellery grinned. *"Quod fugit, usque sequor*—eh, Inspector?"

"Huh?"

Isham rose. "Let's get the hell out of here. There's work to do."

Chapter Seven
FOX AND THE ENGLISH

THEY WALKED MORE DEEPLY into fog. No light appeared anywhere.

It was not to be expected that Mrs. Baxter, the housekeeper, for example, would have anything of importance to contribute. Yet it was necessary, in the interests of thoroughness, to question her. They returned to the drawing room and went through the dreary business. Mrs. Baxter, in a flutter, merely confirmed Stallings's story of the excursion the night before. No, Mr. Brad had said nothing to her about visitors. No, when she served dinner to Mr. Brad alone in the dining room he did not seem particularly upset, or nervous. Just a little absent-minded, perhaps. Yes, Fox had dropped them off at the Roxy. Yes, she and Stallings had returned to Bradwood by train and taxicab, arriving a little past midnight. No, she didn't believe Mrs. Brad or the others had come home yet, but she wasn't certain. The house was dark? Yes, sir. Anything seem wrong? No, sir.

All right, Mrs. Baxter. . . . The elderly housekeeper retreated hastily and the Inspector swore with fluency.

Ellery looked on, preoccupied with a spot at the base of a fingernail at odd moments. The name Andrew Van kept swimming about in the channels of his brain.

"Come on," said Isham. "Let's talk to that chauffeur, Fox."

He strode out of the house with Vaughn, and Ellery ambled after, sniffing the June roses and wondering when his colleagues would stop chasing their tails and embark for that very interesting patch of earth and trees in the Sound, Oyster Island.

Isham led the way around the left wing of the main house, along a narrow gravel path which very soon entered a carefully wild grove. A short walk, and they emerged from under the trees to a clearing in the center of which stood a pleasant little cabin built of shaven logs. A county trooper lounged conspicuously in the sun before the hut.

Isham knocked on the stout door, and a man's deep voice said: "Come on in."

When they entered, he was on his feet, planted like an oak, fists doubled, his face curiously mottled with spots of pallor. He was a tall straight man, thin and tough as a bamboo shoot. When he saw who his visitors were, his fists unclenched, his shoulders sagged, and he groped for the back of the homemade chair before which he was standing.

"Fox," said Isham peremptorily, "I didn't get much of an opportunity this morning to talk to you."

"No, sir," said Fox. The pallor, Ellery saw with a little sensation of surprise, was not temporary; it was the man's natural complexion.

"We know how you found the body," contributed the District Attorney, dropping into the only other chair in the hut.

"Yes, sir," muttered Fox. "It was an awful exp—"

"What we want to know now," said Isham without inflection, "is why you left Stallings and Mrs. Baxter last night, where you went, and when you got home."

Curiously, the man did not blanch or cringe; the expression on his mottled features did not change. "I just drove around town," he said. "I got back to Bradwood a little before midnight."

Inspector Vaughn came forward deliberately and clamped his hand on Fox's limp arm. "Look here," he said, almost pleasantly. "We're not trying to hurt you, or frame you, you understand. If you're on the level, we'll let you alone."

"I'm on the level," said Fox. Ellery thought he detected traces of culture in the man's pronunciation and intonations. He watched him with growing interest.

"All right," said Vaughn. "That's fine. Now forget all that bunk about just driving around town. Give it to us straight. Where did you go?"

"I'm giving it to you straight," replied Fox in a dead, even voice. "I drove around Fifth Avenue and through the Park and on Riverside Drive for a long time. It was nice out, and I enjoyed the air."

The Inspector dropped his arm suddenly and grinned at Isham. "He enjoyed the air. Why didn't you call for Stallings and Mrs. Baxter after they got out of the movie?"

Fox's broad shoulders twitched in the suspicion of a shrug. "No one told me to."

Isham looked at Vaughn, and Vaughn looked at Isham. Ellery, however, looked at Fox; and he was surprised to see the man's eyes—it seemed impossible—fill with tears.

"Okay," said Isham finally. "If that's your story, you're stuck with it, and God help you if we find out otherwise. How long have you worked here?"

"Since the first of the year, sir."

"References?"

"Yes, sir." Silently he turned and went to an old sideboard. He fumbled in a drawer and brought out a clean, carefully preserved envelope.

The District Attorney ripped it open, glanced over the letter inside, and handed it to Vaughn. The Inspector read it more carefully, then, flipping it on the table, inexplicably strode out of the hut.

"Seems all right," said Isham, rising. "By the way, you, Stallings, and Mrs. Baxter are the only people employed here, aren't you?"

"Yes, sir," said Fox without raising his eyes. He picked up his references and kept turning the envelope and paper over between his fingers.

"Er—Fox," said Ellery. "When you got home last night, did you see or hear anything unusual?"

"No, sir."

"You stay put," said Isham, and left the hut. Outside, Inspector Vaughn joined him, and Ellery paused in the doorway. Fox, inside, had not moved.

"He's lying in his teeth about last night," said Vaughn loudly; Fox could not help but hear. "We'll check up right away."

Ellery winced. There was something ruthless about the tactics of both men, and he could not forget the tears in Fox's eyes.

In silence they cut over toward the west. Fox's hut was not far from the waters of Ketcham's Cove, and they could see the sunny glint of blue through the trees as they stumbled along. A short distance from the hut they struck a narrow road, unfenced.

"Brad's property," grunted Isham. "He wouldn't fence it. The house those Lynn people rented must he over in that stretch beyond the road."

They crossed the road and at once plunged into cathedral woods. It was five minutes before Vaughn found the footpath which led through the dense underbrush toward the west. Shortly after the path widened, the woods grew sparser, and they saw a low rambling stone house set in the heart of the trees. A man and a woman were sitting on the open porch. The man rose rather hastily as the figures of the three visitors came into view.

"Mr. and Mrs. Lynn?" said the District Attorney, as they paused at the foot of the porch.

"In the flesh," said the man. "I'm Percy Lynn. My wife here . . . You gentlemen are from Bradwood?"

Lynn was a tall, dark, sharp-featured Englishman with close-cropped oily hair and shrewd eyes. Elizabeth Lynn was blonde and fat; the smile on her face seemed fixed there.

Isham nodded, and Lynn said: "Well . . . Won't you come up?"

"It's all right," said Inspector Vaughn pleasantly. "We won't stay but a minute. Heard the news?"

The Englishman nodded soberly; his wife's smile, however, did not fade. "Shocking, really," said Lynn. "The first we knew about it was when I walked down to the road and bumped into a bobby. He told me about the tragedy."

"Naturally," said Mrs. Lynn in a shrill voice, "we wouldn't dream of going over *then*."

"No, naturally not," agreed her husband.

There was a little silence, in which Isham and Vaughn conversed in the language of the eyes. The Lynns remained motionless; there was a pipe in the tall man's hand, and a little curl of smoke rose without trembling into his face.

He gestured with the pipe suddenly. "Come now," he said, "I realize perfectly well how deuced awkward it is, gentlemen. You're the police, I presume?"

"That's right," said Isham. He seemed content to permit Lynn to make all the advances, and Vaughn remained in the background. As for Ellery, he was fascinated by that awful smile on the woman's face. Then he grinned himself; he knew now why it was so rigid. Mrs. Lynn had false teeth.

"You'll want to see our passports, I fancy," Lynn went on in a grave voice. "Check up on the neighbors and friends, and all that sort of thing. Eh?"

The passports proved in order.

"I fancy too you'll want to know just how we come—Mrs. Lynn and I—to be living here . . ." began the Englishman when Isham returned the passports.

"We've heard all that from Miss Brad," said Isham. He moved up two steps suddenly, and the Lynns stiffened. "Where were you people last night?"

Lynn cleared his throat noisily. "Ah—yes. Of course. As a matter of fact, we were in the city. . . ."

"New York?"

"Quite so. We went into town for dinner and to see a play—crumby sort of thing."

"What time did you get back here?"

Mrs. Lynn shrilled unexpectedly: "Oh, we didn't. We spent the night at a hotel. It was much too late to—"

"What hotel?" asked the Inspector.

"The Roosevelt."

Isham grinned. "Say, how late was it, anyway?"

"Oh, past midnight," replied the Englishman. "We had a snack after the play, and—"

"That's fine," said the Inspector. "Know many people around here?"

They shook their heads together. "Scarcely any one," said Lynn. "Except the Brads and that very interesting chap, Professor Yardley, and Dr. Temple. That's all, really."

Ellery smiled ingratiatingly. "Have either of you by any chance ever visited Oyster Island?"

The Englishman smiled briefly in return. "Blank there, old chap. Nudism is nothing new to us. We had our fill of it in Germany."

"Besides," put in Mrs. Lynn, "the people on that island—" She shuddered delicately. "I quite agreed with poor Mr. Brad that they should be ejected."

"Hmm," said Isham. "Any explanation to offer for the tragedy?"

"We're quite at a loss, sir. Quite. Fearful thing, though. Savage." Lynn tchk-tchked. "Sort of thing that gives your splendid country a black eye on the Continent."

"Yes, indeed," said Isham dryly. "Thanks . . . Come along."

Chapter Eight
OYSTER ISLAND

KETCHAM'S COVE WAS A rough semicircle torn out of the shore of Thomas Brad's estate. In the center of the arc of beach bobbed a large slip, to which several motorboats and a launch lay moored. Ellery, who had returned with his two companions to the westward road and followed it toward the water, found himself standing on a smaller slip several hundred yards from the main moorings. Across the water, not a mile away, sprawled Oyster Island. Its shoreline looked as if the Island had been wrenched bodily out of the mainland, becoming slightly distended in the process. Ellery could not see the other side of the Island, but he judged that its contour had inspired its name.

Oyster Island, set like a green gem in the turquoise background of Long Island Sound, was so far as any outward appearance indicated a primeval tangle of forest. The trees and wild shrubs ran almost to the water's edge. No . . . there *was* a small landing dock. By straining his eyes he could make out its gray rickety outline. But there was no other man-made structure in sight.

Isham strode out on the slip and yelled: "Hi!" to a police launch idly cruising back and forth between the mainland and Oyster Island. Through the little strait to the west Ellery saw the stern of another police launch; it was patrolling close to shore, he realized, as it disappeared behind the Island.

The first launch shot landward and made fast to the slip.

"Well, here goes," said Vaughn in a rather tense voice, as he stepped into the launch. "Come on, Mr. Queen. This may be the end."

Ellery and Isham jumped in, and the launch swerved widely as it headed directly for the center of the oyster.

They knifed across the Cove. Gradually they got a clearer view of the Island and the mainland. Not far from the slip at which they had embarked, they now saw, lay a similar slip to the west—evidently for the use of the Lynns. A rowboat, moored to one of the bitts, bleached there in the sun. At a corresponding point eastward across the Cove a replica of the Lynns' slip was visible.

"Dr. Temple lives off there, doesn't he?" asked Ellery.

"Yes. That must be his landing place." The eastern slip was empty of craft.

The launch sheared the water. As they drew nearer the little dock on Oyster Island, its details leaped into view. They sat silently watching it grow.

Suddenly Inspector Vaughn sprang to his feet, his face suffused with excitement, and yelled: "Something's happening over there!"

They stared at the dock. The figure of a man, carrying a struggling, faintly screaming woman in his arms, had dashed out of the brush, leaped heavily into a tiny outboard motorboat which they now saw was tied to the western side of the dock, dumped the woman unceremoniously on the bow thwart, turned the engine over, and with a rush drove the boat away from the dock, heading directly for the oncoming police launch. The woman, as if stunned, lay still; they could see the man's dark face as he turned quickly to look back at the Island.

Not ten seconds after the escape—if indeed it was an escape—an astonishing apparition burst out of the woods, following the same path the runaways had taken.

It was a nude man. A tall, wide, brown and heavily muscled fellow, with a mane of black hair tossing with the wind of his passage. Tarzan, thought Ellery; he was half-prepared to see the trunk of Tarzan's elephantine and improbable companion appear from the brush behind him. But where was the loin skin? . . . They could make out his curse of disappointment as he stopped short on the dock, glaring after the departing boat. He stood there for a moment, ropy arms hanging loosely, utterly unconscious of his nakedness. He had eyes only for the outboard, and the man in the boat was looking back tensely, apparently unaware of what lay in the path of his craft.

Then, so suddenly that Ellery blinked, the nude man vanished. He had executed a swift dive from the edge of the dock, cleaving the water like a harpoon. He reappeared almost at once and broke into a fast, distance-eating crawl, heading for the runaways.

"The damned fool!" exclaimed Isham. "Does he expect to overhaul a motorboat?"

"The motorboat's stopped," observed Ellery dryly.

Isham, startled, looked sharply at the outboard. It lay dead in the water a hundred yards offshore; and its pilot was working frantically over the trailing motor.

"Hit 'er up!" shouted Inspector Vaughn to the police pilot. "That guy's got murder in his eyes!"

The launch roared, and its siren let out a deep-throated whine that raised echoes behind the Island. As if for the first time conscious of the launch's presence, the man in the boat and the man in the water froze to search out the source of the warning. The swimmer, treading water, stared for an instant, then shook a cascade from his hair savagely and dived. He reappeared a moment later in another fast crawl, but this time he was retreating to the Island as if all the devils out of hell were in his wake.

The girl on the thwart sat up and stared. The man dropped into the sternsheets limply and waved his hand to the launch.

They pulled alongside just as the naked man leaped out of the water to shore. Without looking back he tore into the protection of the woods, and disappeared.

Astonishingly, as the police craft hooked onto the dead outboard, the man threw back his head and laughed—a deep, hearty laugh of pure relief and enjoyment.

He was a thin wiry individual of indeterminate age, with brownish hair and a face burnt almost purple—a complexion which could only be the result of long years under the equatorial sun. His eyes, too, looked bleached; they were water-gray, almost colorless. His mouth was a trap in flesh; the muscles of his jaw braced his purple cheek like girder-steel. Altogether a formidable person despite his flight, Ellery decided, as he watched the man roll on the sternsheets in the full ecstasy of his glee.

The female this remarkable man had abducted could only be, from her resemblance to Jonah Lincoln, the rebellious Hester. She was a plain but well-made young woman. Well-made, as the embarrassed men in the police launch had no difficulty in seeing; although a man's coat was draped about her shoulders—the laughing man, Ellery noted, was coatless—beneath it she was scantily concealed in a dirty piece of canvas, as if someone had forcibly covered her nakedness with the first scrap of material which lay at hand.

She returned their stares out of troubled blue eyes, and then she blushed and shivered, hanging her head. Her hands crept insensibly into her lap.

"What the hell are you laughing at?" demanded the Inspector. "And who are you? What d'ye mean by kidnaping this woman?"

The coatless man dashed a tear from his eyes. "Don't blame you," he gasped. "Gad, that was funny!" He shook the last remnants of mirth out of his somber face, and stood up. "Sorry. My name's Temple. This is Miss Hester Lincoln. Thanks for the rescue."

"Come aboard," growled Vaughn.

Isham and Ellery helped the silent woman into the launch. "I say, wait a minute," snapped Dr. Temple. There was no humor in his face now; it was black with suspicion. "Who the devil are you people, anyway?"

"Police. Come on, come on!"

"Police!" The man's eyes narrowed, and he clambered slowly into the launch. A detective fastened the outboard to the painter of the bigger craft. Dr. Temple looked from Vaughn to Isham to Ellery. The girl had slumped into a seat and was studying the floor. "Now, that's queer. What's happened?"

District Attorney Isham told him. His face went ghastly pale; and Hester Lincoln looked up with eyes full of horror.

"Brad!" muttered Dr. Temple. "Murdered . . . It doesn't seem possible! Why, only yesterday morning I saw him and—"

"Jonah," began Hester; she was trembling. "Is—is he all right?"

No one answered her. Dr. Temple was biting his lower lip; a very thoughtful look had come into his pallid eyes. "Have you seen—the Lynns?" he asked in a peculiar voice.

"Why?"

Temple was silent; then he smiled and shrugged. "Oh, nothing. Just a friendly question . . . Poor Tom." He sat down suddenly and gazed over the water at Oyster Island.

"Head back to Brad's landing," ordered Vaughn. The launch churned the water and began to move back toward the mainland.

Ellery noticed the tall outlandish figure of Professor Yardley standing on the big slip, and waved. Yardley waved his gangling arm in reply.

"Now, Dr. Temple," said District Attorney Isham grimly, "suppose you go into your song-and-dance. What's the idea of the big kidnaping scene, and who in the name of God is that naked lunatic who was chasing you?"

"It's unfortunate . . . I suppose I'd better come out with the truth. Hester—forgive me."

The girl did not answer; she seemed stunned by the news of Thomas Brad's death.

"Miss Lincoln," went on the sun-blackened man, "has been—well, let's say a little impulsive. She's young, and certain things make young people lose their heads."

"Oh, Victor," said Hester in an infinitely weary voice.

"Jonah Lincoln," continued Dr. Temple with a frown, "hasn't taken—how shall I say it?—he hasn't done his duty, as I see it, toward his sister."

"As *you* see it," said the girl bitterly.

"Yes, Hester, because I feel—" He bit his lip again. "At any rate, when a week passed and Hester hadn't returned from that damned Island, I thought it was high time someone brought her to her senses. Since nobody else seemed capable of doing it, I assumed the duty. Nudism!" He snorted. "Perversion, as those people practice it. I haven't been a medical man for nothing. They're a bunch of fakers trading on the inhibitions of decent people."

The girl gasped. "Victor Temple! Do you realize what you're saying?"

"Excuse me for butting in," said the Inspector mildly, "but might I ask what business it is of yours if Miss Lincoln wants to prance around without any clothes on? She looks of age."

Dr. Temple snapped his jaws together. "If you must know," he said angrily, "I feel I have the right to interfere. Emotionally, she's just a child, an adolescent. She's been carried away by a handsome physique and a smooth line of talk."

"That was Paul Romaine, I take it?" put in Ellery with a dry smile.

The physician nodded. "Yes, the insidious blackguard! He's the living trademark of that crazy cult of the sun. Sun's all right in its place. . . . I went over there this morning to scout around. Romaine and I had a little tussle. Like cavemen! It was ridiculous, and that's why I laughed a moment ago. But it was serious then, and he's a good deal stronger than I. I saw I was in for it, grabbed Miss Lincoln in the approved fashion, and ran for it." He grinned wryly. "If it wasn't for the fact that Romaine stumbled and hit his thick head against a rock, I'm afraid I should have been properly thrashed. And there's the story of the great abduction."

Hester stared at him dully; she was shivering in her fright.

"But I still don't see what right you had—" began Isham.

Dr. Temple rose, and something fierce came into his eye. "It's really none of your damned business, whoever you may be. But I expect to make this young lady my wife someday. *That's* what right I have. . . . She's in love with me, but she doesn't know it. And, by God, I'll *make* her know it!"

He glared at her, and for a moment her eyes sparked with his in an answering glare.

"'This,'" murmured Ellery to Isham, "'is the very ecstasy of Love.'"

"Huh?" said Isham.

A trooper caught the line on the main slip. Professor Yardley said: "Hello, Queen! Drifted back to see how you were coming on. . . . 'Lo, Temple! Anything the matter?"

Dr. Temple nodded. "I've just kidnaped Hester, and these gentlemen want to hang me."

Yardley's smile faded. "I'm sorry. . . ."

"Er—you come along with us, Professor," said Ellery. "I think we'll need you on the Island."

Inspector Vaughn added: "Good idea. Dr. Temple, you said you saw Brad yesterday morning?"

"Just for a moment. As he was leaving for the city. I saw him Monday night, too—night before last. He seemed perfectly normal. I can't understand it, I really can't. Any suspicions?"

"I'm asking," said Vaughn. "How'd you spend last night, Doctor?"

Temple grinned. "You're not starting with me? I was home all evening—I live alone, you know. A woman comes in every day to cook and clean up."

"Just as a matter of form," said Isham, "we'd like to know a little more about you."

Temple waved a dejected arm. "Anything you want."

"How long have you lived here?"

"Since 1921. I'm a retired army officer, you know—a medical man. I was in Italy at the outbreak of the war and joined the Italian Medical Corps rather impulsively; I was just a shaver out of diapers and Med School. Rank of Major, shot up once or twice—I was in the Balkan campaign and got myself taken prisoner. It wasn't much fun." He smiled briefly. "That ended my military career. I was interned by the Austrians in Graz for the duration of the war."

"And then you came to the States?"

"I knocked about for several years—I'd come into a sizable inheritance during the war—and then drifted back home. Well, you know how things were for many of us. Old friends gone, no family—the usual thing. I settled here, and I've been here ever since playing the country gentleman."

"Thanks, Doctor," said Isham with more cordiality. "We'll drop you here and—" A thought struck him. "You'd better go back to the Brad house, Miss Lincoln. There may be fireworks over on the Island. I'll have your things sent back."

Hester Lincoln did not raise her eyes. But there was a stubborn hardness in her tone as she said: "I'm *not* staying here. I'm going back."

Dr. Temple dropped his smile. "Going back!" he cried. "Are you insane, Hester? After everything that's hap—"

She flung his coat off her shoulders; the sun blazed on her brown shoulders and her eyes blazed in sympathy with it. "I won't be told what to do by you or anybody else, Dr. Temple! I'm going back, and you shan't stop me. Don't you *dare.*"

Vaughn looked helplessly at Isham, and Isham began to work up a muttering rage.

Ellery drawled: "Oh, come, now. Let's all go back. I think it may prove rather a lark."

And so once more the launch cut across the waters of Ketcham's Cove, this time achieving the little landing dock without incident. As they stepped to the dock, Hester grimly refusing assistance, they started at the appearance of what at first glance seemed to be a ghost.

It was a little old man, unkempt and brown-bearded, with fanatical eyes. He was swathed in a pure white robe. He wore curious sandals. In his right hand he held a crude and peculiar baton topped with a badly carved representation of a snake. . . . He strode out of the bushes, stuck out his skinny chest, and stared haughtily at them.

Behind him towered the naked swimmer—except that he had in the interim donned white duck trousers and an undershirt. His brown feet were bare.

The two parties eyed each other for an instant, and then Ellery said, with warm appreciation: "Well, if it isn't Harakht himself!" Professor Yardley smiled in his beard.

The little ghost started, his eyes rolling toward Ellery. But the shimmer in them did not reflect a glint of recognition. "That is my name," he announced in a shrill clear voice. "Are you worshipers at the shrine?"

"I'll worship at *your* shrine, you little peanut," snarled Inspector Vaughn, striding forward and gripping Harakht's arm. "You're the boss grifter of this carnival, aren't you? Where's your shack? We want to talk to you."

Harakht looked helpless, and turned to his companion. "Paul, you see? Paul!"

"He must have liked the name," murmured Professor Yardley. "A rare disciple!"

Paul Romaine did not shift his gaze; he was glaring at Dr. Temple, who returned the glare with interest. Hester, Ellery noticed, had slipped off into the underbrush.

Harakht turned back. "Who are ye? What is your mission? We are peaceful folk here."

Isham snorted, and Vaughn grumbled: "Old man Moses himself. Look here, grandpa. We're the police, understand, and we're looking for a murderer!"

The little old man shrank as if Vaughn had struck him; his slate lips trembled, and he gasped: "Again! Again! Again!"

Paul Romaine came to life. He brushed Harakht aside roughly and stepped forward to confront the Inspector. "You talk to me, whoever you are. The old man's a little batty. You're looking for a murderer? Go ahead and look. But what the hell has that got to do with us?"

Ellery admired him; the man was a splendid animal physically, handsome with a magnetic masculinity that made it easy to understand why women of repressed or sentimental natures would lose their hearts to him.

Isham said quietly: "Where were you and this lunatic last night?"

"Right here on the Island. Who's been killed?"

"Don't you know?"

"No! Who?"

"Thomas Brad."

Romaine blinked. "Brad! Well, it was probably coming to him. . . . What of it? We're in the clear. We haven't anything to do with those sniveling old women on the mainland. All we want is to be let alone!"

Inspector Vaughn pushed Isham gently aside; the Inspector himself was no weakling of a man, and his eyes were well on a level with Romaine's as they locked glances. "Now you," said Vaughn, digging his fingers into the man's wrist, "keep a civil tongue in your head. You're talking to the District Attorney of this county, and the boss cop of the roost. You answer questions like a good little boy, see?"

Romaine wrenched at his arm; but Vaughn's fingers were iron, and they remained clamped about the thick wrist. "Oh, all right," he mumbled, "if that's the way you feel about it. It's just that nobody lets us alone. What do you want to know?"

"When was the last time you and Chief Bilgewater behind you left the Island?"

Harakht began shrilly: "Paul, come away! These are infidels!"

"Keep quiet! . . . The old man here hasn't left the place since we got here. I went into the village a week ago for supplies."

"That's the ticket." The Inspector released Romaine's arm. "Get going. We want to see your headquarters, or temple, or whatever the hell you call it."

In single file they followed the incongruous figure of Harakht along a footpath which led from the shore directly into the brush toward the heart of the Island. The Island was curiously still; there seemed to be little bird and insect life, and no human life whatever. Romaine stamped along noncommittally; he seemed to have forgotten the presence of Dr. Temple, who followed in his footsteps, watching the brawny back with unwavering eyes.

Evidently Romaine had sounded a warning before the arrival of the investigating party, for when they emerged from the woods into a large clearing, where the house stood—a sparsely slatted, huge wooden structure crudely put together—the members of Harakht's cult were awaiting them, all clothed. It had been a hasty warning, for the neophytes, numbering some twenty men and women of all ages and descriptions, were attired in scraps of garments. Romaine growled something indistinguishable, and like a tribe of troglodytes they scuttled back into various wings of the house.

The Inspector said nothing; he was not at the moment interested in infractions of the public decency law.

Harakht glided on, oblivious; he held the home-made uraeus high before him, and his lips moved presumably in prayer. He led the way up the steps of the central building into what was apparently the "shrine"—an amazing room, vast in extent, rigged out with astronomical charts, plastercast statues of Horus, the falcon-headed Egyptian god, cows' horns, a sistrum, an emblematic disc supporting a throne, and a curious sort of pulpit which was surrounded by bare wooden slabs whose use was, to Ellery at least, obscure. The room was roofless, and the late afternoon sun cast long shadows on the walls.

Harakht went directly to his altar, as if safety lay there, and disregarding his visitors he raised knotted fleshless arms to the sky and began to mumble in a strange tongue.

Ellery looked inquiringly at Professor Yardley, who stood, tall and ugly, listening intently a foot away. "Extraordinary," muttered the Professor. "The man is an anachronism. To hear a twentieth-century human being speak in ancient Egyptian . . ."

Ellery was astonished. "Do you mean to say that this man actually knows what he's talking about?"

Yardley smiled sadly, and whispered: "The man is insane. But he had good reason to go insane, and as for the genuineness of his speech . . . He calls himself Ra-Harakht. Actually he is—or was—one of the world's great Egyptologists!"

The sonorous words rolled on. Ellery shook his head.

"I meant to tell you," whispered the Professor, "but I really haven't had a moment with you alone. I recognized him the instant I saw him—which was a few weeks ago, when I rowed out to the Island on a purely curiosity-satisfying exploration. . . . Curious story. His name is Stryker. He suffered a horrible sunstroke while excavating in the Valley of the Kings years ago, and never recovered. Poor chap."

"But—speaking ancient Egyptian!" protested Ellery.

"He's intoning a priestly prayer to Horus—in the hieratic language. This man," said Yardley soberly, "was the real thing, please understand. Naturally, he's addled now, and his memory isn't what it should be. His lunacy has garbled everything he ever knew. There's nothing like this room, for example, in an Egyptological sense. Conglomerate—the sistrum and cows' horns are sacred to Isis, the uraeus is the symbol of the godhead, and there's Horus floating about. As for the fixtures, the wooden slabs where, I suppose, the worshipers recline during services, his own Biblical turn of speech . . ." The Professor shrugged. "It's all been thrown together out of his imagination and the wreckage of his brain."

Harakht lowered his arms, took an odd censer from a recess of the altar, sprinkled his eyelids, and then descended from the rostrum quietly. He was even smiling, and he seemed more rational.

Ellery regarded him with newborn vision. Insane or not, the man as an authentic figure became a totally different problem. The name Stryker, now that he masticated it in his memory, raised a faint flavor of recollection. Years ago, when he had been in preparatory school . . . Yes, it was the same man he had read about. Stryker the Egyptologist! Mumbling a language dead for centuries . . .

Ellery turned to find Hester Lincoln, attired in a brief skirt and sweater, facing them from a low doorway on the opposite side of the altar room. Her plain face, white though it was, showed a steely determination. She did not look at Dr. Temple, but walked across the room to stand openly by Paul Romaine's side. Her hand took his. Surprisingly, he turned beet red and edged a step away.

Dr. Temple smiled.

Inspector Vaughn was not to be sheered off by trifles. He strode up to Stryker, who was standing quietly regarding his inquisitors, and said: "Can you answer a few simple questions?"

The madman inclined his head. "Ask."

"When did you leave Weirton, West Virginia?"

The eyes flickered. "After the rite of *kuphi* five moons ago."

"When?" shrieked Vaughn.

Professor Yardley coughed. "I think I can tell you what he's trying to say, Inspector. The rite of *kuphi,* as he calls it, was practiced by the ancient Egyptian priests at sunset. It consisted of an elaborate ceremony in which *kuphi,* a confection made of some sixteen ingredients—honey, wine, resin, myrrh and so on—was mixed in a bronze censer while the holy writings were read. Naturally, he's referring to a similar ceremony held five moons ago at sunset—January, of course."

It was as Inspector Vaughn nodded and Stryker smiled gravely at the Professor that Ellery let loose a resonant bellow that made them all jump.

"Krosac!"

His eyes were bright as he watched the sun god and his business manager.

Stryker's smile vanished, and the muscles about his mouth began to twitch. He cringed toward his altar. Romaine was unmoved; rather astonished, from his expression.

"I'm sorry," drawled Ellery. "I get that way sometimes. Proceed, Inspector."

"Not so dumb," grinned Vaughn. "Harakht, where is Velja Krosac?"

Stryker wet his lips. "Krosac . . . No, no! I do not know. He has deserted the shrine. He has run away."

"When did *you* tie up with this goof?" demanded Isham, leveling his forefinger at Romaine.

"What's all this Krosac business?" growled Romaine. "All I know is I met up with the old man in February. Seemed as if he had a good idea."

"Where was this?"

"Pittsburgh. Looked like a swell opportunity to me," continued Romaine with a shrug of his broad shoulders. "Of course, all this"— he lowered his voice—"this bunk about sun gods . . . It's good stuff for the yokels but the only thing I'm interested in is getting people to take their stinking clothes off and get into the sun. Look at me!" He inhaled deeply and his magnificent chest rose like a balloon. "I'm not sick, am I? That's because I let the beneficial rays of the sun get at my skin and under my skin. . . ."

"Oh can it," said the Inspector. "I know the line, the usual sales talk. I've been wearing clothes since I jumped out of my cradle, and I could twist you around my little finger. How's it happen that you came here, to Oyster Island?"

"You could, could you?" Romaine's back swelled. "Well, cop or no cop, suppose you try it some time! I'd—"

"It was arranged," shrilled Stryker anxiously.

"Arranged?" Isham frowned. "By whom?"

Stryker retreated. "It was arranged."

"Ah, don't listen to him!" snarled Romaine. "When he gets stubborn, you can't get a sensible word out of him. When I joined up with him, he said the same thing. It was arranged—to come to Oyster Island."

"Before you became his—er—fellow-divinity, eh?" asked Ellery.

"That's right."

They seemed to have arrived at a dead end. It was evident that, mad or not, the sunstruck Egyptologist could not be prevailed upon to divulge another coherent thought. Romaine knew, or professed to know, nothing about the events of six months before.

Inquiry revealed the information that there were twenty-three nudists living on the Island, most of them from New York City, who had been attracted to this doubtful Arcadia by adroit newspaper advertisements and Romaine's personal missionary work. Their transportation was provided from the local railroad station; taxicabs brought them to a public landing on the farther boundary of Dr. Temple's estate; and Ketcham, the owner of the Island, ferried them across in an ancient dory for a small consideration.

Old Man Ketcham, it appeared, lived with his wife on the eastern tip of the oyster.

Inspector Vaughn rounded up the sun god's twenty-three shrinking neophytes of sun worship and nudism, and a badly frightened lot they were. Most of them, now that their excursion into the forbidden delights of nakedness was held up to the light of public investigation, seemed heartily ashamed of themselves; and several appeared in full regalia dragging hand luggage. But the Inspector grimly shook his head; no one was to leave the Island until he granted permission. He took their names and city addresses, smiling sardonically at the array of Smiths, Joneses, and Browns the pages of his notebook began to display.

"Any of you leave the Island yesterday?" demanded Isham.

A quick shaking of heads; no one, it seemed, had set foot on the mainland for several days.

The investigating party turned to go. Hester Lincoln still stood by Romaine's side. Dr. Temple, who had patiently waited without once uttering a word, now said: "Hester, come along."

She shook her head.

"You're just being stubborn," said Temple. "I know you, Hester. Be sensible—don't stay here with this bunch of fakers, grafters, and inhibited morons."

Romaine leaped forward. "What did you say?" he growled. "What did you call me?"

"You heard me, you fourflushing thickhead!" All the venom and baffled anger in the good doctor's soul bubbled over; his right arm lashed out, and his fist struck Romaine's jaw with a dull snick.

Hester stood frozen to the floor for a moment, and then her lips quivered. She turned and ran into the woods, sobbing convulsively.

Inspector Vaughn sprang; but Romaine, after a single instant of stupefaction, threw back his shoulders and laughed. "If that's the best you can do, you little weasel . . ." His ears were fiery red. "I warn you, Temple; you stay away from here. If I catch you on this Island again, I'll break every bone in your damned nosy body! Now get out."

Ellery sighed.

Chapter Nine
THE $100 DEPOSIT

DENSE AND DENSER FOG. The "important" visit was over.

They left the Island in gloomy spirits. A maniac with the usual complement of cunning and incoherence; a dead trail to a vanished man . . . the mystery was deeper than ever. They all felt that in some way the presence in the vicinity of Bradwood of the man who called himself Harakht was significant. It could not be coincidence. Yet what possible connection could there be between the murder of a country schoolteacher and the murder of a millionaire hundreds of miles away?

The police launch sputtered out from the landing dock and headed east along the shore of Oyster Island, skirting the green-walled ribbon of beach. At the extreme eastern tip of the Island they saw a similar structure in the water.

"That must be Ketcham's private slip," said Vaughn. "Head in."

The Island at this point was even more desolate than on the western side. From where they stood on the wooden platform they had an unobstructed view of the Sound and the New York shoreline to the north. It was windy, a salty spot.

Dr. Temple, much subdued, and Professor Yardley remained in the launch. District Attorney Isham, Vaughn, and Ellery rattled off the ramshackle landing and followed a crooked path through the woods. It was cool here, and except for the path—which looked as if it had been last trodden by Indian feet—they might have been in virgin forest. Within a hundred and fifty yards, however they came upon a rude evidence of civilization, a cabin constructed of years-tempered, roughly hewn logs. Seated on the doorstep, placidly smoking, a corncob, was a big sunbitten old man. He rose quickly as he saw his visitors, and his white-tufted eyebrows bunched over remarkably clear eyes.

"What might ye be doin' here?" he demanded in an unfriendly drawl. "Don't ye know this is private prop'ty, this whole Island?"

"Police," said Inspector Vaughn succinctly. "You Mr. Ketcham?"

The old man nodded. "P'lice, hey? After them noodists, I'll warrant. Well, y'ain't got nothin' on Mrs. Ketcham and me, gentlem'n. I jest own this here scoop o' dirt. Ef my tenants been cuttin' up, that's their hard luck. I ain't respon—"

"Nobody's taking you to task," snapped Isham. "Don't you know there's been a crime committed on the mainland—at Bradwood?"

"Ye don't tell me!" Ketcham's jaw dropped, and his pipe seesawed between two brown teeth. "Hear that, Maw?" He turned his head toward the interior of the cabin, and they could discern an old crone's wrinkled face between his outstretched arm and the jamb of the door. "Been a crime over to Bradwood. . . . Well, well, ain't that too bad. What's it got to do with us?"

"Nothing—I hope," said Isham darkly. "Thomas Brad's been murdered."

"Not Mr. Brad!" screamed an old feminine voice from the cabin; and Mrs. Ketcham popped her head out. "Ain't that *awful!* Well, I allus said—"

"You git back in there, Maw," said old Ketcham; his eyes were frosty. The old woman's head vanished. "Well, gentlem'n, I ain't what you might say s'prised t' hear it."

"Good!" said Vaughn. "Why?"

"Well, there's been goin's-on."

"What do you mean? What kind of goings-on?"

Old Ketcham winked one eye. "Well, Mr. Brad an' the loonatic"—he jerked a dirt-crusted thumb over his shoulder—"they been havin' ruckuses ever since them people rented Oyst'r Island from me fer th' summer season. I own this here Island, ye know. Fam'ly been here over four gen'rations. Since Injun days, I reckon."

"Yes, we know that," said Vaughn impatiently. "So Mr. Brad didn't like the idea of Harakht and his bunch so close to him, eh? Did you—?"

"One moment, Inspector," said Ellery; his eyes were bright. "Mr. Ketcham, who leased the Island from you?"

Ketcham's corncob vomited yellow smoke. "Not th' nutty feller. A man with a durned funny name. Foreign sort o' name. Kro-sac." He pronounced it with difficulty.

The three men exchanged glances. Krosac—a trail at last. The mysterious limping man of the Arroyo murder. . . .

"Did he limp?" asked Ellery eagerly.

"Seein'," drawled Ketcham, "as I never seen him, I can't say. Wait a minute; I got somethin' ye might be int'rested in." He turned and disappeared in the darkness of the cabin.

"Well, Mr. Queen," said the District Attorney thoughtfully, "it looks as if you called the turn. Krosac . . . With Van an Armenian, and Brad a Roumanian—well, maybe not, but anyway certainly Central Europeans—and Krosac floating around somewhere after last being seen at the scene of the first crime . . . It's hot, Vaughn."

"Looks that way," muttered the Inspector. "We'll have to do something about that right away. . . . Here he comes."

Old Ketcham reappeared, his face red with perspiration, triumphantly waving a dirty, much-fingermarked sheet of paper.

"This here letter now," he said, "it come from this Krosac. Y'can see fer y'rselves."

Vaughn snatched it from him, and Ellery and Isham examined it over his shoulder. It was a typewritten communication on a sheet of undistinguished stationery, dated October thirtieth of the previous year. It was answering, it said, an advertisement in a New York newspaper offering Oyster Island for summer rental. The writer was enclosing, the letter said, a money order for one hundred dollars as a binder until occupancy should be taken, which would be on March first following. The letter was signed—in type—Velja Krosac.

"The money order was enclosed, Mr. Ketcham?" said Vaughn quickly.

"Sure was."

"Good," exclaimed Isham, rubbing his hands. "We'll trace it and get hold of the slip Krosac must have made out in whatever post office he sent it from. It will bear his signature, and that'll be plenty."

"I'm afraid," drawled Ellery, "that if Mr. Velja Krosac, our esteemed and slippery quarry, is as canny as his activity to date indicates, you'll find the money-order application made out by friend Harakht. There were no samples of Krosac's handwriting to be found in the Van investigation, remember."

"Did this man Krosac appear in person on March first?" asked the District Attorney.

"Noss'r. Nob'dy o' that name ever did come, but the ol' banshee back yonder—Har—Harakht's his name?—he come, an' the feller who come with him, Romaine, they paid over th' balance o' the rent in cash an' took occup'ncy."

By mutual consent Vaughn and Isham dropped the Krosac line of inquiry. Obviously this old character could contribute nothing more in that direction. The Inspector slipped the letter into his pocket, and began to ask questions concerning the Brad-Harakht quarrel. He discovered that from the beginning, when it was evident that the cult was really a colony of nudists, Brad had come to the Island personally to voice the joint objection of the mainland community. Harakht, it appeared, had been impervious to cajolery or threats; and Romaine had bared his teeth. Brad, in desperation, had offered to reimburse them many times over; he had named a preposterous sum for their lease.

"Who signed the lease, incidentally?" asked Isham.

"The ol' polecat," replied Ketcham.

Harakht and Romaine had refused Brad's offer. Then Brad had threatened legal action on the ground that the two men were maintaining a public nuisance. Romaine had retorted that they were harming no one, that the Island was off the public highways, that for the duration of their lease it virtually belonged to them. Whereupon Brad had endeavored to persuade Ketcham to oust them by legal action on the same ground.

"But they weren't hurtin' me an' Mrs. Ketcham none," said the old man. "Mr. Brad offered to give me a thousand dollars ef I'd do it. No, sir, says I, not ol' man Ketcham; no lawsuits fer ol' man Ketcham."

The last quarrel, and the most violent, had taken place just three days before, continued Ketcham—on Sunday. Brad had sailed across the waters of the Cove like Troy-bound Menelaus, had met Stryker in the woods, and they had had a fierce battle of words, in the course of which the little brown-bearded man went into a frenzy. "Thought he'd throw a fit, I did," remarked Ketcham placidly. "This feller Romaine—pow'rful brute, he is—he mixes in an' orders Mr. Brad offen the Island. Me, I'm watchin' from the woods; none o' my business, 'twa'nt. So Mr. Brad, he won't go, an' Romaine, he grabs Mr. Brad by th' neck an' he says: 'Now, git, damn ye, or I'll wallop the everlastin' daylights outa ye till yer own mother wouldn't know ye!' an' Mr. Brad, he gits, yellin' that he'd git even with 'em ef it took every cent he had."

Isham rubbed his hands again. "Good man, Mr. Ketcham. Wish there were more like you around here. Tell me—did any one else from the mainland ever have a run-in with Harakht and Romaine?"

"Betcha." Old Ketcham looked gratified, and smiled cunningly. "That feller Jonah Lincoln—lives at Bradwood. Had a fist fight with Romaine last week, right here on this Island." He smacked his leathery lips. "Man, that *was* a battle! Reg'lar champeenship shindy. Lincoln, he'd come over to git his sister Hester, who'd jest arrived."

"Well, well?"

Old Ketcham waxed eloquent; his eyes sparkled. "Nice figger, that gal. She went an' tore off her clothes, durned ef she didn't, right in front o' the two of 'em! She was that mad at her brother fer interferin'. Said he'd sat on 'er an' ruled 'er life since she was a mite, an' she could do what she dum' pleased now. . . . I tell ye, that was *somethin'*. I was lookin' through the trees. . . ."

"Ketcham, you o' he-bull!" shrieked the feminine voice from the interior of the cabin. "Y'oughta feel 'shamed o' yr'self!"

"Mm," said Ketcham, sobering. "Anyways, when Lincoln hears his sister won't go back, an' sees 'er standin' there nekkid as the day she was born, right there, mind ye, in front o' Romaine—an' didn't he like it!—he hauls off an' cracks Romaine one, an' they had their little tussle. Lincoln, he took a pow'rful beatin', but he's game, he is—took it like a man. Romaine threw 'im smack into th' Cove, by thunder. Pow'rful feller, Romaine."

There was nothing more to be learned from the garrulous old man. They returned to the launch. Professor Yardley was quietly smoking, and Dr. Temple was pacing up and down the deck, his purple face stormy.

"Learn anything?" inquired Yardley mildly.

"A little."

They were all thoughtful as the launch spluttered and swung about for the mainland.

Chapter Ten

DR. TEMPLE'S ADVENTURE

THE AFTERNOON LENGTHENED. DISTRICT Attorney Isham departed. Inspector Vaughn issued orders and received reports in an unending—and inconsequential—stream. Oyster Island was quiet. Mrs. Brad was closeted in her bedroom; ill, it was reported, and her daughter Helene was attending her. Jonah Lincoln paced the grounds restlessly. Troopers and detectives yawned all over Bradwood. Reporters came and went, and the evening air was thick with flashlight powder.

Ellery, not a little weary, followed Professor Yardley across the main road, through a gate in a high stone fence, up a gravel walk to Yardley's house. Both men were subdued and wrapped in their own thoughts.

Evening came, and then a black night unilluminated by any star. Oyster Island as the darkness fell seemed to sink into the Sound.

By tacit consent neither Ellery nor his host discussed the odd problem with which they were grappling. They talked of old and pleasanter things—university days, the crusty old Chancellor, Ellery's maiden excursions into criminal investigation, Yardley's placid career in the years since they had parted. At eleven o'clock Ellery girded his loins in a pair of seersucker pajamas, grinned, and went to sleep. The Professor smoked serenely in his study for an hour, wrote several letters, and then retired.

It was nearly midnight when there was a stir on the porch of Dr. Temple's stone house, and the physician, attired in black trousers, black sweater, and black moccasins, extinguished his pipe and stepped noiselessly off the porch to disappear among the dark trees between his house and the eastern boundary of Bradwood.

The countryside, except for the singsong rasping of crickets, seemed asleep.

Against the black background of the woods and shrubbery he was invisible—a stealthy blob of nothing unbetrayed even by the color of his skin. A few feet from the side of the easterly road he froze behind the shelter of a tree. Someone was pounding along the road, coming in his direction. From the dim silhouette Dr. Temple made out the figure of a uniformed county trooper, evidently on patrol. The trooper passed on, moving toward Ketcham's Cove.

When the guard's footsteps were no longer audible, Dr. Temple ran lightly across the road to the cover of the Bradwood trees and began to work his soundless way westward. It took him half an hour to cross Bradwood proper without arousing the suspicions of the occasional dark figures strolling about. Past the summerhouse and the totem post, past the high wire screen which marked off a tennis court, past the main house and the central walk to the Bradwood landing, past Fox's little cabin to the westerly road separating Bradwood from the Lynn estate.

Here, his wiry body tense, Dr. Temple redoubled his caution, slipping among the trees of the Lynn woods like a wraith until the dark bulk of the house loomed ahead. He had approached it from the front; now he groped his way to the north side, where the trees grew thick almost to the house itself.

There was a light burning in the window nearest him, not five feet from where he crouched behind the trunk of an old sycamore. The blind was completely drawn.

He could hear shuffling footsteps from the room—a bedroom. Once the fat shadow of Mrs. Lynn crossed the window shade. Dr.

Temple crept on hands and knees, feeling every inch of the ground before him, until he lay directly beneath the window.

Almost at once he heard the sound of a closing door, and Mrs. Lynn's high-pitched voice, shriller than usual, say: "Percy! *Did you bury it?*"

Dr. Temple gritted his teeth, the perspiration poured down his cheeks. But he made no sound.

"Yes, yes. For heaven's sake, Beth, don't talk so loudly!" The voice of Percy Lynn was strained. "The bally place is alive with bobbies!"

Footsteps near the window; Dr. Temple hugged the base of the wall, holding his breath. The shade slid up, and Lynn peered out. Then the sound of the shade being drawn again.

"Where?" whispered Elizabeth Lynn.

Dr. Temple tightened all his muscles, strained his ears with an effort that made him tremble. But try as he might, he could not catch the words of Lynn's whispered reply. . . .

Then—"They'll never find it," said Lynn in a more normal tone. "We're safe enough if we lie doggo."

"But Dr. Temple—I'm frightened, Percy!"

Lynn swore grimly. "I remember, all right. It was in Budapest after the war. The Bundelein affair . . . Damn his eyes! It's the same man, I'd take my oath."

"He hasn't said anything," whispered Mrs. Lynn. "Perhaps he's forgotten."

"Not he! Last week, at the Brads . . . he kept watching me. Careful, Beth. We're in deuced deep water—"

The light blinked out; a bedspring creaked; the voices sank to an indistinguishable murmur.

Dr. Temple crouched there for a long time; but he heard no further sound. The Lynns had retired.

He rose to his full height, listened intently for a few seconds, and then stole back into the woods. A shadow gliding from tree to tree . . . As he crept through the woods which fringed the semicircle of

Ketcham's Cove, he could hear the lapping of the water against the Bradwood landing.

And then once more he froze behind a tree; faint voices were coming from the general direction of the landing. He crept with infinite caution closer to the shoreline. Suddenly the black waters gurgled almost at his feet. He strained his eyes: ten feet offshore, a short distance from the murky dock, a rowboat swayed. Two dim figures were visible, seated in the middle of the boat. A man and a woman. The woman's arms were about the man, and she was pleading with him passionately.

"Why are you so cold? Take me to the Island. We'll be safer there—under the trees. . . ."

The man's voice, low and guarded: "You're acting like a fool. It's dangerous, I tell you. Tonight of all nights! Are you crazy? Somebody will miss you, and there'll be hell to pay. I told you we should keep apart, at least until this blows over!"

The woman tore her arms from the man's neck; she cried in a desperate soprano: "I knew it! You don't love me any more. Oh, it's—"

He clapped his palm over her mouth, whispering fiercely: "Shut up! There are troopers around!"

She relaxed in his arms. Then she pushed him away with both hands and slowly sat up. "No. You shan't have her. I'll see to that."

The man was silent. He picked up an oar and poled the boat to shore. The woman rose, and he pushed her roughly out of the boat. Hastily he shoved off and began to row—toward Oyster Island.

The moon came up, then, and Dr. Temple saw that the man rowing away was Paul Romaine.

And the woman standing white-faced and quivering on the shore was Mrs. Brad. Dr. Temple scowled and vanished among the trees.

Chapter Eleven
YOICKS!

WHEN ELLERY WALKED UP the gravel path of Bradwood the next morning he saw District Attorney Isham's car parked in the driveway. There was a grim expectancy in the faces of the detectives standing about. With a suspicion that something of importance was occurring, he hurried up the steps of the colonial porch and into the house.

He brushed by a pale Stallings and made for the drawing room. There he found a wolfishly grinning Isham and a most menacing Inspector Vaughn confronting Fox, the gardener-chauffeur. Fox was standing before Isham, a silent figure, his hands tightly clenched; only his eyes betrayed his perturbation. Mrs. Brad, Helene, and Jonah Lincoln were at one side, like the Three Fates.

"Come in, Mr. Queen," said Isham pleasantly. "You're just in time. Fox, you're caught with the goods. Why not speak up?"

Ellery advanced softly into the room. Fox did not stir. Even his lips were taut. "I don't understand," he said, but it was apparent that he did understand, and that he was bracing himself for a blow.

Vaughn bared his teeth. "Stop stalling. You visited Patsy Malone Tuesday night—the night Brad was murdered!"

"The night," added Isham with meaning, "that you dropped Stallings and Mrs. Baxter off at the Roxy. At eight o'clock, Fox."

Fox stood like stone. His lips turned white.

"Well?" snarled the Inspector. "What have you got to say for yourself, you mug? Why should an innocent chauffeur visit the mob headquarters of a New York gangster?"

Fox blinked once; but he did not reply.

"Won't talk, eh?" The Inspector went to the door. "Mike, bring that inking pad here!"

A plainclothesman appeared at once carrying an inking pad and paper. Fox uttered a strangled cry and lunged forward toward the door. The plainclothesman dropped pad and paper and grasped Fox's arms, and the Inspector secured a vicious hold on the man's legs and brought him, struggling fiercely, to the floor. Overpowered, he ceased his struggles and permitted Vaughn to yank him to his feet unresisting.

Helene Brad looked on with horrified eyes. Mrs. Brad seemed unmoved. Lincoln rose and turned his back.

"Take his prints," said the Inspector grimly. The plainclothesman gripped Fox's right hand, pressed the fingers to the pad and then expertly to the paper; he repeated the procedure with the left hand. Fox wore a look of agony.

"Check those right away." The fingerprint man hurried off. "Now, Fox, my lad—if that's your name, which I know damned well it isn't—suppose you get a little sense into you and answer my questions. Why did you pay a visit to Malone?"

No answer.

"What's your real handle? Where do you come from?"

No answer. The Inspector went to the door again and beckoned two detectives standing in the hall. "Take him back to his cabin and keep him locked up there. We'll attend to him later."

Fox's eyes burned as he shambled out between the two detectives. He avoided the eyes of Mrs. Brad and Helene.

"Well!" The Inspector mopped his brow. "Sorry, Mrs. Brad, to raise such a fuss on your drawing-room floor. But the man's evidently a bad actor."

Mrs. Brad shook her head. "I can't understand it. He's always been such a nice young man. So polite. So efficient. You don't think he was the one who—"

"If he was, God help him."

"I'm sure he wasn't," said Helene with asperity; her eyes were full of pity. "Fox couldn't be a murderer or a gangster. I'm sure of it. He's always kept to himself, it's true, but he's never been drunk or disorderly or in any way objectionable. He's a cultured man, too. I've often caught him reading good books and poetry."

"These fellows are sometimes pretty cagey, Miss Brad," said Isham. "For all we know he may have been playing a part ever since he got the job here. We looked up his references and they were genuine—but he'd worked for the man only a few months."

"May have taken that job just for the references," said Vaughn. "They'll do all sorts of things." He turned to Ellery. "You can score this one for your father, Mr. Queen. We got the tip from Inspector Queen, who's got his fingers on more stool-pigeons and tipsters than any cop in New York."

"I knew Dad couldn't keep from putting his oar in," murmured Ellery. "Was your information so specific?"

"The stoolie saw Fox go into Malone's headquarters, that's all. But it's enough."

Ellery shrugged. Helene said: "The trouble with you people is that you're always ready to think the worst of everybody."

Lincoln sat down and lighted a cigarette. "Perhaps, Helene, we'd better keep out of it."

"Perhaps, Jonah, you'd better mind your own business!"

"Children," began Mrs. Brad weakly.

Ellery sighed. "Any news, Mr. Isham? I'm starved for information."

The Inspector grinned. "Chew on this, then." He took a sheaf of typewritten papers from his pocket and handed it to Ellery. "If you can find anything in 'em, you're a genius. *But . . .*" he said sharply, turning to Lincoln, who had risen and was about to leave the room, "don't go yet, Mr. Lincoln. There's something—I—want to ask you."

It was timed nicely, and Ellery approved the Inspector's adroit and deliberate strategy. Lincoln stopped on the instant, reddening. The two women stiffened in their chairs. All at once, from a subdued atmosphere, the air in the room crackled with tension.

"What's that?" asked Lincoln with difficulty.

"Why," said Vaughn pleasantly, "did you lie to me yesterday when you told me that you, Miss Brad, and her mother had come home together Monday night?"

"I—Why, what do you mean?"

Isham said: "It appears that you people are making every effort to hinder rather than help the investigation of your husband's murder, Mrs. Brad. The Inspector's men have discovered from the taxicab driver who took two of you from the station to Bradwood Monday night—"

"Two?" drawled Ellery.

"—that only Mr. Lincoln and Miss Brad were in the cab, Mrs. Brad!"

Helene sprang to her feet; Mrs. Brad was stricken speechless. "Don't answer, Mother. This is infamous! Are you suggesting that one of *us* is implicated in the murder, Mr. Isham?"

Lincoln muttered: "Look here, Helene, perhaps we'd better—"

"Jonah!" She faced him, quivering. "If you dare to open your mouth I'll—I'll never speak to you again!"

He bit his lips, avoided her eyes, and walked out of the room. Mrs. Brad uttered a puling little cry, and Helene stood in front of her, as if to shield her from harm.

"Well," said Isham, throwing up his hands, "there you are, Mr. Queen. That's what *official* investigators have to contend with. All right, Miss Brad. I want you to know, though, that from this moment on everyone—and I *mean* everyone—is under suspicion for the murder of Thomas Brad!"

Chapter Twelve
THE PROFESSOR TALKS

With the verve of a dog carrying a bone Mr. Ellery Queen, slightly bewildered special investigator, returned posthaste to his host's house across the road bearing the reports on work in progress. The noon sun was hot, too hot for haberdashery, and Ellery sought the cool interior with a panting relief. He found Professor Yardley in a room which might have been transported bodily out of the Arabian Nights, a patio-like affair of tessellated marble and Turkish arabesques. It looked like the inner court of a zenana; its chief delight was a pool a-brim to its mosaic lip with water. The Professor was attired in a pair of tight short breeches, and he was dangling long legs in the water while he peacefully puffed on a pipe.

"Phew!" said Ellery. "I'm more than grateful for your little harem, Professor."

"As usual," said the Professor severely, "your choice of words is sloppy. Don't you know that the men's apartments are called the selamik? . . . Get out of your clothes, Queen, and join me here. What's that you're carrying?"

"A message from Garcia. Don't move. We'll go over this together. I'll be back in a moment."

He reappeared shortly in trunks, the upper part of his body smooth and gleaming with perspiration. He dived flatly into the pool, throwing up a wave which drenched the Professor and extinguished his pipe, and proceeded to splash about with energy.

"Another one of your accomplishments," growled Yardley. "You always were a damned poor swimmer. Come out of there before you drown me."

Ellery grinned, clambered out, stretched full length on the marble, and reached for Inspector Vaughn's sheaf of reports.

"What have we here?" He ran his eye down the top sheet. "Hmm. Doesn't look like much. The admirable Inspector hasn't been idle. Check-up with the Hancock County officials."

"Oh," said the Professor, struggling to relight his pipe. "So they've done that, have they? What's been happening down there?"

Ellery sighed. "First, the autopsy findings on the body of Andrew Van. Absolutely devoid of the minutest particle of interest. If you'd read as many autopsy reports as I have, you'd appreciate . . . And a complete synopsis of the original investigation. Nothing I don't already know, or that you didn't read in contemporaneous newspaper accounts . . . Ha! What's this? 'Pursuant'—digest this, please; it sounds just like that fellow Crumit—'Pursuant to District Attorney Isham's inquiry concerning a possible relationship between Andrew Van, the Arroyo schoolteacher, and Thomas Brad, recently murdered Long Island millionaire, we are sorry to state that no such relationship exists; at least insofar as we have been able to determine from a careful study of the deceased Van's old correspondence, and so on.' Neat, eh?"

"A model of rhetoric," grinned the Professor.

"But that's all. *Alors,* we leave Arroyo and return to Ketcham's Grove." Ellery squinted at the fourth sheet. "Dr. Rumsen's autopsy report on the body of Thomas Brad. Nothing that we don't know, really. No marks of violence on the body itself, no indication of poisoning in the internal organs, and so on, and so on, *ad nauseam.* The usual trivialities."

"I remember you asked Dr. Rumsen the other day if Brad mightn't have been strangled. Does he say anything about that?"

"Yes. Lungs show no signs of suffocation. *Ergo,* he wasn't strangled."

"But why did you ask the question in the first place?"

Ellery waved a dripping arm. "Nothing earth-shaking. But since there were no marks of violence on the rest of the body, it might have been important to know exactly how the man was killed. It had to be his head, you see, which bore the brunt of the assault; which suggested strangulation. But Rumsen in this report says that it could only have been a blow with a blunt instrument on the skull, or possibly a revolver shot in the head. I should say the first, all things considered."

The Professor kicked up a column of water. "I suppose that's so. Anything else?"

"Investigation to discover the route the murderer took. Futile, very futile." Ellery shook his head. "Impossible to procure a list of persons who boarded or descended from trains in the neighborhood of the Cove during the crime period. Troopers on the highways, residents near or on the roads, can offer no information. An attempt to find persons who were on or in the vicinity of Ketcham's Cove on Tuesday evening has been unsuccessful. . . . And yachtsmen and others who sailed the Sound Tuesday afternoon and evening report no mysterious or suspicious activity, no strange boat which might have landed the murderer in the Cove by a water route."

"As you say, a futile business." The Professor sighed. "He may have come by train, automobile, or boat, and I suppose we'll never know exactly. Might even have come by hydroplane, to reduce it to an absurdity."

"There's an idea," smiled Ellery. "And don't fall into the error of calling improbabilities absurdities, Professor. I've seen some queer things happen. . . . Let's get on with this." He scanned the next sheet rapidly. "More nothing. The rope used in lashing Brad's arms and legs to the totem pole . . ."

"I suppose it's also futile," grunted Yardley, "to expect you to say 'totem post.'"

"Totem post," continued Ellery dutifully, "has been found to be ordinary cheap-grade clothesline, which can be purchased at any grocer's or hardware store. No dealer within ten miles of Bradwood can offer anything which promises to be a live trail. However, Isham reports that the quest will be carried on by Vaughn's men over a wider area."

"Thorough, these people," said the Professor.

"Unwilling as I am to admit it," said Ellery with a grin, "it's just such routine thoroughness that solves the run of crimes. . . . The knot, Vaughn's pet idea. Result—*zero*. A clumsy inexpert thing, but efficient enough, according to Vaughn's expert. Just such a knot as you or I might tie."

"Not I," said Yardley. "I'm an old mariner, you know. Bowlines, half hitches, and what not."

"You're as close to H2O now as you've ever been—I mean in a nautical capacity. . . . Ah, Paul Romaine. An interesting character. The assertive male with a good healthy streak of practicality in him."

"Your habit," said the Professor, "of misusing words is really to be deplored."

"Background, says Inspector Vaughn's little piece, obscure. Beyond the fact that he joined our Egyptological avatar in Pittsburgh in February, as he himself said, nothing has been discovered about him. His trail before that is a blank."

"The Lynns?"

Ellery put down the paper for a moment. "Yes, the Lynns," he murmured. "What do you know about them?"

The Professor caressed his beard. "Suspicious, my boy? I might have known it wouldn't escape you. There *is* something faintly spurious about their ring. Although they've been quite respectable. Beyond reproach, as far as I know."

Ellery picked up the paper. "Well, Scotland Yard, while it doesn't say so in so many words, thinks otherwise, I'll warrant. Isham cabled the Yard, and the Yard cabled back, according to this report, that they could find no data on a couple named Percy and Elizabeth Lynn, as described. Their passports have also been investigated, but of course they're in order, as might be expected. Perhaps we've been unkind. . . . Scotland Yard intimates that they are continuing a search of civilian records—criminal records, too—in the hope of unearthing information pertinent to the Lynns' activities in English territory, since they claim to be English subjects."

"Lord, what a mess!"

Ellery scowled. "You're just finding it so? I've worked on complicated cases in my brief and brilliant time, but never anything quite so snarled as this. . . . You haven't heard, of course, the latest developments about friend Fox the chauffeur, and Mrs. Brad." The Professor's eyebrows went up. Ellery related what had occurred an hour before in the drawing room at Bradwood. "Clear, isn't it?"

"As the waters of the Ganges," grunted Yardley. "I'm beginning to wonder."

"What?"

The Professor shrugged. "I shan't leap at conclusions. What else does that encyclopedia in your hand disclose?"

"Fast work on Vaughn's part. The doorman of the Park Theater testified that a woman of Mrs. Brad's description left the theater Tuesday night in the middle of the first act—about nine o'clock."

"Alone?"

"Yes . . . Another thing. Vaughn's lines have hooked the original of the money-order application for one hundred dollars which was sent to Ketcham as deposit on the Oyster Island rental. It was made out in the Peoria, Illinois post office in the name of Velja Krosac."

"No!" The Professor's eyes grew round. "Then they've a sample of his handwriting!"

Ellery sighed. "Leaping at conclusions? I thought you were being careful about that. The name was hand-printed. The address was simply Peoria—evidently Stryker's traveling manna-dispenser stopped there to do a little business among the natives. . . . One thing more of local interest. Accountants are at work checking the books of Brad & Megara. Natural line of inquiry, of course. But so far everything seems aboveboard; the firm is well-known and extremely prosperous; finances are quite in order. . . . Incidentally, our peregrinating friend Stephen Megara, who's lolling about somewhere on the high seas, is not active in the business—hasn't been for five years. Brad kept a supervisory eye cocked, but young Jonah Lincoln runs the place almost single-handed. I wonder what's sticking in *his* craw."

"Future mother-in-law troubles, I should say," remarked the Professor dryly.

Ellery tossed the sheaf to the marble floor of the selamik, as Yardley called it, and then leaned forward quickly to retrieve it. An additional sheet had fallen from the rear of the sheaf. "What's this?" He scanned it with omnivorous eyes. "Good lord, here's something!"

Yardley's pipe remained suspended in mid-air. "What?"

Ellery was excited. "Actually information about Krosac! A later report, from the date. Evidently District Attorney Crumit held it back in his first reply, and then decided to wash his hands of the entire affair and shunt it onto poor Isham . . . Six months of investigation. Data galore . . . Velja Krosac is a Montenegrin!"

"Montenegrin? You mean by birth? For there's no such country as Montenegro today, you know," said Yardley with interest. "It became one of the political divisions of present-day Yugoslavia—the Serbs, Croats, and Slovenes merged officially in 1922."

"Hmm. Crumit's investigation revealed that Krosac was one of the first emigrants from Montenegro after peace was declared in 1918. His passport on entry into the United States indicated that he was a Montenegrin by birth but nothing else of value. By the sarcophagus of Tut, the man emerges!"

"Did Crumit discover anything about his American career?"

"Sufficient, although in a sketchy way. He seems to have traveled from city to city, presumably getting acquainted with his adopted country and learning the language. For several years he engaged in a small peddler's enterprise, apparently a legitimate business. He sold fancy needlework, small woven mats, and that sort of thing."

"They all do," remarked the Professor.

Ellery digested the next paragraph. "He met friend Harakht, or Stryker, four years ago in Chattanooga, Tennessee, and the two men joined forces. Stryker at the time was selling a 'sun medicine'— cod-liver oil with a home-made label. Krosac became his business manager and, for the public's benefit, 'disciple,' helping the poor old lunatic build up the sun cult and the health preaching during their nomadic existence on the road."

"Anything on Krosac after the Arroyo murder?"

Ellery's face fell. "No. He's simply vanished. He managed it adroitly enough."

"And Kling, Van's servant?"

"Not a trace of him. It's as if the earth swallowed up both of 'em. This Kling complication disturbs me. Where the deuce is he? If Krosac sped his soul across the Great Divide, what happened to his body—where did Krosac bury it? I tell you, Professor, until we know the actual fate of Kling we shan't solve this case. . . . Crumit made exemplary efforts to find a connection between Kling and Krosac, probably on the assumption that they might have been confederates. But he's found nothing."

"Which doesn't necessarily mean that no connection exists," pointed out the Professor.

"Naturally not. And, of course, so far as Krosac is concerned, we have no way of determining whether he's been in communication with Stryker or not."

"Stryker . . . There's an example of God's wrath for you," muttered Yardley. "Poor devil!"

Ellery grinned. "Stiffen your fibers, sir; this is murder. Incidentally, from this last report the West Virginia people have trailed Harakht to his lair. That is, they have discovered that he is one Alva Stryker, according to Crumit, well-known Egyptologist, who went insane from sunstroke, as you said, many years ago in the Valley of the Kings. He has no kin, as far as could be determined, and he has always seemed a perfectly harmless lunatic. Listen to this—Crumit's note: 'It is the belief of the District Attorney of Hancock County that the man Alva Stryker, who calls himself Harakht, or Ra-Harakht, is blameless in the murder of Andrew Van, but has been for years the prey of unscrupulous opportunists who have utilized his odd appearance, his mild lunacy, and his obsession with a garbled cult-worship in an unusual but nonetheless vicious kind of confidence game. It is our opinion also that a man of this type with undiscovered motive for the murder of Van was responsible for the victim's death. All the facts point to Velja Krosac as this man.' Neatly phrased, eh?"

"A somewhat circumstantial case against Krosac, isn't it?" asked the Professor.

Ellery shook his head. "Circumstantial or not, in selecting Krosac as the probable murderer of Van, Crumit has hit on the essential."

"What makes you think so?"

"The facts. But that Krosac killed Andrew Van isn't the keystone of the case we're attempting to build up. The quintessential problem is"—Ellery leaned forward—"*who is Krosac?*"

"What do you mean?" demanded Professor Yardley.

"I mean that Velja Krosac is known in his true face and figure to only one person in the case," replied Ellery earnestly. "That is Stryker, who cannot be depended upon for reliable testimony. So I say again: Who is Krosac? Who is Krosac *now?* He may be anyone about us!"

"Nonsense," said the Professor uncomfortably. "A Montenegrin, probably with a Croatian accent, a man moreover with a limp in his left leg . . ."

"Not really nonsense, Professor. Nationalists merge fluidly in this country, and certainly when Krosac conversed with Croker, the Weirton garageman, he spoke colloquial, unaccented English. As for the fact that Krosac may be in our midst—I don't believe you've completely analyzed the elements of the Brad crime."

"Oh, haven't I?" snapped Yardley. "Perhaps not. But let me tell you this, young man—you're crossing the river prematurely."

"I've done that before." Ellery rose and dived into the pool again. When his head emerged dripping from the water, he was grinning quizzically at the Professor. "I won't mention the fact," he said, "that it was Krosac who arranged for the sun cult's proximity to Bradwood! Before the Van murder, mind you. Significant? Then he might be about here somewhere. . . . Come on!" he said abruptly, climbing out of the pool and lying down with his hands behind his head. "Let's get together on this. Let's begin with Krosac. A Montenegrin. Who, let us say, kills a Central European with an apparently assumed Roumanian nationality, and a Central European with an apparently assumed Armenian nationality. Three Central Europeans, then, possibly all from the same country; for I'm convinced that, things being what they are, Van and Brad did not come from Armenia and Roumania."

The Professor grunted and applied two matches to his pipe. Ellery, sprawled on the hot marble, lighted a cigarette and closed his eyes. "Now think about this situation in terms of motive. Central Europe? The Balkans? Heart of superstition and violence; almost a platitude. Does that suggest anything to you?"

"I'm uncommonly ignorant about the Balkans," said the Professor indifferently. "The only association that comes to mind when you mention the word is the fact that for centuries that part of the world has been the source of weird and fantastic folklore. I presume it's a result of the generally low level of intelligence and the desolate and mountainous terrain."

"Ha! There's an idea," chuckled Ellery. "Vampirism! Do you recall *Dracula,* Bram Stoker's immortal contribution to the nightmares of innocent burghers? The story of a human vampire, laid in Central Europe. And heads cut off, too!"

"Drivel," said Yardley with an uneasy stare.

"Right," said Ellery promptly. "Drivel if only for the fact that no stakes were hammered into the hearts of Van and Brad. No self-respecting vampirist omits that pleasant little ceremony. If we'd found stakes I'd almost be convinced that we are dealing with a superstition-crazed man doing away with what he considered were human vampires."

"You aren't serious," protested Yardley.

Ellery smoked for a moment. "Hanged if I know whether I am or not. You know, Professor, we may in our divine enlightenment pooh-pooh such nursery horribilia as vampirism, but after all if Mr. Krosac believes in vampires and goes about cutting people's heads off, you can't very well shut your eyes to the reality of his belief. It's almost a statement of the pragmatic philosophy. If it exists for him . . ."

"How about this Egyptian cross business of yours?" asked the Professor gravely; he sat up straighter, shifting about for a more comfortable position, as if he anticipated a long discussion.

Ellery sat up and hugged his brown knees. "Well, how about it? You've something up your sleeve; you hinted as much yesterday. Have I, in the language of the classics, pulled a boner?"

The Professor deliberately knocked out his pipe, placed it on the edge of the pool beside him, ruffled his black beard, and became professorish. "My son," he said solemnly, "you made an ass of yourself."

Ellery frowned. "You mean the *tau* cross is not an Egyptian cross?"

"I mean precisely that."

Ellery rocked gently. "The voice of authority . . . Hmm. You wouldn't want to place a small bet, now, would you, Professor?"

"I'm not a betting man; haven't the income . . . Where did you get the idea that the *crux commissa* is called the Egyptian cross?"

"*Encyclopaedia Britannica.* About a year ago I had occasion to do some research on the general subject of crosses; I was working on a novel at the time. As I recall it now, the *tau,* or T, cross was described as a common Egyptian device, often called the Egyptian cross, or words to that effect. At any rate, my recollection is that the article definitely linked the words *tau* and Egyptian in connection with the cross. Would you care to look it up?"

The Professor chuckled. "I'll take your word for it. I don't know who wrote that article—for all I know it may have been someone of overwhelming erudition. But the *Encyclopaedia Britannica* is as fallible as other man-made institutions, and it isn't always the last authority. I'm not an authority on Egyptian art myself, please understand, but it's one phase of my work, and I tell you without equivocation that I've never encountered the phrase 'Egyptian cross'; I'm sure it's a misnomer. Yes, there is something Egyptian shaped like a T. . . ."

Ellery looked puzzled. "Then why do you say the *tau* isn't—"

"Because it isn't." Yardley smiled. "A certain sacred instrument used by the ancient Egyptians possessed a shape like the Greek T. It occurs frequently in hieroglyphic literature. But that doesn't make it a *tau* cross, which is an old Christian religious symbol. There are many fortuities like that. St. Anthony's Cross, for example, is a name also applied to the *tau* cross, merely because it resembles the crutch with which St. Anthony is generally depicted. It's no more St. Anthony's Cross, strictly speaking, than it is yours or mine."

"Then the T isn't properly an Egyptian cross at all," muttered Ellery. "Damn it all, I would mess it up."

"If you want to call it that," said the Professor, "I can't stop you. It's true that the cross seems to have been a familiar enough symbol for ages—its use has been variegated and universal from the most primitive times. I could give you numerous examples of variations on the cruciform symbol—by the Indian of the Western Hemisphere before the coming of the Spaniards, for instance. But that's irrelevant. The essential point is this." The Professor screwed up his eyes. "If there is one cruciform symbol which you might by stretching a point call an Egyptian cross, it is the *ankh.*"

"The *ankh?*" Ellery looked thoughtful. "Perhaps that was what I really was thinking of. Isn't that the T cross with the circle at the top?"

Yardley shook his head. "Not a circle, my boy, but a drop-or pear-shaped little figure. The *ankh* in substance somewhat resembles a key.

It is called the *crux ansata*, and appears with extreme frequency in Egyptian inscriptions. It connoted divinity, or royalty, and peculiarly enough characterized the holder as a generator of life."

"Generator of life?" Something was brewing in Ellery's eyes. "Good lord!" he cried. "That's it! The Egyptian cross after all! Something tells me we're on the right track now!"

"Elucidate, young man."

"Don't you see? Why, it's as clear as Herodotus!" shouted Ellery. "The *ankh*—symbol of life. Crossbar of the T—the arms. Upright— the body. Pear-shaped dingus at the top—the head. And the head's been cut off! That means something, I tell you—Krosac deliberately changed the symbol of life to the symbol of death!"

The Professor stared at him for a moment, and then broke into a long and derisive chuckle. "Ingenious, my boy, ingenious as the devil, but a million parasangs from the truth."

Ellery's excitement subsided. "What's wrong now?"

"Your inspired interpretation of Mr. Krosac's motive in cutting off his victims' heads might be tenable if the *ankh*, or *crux ansata*, were symbolic of the human *figure*. But it isn't, Queen. It has a much more prosaic origin." The Professor sighed. "You remember the sandals Stryker wears? They're imitations of the typical ancient Egyptian footgear. . . . Now, I shouldn't like to be quoted on this—after all I'm no more an anthropologist than I am an Egyptologist—but the *ankh* is generally considered by experts to have represented a sandal strap like the one Stryker uses—the loop at the top being the part that passes around the ankle. The perpendicular below the loop was that part of the strap which went down over the instep and connected with the sole of the sandal between the great toe and the other toes. The shorter, horizontal pieces went down the sides of the foot to the sole of the sandal."

Ellery was crestfallen. "But I still don't see how that symbol, if its origin was a sandal, could possibly come to represent the creation of life, even in a figurative sense."

The Professor shrugged. "Word- or idea-origins are sometimes incomprehensible to the modern mind. The whole thing's unclear from the scientific standpoint. But since the *ankh* sign was frequently used in writing various words from the stem meaning 'to live,' it came eventually to stand for a symbol of living, or life. So much so that, despite the fact that the material of the true origin was flexible—the sandal generally being made of treated papyrus, of course—eventually the Egyptians employed the sign in rigid forms—amulets of wood, faïence, and so on. But certainly the symbol itself never meant a human figure."

Ellery polished the damp lenses of his pince-nez, squinting thoughtfully meanwhile at the sunny water. "Very well," he said with desperation. "We abandon the *ankh* theory. . . . Tell me, Professor. Did the ancient Egyptians practice crucifixion?"

The Professor smiled. "You refuse to surrender, eh? . . . No, not to my knowledge."

Ellery set the glasses firmly on his nose. "Then we abandon the Egyptological theory altogether! At least *I* do. I went off half-cocked—an alarming symptom of late; I must be getting rusty."

"A little learning, my boy," remarked the Professor, "as Pope said, is a dangerous thing."

"By the same token," retorted Ellery, "*faciunt nae intelligendo, ut nihil intelligant* . . . by too much knowledge they bring it about that they know nothing. That's not personally intended, of course—"

"Of course not," replied Yardley with gravity. "And Terence didn't mean it either, eh? . . . At any rate, I thought you were bending over backwards in an effort to interpret the facts Egyptologically. You were always prone to romanticize, as I recall, even in the classroom. Once, when we were discussing the source of the Atlantean legend as it was transmitted by Plato, Herodotus, and—"

"If I may interrupt the learned gentleman," said Ellery a little testily, "I'm trying to shoulder my way out of a lot of mud, and you're befouling the terrain with irrelevant classicism. Excuse me. . . . If

Krosac by lopping off the heads of his victims and strewing T signs about the scenes of his crimes meant to leave the symbol of a cross, it certainly was not an *ankh* cross and could only have been the *tau* cross. And since there seems to be little if any significance to the existence of the *tau* cross in Pharaonic Egypt, the probabilities are that Krosac had no such thought in mind, despite the fact that he was associated with a madman whose obsession was things religious in the Egyptological sense. . . . Confirmation? Yes. Thomas Brad was hung on a totem pole—pardon, post. Another religious symbol worlds removed from hieraticism. Further confirmation—if Krosac meant an *ankh* cross he would have left the heads rather than removed them. . . . So we have cast doubt upon the Egyptian theory, we have no evidence for the American totem theory except the single fortuitous fact of Brad's place of crucifixion—and that was apparently chosen because of its T-shaped significance rather than any religious significance—and we cannot persist in the cruciform theory at all . . . the *tau* cross in the Christian creed—since decapitation as far as I know has never played a part in the murder of martyrs . . . *Ergo,* we abandon all religious theories—"

"Your credo," chuckled the Professor, "seems to be like the religion of Rabelais—a great Perhaps."

"—and revert to what was leaning against my nose from the beginning," concluded Ellery with a rueful smile.

"What's that?"

"The fact that T probably means T, and not a damned thing else. T in its alphabetical sense. T, T . . ." Suddenly he stopped, and the Professor studied him curiously. Ellery was staring at the pool with eyes that saw nothing so innocent as blue water and sunlight.

"What's the matter?" demanded Yardley.

"Is it possible?" muttered Ellery. "No . . . too pat. And nothing to confirm it. Once before it occurred to me—" His voice trailed off; he had not even heard Yardley's question. The Professor sighed and picked up his pipe again. Neither man said anything for a long time.

They were sitting that way, two nearly naked figures in the peaceful patio, when an old Negress pattered in with a disgusted look on her shiny black face.

"Mistuh Ya'dley," she said in a soft complaining voice, "some un's jest breakin' th' do' down tryin' to git in hyah."

"Eh?" The Professor started and shook off his reverie. "Who is it?"

"Dat 'Spectuh man. He's awful stewy, seems like, suh."

"All right, Nanny. Send him in."

Vaughn burst in upon them a moment later waving a small piece of paper; his face was congested with excitement. "Queen!" he shouted. "Great news!"

Ellery shifted about with abstracted eyes. "Eh? Oh, hello, Inspector. What's this news of yours?"

"Read this." The Inspector hurled the piece of paper on the marble floor and sank to the edge of the pool, panting like an expectant trespasser in a *seraglio*.

Ellery and the Professor looked at each other, and then together at the paper. It was a radiogram from the Island of Jamaica.

MADE PORT HERE TODAY HEARD OF BRADS DEATH SAILING NEW YORK AT ONCE.

The message was signed: *Stephen Megara.*

PART THREE

Crucifixion of a Gentleman

"J'ai découvert comme Officier Judiciaire Principale près le Parquet de Bruxelles que l'opération du cerveau criminel est dirigée par motifs souvent incompréhensibles au citoyen qui observe la loi."

—FÉLIX BROUWAGE

Chapter Thirteen
NEPTUNE'S SECRET

STEPHEN MEGARA'S YACHT *Helene* made a record run from Jamaica north through the peppered islands of the Bahamas, but near New Providence Island she developed serious engine trouble and her master, Captain Swift, was constrained to put her into the port of Nassau for repairs. It was several days before she was able to stand out to sea again.

So it was not until the first of July, eight days after Inspector Vaughn's receipt of Megara's radiogram, that the *Helene* hove into sight of the Long Island coast. Arrangements had been made with the Port authorities to expedite Megara's clearing through New York Harbor, and the *Helene* after a brief delay steamed into Long Island Sound, accompanied by a police boat and a flock of small craft hired by enterprising newspapermen who were kept off the *Helene's* holy-stoned decks only with the greatest difficulty.

Eight days . . . Eight days of singularly halcyon uneventfulness. With the exception of the funeral. And even that was a quiet affair. Brad had been interred in a Long Island cemetery without pomp or untoward circumstance; and Mrs. Brad, it was observed by the gentlemen of the press, bore the ordeal with remarkable fortitude. Even her daughter, no blood-relation of the deceased, was more affected by the interment than the widow.

The search for Velja Krosac had assumed the proportions of a national manhunt. His description had been sent to police headquarters and Sheriffs' offices throughout the United States and to all port officers; he was being watched for by the police of the forty-eight States, Canada, and Mexico. Despite the widening of the seine, however, no Montenegrin fish was caught; the man had disappeared as effectually as if he had flown off the Earth into space. Of Kling, too, not a trace.

The chauffeur, Fox, was still under guard in his hut; not formally arrested, to be sure, but as effectively a prisoner as if he had been behind the bars of Sing Sing. Quietly the inquiry spread about him; but by the time of Megara's arrival no identification of his fingerprints had been made in any of the Eastern rogues' galleries. The Inspector, doggedly, sent copies of the fingerprints farther west. Fox himself maintained his iron silence. He did not complain at his unofficial confinement, but there was a desperate glint in his eye, and the Inspector grimly doubled the guard. It was part of Vaughn's genius to ignore the man completely, except for the silent guards; Fox was not questioned or bullied; he was left strictly alone. Despite this strain on his nerves, however, the man did not break. He sat quietly in his hut, day after day, barely touching the food relayed to him from the kitchen of Mrs. Baxter, barely moving, barely breathing.

Everything was ready on Friday, the first of July, when the *Helene* pushed her way up Long Island Sound and through the western narrows of Ketcham's Cove, anchoring in the deep waters between Oyster Island and the mainland. Bradwood's landing dock was black with people—detectives, police, troopers. They watched the slow maneuvers of the yacht. It was a gleaming white, low-slung and rakish craft. In the magnifying morning air the neat glitter of her brasswork and the tiny moving figures on her deck were clearly visible. Little boats swayed around her narrow belly.

Inspector Vaughn, District Attorney Isham, Ellery Queen, and

Professor Yardley stood on the dock, silently waiting. A launch put out overside, smacked into the waters of the Cove. Several figures could be seen descending the iron staircase and stepping into the launch. Immediately a police boat got under way and the launch followed submissively. They made for the landing. The crowd stirred. . . .

Stephen Megara was a tall, sun-blackened man of powerful physique, with a black mustache and a nose which, from its appearance, had been irremediably battered in a brawl. He was altogether a vital and somehow sinister figure. His leap from the launch to the dock was quick, sure, lithe; all his movements were decisive. Here, Ellery felt as he studied him with keen interest, was the man of action; a richly different person from the paunchy, overfed and prematurely old man that must have been Thomas Brad.

"I'm Stephen Megara," he said abruptly in English, touched by an Etonian accent. "Quite a reception committee. Helene!" He singled her out of the crowd—the chief actors, standing timidly in the background—Helene, her mother, Jonah, Dr. Temple . . . Megara took Helene's hands, ignoring the others, and looked with fierce tenderness into her eyes. She flushed and withdrew her hands slowly. Megara smiled a brief, mustache-raising smile, murmured something into Mrs. Brad's frozen ear, nodded curtly to Dr. Temple, and turned back. "So Tom's been murdered? I'm at the service of any one who cares to introduce himself."

The District Attorney grunted: "Indeed?" and said: "I'm Isham, D.A. of the County. This is Inspector Vaughn of the Nassau County detective bureau. Mr. Ellery Queen, special investigator. Professor Yardley, a new neighbor of yours."

Megara shook hands perfunctorily. Then he turned and crooked a dark finger at a hard-faced, frosty old man in blue uniform who had accompanied him in the launch. "Captain Swift, my skipper," said Megara. Swift had champing jaws and eyes like the lenses of a telescope—clear as crystal in a face as weatherbeaten as the wandering Jew's.

"'Meetcha," said Captain Swift to no one in particular, and put his left hand to his cap. Three fingers were missing, Ellery observed. And when they all, by tacit consent, stirred and began to move off the dock toward the path leading to the house, Ellery saw that the sailing master walked with the roll of the deepwater man.

"Too bad I didn't get word before this," said Megara swiftly to Isham, as they strode along. The Brads, Lincoln, Dr. Temple walked behind with expressionless faces. "I've been lolloping about the high seas for months; you don't get news that way. It's been a blow, learning about Tom." Nevertheless, as he said it, it did not seem like a blow; he discussed the murder of his partner as unemotionally as he might discuss the purchase of a new shipment of rugs.

"We've been waiting for you, Mr. Megara," said Inspector Vaughn. "Who to your knowledge might have had motive for killing Mr. Brad?"

"Hmm," said Megara. He twisted his head for an instant to look back at Mrs. Brad, at Helene. "Rather not answer at the moment. Let me know exactly what's happened."

Isham opened his mouth to reply, when Ellery asked in a soft voice: "Have you ever heard of a man called Andrew Van?"

For the fraction of a second Megara's rhythmic stride broke, but his face was inscrutable as he forged on. "Andrew Van, eh? What has he to do with this?"

"Then you know him!" cried Isham.

"He was murdered under circumstances similar to those surrounding the death of your partner, Mr. Megara," said Ellery.

"Van murdered, too!" Something of the yachtsman's poise dropped away from him, there was a flicker of uneasiness in his bold eyes.

"Head cut off, and body crucified in the form of a T," Ellery went on in a matter-of-fact way.

Megara stopped short this time, and the whole cavalcade behind him stopped as well. His face went violet under its mask of sunburn. "T!" he muttered. "Why—Let's get into the house, gentlemen."

He shivered as he said this, and his shoulders sagged; his mahogany complexion was ghastly. He looked suddenly years older.

"Can you explain the T's?" demanded Ellery eagerly.

"I have an idea . . ." Megara clicked his teeth together, and strode on.

They negotiated the rest of the distance to the house in silence.

Stallings opened the front door, and at once his bland face broke into a welcoming smile. "Mr. Megara! I'm happy to welc—"

Megara brushed by him without a glance. He made for the drawing room, followed by the others, and there began to pace the floor with long strides. He seemed to be turning something over in his mind. Mrs. Brad glided up to him and placed her pudgy hand on his arm.

"Stephen . . . if you could only clear up this terrible—"

"Stephen, you *know!*" cried Helene.

"If you know, Megara, for God's sake spill it and end this rotten suspense!" said Lincoln hoarsely. "It's been a nightmare for all of us."

Megara sighed and jammed his hands into his pockets. "Keep cool. Sit down, Captain. Sorry to bring you into a scurvy thing like this." Captain Swift blinked and did not sit down; he seemed uncomfortable, and edged nearer the door. "Gentlemen," said Megara abruptly, "I believe I know who murdered my—who murdered Brad."

"You do, eh?" said Vaughn with no excitement.

"Who?" cried Isham.

Megara threw back his wide shoulders. "A man named Velja Krosac. Krosac . . . No doubt about it in my mind. T, you say? If it means what I think it means, he's the only man in this world who could have left it. T, eh? In a way, it's a living sign that . . . Tell me just what happened. In the murder of Van as well as of Brad."

Vaughn looked at Isham, and Isham nodded. Whereupon the Inspector launched into a terse summary of all that had occurred in both crimes, beginning with the discovery by Old Pete and Michael Orkins of the schoolmaster's body at the crossroads of the Arroyo pike and the New Cumberland-Pughtown highway. When Vaughn related the garageman Croker's testimony concerning the limping man who had hired Croker to drive him to the crossroads, Megara nodded slowly, and said: "That's the man, that's the man," as if he were banishing his last doubt. The story concluded, Megara smiled without humor.

"I have it straight now." He had recovered his poise; there were purpose and courage in his posture. "Now tell me just what you found in the summerhouse. There's something a little queer . . ."

"But Mr. Megara," protested Isham, "I can't see—"

"Take me there at once," said Megara curtly, and strode to the door. Isham looked doubtful, but Ellery caught his eye and nodded. They all streamed after the yachtsman.

As they took the path to the totem post and the summerhouse, Professor Yardley whispered: "Well, Queen, it looks like the finale, eh?"

Ellery shrugged. "I can't see why. What I said about Krosac still applies. Where the devil is he? Unless Megara can identify him in his present personality—"

"That's assuming a lot," said the Professor. "How do you know he's around here?"

"I don't! But it's certainly possible."

The summerhouse had been swathed in canvas, and a trooper stood by on guard. Vaughn flipped the canvas back and, unwinking, Megara went in. The interior of the summerhouse appeared exactly as the investigators had discovered it on the morning after the crime—a bit of forethought on the Inspector's part which, it seemed, was destined to bear fruit.

Megara had eyes for only one thing—he ignored the T, the blood-stain, the signs of a struggle and a butchery—the pipe with its bowl carved into a Neptune's-head and trident. . . .

"I thought so," he said quietly, stooping and picking up the pipe. "The moment you mentioned the Neptune's-head pipe, Inspector Vaughn, I knew that something was wrong."

"Wrong?" Vaughn was disturbed; Ellery's eyes were bright and in-quiring. "What's wrong, Mr. Megara?"

"Everything." Megara looked at the pipe with bitter resignation. "You think this was Tom's pipe? Well, it wasn't!"

"You don't mean to tell me," exclaimed the Inspector, "that the pipe belongs to Krosac!"

"I wish it did," replied Megara savagely. "No. It belongs to me."

For an instant they digested this revelation, turning it over in their minds as if to take what nourishment there was from it. Vaughn was plainly puzzled. "After all," he said, "even if it *is*—"

"Wait a minute, Vaughn," said the District Attorney swiftly. "I think there's more in this than meets the eye. Mr. Megara, we've been under the impression that the pipe was Brad's. Stallings gave us the definite feeling that it was, although now that I think of it, it's easy to have made such a mistake. But it has Brad's fingerprints on it, and it was smoked on the night of the murder with his own brand of tobacco in it. Now you say it's yours. What I can't understand—"

Megara's eyes narrowed; his tone was stubborn. "There's some-thing wrong here, Mr. Isham. That's my pipe. If Stallings said it was Tom's, he either lied or took it to be Tom's just because he'd noticed it in the house before I went away last year. I left it here inadvertently when I sailed away about a year ago."

"What you can't understand," said Ellery softly to Isham, "is why one man should smoke another man's pipe."

"That's it."

"Ridiculous!" snapped Megara. "Tom wouldn't smoke my pipe, or anyone else's. He had plenty of his own, as you can see if you open his drawer in the study. And no man puts another man's bit into his mouth. Especially Tom; he was a fanatic on sanitation." He turned the Neptune's-head over in his fingers with absent affection. "I've missed old Neptune. . . . I've had him for fifteen years. Tom—he knew how much I prized it." He was silent for a moment. "He would no more smoke this pipe than he would put Stallings's false teeth into his mouth."

No one laughed. Ellery said swiftly: "We face an interesting situation, gentlemen. The first ray of light. Don't you see the significance of this identification of the pipe as Mr. Megara's?"

"Significance my hind leg," snorted Vaughn. "It means only one thing—Krosac's trying to frame Mr. Megara."

"Nonsense, Inspector," said Ellery genially. "It means nothing of the sort. Krosac could not possibly expect to make us believe Mr. Megara murdered Brad. Everyone knew that Mr. Megara was off somewhere, thousands of miles away, stretching his sea-legs in a periodic water tramp. And then—the T's, and the tie-up with the murder of Van . . . As good as a signature. No." He turned to the yachtsman, who was still studying the pipe with a frown. "Where were you, sir—your yacht, yourself, your crew—on June twenty-second?"

Megara turned to his sailing master. "We expected that, didn't we, Captain?" His mustache lifted in a brief grin. "Where were we?"

Captain Swift flushed and produced a sheet of paper from one of his bulging blue pockets. "Mem'randum from my log," he said. "Ought to answer ye, mister."

They examined the memorandum. It stated that on June twenty-second, the *Helene* had passed through the Gatun Locks in the Panama Canal, bound for the West Indies. Attached to the memorandum was an official-looking slip which acknowledged payment for passage to the Canal authorities.

"Whole ship's crew aboard," rasped Captain Swift. "My log's open to inspection. We been cruisin' the Pacific workin' east. We been as far as Australia on the westward passage."

Vaughn nodded. "Nobody's doubting you people. But we'll take a look at your log, anyway."

Megara spread his legs and teetered back and forth; it was easy to imagine him straddling a ship's bridge, swaying to the lift and fall of a deep-sea vessel. "Nobody's doubting us. Indeed! Not that I care a damn if you do, you understand . . . The closest we came to death on the whole voyage was a pain in the groin that I developed off Suva."

Isham looked uncomfortable, and the Inspector turned to Ellery. "Well, Mr. Queen, what's buzzing around in your noddle? You've got a notion, I can see that."

"I'm afraid, Inspector, from this material evidence," said Ellery, pointing to the memorandum and the slip, "that we can't very well believe Krosac intended us to think Mr. Megara his partner's murderer." He puffed on a cigarette before continuing. "The pipe . . ." He flicked the ashes of his cigarette toward the odd brier in Megara's hand. "Krosac must have known that Mr. Megara would have an unimpeachable alibi for the general period of the murder. We discount any surmise, therefore, in that direction. *But* from the facts that this is Mr. Megara's pipe and that Brad would not have smoked it, we can now establish a tenable theory."

"Smart," said Professor Yardley, "if true. How?"

"Brad would not have smoked this Neptune's-head pipe, the property of his partner. Yet it has been smoked—handled, apparently, by the victim himself. But if Brad would not have smoked the pipe and yet there are evidences on it that he did, what have we?"

"Ingenious," muttered the Professor. "The pipe was made to *appear* as if Brad smoked it. It would be child's play to place the dead man's fingerprints on its stem."

"Precisely!" cried Ellery. "And the job of making the pipe look as if it had been smoked would be simple. Perhaps the murderer himself actually loaded it, lighted it, and puffed a bowlful. Too bad the Bertillon system doesn't take into account the variations of individual bacteria; there's an idea! . . . Now, who might want to make it appear that Brad had smoked this pipe? Surely only the murderer. Why? To confirm the impression that Brad had wandered out—in a smoking jacket—to the summerhouse smoking the pipe, and had been attacked and killed there."

"Sounds likely," confessed Isham. "But why should Krosac do that with Mr. Megara's pipe? Why didn't he pick one of Brad's own?"

Ellery shrugged. "There's a simple answer to that, if you stop to think about it. Krosac, got the pipe—where? In the drawer of the reading table in the library. Is that right, Mr. Megara?"

"Probably," said Megara. "Tom kept all his pipes there. When he found mine after I left, he must have put it away in the same drawer against my return."

"Thank you. Now, going to the drawer, Krosac sees a number of pipes. He naturally assumes they all belong to Brad. He wants to leave one pipe to make it appear that Brad was smoking in the summer-house. So he selects a pipe which is most distinctive in appearance, going on the excellent theory that the most distinctive-looking pipe will be the most easily identified pipe. *Ergo*—Neptune. Fortunately for us, however, Neptune was the property of Mr. Megara, not Brad.

"Ah," proceeded Ellery in a sharp voice, "but here we come to an interesting deduction. Friend Krosac has gone to considerable trouble, has he not, to make it appear that Brad was attacked and killed while he was smoking *in the summerhouse?* For, you see, had there been no pipe and no evidence of smoking, we should have questioned Brad's presence in the summerhouse, especially since he was wearing a smoking jacket; he might have been dragged there. But when we know that a man was smoking in a certain place, we know that up to a certain point, at least, he was there of his own free will. . . . Now we find, however, that he was *not* smoking there, and we know the murderer wants us to believe he was. The only sane inference is that *the summerhouse was not the scene of the crime,* but that the murderer wanted us very much to believe it was."

Megara was regarding Ellery with a speculative and rather cynical light in his eye. The others kept silent.

Ellery flipped his cigarette out through the doorway. "The next step is surely clear. Since this isn't the scene of the crime, some other place is. We must find that place and examine it. Finding it, I believe, will offer no difficulty. The library, of course. Brad was last seen alive there, occupied in playing checkers with himself. He was waiting for someone, for he had carefully cleared the house of possible witnesses or interrupters."

"Just a minute." Megara's mouth was hard. "That's a pretty speech and good hearing, Mr. Queen, but it happens to be all wrong."

Ellery lost his smile. "Eh? I don't understand. Wherein is the analysis faulty?"

"It's wrong in the assumption that Krosac didn't know the pipe is mine."

Ellery took off his pince-nez and began to swab its lenses with his handkerchief—an infallible sign in him of perturbation, satisfaction, or excitement. "An extraordinary statement, if true, Mr. Megara. How could Krosac know the pipe belonged to you?"

"Because the pipe was in a *case*. Did you find a case in the drawer?"

"No." Ellery's eyes glittered. "Don't tell me that your initials were on the case, sir!"

"Better than that," snapped Megara. "My full name in gilt letters was stamped on the morocco cover. The pipe was in the case when I last saw it. The case naturally has as odd a shape as the pipe, and couldn't possibly be used for another pipe, unless it was a replica of this."

"Oh, splendid!" cried Ellery, smiling broadly. "I take it all back. You've given us a new lease on life, Mr. Megara. It puts an entirely different complexion on matters. Gives us even more to work on . . . Krosac knew it was your pipe, then. Nevertheless, he deliberately selected your pipe to leave in the summerhouse. The case he took away, obviously, since it's gone. Why take away the case? Because if he had left it, we should have found it, seen the resemblance between the shape of the Stephen Megara case and the shape of the supposed Brad pipe, and known at once that the pipe wasn't Brad's. By taking the case away, Krosac made us believe *temporarily* that the pipe was Brad's. You appreciate the inference?"

"Why temporarily?" demanded Vaughn.

"Because," said Ellery triumphantly, "Mr. Megara *did* come back, *did* identify the pipe, *did* tell us about the missing pipe case! Surely Krosac knew Mr. Megara would eventually do this. Conclusion—*until Mr. Megara arrived*, Krosac wanted us to believe that the pipe belonged to Brad, and that therefore the summerhouse was the scene of the crime. *After Mr. Megara arrived*, Krosac was willing that we should know the summerhouse was *not* the scene of the crime; willing, furthermore, since it would be inevitable, to have us look for the *real* scene of the crime. Why do I say willing? Because Krosac could have avoided all this merely by choosing another means of making the summerhouse seem the scene of the crime; merely, in fact, by choosing one of Brad's own pipes!"

"You hold, then," said the Professor slowly, "that the murderer deliberately desires us to return to the real scene of the crime. I can't understand why."

"Sounds funny to me," said Isham, shaking his head.

"It's so abominably plain," grinned Ellery. "Don't you see—Krosac wanted us to look at the scene of the crime *now*—not a week ago, mind you, but *now.*"

"But why, man?" asked Megara impatiently. "It doesn't make sense."

Ellery shrugged. "I can't tell you specifically, but I'm convinced it makes rather remarkable sense, Mr. Megara. Krosac wants us to *find* something now—*while you are at Bradwood*—which he didn't want us to find while you were on the Pacific somewhere."

"Nuts," said Inspector Vaughn with a scowl.

"Whatever it is," said Isham, "I'm prepared to doubt it."

"I suggest," said Ellery, "that we follow along with Messer Krosac. If he wanted us to find it, let's oblige him. Shall we go to the library?"

Chapter Fourteen
THE IVORY KEY

THE LIBRARY HAD BEEN sealed since the morning after the discovery of Brad's mutilated body. Isham, Vaughn, Megara, Professor Yardley, and Ellery went into the room; Captain Swift had rolled back to the dock, and the Brads and Lincoln were in their own quarters. Dr. Temple had vanished long before.

Megara stood to one side as the search was made—no perfunctory examination, this time, but a crevice-exploring expedition which left not a particle of dust undisturbed. Isham turned the secretary into a scene of carnage, strewing it with the crumpled bodies of vagrant papers. Vaughn took it upon himself to go over the furniture, piece by piece. Professor Yardley, self-delegated, retired to the alcove where the grand piano stood and amused himself by ravishing the music cabinet.

Almost at once the discovery was made—or at least a discovery, whether it were the one Velja Krosac had intended or not being at the moment of no consequence. It was a discovery of major importance— and made by Ellery, who was prowling by the Inspector's side. Quite by accident, or in the interest of thoroughness, Ellery grasped a corner of the divan and pulled it back from before the book-filled wall so that it stood completely on the Chinese rug, where before its rear legs had rested on the bare floor. As he did this he exclaimed aloud and stooped swiftly to examine something on the part of the rug which had been hidden under the divan. Isham, Vaughn, and Yardley hurried to his side; Megara craned, but did not move. "What is it?"

"Good grief," muttered the Inspector. "Of all the obvious places. A stain!"

"A bloodstain," said Ellery softly, "unless experience, like my reverend Professor here, is a poor teacher."

It was a dried blackish stain, standing out with the crudity of a wax seal on the golden colors of the rug. Near it—no more than a few inches away—there was a square depression in the fabric of the rug, the sort of impressment made by the weight of a chair- or table-leg which has stood on one spot for a long time. The shape of the depression could not be laid to the feet of the divan, which at the base were round.

Ellery, kneeling, looked around. His eyes wavered for a moment, and then went to the secretary, which stood on the opposite wall.

"There should be—" he began, and shoved the divan toward the center of the room. He nodded at once: three feet from the first depression was its mate in the pressed nap.

"But the stain," frowned Isham, "how the devil did it get under the divan? Stallings told me when I first questioned him that nothing had been moved in this room."

"That doesn't require explanation, does it?" remarked Ellery dryly as he rose to his feet. "Nothing was moved—except the rug itself, and you could scarcely expect Stallings to have noticed *that*."

His eyes gleamed as he looked about the library. He had been right about the secretary; it was the only article of furniture in the room whose legs could have made depressions the exact shape and size of the two under the divan. He crossed the room and lifted one of the secretary's square-tipped legs. On the rug directly beneath the tip, plain enough, was a depression like the two on the other side of the room, except that it was not so deep or sharply defined.

"We might conduct an entertaining little experiment," said Ellery, straightening up. "Let's shift this rug about."

"Shift it about?" asked Isham. "What for?"

"So that it will lie as it did Tuesday night, before Krosac changed its position."

A great light broke over Inspector Vaughn's face. "By God," he cried, "I see it now. He didn't want us to find the bloodstain, and he couldn't get rid of it!"

"That's just half the story, Inspector," remarked Professor Yardley, "if I understand Queen's implications."

"You do," said Ellery equably. "It's just a matter of getting this table out of the way. The rest is easy." Stephen Megara still stood in a corner, silently listening; he made no move to help the four men. Vaughn lifted the round table without effort and carried it out into the hall. In a very few moments, by placing a man at each corner of the rug, they were able to jerk it from under all the small articles of furniture and turn it about, so that the part which had been hidden beneath the divan now lay where it must have lain the night of Brad's murder—on the opposite side of the room. The two depressions, they saw instantly, fitted with precision under the two front legs of the secretary. And the dried bloodstain . . .

Isham stared. "Behind the checker chair!"

"Hmm. The scene begins to materialize," drawled Ellery. The bloodstain lay two feet behind the collapsible wall chair of the checker table which stood next to the secretary.

"Struck from behind," mumbled Professor Yardley, "as he was experimenting with his infernal checkers. Might have known that obsession would get him into trouble some day."

"What do you think, Mr. Megara?" asked Ellery suddenly, turning to the silent yachtsman.

Megara shrugged. "That's your job, gentlemen."

"I think," said Ellery, sitting down in a club chair and lighting a cigarette, "that we'll save time by a little rapid-fire analysis. Any objections, Inspector?"

"I still can't see," complained Vaughn, "why he should have swung the rug around. Whom was he trying to fool? We wouldn't have found it at all if he hadn't, as you pointed out, deliberately left a trail back to this room by that pipe of Mr. Megara's."

"Gently, Inspector. Let me have my head for a moment . . . It's apparent now—there can't be any disagreement on the point—the Krosac never intended *permanently* to conceal the fact that this room was the scene of the crime. Not only didn't he want permanently to conceal this fact, but he even arranged matters in a deucedly clever way to lead us back to this room, at his own good time, when he knew a more careful examination of the room would disclose the bloodstain. Had he wanted permanently to conceal this fact, he would not in the first place have left the pipe trail back to the library, nor would he have left that bloodstain as it is. For observe." Ellery pointed to the open dropleaf of the secretary. "Right at hand, almost above the bloodstain, were two bottles of ink. Suppose Krosac had left the rug in its original position, and had deliberately turned over one of these two bottles of ink by accident. The police would have found bottle and stain, would have assumed the superficial truth—that the ink had been tipped over, by Brad or some one else—and would never have thought of looking beneath the ink for a bloodstain. . . . Instead of adopting this perfectly simple procedure, Krosac went to the vast trouble of shifting the rug around, contriving matters so that we would miss the bloodstain on first examination, would be brought back to it by Mr. Megara's identification of the pipe as his, and would thereby find it on second examination. The essential point being that nothing was gained by Krosac in these complex maneuvers except—*time*."

"All very well," said the Professor in a nettled tone, "but I'll be drawn and quartered if I see why he wanted us to find it at all."

"Professor darling," said Ellery, "don't anticipate. This is my recitation. You're swell on ancient history, but my forte is logic and I yield the palm to no man in my own province. Ha, ha! Well, let it go."

He dropped his grin. "Krosac wanted not permanent concealment of the scene of the crime, but delay of its discovery. Why? Three possible reasons. Follow closely—Mr. Megara especially; you may be able to help us here."

Megara nodded and dropped on the divan, which had been restored to its proper position before the wall.

"One: There was something in this room dangerous to Krosac which he wanted to take away later, since for some peculiar reason he could not take it away on the night of the murder. . . . Two: There was something Krosac wanted to add or bring back to this room later, which he could not add or bring back on the night of the murder—"

"Hold your horses a minute," said the District Attorney, who for a moment had been fiercely frowning. "Both of those sound reasonable, for in either case making the summerhouse seem the scene of the crime would draw attention away from the library, perhaps leaving it during that period accessible to the murderer."

"Contradiction in order. Wrong, Mr. Isham," drawled Ellery. "Krosac had to expect, even if the stain were missed in the first search—as he planned—and the summerhouse accepted as the scene of the crime . . . Krosac had to expect, I repeat, that the house would be guarded and that he would be prevented by purely precautionary police measures from taking something away later or bringing something back later. But there's an even more important objection to the first two possibilities, gentlemen.

"If Krosac wanted to come back here and therefore deliberately made the summerhouse appear the scene of the crime, it would certainly be to his advantage to make the summerhouse appear the scene of the crime permanently. This would give him unlimited time and opportunity in which to gain access to the library. But he didn't—he deliberately left a trail back to this room which, if the surmise I've just mentioned were correct, would be about the last thing he'd do. So I say, neither of the first two theories is tenable."

"Over my head," said Vaughn disgustedly. "Too fancy for me.

"Shut up like a good fellow," snapped Isham. "This isn't slap-me-down police methods, Vaughn. I'll admit it's an unorthodox way to go about solving a crime, but it sounds like the real stuff. Go on, Mr. Queen. We're all ears."

"Inspector, consider yourself publicly reprimanded," said Ellery severely. "Third possibility: That there is something now in the library which was also there the night of the murder, which—a plethora of whiches—is not dangerous to the criminal, which he didn't plan to take away later, which he wanted the police to discover, but which he did not want discovered by the police until Mr. Megara's return."

"Phew," said Vaughn, throwing up his hands. "Let me out of here."

"Don't mind him, Mr. Queen," said Isham.

Megara squinted steadily at Ellery. "Go ahead, Mr. Queen."

"Since we are obliging souls," continued Ellery, "obviously we must look for and find what Krosac planned us to find only when you, Mr. Megara, were on the scene. . . . You know," he added contemplatively, "I've always found—and I think you'll bear me out, inspector—that the more involved a murderer becomes the more errors he's apt to make. Suppose we get friend Stallings in here for a moment."

The detective at the door yelled "Stallings!" and the butler appeared in dignified haste.

"Stallings," said Ellery abruptly, "you know this room pretty well, don't you?"

Stallings coughed. "If I do say so, sir, as well as Mr. Brad himself knew it."

"I'm ravished to hear it. Take a look about." Stallings dutifully took a look about. "Is everything in order? Has anything been added? Is there anything here which shouldn't be here?"

Stallings smiled briefly and began a stately stalk about the library. He poked in corners, opened drawers, investigated the interior of the secretary. . . . It took him ten minutes, but when he concluded his tour of inspection and said: "This room is exactly as I saw it last, sir—I mean before Mr. Brad was killed . . . except, sir, that the table is gone," they all felt that there was nothing more to ask.

But Ellery was persistent. "Nothing else has been disturbed or taken away?"

The butler shook his head emphatically. "No, sir. The only thing that's really different is that stain, sir," he said, pointing to the rug. "It wasn't there Tuesday evening when I left the house. And the checker table . . ."

"What about the checker table?" asked Ellery sharply.

Stallings shrugged with decorum. "The pieces. Of course, their position is different. Mr. Brad naturally played on after I left."

"Oh," said Ellery with relief. "That's excellent, Stallings. You have within you the delicate makings of a Sherlock, the camera eye. . . . That's all."

Stallings cast a reproachful look at Stephen Megara, who was staring moodily at the wall and puffing at a West Indian cheroot, and left the room.

"Now," said Ellery briskly, "let's scatter."

"But what the hell do we look for?" grumbled Vaughn.

"Heavens, Inspector, if I knew a search wouldn't be necessary!"

The scene that ensued would have been ludicrous to any observer except Stephen Megara; that man, it seemed, was minus the faculty of laughter. The spectacle of four grown men crawling about a room on hands and knees, doing their best to climb up the walls and tap plaster and wood, going through the stuffing of the divan's pillows, wrenching experimentally at the legs and arms of chairs, divan, secretary, checker-table . . . an Alice-in-Wonderland situation. After fifteen minutes of fruitless search Ellery, rumpled, hot, and much annoyed rose and sat down by Megara's side, to sink instantly into a reverie. The daydream was, from the expression on his face, more in the nature of a nightmare. The Professor, nothing daunted, toiled on; he was enjoying himself hugely as he crawled, his ungainly length doubled up, over the rug. Once he straightened and looked up at the old-fashioned chandelier.

"Now that would be an unusual hiding place," he muttered,

and forthwith proceeded to stand on a chair and tinker with the crystal ornaments of the chandelier. There was a defective or exposed wire somewhere, for he suddenly yelped and crashed to the floor. Vaughn grunted and held another piece of paper up to the light; the Inspector working on the theory, apparently, that a message had been written in invisible ink. Isham was shaking out the draperies; he had already unwound the window shades and searched for hollow interiors in the lamps. It was all pleasant and unreal and useless.

All of them, at one time or another, had cast speculative glances at the books bristling in their built-in cases, but no one had made a move toward examining them. The enormity of the task of going through those myriad volumes one by one seemed to discourage even a beginning.

Ellery leaned back suddenly and drawled: "What a pack of prime fools we are! Chasing our tails like pups . . . Krosac wanted us to come back and search this room for something. Then he wanted us to find it. He wouldn't put it in a place which would take the combined ingenuity of a Houdini and a bloodhound to discover. On the other hand, he would secrete it in a place not so obvious as to be found in a superficial search, yet not in so obscure a place as never to be found, even in a thorough search. As for you, Professor, please remember when you attempt to explore chandeliers again that Krosac probably isn't so well acquainted with this room that he knew where there would be hollows in furniture legs, or in lamps. . . . No, it's in a clever, but accessible, hiding place."

"Swell talk," said Vaughn sarcastically, "but where?" He was tired and dripping. "Know of any hiding places here, Mr. Megara?"

Professor Yardley's chin-brush jutted out like the false beard of an Egyptian Pharaoh as Megara shook his head.

Ellery said: "Reminds me of a remarkably similar search my father, Assistant D.A. Cronin, and I made not long ago when we were investigating the murder of that crooked lawyer, Monte Field who was poisoned—you recall?—in the Roman Theater during a performance of *Gunplay*. We found it in—"

The Professor's eyes glistened, and he hurried across the room to the alcove in which the grand piano was ensconced. Isham had gone through the alcove some minutes before. But Yardley did not bother with the body of the instrument, or the piano chair, or the music cabinet. He merely sat down in the chair and, with all the gravity Ellery remembered from the Professor's lectures at the university, began at the first bass note on the keyboard and wended his digital way up toward the treble, one note at a time, depressing each key slowly.

"A canny analysis, Queen," he said as he sounded one note after another. "Gave me a positive inspiration. . . . Suppose I were Krosac. I want to hide something—small, let us say, flat. I have only a limited time and a limited knowledge of the premises. What shall I do? Where shall—" He stopped for a moment; the note he had struck was off-key. He pressed it several times, but when it was apparent that the note was merely out of tune, he continued his ascending exploration. "Krosac wants a place which won't be discovered until he's ready—won't be discovered even by accident. He looks about—and there's the piano. Now mark this: Brad is dead; this is Brad's room. Certainly, he reasons, no one is going to play a piano in the private study of a dead man—not for a long time, anyway. And so . . ."

"A positive triumph of the intellect, Professor!" cried Ellery. "I couldn't have done better myself!"

And just as if the concert had been scheduled to begin at the immediate conclusion of this modest program note, the Professor made his discovery. The even ripple of the scale had been interrupted; he had come to a key which stubbornly refused to be depressed.

"Eureka," said Yardley, with an expression of utter disbelief on his ugly face. He looked like a man who has been taught a trick of legerdemain and is astonished to find at his first attempt that the trick was successful.

They crowded around now, Megara as eager as the rest. The note refused to descend more than a quarter of an inch, despite all of the Professor's efforts. And suddenly it stuck completely, refusing even to rise again.

Ellery said sharply: "Just a sec," and took out of his pocket the little kit he always carried in defiance of his father's derision. He selected a longish needle from this kit and began to probe the crevices between the stubborn key and the note on either side. A moment's work, and between two of the ivory slabs the tiny edge of a wad of paper appeared.

They all straightened up, sighing. Ellery gently worked the wad out. In silence they surrounded him and backed into the library. The paper had been flattened and crushed; Ellery unfolded it with care and spread it out on the table.

Megara's face was inscrutable. As for the others, not one of them, including Ellery himself, could have prophesied the extraordinary message conveyed by the heavily scrawled writing on the sheet.

TO THE POLICE:

If I am murdered—and I have good reason to believe that an attempt will be made on my life—investigate immediately the murder of the Arroyo (W. Va.) schoolmaster, Andrew Van, who was found crucified and beheaded last Christmas Day.

At the same time notify Stephen Megara, wherever he may be, to return posthaste to Bradwood.

Tell him not to believe that Andrew Van is dead. Only Stephen Megara will know where to find him.

Please, if you value the lives of innocent people, keep this absolutely confidential. Do not make any move until Megara advises what to do. Van as well as Megara will need every protection.

This is so important that I must repeat my admonition to let Megara lead the way. You are dealing with a monomaniac who will stop at nothing.

The note was signed—it was unmistakably genuine, as an immediate comparison with other samples of the man's handwriting in the secretary proved—*Thomas Brad.*

Chapter Fifteen
LAZARUS

STEPHEN MEGARA'S FACE WAS a study in boiling expression. The metamorphosis in this vital, self-possessed man was startling. The pressure of the unknown had finally torn the mask of will from his face. His eyes glittered with an icy unrest. He looked rapidly about the room—at the windows, as if he anticipated the phenomenon of a phantasmal Velja Krosac leaping at him; at the door, where the detective leaned indifferently. He took a squat automatic from his hip pocket and examined its mechanism with lightning fingers. Then he shook himself and strode to the door, closing it in the detective's face. He went to the windows, and with hard eyes looked out. He stood there quietly for a moment, uttered a short laugh, and slipped the automatic into his coat pocket.

Isham growled: "Mr. Megara."

The yachtsman turned swiftly, his face set. "Tom was a weakling," he said curtly. "He won't get me—that way."

"Where is Van? How is it he's alive? What does this note mean? Why—?"

"Just a minute," drawled Ellery. "Not too fast, Mr. Isham. We've much to chew upon before we're served another portion. . . . It's apparent now that Brad placed this note in an immediately accessible place—the secretary or the drawer of the round table—intending it to be found at once if he were murdered. But he didn't reckon with the thoroughness of Krosac, who gains more of my admiration with each passing incident of the investigation.

"Murdering Brad, Krosac didn't neglect to search the room afterward. Perhaps he had a presentiment that such a note, or warning, existed. At any rate, he found the note and, since he saw that it was in no way dangerous to himself—"

"How do you figure that?" demanded Vaughn. "It seems to me like the last thing any murderer would do—leave his victim's note to be found!"

"It doesn't require gigantic ratiocination, Inspector," said Ellery dryly, "to understand this amazing man's motive for an apparently foolish act. Had Krosac considered the note dangerous to his safety, certainly he would have destroyed it. Or at the very least, taken it away with him. But not only didn't he destroy it, he actually—in the face of all seeming reason, as you point out—left it on the scene of the crime, falling in with his victim's last wishes."

"Why?" asked Isham.

"Why?" Ellery's thin nostrils oscillated fiercely. "Because he considered the finding of the note by the police, far from perilous to his safety, actually *advantageous* to himself! Ah, but here we put our fingers on the crux of the situation. What does the note say?" Megara's shoulders twitched suddenly, and a sinister determination took possession of his vital features. "The note says that *Andrew Van is still alive, and that only Stephen Megara will know where to find him!*"

Professor Yardley's eyes widened. "Devilishly clever. He doesn't know where Van is!"

"That's it exactly. Krosac, it's a certainty now, somehow killed *the wrong man* in Arroyo. He thought he had murdered Andrew Van; Thomas Brad was next on his list, and when he had found and killed Brad he discovered this note. It told him that Van was still alive. But if he had motive to seek the life of Van six months ago, he surely has motive—and desire—still. If Van is alive—and brushing aside the petty consideration of the poor devil Krosac killed by mistake," Ellery interpolated grimly, "Van must be sought out once more and exterminated. But where was Van? That he disappeared—took to his heels on learning that Krosac was after him and had actually killed another man through some error—was self-evident."

Ellery brandished his forefinger. "Now consider the problem our brilliant Krosac faces. The note does not say where Van is. It says that only one man, Megara, knows where Van is. . . ."

"Hold on," said Isham. "I see what you're driving at. But why the dickens didn't Krosac just destroy the note and wait for Megara to return? Then Megara would reveal to us where Van is, and Krosac, as I suppose you're going to say, would in some way learn from us where Van is, too."

"An excellent question, on the surface. Actually, unnecessary." Ellery lighted a cigarette with slightly trembling fingers. "Don't you see that if no note were left and Megara returned, Megara would have no reason to *doubt* Van's death! Would you, Mr. Megara?"

"I would. But Krosac couldn't know that." The austerity of Megara's character, the iron will of the man, dominated even the pitch of his voice.

Ellery was taken aback. "I don't see . . . Krosac wouldn't know? At least that proves my point. By leaving the note here to be found by the police—at once, I mean, with the police knowing immediately on discovering the body that the library was the scene of the crime— the police would institute an immediate search for Van. But Krosac himself wants to look for Van, and a contemporaneous police search would hinder his own investigation—naturally! By *delaying* the discovery of the note, Krosac accomplishes two ends: One, in the interval between the murder of Brad and Mr. Megara's arrival, he can himself search for Van unhampered by the police; who, not yet having found the note, would know nothing of Van's being still alive. Two, if Krosac in that interval doesn't succeed in finding Van, he has lost nothing; for when Mr. Megara arrived on the scene, he would identify the pipe, the pipe would uncover a new investigation—as it did—leading ultimately to the discovery of the library as the real scene of the crime, the library would be thoroughly combed, the note then found, Megara would learn that Van was not dead, would disclose Van's whereabouts to the police . . . and Krosac has merely to follow us in order to discover exactly where Van is hiding!"

Megara muttered savagely: "Maybe it's all over already!"

Ellery wheeled. "You mean you think that Krosac in the interim did find Van?"

Megara spread his hands and shrugged—a Continental gesture, incongruous in this virile, American-looking man. "It's possible. With that devil, anything is possible."

"Listen," snapped the Inspector. "We're wasting valuable time gassing when we might be getting real information. Just a minute, Mr. Queen; this isn't a *Kaffeeklatsch;* you've had the floor long enough. . . . Spill it, Mr. Megara. What the devil is the connection between Van, your partner Brad, and yourself?"

The yachtsman hesitated. "We are—we were—" Instinctively his hand darted into the pocket which bulged.

"Well?" cried the District Attorney.

"Brothers."

"Brothers!"

Ellery's eyes were fixed on the tall man's lips. Isham said with excitement: "Then you were right, Mr. Queen! Those aren't their real names. Can't be Brad, Megara, or Van. What are—"

Megara sat down abruptly. "No. None of those. When I tell you—" His eyes clouded; he looked at something far beyond the confines of the library.

"What is it?" asked the Inspector slowly.

"When I tell you, you'll understand what to this moment has probably been a deep mystery to you. The instant you told me about the T's—that crazy business of the T's—the headless bodies and rigid arrangement of the arms and legs, the T's in blood on the door and the summerhouse floor, the crossroads, the totem pole—"

"Don't tell me," said Ellery harshly, "that *your real name begins with T!*"

Megara nodded as if his head weighed a ton. "Yes," he said in a low voice. "Our name is Tvar. T-v-a-r. . . . The T, you see."

They were silent for a moment. Then the Professor remarked: "You were right, Queen, as usual. A literal significance, nothing more. Merely a T—no cross, no Egyptology, no garbled religious implication . . . Strange. Incredible, really."

A shade of disappointment tinged Ellery's face; he watched Megara with unwavering eyes.

"I don't believe it," asserted Vaughn out of a vast disgust. "I've never heard of such a thing."

"Carving a man into the initial of his name!" muttered Isham. "Why, we'd be the laughingstock of the East, Vaughn, if we let this out."

Megara leaped to his feet, his whole body elastic with rage. "You don't know Central Europe!" he snarled. "You fools, he's flinging those T's—the symbol of our hated name—in our faces! The man's insane, I tell you! It's so damned clear. . . ." His rage went out of him, and he sank back into the chair. "Hard to believe," he murmured. "Yes, but not what's troubling you. It's hard to believe that he's been hunting us all these years. Like a movie. But that he'd mutilate the bodies—" His voice hardened again. "Andreja knew!"

"Tvar," said Ellery quietly. "A triple alias for years. Obviously for grave reasons. And Central Europe . . . I imagine it's vengeance, Mr. Megara."

Megara nodded; his voice was becoming weary. "Yes, that's so. But how did he find us? I can't understand it. When Andreja, Tomislav and I agreed—God, how many years ago—to disguise our identities, we agreed also that no one—no one, you understand—must learn our old family name. It was to be a secret, and the secret's been kept, I'd swear. Not even Tom's wife—Margaret—or her daughter Helene knows that our name is Tvar."

"You mean," demanded Ellery, "that Krosac is the *only* person who knows?"

"Yes. That's why I can't imagine how even he got on our track. The names we selected . . ."

"Come on," growled Vaughn. "Get going. I want information. First—who in hell *is* this Krosac? What's he got against you people? Second—"

"Don't go off half-cocked, Vaughn," said Isham irritably. "I want to digest this T business for a minute. I don't altogether understand. Why should he pick on the initial of their name?"

"To signify," replied Megara in a cavernous voice, "that the Tvars are doomed. Silly, isn't it?" His barking laugh grated on their ears.

"Would you recognize Krosac if you saw him?" asked Ellery thoughtfully.

The yachtsman compressed his lips. "That's the damnable part of it! None of us saw Krosac for twenty years, and at that time he was so young that identification or recognition today would be impossible. He may be anybody. We're up against a man—who's damned near invisible!"

"He has a limp in his left leg, of course?"

"He limped slightly as a child."

"Not necessarily permanent," murmured Professor Yardley. "It may be a dodge. The deliberate assumption of a lost physical deficiency to confuse his trail. It would be consistent with Krosac's diabolical cleverness."

Vaughn suddenly strode forward and drew his lips back from his teeth. "*You* may want to gab here all day, but I'm going to get behind this! Look here, Mr. Megara—or Tvar, or whatever your name is— why doesn't Krosac lie down and be a good boy? What the devil does he want to kill you people for? What's the story?"

"That can wait," said Ellery sharply. "There's one thing more important than anything else at the moment. Mr. Tvar, this note left by your brother says you know where to reach Van. How can you know? You've been out of communication with the world for a year, and the Arroyo murder took place only six months ago—last Christmas."

"Prepared, all prepared," muttered Megara. "For a long time, for years . . . I said before that I would have known without the note that Andreja was still alive. The reason was—something you told me in your recital of the Arroyo facts." They stared at him. "You see," he continued gloomily, "when you mentioned the names of the two men who discovered the body at the crossroads . . ."

Ellery's eyes narrowed. "Well?"

Megara again searched the room with his eyes, as if to make sure that the evanescent Krosac could not hear. "I knew. For if Old Pete—the hillman you mentioned—was alive, then Andreja Tvar, my brother, was also alive."

"I'm afraid I—" began the District Attorney blankly.

"Oh perfect!" cried Ellery, turning to Professor Yardley. "Don't you see? Andrew Van is Old Pete!"

Before the others could recover from their astonishment, Megara nodded and continued. "That's it. He assumed the alternate personality of the hillman years ago in preparation for just such an eventuality as this. He's probably in the West Virginia hills now—if Krosac hasn't already found him—hiding away in fear of his life, hoping against hope that Krosac hasn't discovered his mistake. Krosac hasn't seen any of us either for twenty years, remember. At least, I don't believe he has."

"And that's how Krosac made a mistake in his original murder," said Ellery. "Not having seen his victim for so many years, it was easy to fall into the error."

"You mean Kling?" asked Isham thoughtfully.

"Who else?" Ellery smiled. "You want action, Inspector? It looks as if we're going to get some." He rubbed his hands briskly. "Because one thing is sure. We must forestall Krosac and fool him. I don't believe Krosac has found Andreja yet. The Old Pete get-up was perfect; I sat in that courtroom in Weirton and never once suspected that anything might be out of character with the man. We must get to your brother at once, Mr. Megara, but so secretly that Krosac—whoever he is, no matter in what identity he may be masquerading—will still be ignorant of the hillman disguise."

"Suits me," said Vaughn, with a surly grin.

Megara rose; his eyes had become narrow slits of enamel. "I'll do anything you say, gentlemen—for Andreja. As for me," he patted his gun pocket ominously, "if that devil Krosac is looking for trouble, he'll find it. A cartridgeful."

Chapter Sixteen
THE ENVOYS

NOTHING MRS. BRAD—or her daughter—was able to say could persuade Stephen Megara to remain on *terra firma* that night. He spent the rest of the day quietly enough, his old commanding self, with the Brads and Lincoln; but when evening fell, he began to stir restlessly, and by nightfall was on his way to the anchored yacht offshore. Its riding lights pricked the blackness of Oyster Island sharply. Mrs. Brad, to whom the return of her husband's "partner" was a comfort and a reassurance, had followed the yachtsman down the path to the landing in the dark, pleading with him to remain.

"No," he said, "I sleep on the *Helene* tonight, Margaret. I've lived on it so long it's really my home. . . . Nice of you to want me. But Lincoln's with you, and"—his tone was ugly—"my being there won't make the house any safer for you. Good night, Margaret, and don't worry."

The two detectives who accompanied them to the Cove stared curiously. Mrs. Brad lifted a tearful face to the sky, and retraced her steps. It was remarkable how little the tragedy had affected her nerves; she passed the silent totem post, with its brooding wooden eagle, almost indifferently.

It had been quickly agreed by the conspirators that the story of the Tvar brothers was to be kept a secret from every one.

Stephen Megara, under the questioning glances of Captain Swift and the steward, slept under guard that night. Detectives patrolled the decks. Megara locked his cabin door, and the man on duty outside heard the gurgle of liquid and the steady chink of glasses for two hours. Then the light snapped off. Despite his assurance, Megara seemed to welcome the bolster of liquid courage. But he slept quietly enough, for the detective heard no sound all night.

The next morning, Saturday, Bradwood stewed with activity. Very early two police cars—sedans—dashed around the driveway and waited, panting, before the colonial house. Inspector Vaughn, like conquering Caesar, descended and strode in the midst of his uniformed guard down the path toward the landing dock. At the dock the engine of a police launch broke into a roar. The Inspector, very grim and red of face, jumped into the launch and was piloted toward the yacht.

The proceedings were conducted with frankness; there was no attempt at concealment. On Oyster Island several tiny figures could be descried before the greenery craning at the progress of the launch. Dr. Temple, pipe in mouth, stood on his boat landing and watched. The Lynns, under the pretext of rowing about the waters of the Cove, were all eyes.

The Inspector disappeared up the *Helene's* ladder.

Five minutes later he reappeared, accompanied by Stephen Megara, who was dressed in a business suit. Megara's face was drawn, and he reeked of alcohol; he said nothing to his sailing master, but followed Vaughn down the ladder with surprisingly steady steps. They dropped into the launch, which at once put back for shore.

On the Bradwood dock they conversed for a moment in low tones; the guard waited. Then the uniforms closed in, and the two men strode up the path toward the house completely surrounded by police. It was almost a parade.

Before the house a plainclothesman saw them coming, leaped from the tonneau of the first police car, saluted, and stood waiting. Very quickly Vaughn and Megara got into the first car. The second filled with police. And then the two cars, klaxons raucously clearing the road, shot around the drive and into the highway which ran past Bradwood.

At the gate, four county troopers on motorcycles jumped to life. Two preceded the first car; two flanked it; the police car made up the rear. . . . It was an amazing thing, but with the departure of the two cars not a single trooper, policeman, or detective remained on the grounds of Bradwood, or anywhere in the immediate vicinity.

The cavalcade thundered on the main highway, sweeping all traffic aside, proclaiming in gassy roars its intention to reach New York City. . . .

Back at Bradwood the departure of the Inspector and Megara left everything still and peaceful. The Lynns paddled home. Dr. Temple strolled off, smoking, into the woods. The figures on the shore of Oyster Island disappeared. Old man Ketcham rowed out into the Cove in a decrepit old dinghy, bound for the mainland. Jonah Lincoln quietly backed one of the Brad cars out of the garage, and headed it down the drive.

Professor Yardley's house, set well back from the road, was lifeless, from all outward appearances.

But that Vaughn had not taken leave of his senses would have been apparent to anyone who investigated the ends of the highway which separated Bradwood from Yardley's estate. . . . For at each terminal of the road—two junctions, either of which any automobile or pedestrian must pass in order to leave Bradwood by a land route—a powerful car full of detectives was unobtrusively parked.

And in the Sound, behind Oyster Island and so invisible from the mainland, a large launch drifted, motor idling, while men sat on the deck fishing . . . keeping a sharp look out nevertheless for the two horns of Ketcham's Cove, past one of which any craft must come if it attempted to leave the vicinity of Bradwood by water.

Chapter Seventeen
THE OLD MAN OF THE MOUNTAIN

THERE WAS GOOD REASON for the fact that Professor Yardley's house showed no evidence of life Saturday morning. The Professor was under orders, like any officer; as was his old Negress, Nanny. To have exhibited himself openly while Inspector Vaughn and Stephen Megara were making their noisy departure might have been indiscreet. It was known that the Professor entertained a guest—Mr. Ellery Queen, special investigator, of New York City. If the Professor had strolled about alone, it might have raised suspicions in the mind of whoever deemed it necessary to be on the alert. And unfortunately the Professor could not appear with his guest. His guest was gone. His guest, to be exact, at the moment when Megara climbed into the police car, was hundreds of miles from Long Island.

It had been a canny plot. Late Friday night, in the darkness enshrouding Bradwood, Ellery had quietly slipped out of Yardley's grounds in his Duesenberg. Until he reached the main highway he maneuvered the car like a ghost. Then he plunged forward toward Mineola. There he picked up District Attorney Isham and darted toward New York.

At four o'clock Saturday morning the old Duesenberg was in the capital of Pennsylvania. Harrisburg was asleep; both men were tired, and without conversation they checked in at the Senate Hotel and went to their rooms. Ellery had left a call for nine. They dropped into their beds like clubbed men.

Nine-thirty Saturday morning found them miles from Harrisburg, bound for Pittsburgh. They did not stop for luncheon. The racing car was coated with dust, and both Ellery and Isham showed the strain of the tedious grind. . . . The Duesenberg for all its years responded nobly. Twice they were chased by motorcycle policemen when Ellery was sending the old engine along at seventy miles an hour. Isham produced his credentials, and they went on. . . . At three o'clock in the afternoon they were crawling through Pittsburgh.

Isham growled: "The hell with this. He'll keep. I don't know how you do it, but I'm starving. Let's have something to eat."

They wasted precious time while the District Attorney filled his stomach. Ellery was strangely excited; he toyed with his food; although his face was marked with lines of fatigue, his eyes were fresh, and they sparkled at unexpressed thoughts.

At a few minutes to five, the Duesenberg was parked before the frame building which housed the majestic fathers of Arroyo's municipal destiny.

Their joints creaked as they descended. Isham stretched his arms hugely, oblivious of the curious eyes of a fat old German—Ellery recognized him as the worthy Bernheim, Arroyo's storekeeper—and the blue denim-clad countryman who seemed perpetually to be sweeping the sidewalk before the Municipal Hall. Isham yawned: "Well, might as well get it over with right away. Where's this country constable, Mr. Queen?"

Ellery led the way into the rear of the building, where the Constable's office lay. He knocked at the door and a rusty bass voice said: "Come in, durn ye!"

They went in. Constable Luden sat there large and sweaty as life, just as if he had not moved in the six months that had elapsed since

Ellery's last visit to Arroyo. His buck teeth stuck out of his fat red face as he gaped.

"I'll be the son of a so-an'-so," Luden exclaimed, crashing his big feet to the floor, "ef it ain't Mr. Queen! Come in, come in. Still chasin' th' feller that bumped our scoolteacher oft?"

"Still on the scent, Constable," smiled Ellery. "Meet a fellow-preserver of the law. This is District Attorney Isham of Nassau County, New York. Constable Luden—Mr. Isham."

Isham grunted and did not offer to shake hands. The Constable grinned. "Town's seen some mighty big mucks in th' last year, mister, so don't act so stuck-up." Isham gasped. "Y'heard me. . . . What's on y'r mind, Mr. Queen?"

Ellery said hastily: "May we sit down? We've been driving for a few hundred centuries."

"Set."

They sat. Ellery said: "Constable, have you seen that daffy hillman of yours, Old Pete, recently?"

"Ol' Pete? Now, that's queer," said Luden, with a shrewd glance at Isham. "Ain't seen th' old nut fer weeks. Don't often come to town, Ol' Pete, I mean, don't; but this time—durned ef I seen him fer two months! Musta stacked up on vittles a-plenty last time he come down from the mount'n; y'might ask Bernheim."

"Do you know where his hut is located?" demanded Isham.

"Reckon I do. . . . What's all th' shootin' fer far's Ol' Pete's concerned? Ain't goin' t'arrest 'im, now, are ye? Harmless ol' loonatic. . . . Not," added the Constable hastily as Isham frowned, "that it's any o' my affair. . . . Never been up to Ol' Pete's shack—few folks roundabout have. Cave country up there—ol' fellers, thousan's o' years old—an' folks is jest a mite scary. Ol' Pete's shack is some'res in th' hills in a mighty lonely spot. Y' couldn't find it y'rself."

"Will you guide us, Constable?" asked Ellery.

"Sure thing! Reckon I c'n find 'er." Luden stood up and, like a fat old mastiff, shook himself. "Y'don't want word to git round, now, do ye?" he said casually.

"No!" said Isham. "Don't even tell your wife."

The Constable grunted. "No fear o' that. I ain't got no wife, praise be. . . . C'mon."

He conducted them not to the front of the building, where the car was parked on Arroyo's main street, but out through a back door to a side street which was deserted. Luden and Isham waited, and Ellery circled the Municipal Hall quickly and jumped into the Duesenberg. Two minutes later the car was in the side street, and the three men departed in a cloud of choking dust, Luden clinging to the runningboard.

Constable Luden directed them by devious ways to a dirt road which seemed to plunge into the heart of the nearby hills. "Dif'rent road," he explained. "You park 'er here, an' well walk on up."

"Walk?" said Isham doubtfully, eyeing the steep ascent.

"Well," drawled Luden in a cheerful voice: "I c'd carry ye, Mr. Isham."

They left the car in a clump of bushes. The District Attorney looked about, then stooped over the side of the Duesenberg and picked something up from the floor. It was a bulky wrapped bundle. Luden looked at it with frank curiosity, but neither man vouchsafed an explanation.

The Constable lowered his big head and, plodding through a thicket, searched—with the air of a man who does not greatly care whether he finds or not—until he pointed out a faint footpath. Ellery and Isham toiled behind in silence. It was a steadily ascending journey through wild, almost virgin, forest; the trees were so massed that the sky was invisible. The air was sultry, and all three men were soaked with perspiration before they had climbed fifty feet. Isham began to grumble.

Fifteen minutes of back-breaking ascent, with the woods growing denser and the path fainter; and the Constable suddenly halted.

"Matt Hollis, he once tol' me 'bout it," he whispered, pointing. "Crickets! There she is."

They crept closer, Luden leading the way cautiously. And there, as the good Constable had said, she was. . . . In a little clearing, under a massive outcrop of mountainside, nestled a rude shack. The forest had been hacked away for thirty feet to the sides and at the front of the hut; it was protected at the rear by the jutting granite. And—Ellery stared—the entire space of thirty feet, at sides and front, was guarded by a high, tangled, rusty, and dangerous-looking barbed-wire fence.

"Will you look at that!" whispered Isham. "Not even a gate!"

There was no opening anywhere in the barbed-wire fence. The shack inside lay cold and grim—almost a fortress. Even the streamer of smoke that drifted away from the chimney hole was forbidding.

"Cripes," muttered Luden. "Whut's he gone an' fortyfied himself this way fer? Daffy, jest like I told ye."

"A nasty place to stumble on in the dark," murmured Ellery. "Constable, District Attorney Isham and I have a most irregular request to make of you."

Constable Luden, perhaps envisioning his last encounter with Ellery's largess, looked interested at once. "Now, as t'that," he rumbled, "I'm one feller that minds 'is own bus'ness. Got to, round hyah. Plenty o' moonshinin' goin' on up in th' hills roundabout, but y'd not see me stickin' my two cents in. Nossir—whut is it?"

"Forget this entire incident," snapped Isham. "We never came here, understand? You are not to report it to other authorities of Arroyo or Hancock County. You know nothing about Old Pete."

Constable Luden's huge hand closed over something which Ellery had produced from his wallet. "Mr. Isham," he said earnestly, "I'm deef, dumb, an' blind. . . . Find yer way down all right?"

"Yes."

"Then good luck to ye—an' thanks a lot, Mr. Queen."

The very model of disinterest, Luden turned and stole away through the woods. He did not once look back.

Isham and Ellery regarded each other briefly; then each threw back his shoulders and stepped out before the barbed-wire fence.

They had no sooner set foot on the ground before the fence—in fact, Isham was in the act of raising the bundle he carried over the top of the highest strand of wire—when a harsh cracked voice from the interior of the shack cried out: "Halt! Git back!"

They halted, very abruptly; the bundle dropped to the ground. For from the single window of the hut, also protected, they noted, by a curtain of barbed wire, the muzzle of a shotgun had appeared and was trained directly upon them. There was no wavering of the ugly weapon; it meant business, and it was ready to speak for itself.

Ellery gulped, and the District Attorney became rooted to his patch of earth. "That's Old Pete," whispered Ellery. "Consistent voice-maker, at any rate!" He raised his head and bellowed: "Just a minute! Take your finger off that trigger. We're friends."

Silence, while they were scrutinized with slow care by the owner of the shotgun. They stood very still.

Then the harsh voice assailed their ears again: "Don't believe you! Git out. I'll shoot if you don't make tracks in five seconds."

Isham cried: "We're the law, you fool! We've a letter to you from—Megara. Get a move on! For your sake we don't want to be seen here."

The muzzle did not move; but the bushy head of the old hillman appeared dimly behind the curtain of wire, and a pair of bright eyes regarded them with suspicion. They could sense the man's indecision.

The head disappeared, and so did the shotgun. An instant later the heavy nail-studded door creaked inward and Old Pete himself stood there—gray-bearded, disheveled, clad in rags. The shotgun was lowered, but its muzzle covered them.

"Climb that fence, men. No other way in." The voice was the same, but a new note had crept in.

They looked at the fence with dismay. Then Ellery sighed and very delicately raised one leg and rested it on the lowest strand of wire. He tried gingerly to find a safe handhold.

"Come on," said Old Pete impatiently. "And no tricks, either of you."

Isham fished about the ground for a stick; he found one, propped it between the two lowest strands, and Ellery crawled through, not without ripping the shoulder of his suit, however. The District Attorney followed clumsily; neither said a word, and the shotgun never shifted from their bodies.

Quickly they ran toward the man, and he retreated into his hut. Isham swung the heavy door to when they were inside, and dropped the bolt into place. It was the crudest of habitations, but a careful hand had fitted it out. The floor was stone, well swept, and strewn with mats. There was a full larder in one corner, and to the side of the fireplace a neat pile of firewood. A basin-like arrangement at the rear wall, opposite the single door, was obviously the hillman's lavatory; above it hung a shelf stocked with medicinal supplies. Above the basin there was a small hand-pump; the well was apparently beneath the house.

"The letter," said Old Pete hoarsely.

Isham produced a note. The hillman did not lower his weapon; he read the note in snatches, his eyes never off his guests for more than an instant. As he read, however, his demeanor changed. The beard was still there, and the rags, and all the superficial garments of Old Pete; but the man himself was different. He propped the shotgun slowly against the table and sat down, fingering the note.

"Then Tomislav is dead," he said. The voice struck them with a sense of shock. It was not pitched in Old Pete's cracked tones; it was low and cultured, the voice of an educated man in the prime of life.

"Yes, murdered," replied Isham. "He left a message—would you care to read it?"

"Please." The man took Brad's note from Isham and read it rapidly and without emotion. He nodded. "I see . . . Well, gentlemen, here I am. Andrew Van—once Andreja Tvar. Still alive, while Tom, the stubborn fool—"

His bright eyes glazed, and rather precipitately he rose and went to the iron basin. Ellery and Isham looked at each other. A queer one, this fellow! Van ripped off the bushy beard, removed the thatch of white wig from his head. And he washed and wiped the gum from his face. . . . When he turned back he was a vastly different figure from the one which had challenged them from the window. Tall, erect, with close-cropped dark hair, and the keen face of an ascetic, drawn with hardship. The rags hung from his strong body, thought Ellery, "above the pitch, out of tune, and off the hinges," in the phrase of Rabelais.

"I'm sorry I can't offer you chairs, gentlemen. You're District Attorney Isham, I take it, and you . . . I believe I saw you, Mr. Queen, sitting in the first row in the Weirton courthouse on the day of the inquest."

"Yes," said Ellery.

The man was remarkable. An eccentric, certainly. Having apologized for his one chair, he proceeded to seat himself in it, leaving his two visitors standing. "My hideaway. A pleasant place?" His tone was bitter. "I suppose it was Krosac?"

"So it seems," said Isham in a low voice. Both he and Ellery were struck by the man's resemblance to Stephen Megara; there was a strong family likeness. "Stephen writes that he"—Van shivered—"he used the T's."

"Yes. Head cut off. Quite horrible. So you're Andrew Tvar!"

The schoolmaster smiled wanly. "In the old country it was Andreja, and my brothers were Stefan and Tomislav. When we came here, hoping to—" He shrugged, and then sat up stiffly, gripping the seat of the clumsy chair. His eyes rolled like the eyes of a frightened horse toward the heavy door and the wired window. "You're sure," he said harshly, "you weren't followed?"

Isham tried to look reassuring: "Positive. We've taken every precaution, Mr. Tvar. Your brother Stephen was escorted open-ly by Inspector Vaughn of the Nassau County police along one of the main Long Island highways, headed for New York City." The schoolmaster nodded slowly. "If anyone—Krosac, in whatever guise he may be—should follow, there were plenty of men spot-ted about to pick up his trail. Mr. Queen and I left secretly last night."

Andreja Tvar gnawed at his thin upper lip. "It's come, it's come. . . . It—I can't tell you how appalling all this is. To see a horrid specter materialize after years of empty dread . . . You want my story?"

"Under the circumstances," said Ellery dryly, "don't you think we're entitled to it?"

"Yes," replied the schoolmaster heavily. "Stephen and I will need all possible assistance. . . . What has he told you?"

"Only that you and Brad and he were brothers," said Isham. "Now what we want to know—"

Andrew Van rose, and his eyes hardened. "Not a word now! I say nothing until I see Stephen."

His change of bearing and attitude was so sudden that they both stared at him. "But why, man?" cried Isham. "We've traveled hun-dreds of miles to come here—"

The man snatched the shotgun, and Isham took a backward step. "I don't say either of you is not exactly what you claim to be. The note is in Stephen's handwriting. The other is in Tom's. But these things can be arranged. I haven't taken these precautions to be fooled at the last by a clever trick. Where is Stephen now?"

"At Bradwood," drawled Ellery. "Don't act like a child, man; drop that gun. As for not saying anything until you see your brother—why, Mr. Megara anticipated that and we've provided for it. You're perfectly right to be suspicious, and we'll accede to any reasonable suggestion; eh, Isham?"

"Yes," growled the District Attorney. He picked up the bundle he had carried all the way up the mountain trail. "That's the way we'll do it, Mr. Tvar. What do you say?"

The man looked uncertainly at the bundle; that he was torn between desire and indecision was evident from his manner. Finally he said: "Open it."

Isham ripped the brown paper off. The bundle contained a Nassau County trooper's uniform, complete to shoes and revolver.

"Can't possibly arouse suspicion," said Ellery. "Once we get to Bradwood you're a trooper. There are fistfuls of them about the place. A man in uniform is always just a uniform, Mr. Tvar."

The schoolmaster paced up and down his stone floor. "Leave the shack . . ." he muttered. "I've been here safely for months. I—"

"The revolver is loaded," said Isham dryly, "and there's plenty of ammunition in your belt. What can happen to you with a loaded weapon and an escort of two able-bodied men?"

He flushed. "I suppose I seem a coward to you gentlemen. . . .Very well."

He began to fling off his rags; he was dressed in clean and decent underwear beneath, they noted—another note of incongruity. He began, rather awkwardly, to don the trooper's uniform.

"Fits," remarked Ellery. "Megara was right about the size."

The schoolmaster said nothing. . . . When he was fully clothed, the revolver in its heavy leather holster at his side, he presented a fine figure—tall, powerful and, in a way, handsome. His hand strayed to the weapon and caressed it; and he seemed to gather strength from it.

"I'm ready," he said, in a steady voice.

"Good!" Isham went to the door; Ellery peeped out of the wired window. "All clear, Mr. Queen?"

"It seems to be." Isham unbolted the door, and they stepped out quickly. . . . The clearing was deserted; the sun was setting, and the woods were already touched with the dimness of dusk. Ellery scrambled through the lower strands of the fence, Isham followed, and they both stood watching while their uniformed charge climbed—with a litheness Ellery envied—after them.

The door—Andrew Tvar had seen to that—was closed. Smoke still curled from the chimney. To anyone prowling in the edge of the forest the shack would still seem tenanted and impregnable.

The three men darted for the woods, and it closed over their heads. They made their way very cautiously down the faint trail to the clump of bushes where, like Old Faithful, the Duesenberg waited for them. They saw no one in the hills or on the road.

Chapter Eighteen
FOX TALKS

THE QUIET DEPARTURE OF Ellery and Isham on Friday night and their absence all day Saturday did not leave Bradwood eventless. The mysterious trip of Inspector Vaughn and Stephen Megara, watched, it seemed, by the entire community, was on everyone's lips. Even Oyster Island felt its percussion; Hester Lincoln tramped all the tangled way through the woods between Harakht's "temple" and the eastern tip of the Island to ask old man Ketcham what had happened.

Until the return of Vaughn and Megara, however, Bradwood lay sunning itself in peace. Professor Yardley, true to his promise, remained in the sanctuary of his bizarre estate.

About noon—while Ellery and Isham were speeding through southern Pennsylvania between Harrisburg and Pittsburgh, bound for Arroyo—the impressive cavalcade returned to Bradwood. Preceded and flanked by motorcycled troopers, with the rearguard of police, it swept into the drive and snorted to a stop. The sedan door opened and Inspector Vaughn jumped out. He was followed more slowly by Stephen Megara, ugly and silent, eyes roving with mercurial alertness. Megara was instantly surrounded by his guard, and proceeded around the house to the landing dock on the Cove. His own launch was waiting for him. Tagged by the police boat, he returned to the *Helene* and disappeared up the ladder. The police boat kept circling the yacht.

On the porch of the colonial house a detective, who had been amiably rocking himself, got to his feet and handed the Inspector a bulky envelope. Vaughn, who was feeling particularly helpless this morning, snatched at it as if it were a life preserver. The helpless look vanished. His face became grim as he read it.

"Just delivered about a half-hour ago by special messenger," explained the detective.

Helene Brad appeared in the doorway, and the Inspector put the envelope very hastily into his pocket.

"What's going on here?" demanded Helene. "Where is Stephen? I think you owe us some explanation of all this mystery, Inspector!"

"Mr. Megara's on his yacht," replied Vaughn. "No, Miss Brad, I owe you no explanation. If you'll excuse me—"

"I shan't excuse you," said Helene angrily; her eyes flashed. "I think you people have been acting in a beastly manner. Where did you and Stephen go this morning?"

"Sorry," said Vaughn. "Can't tell you. Please, Miss—"

"But Stephen looks ill. You haven't been putting him through those nasty third degrees of yours!"

Vaughn grinned. "Oh, say now—that's a lot of newspaper talk. Nothing like that. Looks sick, does he? Guess he doesn't feel well. He did say something about having severe pains in the groin."

Helene stamped her foot. "Inhuman, all of you! I shall ask Dr. Temple this very moment to go out to the yacht and have a look at him."

"Go ahead and ask," said the Inspector eagerly. "It's all right with me." And he sighed with relief when she marched off the porch and took the path which led past the totem post. Vaughn clamped his jaws at once. "Come along, Johnny. Got a job to do."

Accompanied by the detective, the Inspector descended from the porch and struck out on the western path through the woods. The little hut in which Fox, the gardener-chauffeur, was confined popped into view through the trees. A plainclothesman lounged on the door-step.

"Quiet?" asked Vaughn.

"Not a peep out of him."

Vaughn without ceremony pushed open the door and went into the cabin, followed by his subordinate. Fox's face, lean, gray, black-stubbled, eyes violet with shadows, turned to him at once with eagerness. He had been pacing the floor like any restless prisoner in a cell. When he saw who his visitor was, however, his lips clamped shut and he resumed his pacing.

"I'm giving you one last chance," said the Inspector abruptly. "Will you talk?"

Fox's feet pounded with uninterrupted rhythm.

"Still won't tell me what you went to see Patsy Malone for, hey?"

No answer.

"All right," said Vaughn, sitting down lazily. "That's your funeral—*Pendleton.*"

The man's stride faltered for an instant, and then resumed. His face remained expressionless.

"Good boy," said Vaughn with sarcasm. "Swell nerves. *And* guts. But it won't get you anywhere, Pendleton. Because we know all about you."

Fox muttered: "I don't know what you're talking about."

"You've done time."

"I don't know what you mean."

"Did a stretch in stir and don't know what doing time means? All right, all right," said the Inspector with a smile. "But I'm telling you, Pendleton, you're acting like a damned fool. I don't hold it against you because you used iron bars for curtains. . . ." His smile disappeared. "I mean it, Pendleton. Denying it won't do you any good. You're in a jam—see? You've got a record, and under the circumstances it's best for you to come clean."

The man's eyes were agonized. "I've got nothing to explain."

"No? All right, let's talk about it. Suppose I bumped into a crook below the deadline in New York City. A jeweler's safe had just been cracked. . . . Think my man wouldn't have explaining to do? Guess again."

The tall man stopped and leaned on his doubled hands; his knuckles were white against the dark table. "For God's sake, Inspector," he said, "give me a break! All right, I'm Pendleton. But I tell you I'm innocent in this case! I want to go straight—"

"Hmm," said the Inspector. "That's better. Now we know where we're at. You're Phil Pendleton, you were in State's Prison at Vandalia, Illinois, serving a sentence of five years for robbery. You pulled the hero act in the prison break there last year, and saved the Warden's life. The Governor of Illinois commuted your sentence. You've got a record—assault and battery in California, housebreaking in Michigan. Served time for both crimes. . . . Now, if you're on the level we don't want to hound you. If you're not, come clean and I'll make it as easy for you as I can. Did you bump off Thomas Brad?"

The man who was known in Bradwood as Fox dropped limply into a chair. "No," he whispered. "As God is my judge, Inspector."

"How'd you get that last job—from the man who gave you references?"

He spoke without looking up. "I wanted to start over again. He—he didn't ask questions. Business was bad, and he fired me. That's all."

"Had no ulterior motive in taking this double gardener-chauffeur's job, eh?"

"No, it was outdoors, good pay . . ."

"All right. If you expect consideration, you've got to clear up that visit to Malone's. If you're on the straight, why do you look up a mob like Malone's?"

Fox was silent for a long moment. Then he rose, and his face hardened. "I've got a right to lead my own life. . . ."

"Sure you have, Pendleton," said the Inspector genially. "That's the ticket! We'll help you."

Fox spoke rapidly, looking at the detective in the doorway without seeing him. "In some way an old—an old prison pal traced me here. The first I knew about it was Tuesday morning. He insisted on meeting me. I said no—I was through. He said: 'You wouldn't want me to tip off your boss, would you?' So I went."

Vaughn nodded; he was listening intently. "Go on, son, go on."

"He told me where to go—no names, just an address in New York. Tuesday night, after I dropped Stallings and Mrs. Baxter off at the Roxy, I drove up there, parked the car on the next block. Some gun let me in. I saw—somebody. He made me a—proposition. I said no—I was through with the old life. No more rackets for me. He told me he'd give me till the next day to consider, and if I didn't come through he'd tell Mr. Brad who I was. I went away—and you know the rest."

"Naturally laid off when he heard a murder was committed," muttered Vaughn. "This was Patsy Malone, eh?"

"I—well, I can't say."

Vaughn eyed him shrewdly. "Won't squeal, hey? What was the proposition?"

Fox shook his head. "I won't tell any more, Inspector. You want to help me and all that, but if I spilled it it would be the spot for me."

The Inspector rose. "I see. Well, I can't say, between you and me, that I blame you. That sounds like the straight goods. . . . By the way—Fox . . ." the man's head jerked up, and he looked into Vaughn's eyes with a mixture of astonishment and gratitude—"where were you last Christmas?"

"In New York, Inspector. Looking for a job. I answered Brad's ad and he took me on the day after New Year's."

"Check." The Inspector sighed. "Well, Fox, for your sake I hope it's as you say. Under the circumstances my hands are tied. You'll have to stick around. No guards, no pinch, you understand. But you'll be under observation, and I don't want you to try a lam."

"I won't, Inspector!" cried Fox. New hope had leaped into his face.

"Keep going as if nothing'd happened. If you're in the clear I won't discuss this thing with Mrs. Brad or disclose your record to her."

Before this generosity Fox stood speechless. The Inspector beckoned his man and left the hut.

Fox followed slowly. He stood in the doorway and watched the Inspector and the two detectives stride down the path into the woods. His chest rose, and he breathed deeply of the warm air.

Vaughn found Helene Brad on the porch of the big house.

"Torturing poor Fox again," she sniffed.

"Fox is all right," said the Inspector shortly; his face showed the fatigue and helplessness he felt. "Find Temple?"

"Dr. Temple was out. He took a sail somewhere in his motorboat. I left a note for him to see Stephen the moment he got back."

"Out, eh?"

Vaughn glanced in the general direction of Oyster Island and nodded wearily.

Chapter Nineteen

T

At 9:15 Sunday morning Inspector Vaughn, who had slept overnight at Bradwood, was summoned by Stallings to the telephone. He seemed to be expecting the call, for he looked blank at once and said in an audible mutter: "Wonder who that is." Whether Stallings was deceived or not, he learned little enough from the Inspector's monosyllabic replies to the early caller. "Hmm. . . . Yes. . . . No. All right." The Inspector hung up and, eyes glittering, hurried out of the house.

At 9:45 District Attorney Isham made a grand entrance into Bradwood, driving up in an official county car with three county troopers. They all descended before the colonial house and Inspector Vaughn leaped forward, grasped Isham's hands, and began earnestly to converse with him in an undertone.

Under cover of this diversion Ellery slipped his Duesenberg into the grounds of Yardley's estate a few moments later.

No one apparently noticed that one of the three troopers who had accompanied the District Attorney did not possess the easy military bearing characteristic of his companions. He joined a larger group of troopers, who thereupon dispersed and walked off in various directions.

Professor Yardley, in slacks and sweater, smoking the inevitable pipe, greeted Ellery with a welcoming cry in the selamik of the house.

"Here's our chief guest!" he shouted. "I thought you weren't coming back, my boy!"

"As long as you're in the quotative mood," smiled Ellery, stripping off his coat and flinging himself on the tessellated marble, "you might consider the fact that *hospes nullus tam in amici hospitium diverti potest . . . odiosus siet.*"

"Why butcher Plautus? You haven't been here three days anyway." The Professor's eyes were bright. "Well?"

"Well," said Ellery, "he's with us."

"No!" Yardley became thoughtful. "In uniform? Good as a play, by heaven."

"We rearranged the details in Mineola this morning. Isham got hold of a couple of troopers and an official car, telephoned Vaughn, and set out for Bradwood." Ellery sighed; there were huge circles under his eyes. "That trip! Van was about as communicative as a clam. I'm tired! But there's no rest for the weary. Would you care to witness the great unveiling?"

The Professor scrambled to his feet. "Decidedly! I've been a martyr long enough. Had breakfast?"

"We stuffed our bellies in Mineola. Come along."

They left the house and sauntered across the road to Bradwood, Vaughn was still talking to Isham when they reached the porch. "Just telling the D.A.," said Vaughn, as if Ellery had never been away, "the line we got on Fox."

"Fox?"

The Inspector repeated what he had learned about the man's history.

Ellery shrugged. "Poor devil. . . . Where's Megara?"

"On the yacht." Vaughn lowered his voice. "*He's* gone down to the landing. . . . Megara had some bad pains in his groin yesterday. Miss Brad tried to get Temple, but he was out all day. I think Temple's gone over to the *Helene* this morning."

"Anything evolved from that pretty plot yesterday?"

"Nothing. Decoy didn't pull a real live duck out of the sky. Come on, let's go before these people start getting up. They're all asleep yet—nobody's been about."

They proceeded around the house and took the path to the Cove. On the dock stood three troopers, and the police launch waited to cast off.

No one paid the least attention to the third trooper. Isham, Vaughn, Yardley, and Ellery scrambled into the launch, and the three troopers followed. The boat sputtered off toward the yacht a half-mile away.

The same procedure was observed in boarding the *Helene*. The four men scaled the ladder, and then the troopers followed. The members of the *Helene's* crew who stood about the deck in immaculate whites had eyes only for Inspector Vaughn, who was striding along as if he meant to arrest somebody.

Captain Swift opened the door of his cabin as they passed. "How long—?" he began.

Vaughn tramped along, a deaf man, and the others meekly tramped along, too. The Captain stared after them, his jaw swelling; then he cursed with effortless fluency and retreated into his cabin, slamming the door.

The Inspector knocked on the panels of the main cabin. The door swung inward, and Dr. Temple's taut, blackish face appeared.

"Hullo!" he said. "Out in force, eh? I've just been having a look at Mr. Megara."

"May we come in?" asked Isham.

"Come in!" said Megara in a tight voice from the interior of the cabin. They filed in, silently. Stephen Megara lay on a simple bed, naked where a sheet did not cover him. The yachtsman's face was pale and strained; there were beads of sweat on the edge of his eyebrows. He was doubled up, clutching his groin. He did not look at the troopers; his eyes were fixed on Temple with agony.

"What's the trouble, Doctor?" asked Ellery soberly.

"*Hernia testis,*" said Dr. Temple. "A good case of it. It's not anything to worry about immediately. I've given him temporary relief; he'll feel the effect of it in a moment."

"Got it on this last trip," panted Megara. "All right, Doctor; all right. Leave us, please. These gentlemen want to discuss something with me."

Temple stared; then he shrugged and picked up his medical bag. "As you say. . . . Don't neglect that, Mr. Megara. I suggest surgery, although it isn't absolutely necessary right now."

He bowed with military stiffness to the others and quickly left the cabin. The Inspector followed him out. He did not return until Dr. Temple was in his own motorboat headed for the mainland.

Vaughn closed the cabin door tightly. On deck two troopers set their backs against it.

The third trooper took a step forward, and licked his lips. The man in the bed plucked at the sheet.

They looked at each other, silently; they did not shake hands.

"Stefan," said the schoolmaster.

"Andreja." Ellery felt the alarming impulse to giggle; there was something ludicrous in the situation, tragic as its overtones were. These two straight, clean-cut men with the foreign names—the yacht, the bed of pain, the drab uniform . . . There had never been anything quite like it in all his experience.

"Krosac. Krosac, Andreja," said the sick man. "He's found us, as you always said he would."

Andreja Tvar said harshly: "Had Tom followed my advice . . . I warned him by letter last December. Didn't he get in touch with you?"

Stefan shook his head slowly. "No. He didn't know where to reach me. I was cruising in the Pacific. . . . How have you been, Andr'?"

"Very well. How long is it?"

"Years . . . Five, six?"

They fell silent. The Inspector was watching them with eagerness, and Isham barely breathed. Yardley looked at Ellery, and Ellery said quickly: "Please, gentlemen. The story. Mr.—Van . . ." he indicated the schoolmaster, "must get away from Bradwood as soon as possible. Every moment he lingers in this vicinity increases the danger. Krosac, whoever he is, is clever. He may easily see through our little deception, and we want no possibility of his following Mr. Van back to West Virginia."

"No," said Van heavily, "that's true. Stefan, tell them."

The yachtsman straightened in bed—the pain had either left him or in his excitement he had forgotten it—and stared at the low ceiling of the cabin. "How shall I begin? It happened so damned long ago. Tomislav, Andreja, and I were the last of the Tvar family. A proud and wealthy mountain clan in Montenegro."

"Which has vanished," said the schoolmaster in a frozen voice.

The sick man waved his hand as if it did not matter. "You've got to understand that we came of the hottest Balkan blood. Hot—so hot it sizzled." Megara laughed shortly. "The Tvars had a traditional enemy—the Krosacs, another clan. For generations—"

"Vendetta!" cried the Professor. "Of course. Not properly vendetta, which is Italian, but certainly a blood feud, like the feuds of our own Kentucky mountaineers. I should have thought of it."

"Yes," snapped Megara. "We don't know to this day why there was a feud—the original cause had been so smeared in blood that our generation didn't know why. But from childhood we were taught—"

"Kill the Krosacs," croaked the schoolmaster.

"We'd been the aggressors," continued Megara, scowling, "and twenty years ago, due to the ferocity and ruthlessness of our grandfather and father, only one male Krosac remained—Velja, the man you're after. . . . He was a kid then. He and his mother were the sole survivors of the Krosac family."

"How far away it seems," muttered Van. "How barbaric! You,

Tomislav, and I, in retaliation for the murder of father, killed Krosac's father and two uncles, ambushed them. . . ."

"Utterly incredible," murmured Ellery to the Professor. "It's hard to believe that we're dealing with civilized people."

"What happened to this youngster, Krosac?" demanded Isham.

"His mother fled with him from Montenegro. They went to Italy, hiding there, and the mother died shortly after."

"And that left young Krosac to carry on the feud against you people," said Vaughn thoughtfully. "I suppose his old lady pumped him full of hop before she died. You kept track of the boy?"

"Yes. We had to, in self-protection, because we knew that he would try to kill us when he grew up. Our paid agents tracked him all over Europe, but he disappeared before he was seventeen and we never heard of him again—until now."

"You people didn't see Krosac personally?"

"No. Not since he left our mountainside, when he was eleven or twelve years old."

"Just a moment," said Ellery, frowning. "How can you gentlemen be so sure Krosac wanted to kill you? After all, a child . . ."

"How?" Andrew Van smiled bitterly. "One of our agents wormed his way into the boy's confidence while he was still under observation and heard him swear to wipe us all out, if he had had to follow us to the ends of the earth to spill our blood."

"And you mean to say," demanded Isham, "because of a kid's wild nonsense, you actually ran from your home country and changed your names?"

Both men flushed. "You don't know Croatian feuds," muttered the yachtsman. He avoided their eyes. "A Krosac once followed a Tvar into the heart of southern Arabia—generations ago. . . ."

"Then it's certain that, if you were face to face with Krosac, you wouldn't know him?" asked Ellery abruptly.

"How could we? . . . We were left alone—we three. Father, mother—dead. We decided to leave Montenegro and go to America. There wasn't a tie to hold us—Andrew here and I were unmarried, and while Tom had been married, his wife had died and there were no children.

"We were a rich family; and our estates were valuable. We sold all our property and under assumed names, separately, we came to this country, meeting by prearrangement in New York. We had decided to take our names"—Ellery started, and then smiled—"from different countries; we consulted an atlas, and each of us assumed a different nationality—I Greek, Tom Roumanian, and Andrew Armenian, since at that time we were unmistakably Southern European in appearance and speech, and couldn't pass for native Americans."

"I warned you about Krosac," said the schoolmaster darkly.

"Tom and I—we'd all been well educated—went into our present business. Andrew here was always a restless soul and he had preferred to work alone, studying the English language by himself, and ultimately becoming a schoolteacher. We all, of course, became American citizens. And gradually, as the years passed, since we'd heard nothing of or from Krosac, we almost forgot him. He became—at least to Tom and me—a legend, a myth. We thought him dead or hopelessly off the trail." The yachtsman set his jaw. "If we'd known—At any rate, Tom married. We did well in business. And Andrew went out to Arroyo."

"If you'd taken my advice," snapped Van, "this would not have happened, and Tom would be alive today. I told you repeatedly that Krosac would come back and take his revenge!"

"Please, Andr'," said Megara in a hard voice; but there was something pitying in his eyes as he looked at his brother. "I know. And you didn't see us often. Your own fault, as you must realize. Perhaps if you'd been more fraternal . . ."

"Stay with you and Tom where Krosac could wipe us out with one blow?" cried the man from Arroyo. "Why do you think I buried myself in that hole? I love life, too, Stephen! But I was wise, and you—"

"Not so wise, Andr'," said the yachtsman. "After all, Krosac found you first. And—"

"Yes," said the Inspector. "So he did. I'd like to get that little business of the Arroyo murder straight, Mr. Van, if you don't mind."

The schoolmaster stiffened at some bleak memory. "Arroyo," he said hoarsely. "A place of horrors. It was my fear that led me, years ago, to assume the character of Old Pete. A dual personality, I felt, would stand me in good stead, should Krosac"—he snarled—"find me. He found—" He stopped and then said rapidly: "For years I kept that hut, which I had discovered by accident, abandoned, when I was exploring some old caves in the hills. I set up the barbed wire. I purchased my disguise in Pittsburgh. Once in a great while, when I was free from my regular duties as the schoolmaster, I stole up into the hills and dressed as Old Pete, appearing in town often enough to make the personality real in the minds of the Arroyo people. Tom and Stephen—they always laughed at this subterfuge. They said it was a childish thing to do. Was it childish, Stephen? Do you think so now? Don't you think that Tom, in his grave, is sorry he didn't follow my example?"

"Yes, yes," said Megara quickly. "Tell the story, Andr'."

The eccentric schoolmaster took a turn about the cabin, hands behind the back of the borrowed uniform, eyes distraught. . . . They listened to an amazing tale.

With the coming of Christmas—he said in the intense voice characteristic of all his utterances—he realized that for two months he had not appeared in Arroyo as the old hillman. His absence over such a long period might well have led some of the townspeople—Constable Luden, perhaps—to seek out the ancient hill-dweller and investigate his cabin . . . an event which, he pointed out, would have been disastrous to his carefully maintained deception. He faced more than a week between Christmas Day and New Year's when his tiny school was closed; and he saw that for several days at least he could act the eremitic Pete with impunity. On previous occasions when he had assumed the ragged character it had been when the schoolmaster was supposedly on a holiday, or over weekends.

"How did you explain these absences to Kling?" asked Ellery. "Or was your servant in the secret?"

"No!" cried Van. "He was stupid, a halfwit. I merely told him that I was going into Wheeling or Pittsburgh for a holiday."

On Christmas Eve, then, he had informed Kling that he was bound for Pittsburgh to celebrate the Yuletide. He had left in the evening for the shack in the hills—all his hillman's trappings, of course, he kept in the hut. There he became Old Pete again. Rising very early the next morning—Christmas morning—he set out on foot for town, for he needed food supplies and he knew that he could get them from Bernheim, the storekeeper, despite the fact that it was Christmas Day and the general store was closed. He had struck the road at the junction of the main highway and the Arroyo pike and there, alone, at half-past six in the morning, had made the horrifying discovery of the crucified body. The significance of the diverse T's had struck him at once. He hurried to his house a hundred yards up the Arroyo road. The shambles that the others had seen later had painful meaning for him; he realized instantly that by sheer accident Krosac had come the night before, killed poor old Kling (thinking him to be Andreja Tvar), had cut off his head, and crucified him to the signpost.

He had had to think rapidly. What was he to do? Through an unexpected generosity of fate, Krosac now believed he had fulfilled his vengeance against Andreja Tvar; why not keep him believing it? By taking the character of Old Pete permanently not only would Krosac be deceived but the little West Virginia world in which Van lived, as well. . . . Fortunately the suit of clothes which Kling had been wearing when he was murdered was one which Van himself had given the man a few days before, an old and well-worn garment. He knew that the Arroyo townspeople would recognize the suit as Andrew Van's, their schoolmaster's; and if he should put some papers in the pockets identifiable with Andrew Van, there would be no question of identification.

Securing letters and keys from old suits of his, the schoolmaster had stolen back to the crossroads, taken from Kling's mutilated body all objects identifiable with Kling—a gruesome task, and the man in uniform shuddered at the recollection—put on the dead man the Van objects, and then deliberately hurried farther up the road into the woods. Here he built a guarded little fire, burned Kling's personal possessions, and waited for someone to come along.

"Why?" demanded Vaughn. "Why didn't you beat it back to your shack and lie low?"

"Because," said Van simply, "it was necessary for me to get to town at once and by some means warn my brothers of Krosac's appearance. If I went into town and said nothing about the body at the crossroads, I should be regarded with suspicion, for it was necessary to pass the junction on the way to town. If I went into town and related the story of my discovery of the body—alone—I might very well come under suspicion. But if I waited for someone to come along, an innocent citizen of the neighborhood, I should have a companion for the 'discovery' of the body, and at the same time would be able to get to town, stock up on provisions, and notify my brothers."

Michael Orkins, the farmer, had come along in an hour or so. Van, or Old Pete, contrived to be tramping the road in the direction of the junction. He had hailed Orkins, the farmer told him to jump in, they found the body . . . the rest, as Van said soberly, "Mr. Queen knows from having attended the inquest."

"And you managed to notify your brothers?" asked Isham.

"Yes. While I was in my own house, after discovering Kling's body at the crossroads, I scribbled a hasty note to Tomis—to the man you know as Thomas Brad. In the excitement when we got to town, I managed to slip the letter through the slot in the post-office door— the post office being closed. I told Tom in the letter briefly what had occurred, warned him that Krosac was probably heading his way bent on vengeance. I wrote too that from then on I meant to be Old Pete, and neither he nor Stephen was to say anything of this. I, at least, meant to be protected from Krosac; for I was dead."

"You were lucky," said Megara bitterly. "When Tom couldn't reach me after receiving your letter, he must have written that note we found addressed to the police—as a last warning to me, should anything happen to him before I returned to Bradwood."

The brothers were pale and tense; both men showed plainly the nerve strain they were experiencing. Even Megara had succumbed to the spell. From the deck outside came a man's coarse laugh; they looked startled, and then relaxed as they realized that it was only one of the *Helene's* crew bantering a trooper.

"Well," said Isham at last, rather helplessly, "that's all well and good, but where the devil does it leave us? Still up a tree, as far as nabbing Krosac is concerned."

"A pessimistic attitude," said Ellery, "royally justified. Gentlemen, who knows or knew about the Tvar-Krosac feud? A little investigation along that line may help us narrow the field of suspects."

"No one but ourselves," said the schoolmaster darkly. "I naturally told no one."

"There are no written records of the feud?"

"No."

"Very well," said Ellery thoughtfully. "That leaves only Krosac as a possible disseminator of the story. While it's conceivable that he may have told somebody, it isn't probable; why should he? Krosac is now an adult—a maniac obsessed with a vengeance-fixation, besides. His vengeance, he would feel, must be personally consummated; those things aren't delegated to agents or accomplices. Eh, Mr. Megara?"

"Not in Montenegro," replied the yachtsman grimly.

"Of course; it's axiomatic to anyone who knows the psychology of feudism," said Professor Yardley. "And in the old Balkan feuds, which were considerably more gory than even our own mountaineer feuds, only a member of the family could wipe out the stain."

Ellery nodded. "Would Krosac have told anyone in this country? Hardly. It would place him in such an individual's power, or would leave a trail to himself and Krosac is, from the cleverness he has displayed, a wary scoundrel despite his monomania. And if he took an accomplice—which he would not do—what had he to offer such a creature?"

"A good point," conceded Isham.

"The very fact that he rifled Mr. Van's house of whatever cash the tin box contained—"

"There were a hundred and forty dollars in the box," muttered Van.

"—indicates that Krosac was hard up and took what he could find. But your brother Tomislav's house was not looted. Certainly no accomplice, then, for had there been one the accomplice would not have passed up the opportunity to steal what he could. These have been murders for revenge, not gain. . . . Other signs of the nonexistence of an accomplice? Yes. In the murder of Kling, only one person was seen in the vicinity of the crossroads, and that man was Velja Krosac."

"What are you trying to prove?" growled Vaughn.

"Simply that the chances are overwhelmingly in favor of Krosac's having worked entirely alone and having told no one of his intended crimes—judging from the individualistic motive, the horrible method, and the trail of a lone man which he made no attempt to conceal up to a certain point. Remember that Krosac practically signed his name to his crimes by plastering T's over the scenes of both. He must have realized this, insane or not, and it's unbelievable that an accomplice would ally himself—after that first murder especially—with such a depraved and brazen maniac."

"And all that gets you exactly nowhere," snapped the Inspector. "Why worry about a mythical accomplice? We haven't made an inch of progress toward finding the principal, Mr. Queen!"

Ellery shrugged; evidently to his mind the elimination of a possible accomplice or sharer in Krosac's secret was a pertinent and prime necessity.

District Attorney Isham paced between the two brothers restlessly. "Look here," he said at last. "After all we mustn't be stampeded by this thing. It isn't sensible that a man will disappear so damned completely he can't even be traced. We must know more about his appearance. Granted you gentlemen don't know what Krosac looks like today, can't you tell us more about him—characteristics that wouldn't change from childhood to maturity?"

The brothers glanced at each other. "The limp," said Van, shrugging.

"I told you that," said Megara. "As a child Krosac contracted a mild hip disease—not disfiguring, but enough to make him limp on his left leg."

"A permanent limp?" demanded Ellery.

The Tvars looked blank.

"It's possible that the limp has been cured in the twenty years that have elapsed since then, you know. In which case the testimony of Croker, the Weirton garageman, would indicate another facet of Krosac's cleverness. Remembering that you people knew he had limped as a child, he might, as Professor Yardley has already suggested, have been *pretending* a limp . . . provided, of course, he has been cured in the interim."

"On the other hand," snapped the Inspector, "the limp may be authentic. Why on earth you should throw a monkey wrench into every piece of evidence we get, Mr. Queen—"

"Oh, very well," said Ellery dryly. "Krosac limps. Does that satisfy you, Inspector?" He smiled. "Depend on it, though. Whether he really limps or not, he'll continue to limp whenever he makes one of his infrequent public appearances."

"We've wasted enough time," grumbled Vaughn. "One thing is sure. You gentlemen have to get plenty of protection from now on. I think you'd better get right back to Arroyo, Mr. Van, and keep out of sight. I'll send a half-dozen guards back to West Virginia with you, and leave 'em there."

"Oh, my dear God," groaned Ellery. "Inspector, do you realize what you're saying? You'll be playing directly into Krosac's hands! We may assume that our ruse has been successful, that Krosac still doesn't know where Andreja Tvar is, although he knows he's alive. Any attention we focus on Andreja Tvar, then, is bound to come to Krosac's notice if he is on the watch, as he must be."

"Well, what would you do?" said Vaughn belligerently.

"Mr. Van should be escorted back to his hut in the hills as unostentatiously as possible—by one man, not a half-dozen, Inspector. Why don't you send an army? And then he must be left alone. As Old Pete he is safe. The less fuss we make, the better off he'll be."

"And how about Mr. Megara—er—Mr. Megara?" asked Isham. He seemed to have difficulty in selecting a proper name for the binominal brothers. "Leave him alone, too?"

"Certainly not!" cried Ellery. "Krosac expects him to be guarded, and he must be. Openly, as openly as you please."

The brothers said nothing as their fate was being argued by these outsiders; surreptitiously they regarded each other, and Megara's stern face grew sterner, while the schoolmaster blinked and moved restlessly about.

"Is there anything else you gentlemen wish to discuss before you're separated?" asked Isham. "Quickly, now, please."

"I've been thinking it over," muttered Van, "and I—I don't think it would be wise for me to return to West Virginia. I have the feeling that Krosac—" his voice trembled. . . . "I think I'll go as far away from this cursed country as I can get. As far from Krosac—"

"No," said Ellery firmly. "If Krosac has any suspicion that you're Old Pete, your relinquishment of that character and your flight would leave an open trail for him to follow. You must remain Old Pete until we've netted our man, or at least until we have proof that Krosac has penetrated your disguise."

"I thought—" Van wet his lips. "I'm not a very wealthy man, Mr. Queen. You probably think me a coward. But I've lived under the shadow of that devil . . ." His strange eyes burned. "There is money coming to me under the will of my brother Tomislav. I relinquish it. I only want to get away. . . ." The inconsistency, the incoherence of his remark made them all uncomfortable.

"No, Andr'," said Megara heavily. "If you want to run out—well, you know best. But the money . . . I'll advance it. You'll need it wherever you're going."

"How much is it?" demanded Vaughn suspiciously.

"Little enough." Megara's hard eyes became harder. "Five thousand dollars. Tom could well have afforded . . . But Andreja is a youngest, and in the old country ideas on the subject of inheritance were rigid. I mys—"

"Your brother Tom was the eldest son?" asked Ellery.

Megara's face reddened. "No. I am. But I'll make up for it, Andr'—"

"Well, do what you please about that," said Vaughn. "But I'll tell you one thing, Mr. Van; you can't skip. Mr. Queen is right as far as that's concerned."

The schoolmaster's face was pale. "If you think he doesn't know—"

"How the devil can he?" said Vaughn irritably. "If it will make you feel any better, Mr. Megara can arrange to give you your money, and you can take it back with you. If you have to beat it without notice, you won't go penniless. But that's the best we can do."

"With my own savings in the hut," muttered Van, "it makes a tidy sum. More than enough, wherever I go. . . Very well. I return to Arroyo. And, Stephen—thank you."

"Perhaps," said the yachtsman lamely, "you'll need more. Suppose I give you ten instead of five. . . ."

"No." The Schoolmaster squared his shoulders. "I want only what's due me. I've always made my own way, Stephen, as you know."

Megara winced as he crawled out of bed and went to a desk. He sat down and began to write. Andreja Tvar paced up and down. Now that his immediate fate had been decided for him, he seemed anxious to leave. The yachtsman rose, waving a check.

"You'll have to wait until tomorrow morning, Andr'," he said. "I'll cash it for you myself and then you can pick up the money in the morning on your way back to West Virginia."

Van looked about quickly. "I must go now. Where can I stay, Inspector?"

"We'll let the troopers take care of you overnight."

The two brothers regarded each other. "Take care of yourself, Andr'."

"And you." Their eyes held, and the intangible barrier between them trembled and almost fell. But it did not. Megara turned away, and the schoolmaster with sloping shoulders walked to the door.

When they had returned to the mainland and Andreja Tvar had marched off in the midst of a group of troopers, Ellery drawled: "Did anything strike you—? No, something did strike you, and the question is superfluous. Why did you seem disturbed, Mr. Isham, by Stephen Megara's explanation for the Tvar brothers' flight from Montenegro?"

"Because," said the District Attorney, "it's preposterous. Feud or no feud. Nobody can tell me that three grown men will quit their homes and country and change their names just because a little shaver has the emotional incentive to kill them."

"Very true," said Ellery, gulping in the warm piny air. "So true that I wonder Inspector Vaughn didn't arrest 'em on the spot for perjury." Inspector Vaughn snorted. "It convinces me that, while the Krosac story is undoubtedly true, there was more to their departure than the fear of an eleven-year-old's problematical vengeance."

"What do you mean, Queen?" asked Professor Yardley. "I can't see—"

"Surely it's obvious! Why should three adults, as Mr. Isham says, desert their homeland and flee to a foreign country under assumed names? Eh?"

"The police!" muttered Vaughn.

"Precisely. They left because they *had* to leave, pursued by a danger much more immediate, I assure you, than the boy Krosac's revenge. If I were you, Inspector, I'd make an overseas inquiry."

"Cable Yugoslavia," said the Inspector. "Good idea. I'll do it to-night."

"You see," drawled Ellery to Professor Yardley, "life, as usual, plays shoddy tricks. They flee from a real danger, and twenty years later the potential danger catches up with them."

Chapter Twenty

TWO TRIANGLES

As Ellery, Professor Yardley, Isham, and Vaughn rounded the eastern wing of the house, someone hailed them from the rear. They all turned quickly; it was Dr. Temple.

"All through with the big powwow?" asked Temple; he had deposited his medical bag somewhere, and was strolling along the path empty-handed, smoking.

"Ah—yes," said Isham.

At the same instant the tall figure of Jonah Lincoln came dashing along the path around the corner; he and Ellery collided, and Jonah stepped back with a scant mutter of apology.

"Temple!" he cried, ignoring the others. "What's the matter with Megara?"

"Don't excite yourself, Mr. Lincoln," said the Inspector dryly. "Megara's all right. Just a hernia. What's eating you?"

Jonah wiped his forehead; he was panting. "Oh, everything's so mysterious around here. Damn it all, haven't we any rights left? I heard that the pack of you had gone over to the yacht after Temple, and I thought—"

"That Mr. Megara had met with foul play?" asked Isham. "No, it's as Inspector Vaughn says."

"Well!" The red tide ebbed from Lincoln's sharp features, and he grew a little calmer. Dr. Temple was smoking peacefully, regarding him without perturbation. "The place is like a prison, anyway," grumbled Jonah. "My sister had the hardest time getting into Bradwood. Just came back from Oyster Island and the man on the—"

"Miss Lincoln's back?" said the Inspector quickly.

Dr. Temple removed the pipe from his mouth; the serene look went out of his eyes. "When?" he demanded.

"A few minutes ago. The detective wouldn't—"

"Alone?"

"Yes. They—" Poor Lincoln's indignation was fated never to be expressed. His mouth was open, and remained open. The other men stiffened.

From somewhere in the house came a wild screaming laugh.

"Hester!" shouted Dr. Temple, and plunged forward, bowling Lincoln over to one side and disappearing around the corner.

"My God," said Isham hoarsely, "what the devil's that?"

Lincoln scrambled to his feet and dashed after the physician, Ellery at his heels and the others streaming after.

The source of the scream had been the upper floor of the house. As they ran into the reception hall they passed Stallings, the butler, standing near the staircase, his face drained of blood. Mrs. Baxter's rigid neck protruded from a rear door.

The upper floor contained the bedrooms. They reached the landing just in time to see Dr. Temple's wiry figure hurtle through the doorway of one of the rooms. . . . The screams persisted; peal after peal of a woman's shrill hysteria.

They found Dr. Temple holding Hester Lincoln in his arms, smoothing her disheveled hair, hushing her gently. The girl's face was crimson, her eyes fierce and unintelligent, her mouth crookedly open; the screams ripped out as if she had no control over her vocal chords.

"Hysterics!" snapped the physician over his shoulder. "Help me get her on the bed."

Vaughn and Jonah leaped forward; the girl's screaming laughter redoubled in volume, and she began to struggle. It was at this moment that Ellery heard quick steps from the corridor, and turned to see Mrs. Brad, in *négligé* and Helene appear in the doorway.

"What's the matter?" gasped Mrs. Brad. "What's happened?"

Helene hurried forward. Dr. Temple forced the kicking girl back on the bed and sharply slapped her face. A shriek trembled, and died. Hester half-rose on the bed and stared at the pale pudgy face of Mrs. Brad. Intelligence sprang into her eyes, and an inhuman hatred.

"Get out, you—you—Get out of my sight!" she cried. "I hate, hate you, and everything that belongs to you. Get out, I say, *get out!*"

Mrs. Brad flamed; her full lips trembled. Her shoulders shook as she gaped. Then she uttered a low cry, wheeled, and disappeared.

"Hush, Hester!" said Helene fiercely. "You don't mean that. Be a good girl, now, and quiet down. You're making a scene."

Hester's eyes seemed to turn over in their sockets; her head sagged, and she dropped like a crumpled sack on the bed.

"Out!" said Dr. Temple imperiously. "Everybody."

He stretched the unconscious girl flat on her back as the others slowly left the room. Jonah, flushed, nervous, but in a way triumphant, closed the door softly.

"I wonder what gave her hysterics," said Isham with a frown.

"The reaction of a violent emotional experience," drawled Ellery. "Is the psychology correct?"

"The New England conscience," murmured Professor Yardley, "in violent eruption."

"Why'd she leave the Island?" demanded Vaughn.

Jonah grinned feebly. "It's all over now, Inspector, so I guess there's no harm in your knowing; nothing mysterious about it. Hester has been infatuated with that scoundrel Romaine on Oyster Island. But just now she came hotfooting it back. It seems he made—well, a pass at her." His face darkened. "Another little score I have to settle with him, damn his black soul! But in a way I feel grateful to him. He opened her eyes and brought her back to her senses."

The Inspector remarked dryly: "It's none of my business of course, but did your sister think he'd recite poetry to her?"

The door opened and Dr. Temple appeared. "She's quiet now; don't bother her," he growled. "You might go in, Miss Brad." Helene nodded and went in, closing the door quickly behind her. "She'll be all right. I'll give her a sedative—get my bag. . . ." He hurried down the stairs.

Jonah stared after him. "When she came back, she told me that she was through with Romaine and the whole damned nudist business. She wants to leave here and go off somewhere—New York, she said. Wants to be alone. Good thing for her."

"Umm," said Isham. "Where's Romaine now?"

"On the Island, I suppose; he hasn't shown his face around here, the dirty—" Jonah bit his lip and shrugged. "May Hester leave Bradwood, Mr. Isham?"

"Well . . . What do you think, Vaughn?"

The Inspector massaged his jaw. "Can't see any harm in it, if we know where to get her when we want her."

"You'll be responsible for her, Mr. Lincoln?" asked Isham.

Jonah nodded eagerly. "I absolutely vouch—"

"By the way," murmured Ellery, "exactly what has your sister against Mrs. Brad, Mr. Lincoln?"

Jonah's smile faded; something froze behind his eyes. "I haven't the faintest idea," he said flatly. "Don't pay any attention to her; she didn't know what she was saying."

"Strange," said Ellery. "It appeared to me that she spoke with remarkable clarity. I think, Inspector, that it would be politic for us to talk with Mrs. Brad."

"I'm afraid—" said Lincoln quickly. He stopped; they all turned at a step below.

One of Vaughn's detectives stood there.

"This Romaine guy and the old man," said the detective, "are down on the dock. Want to talk to you, Chief."

The Inspector rubbed his hands together. "Now, isn't that nice? All right, Bill, I'm coming. We'll defer that little chat with Mrs. Brad, Mr. Queen; it'll keep."

"Any objection to my coming along?" asked Jonah quietly. His big right fist was already clenched.

"Hmm," said the Inspector. He looked at the fist and grinned. "Not a one. Glad to have you."

They strode down the path. Near the tennis court they met Dr. Temple, who was hurrying along carrying his black bag. Temple smiled briefly; he seemed preoccupied and had not noticed the two visitors from Oyster Island.

Jonah walked along grimly.

The big brown figure of Paul Romaine towered on the landing dock. Skinny little Stryker, the mad Egyptologist, sat shivering in a small motorboat tied to the dock. Both men were clothed; immortal Ra-Harakht for this visit, it seemed, had eschewed the baton and snowy robes of his mangled divinity, vaguely sensing that he might accomplish more as mortal than as god. The police launch hovered nearby, and several detectives stood by Romaine's side.

Romaine's legs were stockily planted on the wooden boards. The toy green treeline of Oyster Island, the slowly riding white length of the *Helene* behind him, somehow served him as a suitable background. Whatever else he might be, he was assuredly a man of the open. But there was indecision on his face and a half-grinning desire to please that placed his state of mind instantly.

He said at once: "We don't want to be bothering you, Inspector. But we'd like to settle something." His tone was agreeable. He kept his eyes steadfastly on Vaughn, ignoring Jonah Lincoln. Jonah breathed evenly; he examined Romaine almost with curiosity.

"Go ahead," growled the Inspector. "What do you want?"

Romaine glanced briefly behind him at the cringing figure of

Stryker. "You've just about ruined the business of His Nibs and me. You're keeping our guests cooped up on the Island."

"Well, isn't that jake for you?"

"Yes," said Romaine patiently, "but not this way. They're all scared, like a bunch of kids. Want to quit, and you won't let 'em. But I'm not worried about them. It's the others. Sure won't get any more customers."

"So?"

"We want permission to leave."

Very suddenly old Stryker stood up in the motorboat. "This is persecution!" he shrieked. "A prophet is not without honor save in his own country! Harakht demands the right to preach the gospel—"

"Quiet," said Romaine savagely. The madman gaped and sat down.

"Gibberish," muttered Professor Yardley; he was pale. "Utter gibberish. The man's a stark lunatic. Quotes Matthew; garbles Egyptian and Christian theology . . ."

"Well, you can't have it," said Inspector Vaughn calmly.

Romaine's handsome face at once became threatening. He took a step forward, doubled his fists. The detectives about him edged nearer, expectantly. But the obscure desire to please smothered his seething temper, and he relaxed.

"Why?" he asked, swallowing mightily. "You haven't got anything on us, Inspector. We've been good little boys, haven't we?"

"You heard me. I'm not letting you and that old he-goat skip out on me—not by a long shot. Sure you've been good. But as far as I'm concerned you're both on the teetery edge, Romaine. Where were you the night Thomas Brad was murdered?"

"I told you! On the Island."

"Oh, yeah?" said the Inspector pleasantly. Instead of flaring into anger again Romaine, to Ellery's astonishment, grew thoughtful. The Inspector's nostrils quivered; quite by accident, it seemed, he had stumbled upon something. Isham opened his mouth, and Vaughn nudged him; so Isham closed his mouth.

"Well?" barked Vaughn. "I haven't got all day. Spit it out!"

"Suppose," said Romaine slowly, "suppose I can absolutely prove where I was that night—by a reliable witness, I mean. Would that clear me?"

"Ah," said Isham. "It certainly would, Romaine."

There was a little stir behind them which no one noticed except Ellery. Jonah Lincoln's aplomb had fled; he was growling into his throat and trying to push into the van of the group. Ellery's fingers closed insistently about Lincoln's biceps; they swelled and hardened under his touch, but he stopped short.

"All right," said Romaine abruptly; he was rather white about the nostrils. "I wasn't going to spill this, because it involves—well, some people might misinterpret it. But we've got to get out of here. . . . I was—"

"Romaine," came Jonah's voice clearly, "if you say another word I promise I'll kill you."

Vaughn swung on his heel. "Here, here!" he snarled. "What kind of talk is that? Keep out of this, Lincoln!"

"You heard me, Romaine," said Jonah.

Romaine shook his big head and laughed—a barking little laugh that raised the short hair on Ellery's nape. "Nuts," he said curtly. "I threw you into the Cove once, and I can do it again. I don't give a damn about you or anybody else in this lousy place. Here's the dope, Inspector. Between half-past ten and about half-past eleven that night—"

Silently Jonah lunged forward, arms flailing. Ellery with a grunt threw one arm about his neck and bore him backward. A detective jumped into the fray and grasped Jonah's collar in a stranglehold. After a brief struggle Jonah subsided; he was panting, and he glared at Romaine with murder in his hot eyes.

Romaine said hastily: "I was on Oyster Island with Mrs. Brad."

Jonah shook off Ellery's arm. "All right, Mr. Queen," he said coldly. "I'm quite all right now. He's done it. Let him speak his little piece."

"What d'ye mean—on Oyster Island with Mrs. Brad?" demanded, the Inspector; his eyes were narrowed. "Alone with her?"

"Ah, be your age," snapped Romaine. "That's what I said. We spent an hour together near shore, under the trees."

"How did Mrs. Brad get to the Island that night?"

"We had a date. I waited for her at the Bradwood landing in my boat. She showed up just as I got there. A little before half-past ten."

Inspector Vaughn took a sadly frayed cigar from one of his pockets and jabbed it in his mouth. "You go back to the Island," he said, "and we'll investigate your story. Take the nut with you. . . . And now, Mr. Lincoln," he said thoughtfully, turning his back on Romaine, "if you'd care to take a couple of pokes at this dirty specimen of a hyena's stinking brood, go ahead. I—er—I'm going back to the house."

Romaine stood blinking on the dock. The detectives moved away from him. Jonah stripped off his coat, rolled up his sleeves, and stepped forward.

"One," said Jonah, "for getting funny with my sister. Two," he said, "for turning the head of a very foolish woman. . . . Put 'em up, Romaine."

The madman clutched the gunwale of the boat and screeched: "Paul, come away!"

Romaine looked quickly around at the hostile faces. "Go take off your diapers first," he said, shrugging his big shoulders, and half-turned away.

Jonah's fist collided with the man's jaw. It was a lusty blow, well planted, and had behind it all the bitter rage which Jonah had been nursing for weeks. It would have knocked a man of ordinary strength unconscious; but Romaine was an ox, and the blow merely staggered him. He blinked again, a feline snarl wiped out his handsomeness, and he brought his bludgeon of a right fist up once in a short, powerful uppercut that lifted Jonah an inch from the wooden dock and dropped him, a senseless lump, to the boards.

Inspector Vaughn's geniality vanished. He shouted: "Keep back!" to his men, and sprang forward like a dart. Romaine, moving with extraordinary speed for his bulk, leaped from the dock into the motorboat where Stryker cowered, almost foundering the boat, and shoved off with a gargantuan sweep of his paw. The motor sputtered, and the boat shot away toward Oyster Island.

"I'm getting into the launch," said the Inspector calmly. "You men take this poor guy back—I'll join you in a couple of minutes. That bird needs a lesson."

As the launch swished away from the dock in pursuit of the motorboat, Ellery knelt by the fallen gladiator and slapped his pallid cheeks gently. Professor Yardley flung himself prone on the dock and scooped a palmful of water from the Sound.

The detectives yelled encouragement to the Inspector, who was standing in the prow of the launch, like Captain Ahab, and stripping off his coat.

Ellery dripped water onto Jonah's face. "A remarkable example," he observed dryly to the Professor, "of the triumph of justice. Wake up, Lincoln; the war's over!"

They were sitting on the colonial porch fifteen minutes later when Inspector Vaughn rounded the corner. Jonah Lincoln sat in a rocker holding his jaw in both hands as if he were surprised it was still attached to his face. Ellery, Isham, and Yardley ignored him, smoking peacefully with their backs to him.

The Inspector's face, while not precisely angelic, since there were traces of blood about his nose and a cut under one eye, nevertheless indicated that he felt satisfied with his knightly joust.

"Hullo," he said cheerfully, pounding up the porch steps between the pillars. "Well, Mr. Lincoln, you knocked him kicking by proxy. It was a battle royal, but there's one ladies' man who'll keep away from mirrors for a month."

Jonah groaned. "I—Lord, I just haven't got the strength. I'm not really a coward. But that man—he's a Goliath."

"Well, I'm his little David." Vaughn sucked a torn knuckle. "I thought the old lunatic would throw a fit. I actually knocked out the chief disciple! Heresy, hey, Professor? Better get washed up, Mr. Lincoln." He stopped smiling. "Let's get back to business. Seen Mrs. Brad?"

Abruptly Jonah rose and went into the house.

"I guess she's still upstairs," said Isham.

"Well," said the Inspector, striding after Jonah, "let's get to her before Lincoln does. He's been acting the gentleman, and all that, but this is an official investigation and it's time we got the truth from somebody."

Helene, it seemed, was still in Hester Lincoln's room. Stallings thought that Dr. Temple was upstairs, as well; the physician had not reappeared after going upstairs some time before with his medical bag.

They reached the bedroom floor just in time to see Jonah disappear into his bedroom. Following Stallings's directions, they went to a door at the rear of the house and the Inspector knocked.

Mrs. Brad's tremulous voice said: "Who is it?"

"Inspector Vaughn. May we come in?"

"Who? Oh, one moment!" There was panic in the woman's tones. They waited, and the door opened slightly. Mrs. Brad's rather handsome face appeared; her eyes were moist and apprehensive. "What is it, Inspector? I—I'm ill."

Vaughn pushed the door gently. "I know. But this is important."

She retreated, and they entered. It was heavily feminine, this room: scented, frilled, profusely mirrored, and its dressing-table was covered with cosmetics. She kept backing away, drawing her *négligé* more tightly about her.

"Mrs. Brad," said Isham, "where were you between ten-thirty and eleven-thirty the night your husband was murdered?"

She stopped drawing the *négligé* about her, stopped backing away; almost, it seemed, stopped breathing. "What do you mean?" she asked tonelessly at last. "I was at the theater with my daughter, with—"

"Paul Romaine," said Inspector Vaughn gently, "says you were with him, on Oyster Island."

She faltered: "Paul . . ." Her large dark eyes were haunting. "He— he said that?"

"Yes, Mrs. Brad," replied Isham gravely. "We realize how painful this must be to you. It's admittedly none of our business provided it's just that and nothing more. Tell us the truth, and we shan't refer to it again."

"It's a lie!" she cried. She sat down suddenly in a chintz chair.

"No, Mrs. Brad. It's the truth. It matches the fact that, although you and Miss Brad went to the Park Theater that night, only Mr. Lincoln and your daughter returned to this house in a taxicab. It matches the fact that the doorman of the Park Theater saw a woman of your description leave in the middle of the first act that night, about nine o'clock. . . . Romaine says he had an appointment with you, that you met him near the dock."

She covered her ears. "Please," she moaned. "I was crazy. I don't know how it happened. I was a fool. . . ." They looked at each other. "Hester hates me. She wanted him, too. She thought—she thought he was decent . . ." The age-lines showed with startling clarity, as if newly etched, on her face. "But he's the worst sort of beast!"

"He won't be doing that sort of thing for a long time, Mrs. Brad," said Inspector Vaughn grimly. "Nobody's judging you, or trying to. Your life is your own, and if you were fool enough to get mixed up with that high-binder, you've suffered enough, I suppose. All we're interested in is: How'd you get home and exactly what happened that night?"

She twisted her fingers in her lap; a dry sob choked her. "I—I slipped out of the theater early during the performance; I told Helene I didn't feel well and insisted that she remain and wait for Jonah. . . . I went to Pennsylvania Station and took the first train back—luckily there was one nearly at once. I—I got off a station ahead and hired a taxi to a point near Bradwood. I walked the rest of the way and no one seemed to be about, so—so . . ."

"Naturally," said Isham, "you didn't want Mr. Brad to know you had returned. We understand."

"Yes," she whispered; her face was dyed a dull unhealthy red. "I met—him at the dock."

"What time was it?"

"A trifle before ten-thirty."

"You're sure you saw and heard nothing? You didn't meet anyone?"

"Yes." She looked up with agony in her eyes. "Oh, don't you think I'd have told—everything—if I *had* seen something or someone? And when—when I came back, I slipped into the house and right to my room."

Isham was about to ask another question, when the door opened quietly and Helene Brad appeared. She stood still, looking from her mother's torn face to the faces of the men. "What is it, Mother?" she said, her eyes steady.

Mrs. Brad buried her head in her hands and began to weep.

"So it's come out," whispered Helene. She closed the door, slowly. "You were too weak to keep it back." She glanced with contempt from Vaughn to Isham and went to the sobbing woman. "Stop crying, Mother. If it's known, it's known; other women have tried to recapture romance and failed. God knows . . ."

"Let's get through," said Vaughn. "It's as rotten for us as for you people. How did you and Lincoln know where your mother was that night, Miss Brad?"

Helene sat down by her mother's side and patted the broad twitching back. "There, Mother . . . When Mother left me that night—well, I knew. But she didn't know I knew. I was weak myself." She stared at the floor. "I decided to wait for Jonah; we had both noticed—well, certain things before. When he came, I told him, and we returned home. I looked into this room; Mother was in bed, asleep. . . . The next morning, though, when you found the—the body . . ."

"She confessed to you?"

"Yes."

"If I may ask two questions," said Ellery soberly. The girl's large eyes, so like her mother's, turned on him. "When did you first suspect what was going on, Miss Brad?"

"Oh!" She shook her head, as if she were in pain. "Weeks, weeks ago."

"Do you think your stepfather knew?" Mrs. Brad raised her head suddenly; her face was mottled with tears and rouge. "No!" she cried. "No!"

Helene whispered: "I'm sure he didn't."

District Attorney Isham said: "I think that's enough," curtly, and went to the door. "Come along." He stepped into the hall.

Meekly Inspector Vaughn, Professor Yardley, and Ellery followed.

Chapter Twenty-One
LOVERS' QUARREL

"A PLETHORA OF NOTHING," remarked Ellery the next night, as he and Professor Yardley sat on Yardley's lawn watching the star-pricked sky above Long Island.

"Hmm," said the Professor. Sparks of burning tobacco fell from his pipe as he sighed. "To tell the truth, I've been waiting for the fireworks to begin, Queen."

"Patience. In a way, since this is the night of our celebrated Independence Day, you might expect the scene to crackle with fireworks. . . . There! There's a star-shell now!"

They were silent as they watched a long finger of brilliant light zoom into the dark sky and burst in a flash of dropping velvet colors. The single shell seemed to be a signal; instantly the entire coast of Long Island erupted, and for a space they sat and observed the celebration of the North Shore. Faintly, in the sky above the distant New York shore across the Sound, they made out answering flares, like tiny fireflies.

The Professor grunted. "I've heard so damned much about your pyrotechnical ability as a detective that the reality—sorry if I'm sacrilegious—lets me down. When do you commence, Queen? I mean—when does Sherlock leap to his feet and clamp the irons about the wrists of the dastardly murderer?"

Ellery stared glumly at the crazy light-patterns darting and swirling before the Big Dipper. "I'm beginning to think there won't be a commencement—or a denouement. . . ."

"Doesn't look like it." Yardley took the pipe out of his mouth. "Don't you think it was ill-advised to withdraw the troopers? Temple told me about it this morning; he said that the Colonel of the county forces had issued the withdrawal order. Can't see why, myself."

Ellery shrugged. "Why not? Obviously Krosac is after only two people—Stephen Megara and Andrew Van, or the Tvars, whichever you choose to call them. Megara has sufficient protection from his watery isolation and Vaughn's squad, and Van is well enough guarded by his disguise.

"There are a great many elements in this second crime, Professor, which would bear discussion; in their way they're extraordinarily enlightening. But they don't seem to go anywhere."

"I can't think of any."

"Really?" Ellery stopped to watch a hissing Roman candle. "Do you mean to say you didn't read the full—and extremely interesting—story of the checkers?"

"Checkers, eh?" Yardley's short beard showed dimly before the glow of his pipe bowl. "I confess nothing about Brad's last supper, so to speak, struck me as significant."

"Then I regain some of my lost self-esteem," murmured Ellery. "The story was very clear. But, hang it all, while it's more conclusive than the mere guesses Vaughn and Isham have been making . . ." He rose and plunged his hands into his pockets. "I wonder if you'd excuse me? I've got to walk off this fog in my brain."

"Of course." The Professor leaned back and sucked at his pipe, staring after Ellery with a curious intentness.

Ellery maundered on under the stars and the fireworks. Except for spasmodic flares, it was heavily dark; the dark of the countryside.

He crossed the road between Yardley's place and Bradwood, groping blindly, sniffing the night air, listening to the faint sounds of festive boats on the water, worrying the bones of his brain like a frustrated terrier.

Bradwood, except for a night light on the front porch—Ellery could make out, as he blundered up the driveway, two detectives smoking there—was bleak and comfortless. The trees loomed vaguely to his right, and more distantly to his left. As he passed the house one of the detectives rose and cried: "Who's there?"

Ellery put up one hand to shut off the blinding beam of a powerful flashlight.

"Oh," said the detective. "Excuse me, Mr. Queen." The beam snapped off.

"Such alertness," muttered Ellery, and walked on around the house.

He wondered now why his feet should have turned in this direction. He was approaching the little path which led to the grim totem post and the summerhouse. The effluvium of fear which emanated from the path and its goal—or perhaps it was his subconscious sensitivity to scenes of horror—gripped him, and he hastened by. The main path was black before him.

Suddenly he stopped. Not far to the right, where the tennis court lay, people were talking.

Now Ellery Queen was a gentleman, as gentlemen go, but one thing he had learned from the good Inspector, his father, who was a gentle soul in everything except his cynical familiarity with crime. And that was: "Always listen to conversations." The old man would say: "The only evidence that's worth a red cent, son, is the conversation of people who think they're not being overheard. You listen at times like that and you'll find out more than you could in a hundred quizzes at the line-up."

So Ellery, a dutiful son, remained where he was and listened.

The voices were a man's and a woman's. The tones of both were fa miliar to his ears, but he could not hear the words. Having stooped so low, there was nothing to keep him from stooping even lower. With the stealth of an Indian he leaped from the noisy gravel onto the grass bordering the path, and began a cautious advance toward the source of the voices.

A consciousness of their owners' identities filtered through his brain. They were Jonah Lincoln and Helene Brad.

They were seated, it seemed, at a garden table to the west side of the tennis court; Ellery dimly recalled the lay of the land. He crept up to within five feet of them and became rigid behind a tree.

"It won't do you any good to deny it, Jonah Lincoln," he heard Helene say in freezing tones.

"But, Helene," said Jonah, "I've told you a dozen times that Romaine—"

"Bosh! He wouldn't be so indiscreet. Only—only you, with your peculiar ideas, your—your beastly cowardice . . ."

"Helene!" Jonah was mortally wounded. "How can you say that? It's true that, like Sir Galahad, I tried to lambaste him a couple, and that he knocked me cold, but I—"

"Well," she said, "perhaps that was unjust, Jonah." There was a silence; Ellery knew that she was struggling to keep back the tears. "I can't say you didn't try, of course. But you're always—oh, interfering."

Ellery visualized the scene as well as if he could see. The young man, he was sure, had stiffened. "Is that so?" said Jonah bitterly. "Very well, that's all I wanted to know. Interfering, hey? Just an outsider. No right. Very well, Helene. I shan't interfere any more. I'm going—"

"Jonah!" There was panic in her voice now. "What do you mean? I didn't—"

"I mean what I said," growled Jonah. "For years I've been just a good fellow, slaving like a dog for one man who spends all his time at sea and another who stayed home playing checkers. Well, that's out! The damned salary isn't worth it. I'm going to leave with Hester, by God, and I've told your precious Megara so! Told him this afternoon on the yacht. Let him run his own business for a change; I'm sick and tired of doing it for him."

There was a taut little interval during which neither antagonist said a word. Ellery, behind the security of his tree, sighed. He could imagine what was coming.

He heard the soft escape of Helene's breath, and sensed Jonah's defensive rigidity. "After all, Joe," she whispered, "it isn't as if—as if you didn't owe Father's memory something. He—he did a lot for you, now, didn't he?" No remark from Mr. Lincoln. "And as for Stephen . . . oh, you haven't said it this time, but I've told you so often before that there's nothing between us. Why should you be so—so poisonous about him?"

"I'm not being poisonous," said Jonah with dignity.

"You are! Oh, Jonah . . ." Another silence, during which Ellery visualized the young lady either moving her chair closer or leaning, like Calypso, toward her victim. "I'll tell you something I've never told you before!"

"Eh?" Jonah was startled. Then he said hastily: "You needn't, Helene. I'm not at all interested—if it's about Megara, I mean."

"Don't be silly, Joe. Why do you think Stephen stayed away a whole year on this last trip of his?"

"I'm sure *I* don't know. Probably found a hula-hula girl in Hawaii whose style he liked."

"Jonah! That's unkind. Stephen isn't that sort, and you know it. . . . I'll tell you. It's because he asked me to *marry* him. There! That's why." She paused triumphantly.

"Oh, yes? Well," growled Jonah, "that's one heck of a way to treat your intended bride. Go away for a year! I wish both of you lots of luck."

"But I—I refused him!"

Ellery sighed again and crept back toward the path. The night was still bleak, as far as he was concerned. As for Mr. Lincoln and Miss Brad . . . Silence. Ellery rather fancied he knew what was happening.

Chapter Twenty-Two
FOREIGN CORRESPONDENCE

"ALL THE SIGNS," SAID Ellery to Professor Yardley two days later, on Wednesday, "tell me that justice is wagging her tail and scuttling for home."

"Which means?"

"There are certain universal indications among balked policemen. I've lived with one, you know, all my life. . . . Inspector Vaughn is, in the modest word of the press, baffled. He can't put his finger on anything concrete. So he becomes the aggressive defender of law, chases people, whips his men into a frenzy of useless activity, barks at his friends, ignores his colleagues, and generally acts like little Rollo in a pet."

The Professor chuckled. "If I were you, I'd forget this case entirely. Relax and read the *Iliad*. Or something as nicely literary and heroic. You're paddling the same canoe as Vaughn. Except that you're more graceful about the fact that it's sinking."

Ellery grunted and flipped his cigarette butt into the grass.

He was chagrined; more than that, he was worried. That the case offered no logical solution to his mind did not disturb him half so much as that it seemed to have expired of inertia. Where was Krosac? For what was he waiting?

Mrs. Brad wept over her sins in the privacy of her boudoir. Jonah Lincoln, despite his threats, had returned to the offices of Brad & Megara and was continuing to distribute rugs to a rug-conscious America. Helene Brad floated about in a glow, barely touching the earth. Hester Lincoln, after a stormy session with Dr. Temple, had departed bag and baggage for New York. Dr. Temple thereafter prowled about Bradwood, pipe in mouth, his black face blacker than ever. From Oyster Island there was silence; occasionally old man Ketcham appeared, but he tended his own business as he rowed his dinghy back and forth with supplies and mail. Fox quietly continued to massage the lawns and drive the Brad cars.

Andrew Van skulked in the West Virginia hills. Stephen Megara kept to his yacht; the crew, with the exception of Captain Swift, had been paid off and sent away with Inspector Vaughn's permission. Megara's personal bodyguard of two detectives, who had lolled on the *Helene's* deck—drinking, smoking, playing casino—Megara insisted on dismissing; he was perfectly capable, he said curtly, of taking care of himself. The water police, however, continued to patrol the Sound.

A cable from Scotland Yard had barely ruffled the monotony. It ran:

FURTHER INVESTIGATION PERCY AND ELIZABETH LYNN IN ENGLAND UNSUCCESSFUL SUGGEST CHECK WITH CONTINENTAL POLICE

So Inspector Vaughn acted, as Ellery said, like little Rollo in a pet, and District Attorney Isham shrewdly eased himself out of the case by the simple expedient of remaining in his office, and Ellery cooled himself in Professor Yardley's pool, read Professor Yardley's excellent books, and thanked his multifarious gods for a vacation—both of the body and the mind. At the same time, he kept one worried eye cocked on the big house across the road.

On Thursday morning Ellery strolled over to Bradwood and found

Inspector Vaughn sitting on the porch, a handkerchief between his sunburned neck and his wilted collar, fanning himself and cursing the heat, the police force, Bradwood, the case, and himself in the same breath.

"Nothing, Inspector?"

"Not a damned thing!"

Helene Brad came out of the house, cool as a spring cloud in her white organdie dress. She murmured a good morning and, descending the steps, turned into the westerly path.

"I've just been giving the old oil to the newspapermen," growled Vaughn. "Progress. Improvement. This case'll die of improvements, Mr. Queen. Where the hell is Krosac?"

"A rhetorical question." Ellery frowned over his cigarette. "Frankly, I'm puzzled. Has he given up? It doesn't seem possible. A madman never gives up. Then why is he marking time? Waiting for us to retreat, to give up the case as a bad job?"

"You tell *me*." Vaughn muttered to himself, and then added, "I'll stay here, by God, till Doomsday."

They lapsed into silence. In the garden circled by the driveway moved the tall figure of Fox, clad in corduroys, accompanied by the rattle of a lawn mower.

The Inspector sat up suddenly and Ellery, smoking with his eyes half-shut, started. The rattle had stopped. Fox was standing as still as a scouting brave, head cocked toward the west. Then he dropped the mower and broke into a run, vaulting a bed of flowers. He ran toward the west.

They jumped up, and the Inspector shouted: "Fox! What's the matter?"

The man did not halt his leaping strides. He gestured toward the trees and yelled something which they could not make out.

Then they heard it. A faint scream. It came from somewhere on the Lynn estate.

"Helene Brad!" cried Vaughn. "Come on."

When they burst into the clearing before the Lynn house they found Fox before them, kneeling on the grass and holding on his knee the head of a recumbent man. Helene, her face as white as her frock, stood over them clutching her breast.

"What's happened?" panted Vaughn. "Why, it's Temple!"

"He—I thought he was dead," quavered Helene.

Dr. Temple lay limply, eyes closed, his dark face ashen. There was a deep welt on his forehead.

"Bad knock, Inspector," said Fox gravely. "I can't bring him to."

"Let's get him into the house," snapped the Inspector. "Fox, you phone for a doctor. Here, Mr. Queen, help me lift him."

Fox sprang to his feet and hurried up the stone steps of the Lynn house. Ellery and Vaughn raised the still figure gently and followed.

They entered a charming living room—a living room which once had been charming, but which now looked as if vandals had swept through it. Two chairs were overturned, the drawers of a secretary protruded from their slots, a clock had been upset and its glass smashed. . . . Helene hurried away as they deposited the unconscious man on a settee, and returned a moment later with a basin of water.

Fox was telephoning frantically. "Can't get Dr. Marsh, the nearest doctor," he said. "I'll try—"

"Wait a minute," said Vaughn. "I think he's coming to."

Helene bathed Dr. Temple's forehead, dripped water between his lips. He groaned, and his eyes fluttered; he groaned again, his arms quivered, and he made a weak attempt to sit up.

He gasped: "I—"

"Don't try to talk yet," said Helene softly. "Just lie down and rest a moment." Dr. Temple slumped back and closed his eyes, sighing.

"Well," said the Inspector, "this is a nice how-d'ye-do. Where the devil are the Lynns?"

"From the appearance of this room," said Ellery dryly, "I should say they've skipped."

Vaughn strode through the doorway into the next room. Ellery stood and watched Helene stroke Dr. Temple's cheeks; he heard the Inspector stalking about the rest of the house. Fox went to the front door and hesitated there.

Vaughn came back. He went to the telephone and called the Brad house. "Stallings? Inspector Vaughn. Get one of my men to the phone right away. . . . Bill? Listen. The Lynns have taken it on the lam. You've got their description. Charge—assault and battery. Get busy. I'll give you more facts later."

He jiggled the hook. "Get me District Attorney Isham's office in Mineola. . . . Isham? Vaughn. Start the ball rolling. Lynns skipped out."

He hung up and strode over to the settee. Dr. Temple opened his eyes and grinned feebly. "All right, now, Temple?"

"Gad, what a whack! I'm lucky he didn't crack my skull."

Helene said: "I walked over here to pay a morning visit to the Lynns." Her voice trembled. "I really can't understand it. When I got here I saw Dr. Temple lying on the ground."

"What time is it?" asked the physician, sitting up with a start.

"Ten-thirty."

He sank back. "Out for two and a half hours. It doesn't seem possible. I remember coming to a long time ago, and I crawled toward the house—tried to, anyway. But I must have fainted."

As Inspector Vaughn went to the telephone again to transmit this item to his lieutenant, Ellery said: "You crawled? Then you weren't struck at the spot at which we found you?"

"I don't know where you found me," groaned Temple, "but if you ask that question—no. It's a long story." He waited until Vaughn hung up. "For certain reasons I suspected the Lynns weren't all they pretended to be. I suspected it the moment I laid eyes on them. Two weeks ago Wednesday night I came up here in the dark and heard them talk. What they said made me believe I was right. Lynn had just come back from burying something. . . ."

"Burying something!" yelled Vaughn. Ellery's brows contracted;

he looked at the Inspector, and the same thought was behind both men's eyes. "My God, Temple, why didn't you tell us this at that time? Do you realize what it was he must have buried?"

"Realize?" Temple stared, and then groaned again as pain stabbed across his bruised forehead. "Why, of course. Do you know, too?"

"Do we know! The head, Brad's head!"

Dr. Temple's eyes were mirrors of astonishment. "The head," he repeated slowly. "I never thought of that . . . No, I thought it was something else."

Ellery said swiftly: "What?"

"It was a few years after the war. I'd been released from the Austrian internment camp and was knocking about Europe, getting the feel of free legs again. In Budapest . . . well, I became acquainted with a certain couple. We were stopping at the same hotel. One of the guests, a German jeweler named Bundelein, was found trussed up in his room, and a valuable consignment of jewels which he was taking back to Berlin was missing. He accused the couple; they had disappeared. . . . When I saw the Lynns here, I was almost positive they were the same people. Their name at that time was Truxton—Mr. and Mrs. Percy Truxton. . . . Gad, my head. From the alterations Lynn made in my vision, I could almost qualify as a telescope capable of seeing stars of the fifteenth magnitude!"

"I can't believe it," murmured Helene. "Such nice people! They were lovely to me in Rome. Cultured, apparently wealthy, pleasant . . ."

"If it's true," said Ellery thoughtfully, "that the Lynns are what Dr. Temple accuses them of being, then they had good reason to be nice to you, Miss Brad. It would have been child's play for them to look you up and discover you were the daughter of an American millionaire. And then, if they had pulled a job in Europe . . ."

"Combine business and pleasure," snapped the Inspector. "I guess you're right, Doc. They must have buried some loot. What happened this morning?"

Dr. Temple smiled thinly. "This morning? I've been snooping around here at odd times for the past two weeks. . . . This morning I came over, certain at last that I knew where the stuff was buried, for I'd been searching for it. I went directly to the spot and had begun to dig when I looked up to find the man in front of me. Then the whole world fell on my head and that was the last I knew. I suppose Lynn, or Truxton, or whatever his name is, spied me, realized the game was up, knocked me out, dug up the loot, and beat it with his wife."

Dr. Temple insisted he was able to walk. With Fox supporting him he staggered out of the house and into the woods, the others following. They found, only thirty feet in the woods, a gaping hole in the grassy earth. It was roughly a foot square.

"No wonder Scotland Yard couldn't trace 'em," remarked Vaughn as they made their way back to Bradwood. "Phony names . . . I've got a nice juicy bone to pick with you, Temple. Why in hell didn't you come to me with your story?"

"Because I was a fool," said the physician glumly. "I wanted the full glory of the revelation. And then I wasn't sure—didn't feel like accusing possibly innocent people. I'd hate to see them get away!"

"No fear of that. We'll have 'em under lock and key tonight."

But, as it turned out, Inspector Vaughn was oversanguine. Night came, and the Lynns were still at liberty. No trace whatever was found of them, or of a couple answering to their description.

"Must have split up and disguised themselves," growled Vaughn. He sent a cable to police offices in Paris, Berlin, Budapest, and Vienna.

Friday came and went, and still no news from the farflung draggers seeking the escaped English couple. Their descriptions were posted, with copies of their passport photographs, on a thousand bulletin boards in sheriffs' offices and police headquarters throughout the country. The Canadian and Mexican borders were closely watched. But the Lynns proved once again the difficulty of plucking two ants out of the enormous nest of metropolitan America.

"Must have had a hideaway all fixed up for just such an emergency," said Inspector Vaughn disconsolately. "But we're bound to get 'em after a while. They can't hide out forever."

On Saturday morning three cables arrived from abroad. One was from the Prefect of Police in Paris:

PAIR AS DESCRIBED WANTED BY PARIS POLICE FOR ASSAULT AND ROBBERY IN 1925 KNOWN HERE AS MISTER AND MRS. PERCY STRANG

The second came from Budapest:

A PERCY TRUXTON AND WIFE WANTED BY BUDAPEST POLICE FOR JEWEL THEFT SINCE 1920 FIT YOUR DESCRIPTION

The third, and most informative, came from Vienna:

PAIR ANSWERING DESCRIPTION KNOWN HERE AS PERCY AND BETH ANNIXTER WANTED FOR SWINDLING FRENCH TOURIST OUT OF FIFTY THOUSAND FRANCS AND THEFT OF VALUABLE JEWELRY IN SPRING OF LAST YEAR IF SUCH PAIR HELD BY AMERICAN POLICE DESIRE IMMEDIATE EXTRADITION BOOTY NEVER RECOVERED

There followed a detailed description of the stolen jewels.

"There's going to be a sweet international tangle when we lay hands on 'em," muttered the Inspector as he, Ellery, and Professor Yardley sat on the Bradwood porch. "Wanted by France, Hungary, and Austria."

"Perhaps the World Court will call a special session," remarked Ellery.

The Professor made a face. "Sometimes you annoy me. Why can't you be precise? It's the Permanent Court of International Justice, and such a session would be termed 'extraordinary,' not special."

"Oh, Lord!" said Ellery, rolling his eyes.

"Guess Budapest has first sock," said Vaughn. "Nineteen-twenty."

"I shouldn't be surprised," ventured the Professor, "if Scotland Yard wants them, too."

"Not likely. They're a thorough bunch. If they didn't recognize the description, you can bet your last bib that there's no criminal record against them in London."

"If they really are British," said Ellery, "they'd have kept away from England. Although the man might very well have been Central European in origin. An Oxford accent is one of the most easily acquired of elegances."

"One thing is sure," said the Inspector. "That swag they buried was the ice and the dough from the Vienna job. I'll send the alarm out to the Jewelers' Association and the regular channels. But it's a waste of time. It isn't likely they're well enough acquainted with American fences; and they won't dare go near legitimate dealers unless they're short of cash."

"I wonder," murmured Ellery with a faraway look in his eyes, "why your correspondent in Yugoslavia hasn't answered?"

There was an excellent reason, it turned out later in the day, for the tardiness of Inspector Vaughn's Yugoslavian colleague. They were examining reports on the progress of the Lynn search as they came in by telegraph and telephone every few minutes.

A detective galloped up waving an envelope. "Cable, Chief!"

"Ah," said Vaughn, snatching the message, "now we'll know."

But the cable, which came from Belgrade, capital of Yugoslavia, sent by the Minister of Police, merely said:

EXCUSE DELAY REPORT ON TVAR BROTHERS AND VELJA KROSAC DUE TO OFFICIAL DISAPPEARANCE OF MONTENEGRO AS SEPARATE NATION MONTENEGRIN RECORDS DIFFICULT TO LOCATE ESPECIALLY OF TWENTY YEARS AGO NO QUESTION AS TO AUTHENTICITY OF BOTH FAMILIES HOWEVER AND EXISTENCE OF BLOOD FEUD OUR AGENTS WORKING ON CASE AND WILL CABLE REPORT OF SUCCESS OR FAILURE WITHIN FORTNIGHT

Chapter Twenty-Three
COUNCIL OF WAR

SUNDAY, MONDAY . . . IT WAS remarkable how little was accomplished, how tiny was the store of genuine facts they had been able to save from the wreckage of the murders. The Inspector, Ellery felt sure, would succumb to apoplexy as the ubiquitous British evaders of the law continued at large. And always the same question arose to plague their dreary conferences, their desperate discussions of ways and means: Where was Krosac? Or, if in his amazing way he was one of the chief actors in the drama, who was he and why did he delay? His vengeance was incomplete; that he had been swayed by fear of apprehension or the constant presence of the police from attempting the lives of the two remaining Tvar brothers was incredible, considering the nature of his crimes.

"Our defense of Andreja," said Ellery sadly on Monday evening to the Professor, "has been too perfect. The only explanation I can offer for Krosac's continued inactivity is that he still doesn't know where—and in what guise—Van is. We've fooled him—"

"And ourselves," remarked Yardley. "I'm becoming the least bit bored, Queen. If this is the exciting life of a man-hunter, I'm content to track down the source of a historical fact for the rest of my sedentary days. I invite you to join me. You'll find it infinitely more turbulent than this. Did I ever tell you how Boussard, the French army officer, found that famous basaltic stele in Lower Egypt which has meant so much to Egyptologists—the Rosetta Stone? And how for thirty-two years, until Champollion came along to decipher its triple message of the reign of Ptolemy V, it remained—?"

"It remains," said Ellery disconsolately, "a miniscule compared with the gigantic problem of Krosac. Wells must have had him in mind when he wrote *The Invisible Man.*"

That evening Stephen Megara came to life.

He stood in the center of the drawing room in the colonial mansion of his murdered brother grimly surveying his audience. Inspector Vaughn was there, fuming in a Sheraton chair, and gnawing his fingernails with vexation. Ellery sat with Professor Yardley, feeling stupid under the accusing glare of Megara's eyes. Helene Brad and Jonah Lincoln occupied a sofa, both uneasy; their fingers were intertwined. District Attorney Isham, summoned peremptorily from Mineola by the yachtsman, twiddled his thumbs and coughed incessantly in the doorway. Captain Swift, fumbling with his cap, stood behind his employer, his scraggy neck twisting from side to side under the torture of a stiff collar. Dr. Temple, uninvited but asked to remain, stood before the dark fireplace.

"Now everybody listen to me," said Megara in a sharp voice, "but you especially—Inspector Vaughn and Mr. Isham. It's three weeks since my—since Brad was done in. I'm back ten days. Please tell me what you've accomplished."

Inspector Vaughn squirmed in the Sheraton, and snarled: "I don't like your tone, mister. You damned well know we've done the best we can."

"Not good enough," snapped Megara. "Not by half, Inspector. You know whom you're after. You've even got a partial description of him. It seems to me that with all the forces at your command and disposal it would be a simple matter to collar your man."

"Er—it's just a matter of time, Mr. Megara," said Isham in a placating voice. The bald spot surrounded by his gray hair was wetly red. "It's really not simple, you know."

Vaughn said sarcastically: "You know, Mr. Megara, it hasn't been all God's truth here, either. You people yourselves have wasted a lot of our time. None of you's been strictly on the up-and-up."

"Nonsense!"

Vaughn rose. "And that," he added with a wolfish smile, "goes for you, too, Megara!"

The yachtsman's hard face did not change expression. Behind him Captain Swift swiped at his lips with a blue sleeve and dug his maimed hand into a bulging pocket. "What the devil do you mean?"

"Now, Vaughn," began the District Attorney, worriedly.

"Now Vaughn nothing! You let me handle this, Isham." The Inspector stamped forward, a solid menace, and stood so close to Megara that their chests touched. "You want a showdown, do you? Okay by me, mister! Mrs. Brad gave us the runaround, and she was upheld in her phony story by her daughter and Lincoln. Fox led us a merry chase, and wasted our valuable time and a lot of effort. Dr. Temple here"—the physician started, then quietly studied Vaughn's harsh profile as he began to fill his pipe—"was in possession of important information and tried to act the shiny hero by nabbing two crooks— and maybe worse—all by his lonesome. Result—the crooks make a clean getaway and he gets a sock on the nut. Deserved it, by Judas!"

"You said something," replied Megara evenly, eyes locked in the Inspector's, "about *me*. In what way have I hindered your investigation?"

"Inspector Vaughn," drawled Ellery. "Don't you think you're acting rather—er—impulsively?"

"And I don't want any of your lip either!" shouted Vaughn without turning. He was thoroughly aroused, and his eyes bulged as the cords of his neck tightened. "All right, Megara. The other day you told us a certain story. . . ."

Megara's tall figure did not stir. "Well?"

Vaughn smiled a nasty smile. "Well. Think it over."

"I don't understand," replied Megara coldly. "Be explicit."

"Vaughn," pleaded Isham.

"I'll be what I damn please. You know what I'm talking about. Three men left a certain place in a hurry a certain number of years ago. Why?"

Megara's eyes dropped for the briefest instant. But when he spoke, his tone was puzzled. "I told you why."

"Sure. Sure you did. I'm not questioning what you *told* us. I'm questioning what you *didn't* tell us."

Megara stepped back, shrugged, smiled. "I really believe, Inspector, that this investigation has gone to your brain. I told you the truth. Naturally, I couldn't give you a twelve-hour autobiography. If I left anything out—"

"It's because you thought it wasn't important?" Vaughn laughed shortly. "I've heard that before." He turned and took two steps toward his chair; then he swung about to face the yachtsman again. "But remember—when you call us to account—that our job isn't just looking for a killer. It's fishing through a lot of tangled motives, concealed facts, and downright lies, too. Just remember that." He sat down, blowing his flat cheeks out.

Megara shook his wide shoulders. "I'm afraid we've strayed from the point. I didn't call this council of war to bicker or to start an argument. If I gave you that impression, Inspector, I apologize." Vaughn grunted. "I have something definite in mind."

"That's fine," said Isham heartily, stepping forward. "Dandy, Mr. Megara. That's the spirit. We can certainly use a constructive suggestion."

"I don't know how constructive it is." Megara spread his legs. "We've all been waiting for Krosac to strike. Well, he hasn't. But you can take my word for it that he's going to."

"What d'ye intend to do?" asked the Inspector tartly. "Send him an invitation?"

"Exactly." Megara's eyes bored into Vaughn's. "Why can't we rig up a trap for him?"

Vaughn was silent. Then: "A trap, hey? What have you in mind?"

The yachtsman's white teeth glistened. "Nothing definite, Inspector. After all, your experience in such matters qualifies you rather than me. . . . But knowing Krosac will come eventually, we have nothing to lose. He wants me, does he? Well, let him have me. . . . I think your continued presence around here has made him lie low. If you stay here for another month, he'll continue to lie low for another month. But if you should go away, for example, confess yourself beaten . . ."

"An excellent idea!" cried the District Attorney. "Mr. Megara, you're to be congratulated. It's deplorable that we haven't thought of it before. Of course Krosac won't strike while the police are infesting the place—"

"And he'll be pretty damned careful not to strike when we fade out of here all of a sudden," grumbled Vaughn. Nevertheless, his eyes were thoughtful. "He's a brainy scalawag, and I'm sure he'd smell a rat. . . . But there is something in what you say," he added grudgingly. "It'll bear thinking about."

Ellery sat forward, eyes gleaming. "Commendable courage, Mr. Megara. Of course, you realize what the consequences of failure will be?"

Megara did not smile. "I haven't knocked about the world without taking chances," he said grimly. "I don't underestimate his slimy cleverness, mind you. But it isn't really taking a chance. If we work it properly, he'll try to do me in. And I'll be ready for him—the Captain and I—eh, Captain?"

The old seaman said gruffly: "I never seen a hard case yet that you couldn't settle his hash with a marlinspike. That was in th' old days.

T'day I got a nice new gun, and so've you, Mr. Megara. We'll handle the dirty lubber."

"Stephen," said Helene; she had withdrawn her hand from Lincoln's and was staring at the yachtsman. "You can't mean to leave yourself without any protection at all from that horrible maniac! Don't—"

"I can take care of myself, Helene. . . . What do you say, Inspector?"

Vaughn got to his feet. "I'm not sure. It's a big responsibility for me to assume. The only way I could do it would be to make a feint at withdrawing my men from the grounds and the Sound, but to lay an ambush aboard your boat. . . ."

Megara frowned. "Too clumsy, Inspector. He'd be sure to suspect."

"Well," said the Inspector stubbornly, "you'll have to give me time to think it over. We'll let 'er ride as she is for a while. I'll let you know in the morning."

"Very well." Megara tapped the pocket of his yachtsman's coat. "Meanwhile, I'm ready. I'm not going to skulk aboard the *Helene* like a lily-livered yellowbelly for the rest of my life. The sooner Krosac takes a crack at me the better I'll like it."

"What do you think?" asked Professor Yardley later, as he and Ellery stood at the eastern wing of the Brad house watching Megara and Captain Swift stride rapidly down the path, in the dim illumination of the house lights, toward the Cove.

"I think," said Ellery with a scowl, "that Stephen Megara is a fool."

Stephen Megara had scant time in which to display his courage—or his foolishness.

The next morning, Tuesday, while Ellery and the Professor were at breakfast, a man ran into the Professor's dining room, unmindful of old Nanny's scandalized protests, with a message from Vaughn.

Captain Swift had been discovered in his cabin aboard the *Helene* a few moments before trussed up and unconscious from a vicious blow at the back of his head.

Stephen Megara's headless body had been discovered, stark and horrible, lashed to one of the antenna masts above the superstructure.

PART FOUR

Crucifixion of a Dead Man

"Many investigations hinge on the detective's observation of a tiny discrepancy. One of the most annoying cases in the records of the Prague police was solved after six weeks of pure darkness when a young sergeant recalled the seemingly insignificant detail that four grains of rice had been found in the trouser cuff of the dead man."

—VITTORIO MALENGHI

Chapter Twenty-Four
T's Again

It was a silent company that embarked from the mainland to the *Helene* that morning. A silence enforced by the horror of this swift and murderous act after long days of lull: a silence of the stunned. Ellery, pale as his linen suit, stood nervously at the rail of the big police launch and stared at the yacht. It did not require a queasy landsman's stomach to make him feel sick; the nerves of his stomach were stabbing and throbbing, and he tasted bitter nausea in his dry mouth. The Professor standing quietly at his side was muttering, over and over: "Incredible. Monstrous." Even the detectives accompanying them were subdued; they all kept studying the trim lines of the yacht as if they had never seen it before.

Men moved rapidly about the deck. The center of activity seemed to be about the superstructure amidships; a little knot of men stood there, the vortex, and grew every instant as police launches anchored alongside and their crews of police and detectives clambered aboard.

And, limned clearly against the placid morning sky, was that ghastly symbol, clad in blood-smeared pajamas. It was stiffly attached to the first of the two antenna masts. It resembled nothing human, least of all that vigorous, warm-blooded man who had spoken to them a bare twelve hours before. It mocked them from its position of eminence; its two legs, strapped to the mast, were attenuated out of all proportion to human shape; the whole dreadful effigy of flesh gave the illusion of heroic size.

"Christ on Golgotha," croaked Professor Yardley. "Lord, it's hard to believe, hard to believe." His lips were ashen.

"I'm not a religious man," said Ellery slowly, "but for God's sake, Professor, don't blaspheme. Yes, it's hard to believe. You read the old stories, history—of Caligula, of the Vandals, of Moloch, of the Assassins, of the Inquisition. Dismemberments, impalements, flayings . . . blood, the pages are written in blood. You read . . . But mere reading doesn't begin to give you the full, the hot and smoking horror of it. Most of us can't grasp the monstrous versatility of madmen bent on destroying the human body. . . . Here in the twentieth century, despite our gang wars, the Great War, the pogroms still raging in Europe, we have no clear conception of the true horror of human vandalism."

"Words, just words," said the Professor stiffly. "You don't know, and I don't know. But I've heard stories of returned soldiers . . ."

"Remote," muttered Ellery. "Impersonal. Mass madness can never be so directly sickening as the orgiastic satanism of individual madness. Oh, hell, let's stop it. I feel sick enough."

Neither man said another word until the launch drew alongside the *Helene* and they had climbed the ladder to the deck.

Of all the busy men holding down the *Helene's* decks that morning, Inspector Vaughn seemed the least touched by the phantasmagoric nuances of the crime. To him this was business—bad business, fantastic and bloody business, to be sure, but quite in the line of duty; and if his eyes rolled and his mouth said bitter things it was not because Stephen Megara—into whose living eyes he had glared the night before—hung like a figure of red and mutilated wax on the antenna mast, but because he was horrified by the shocking inefficiency, as he evidently believed it to be, of his subordinates.

He was storming at a lieutenant of water police. "Nobody got by you last night, you say?"

"No, Inspector. I'd swear to it."

"Stop alibi-ing. Somebody *did* get by!"

"We were on the lookout all night, Inspector. Of course, we had only four boats, and it's physically possible that—"

"Physically possible?" sneered the Inspector. "Hell, man, it was done!"

The lieutenant, a young man, flushed. "Might I suggest, Inspector, that he came from the mainland? After all, we could protect only the north, the Sound side of the yacht. Why couldn't he have come out from Bradwood or nearby?"

"When I want your opinion, Lieutenant, I'll ask for it." The Inspector raised his voice. "Bill!"

A man in plainclothes stepped out of a group of silent detectives.

"What have you got to say for yourself?"

Bill rubbed his unshaven jaw and looked humble. "That's a lot of territory we've got to cover, Chief. I'm not saying he didn't come that way. But if he did, you really can't blame us. You know yourself how easy it is to make a sneak through a bunch of trees."

"Listen, men." The Inspector stepped back and clenched his right fist; they listened. "I don't want any debates or alibis, understand? I want facts. It's important to know how he got to the yacht. If he came across the Sound from the New York shore, that's important. If he came from the Long Island mainland, that's important. Chances are he didn't go through Bradwood itself. He'd know it was patrolled. Bill, I want you to—"

A launch shot alongside, towing a rowboat which Ellery, through the sickish haze before his eyes, dimly recognized. A policeman stood up and shouted: "We got it!"

They all ran to the rail. "What's that?" cried Vaughn.

"Found this rowboat floatin' in the Sound," yelled the officer. "Markings show she belongs to that estate next door to Bradwood."

A light leaped into Vaughn's eyes. "The Lynn boat! Sure, that's the answer. Anything in it, officer?"

"Nothing except the oars."

The Inspector spoke rapidly to the man named Bill: "Take a couple of the boys and go over that Lynn estate. Examine the slip especially, and the ground around it for footprints. Go over every inch of the place. See if you can trace the guy before he got there."

Ellery sighed. A ripple went through the mass of men about him. Orders were shouted, detectives scrambled overside. Vaughn strode about, Professor Yardley leaned against the door of the radio operator's cubicle—above which loomed the antenna masts and Stephen Megara's body. District Attorney Isham bent over the rail with a greenish look about him. A little motorboat scooted up with Dr. Temple, his face startled; on the Bradwood dock a group of tiny men—women, too, from the white skirts.

A little moment of quiet ensued. The Inspector came over to where Ellery stood with the Professor, leaned against the door on his elbow, stuck a cigar into his mouth, and looked contemplatively up at the rigid corpse.

"Well, gentlemen?" he said. "How do you like it?"

"Ghastly," muttered the Professor. "A perfect nightmare of insanity. The T's again."

Ellery was struck by a little blow of surprise. Of course. In the unsettled state of his emotions he had entirely overlooked the significance of the antenna mast as an instrument of crucifixion. The upright of the mast and the horizontal bar at the top from which the aerial wires were strung to the corresponding bar on the other side of the cabin roof resembled nothing so much as a slender steel capital T. . . . He noticed now, for the first time, that two men were on the roof behind the crucified body. One he recognized as Dr. Rumsen, the Medical Examiner; the other he had never seen before—a dark, lean old man with a look of the sea about him.

"They'll be taking the body down in a minute," remarked the Inspector. "That old bird up there is a sailor—expert on knots. I wanted him to have a look at the lashings before we cut the body down. . . . What d'ye say, Rollins?" he shouted at the old man.

The knot expert shook his head and straightened up. "No sailor ever tied them knots, Inspector. Just about as clumsy as a 'prentice hand would tie 'em. And another thing. They're the same kind o' knots as on that clothesline y'gave me three weeks ago."

"Good!" said the Inspector cheerfully. "Take him down, Doc." He turned back. "Used clothesline again—guess he didn't want to waste time looking for rope on board. It isn't as if this were an old sailing vessel, y'know. Same knots as we found on the rope used to lash Brad to the totem pole. Same knots, same man."

"Not necessarily a *sequitur*," said Ellery, "but with the other things you're perfectly right. Exactly what is the story, Inspector? I understand Captain Swift was assaulted."

"Yes. The poor old mutt is still out. Maybe he can tell us something. . . . Come up here, Doc," said Vaughn to Dr. Temple, who was still standing in his motorboat alongside, hesitantly, as if he did not know whether to board the yacht or not, "we'll need you." Temple nodded and climbed the ladder.

"Good God," he said, staring with fascination at the body, and went up to the radio operator's cabin. Vaughn pointed to the wall and Dr. Temple found a skeleton ladder at the side of the cabin, which he climbed.

Ellery clucked to himself; the shock of the tragedy had so unnerved him that he had not observed the unsteady trail of blood on the deck. It ran in gobs and spatters from Megara's cabin farther aft to the ladder leading up to the roof of the radio operator's cabin. . . . On the roof Dr. Temple greeted Dr. Rumsen, introducing himself, and the two men, aided by the old sailor, began the unpleasant task of cutting down the body.

"The story is this," resumed Vaughn quickly. "The body was seen as you see it now from the Bradwood dock this morning by one of my men. We beat it over here and found Captain Swift tied like an old chicken in his cabin, out like a light, with a bloody gash at the back of his head. Gave him a little first aid, and he's resting now. You might take a look at Captain Swift, Doc!" he yelled up at Temple, "as soon as you're through up there." Temple nodded, and the Inspector continued: "Dr. Rumsen fixed the old man up a little as soon as he got here. Far as I can see—damned few facts—it's a plain story. There was nobody aboard here last night except Megara and the Captain. Krosac somehow got to that Lynn estate, took the rowboat which has been tied to the slip there, and rowed out to the yacht. It was plenty dark last night, and the only light on the yacht came from the regular riding lights. Boarded, knocked the Captain on the head, and trussed him up, then sneaked into Megara's cabin and did him in. The cabin's a mess—just like the summerhouse was in the Brad murder."

"There's a bloody T somewhere, of course?" asked Ellery.

"On the door of Megara's cabin." Vaughn scraped his blue jaws. "When I stop to think of it, it's absolutely unbelievable. I've seen plenty of murder in my time, but nothing as coldblooded as this; and don't forget, when we investigate a Camorra kill, for instance, we find fancy carving! You go into that cabin and see what's there. Or maybe you'd rather not. It looks like the inside of a butcher shop. He hacked Megara's head off right on that floor, and there's enough blood splashed about in there to paint the yacht red." The Inspector added thoughtfully: "It must have been a man-size job toting Megara's body from the cabin up that ladder to the top of the radio operator's cubbyhole, but I guess it wasn't any tougher than stringing Brad up on the totem pole. Krosac must be one hefty guy."

"It seems to me," said Professor Yardley, "that he couldn't avoid being splashed with the blood of his victim, Inspector. Don't you think there may be a trail to a man with bloodstained clothes?"

"No," said Ellery before Vaughn could reply. "This crime, like the murder of Kling and the murder of Brad, was planned in advance. Krosac knew that his crime would entail the spilling of blood, so he provided himself in each case with a change of clothing. . . . Really elementary, Professor. I should say, Inspector, that your trail will lead to a limping man who carried either a bundle or a small cheap valise. It isn't likely that he would wear the change of garments underneath those which he knew would become bloodied."

"Never thought of that," confessed Vaughn. "A good point. But I'll take care of both ends—I've got men out all along the line on the prowl for Krosac." He leaned over the side and shouted an order to a man in a launch; the launch departed at once.

By this time the body had been cut down, and Dr. Rumsen was kneeling on the roof of the cabin beneath the denuded antenna mast examining the corpse. Dr. Temple had descended some minutes before, talked to Isham at the rail, and then turned aft. A few moments later they all followed, bound for Captain Swift's cabin.

They found Dr. Temple bending over the prone figure of the old sailing master. Captain Swift was lying in a bunk, eyes closed. The top of his tousled old head was caked with dry blood.

"He's coming around," said the physician. "Bad gash there, worse than the one I got. It's lucky he's such a tough old fellow; it might easily have given him concussion of the brain."

The Captain's cabin was in no way disordered; here, at any rate, the murderer had met with little resistance. Ellery noted that a stubby automatic lay on a table within arm's length of the bunk.

"Not fired," said Vaughn, observing the direction of his glance. "Swift didn't get a chance to grab it, I guess."

The old man uttered a hollow retching groan, and his eyelids twitched open to reveal glassy, faded eyes. He stared up at Dr. Temple fixedly for a moment, and then his head turned in a slow arc to regard the others. A swift spasm of pain contracted his body; it convulsed like a snake from head to foot, and he closed his eyes. When he opened them again, the glassiness had gone.

"Take it easy, Captain," said the physician. "Don't move your head. I've a little decoration for you." They noticed that the wound had been treated. Dr. Temple rummaged in a medicine cabinet, found a roll of bandage, and without a word being spoken by anyone, swathed the wounded head until the old sea dog resembled a war casualty.

"Feel all right now, Captain?" asked District Attorney Isham eagerly. He was panting in his zeal to talk to the old man.

Captain Swift grunted. "Reckon so. What th' devil happened?"

Vaughn said: "Megara's been murdered."

The seaman blinked, and moistened his dry lips. "Got his, eh?"

"Yes. We want your story, Captain."

"Is it th' next day?"

No one laughed; they knew what he meant. "Yes, Captain."

Captain Swift stared up at the ceiling of the cabin. "Mr. Megara 'n' me, we left the house last night an' rolled back to th' *Helene*. Far as I c'd tell, everything was shipshape. We chinned awhile—Mr. Megara said somethin' about maybe makin' a voyage to Africa after everything blew over. Then we turned in—him to his cabin an' me to mine. But first I took a turn on deck, like I always do; no watchman aboard, an' I like to be on th' safe side."

"You saw no evidence of a man hiding on board?" asked Ellery.

"Nope," croaked the Captain. "But I can't say for sure. Might 'a' been skulkin' in one o' the cabins, or below."

"And then you turned in," said Isham encouragingly. "What time was this, Captain?"

"Seven bells."

"Eleven-thirty," murmured Ellery.

"Right. I sleep heavy when I sleep. Can't tell ye what time it was, but I found I was sittin' up in my bunk, listenin'. Felt somethin' was wrong. Then I thought I heard a man breathin hard 'longside the bunk. I made a quick grab for the gun on th' table; but I never reached it. A flash lit in my lamps, an' somethin' hit me a fierce crack on th' head. That's all I knew till just now."

"Little enough," muttered Isham. "Didn't you get a look at whoever it was that struck you?"

The Captain shook his head gingerly. "Not a peep. The room was darker'n pitch, an' when the flash hit me, I was blinded."

They left Captain Swift in Dr. Temple's care and returned to the deck. Ellery was thoughtful; more, he was worried. He seemed to be searching his mind for an idea which persisted in remaining evasive. Finally he shook his head in disgust and gave up the effort.

They found Dr. Rumsen waiting for them on the deck below the antenna masts. The knot expert had disappeared.

"Well, Doc?' asked Vaughn.

The Medical Examiner shrugged. "Nothing startling. If you re-member what I told you about the body of Brad three weeks ago, I don't have to say a word."

"No marks of violence, eh?"

"Not below the neck. And above the neck—" He shrugged again. "As far as identification is concerned, it's all clear. This Dr. Temple that was up here a while ago told me Megara was suffering from a re-cently contracted *hernia testis*. Is that right?"

"Megara said as much himself. It's right, all right."

"Well, this body is his, then, because there's evidence of the her-nia. Don't even need an autopsy. And Temple looked at it directly af-ter we cut the body down, before he went off. Said the body was Meg-ara's—he'd given the man a thorough examination in the nude, he said."

"Good enough. What time do you figure Megara was killed?"

Dr. Rumsen squinted thoughtfully aloft. "All things considered, I'd say between one and one-thirty this morning."

"Okay, Doc. We'll take care of the corpse. Thanks."

"Don't mention it." The physician snorted and crept down the lad-der to a waiting launch below. It immediately made off toward the mainland.

"Did you find anything stolen, Inspector?" frowned Ellery.

"No. There was a little cash in Megara's wallet in the cabin. It wasn't taken. And the wall safe wasn't touched."

"There's one thing more—" began Ellery, when a launch slid up and discharged a group of perspiring men.

"Well?" demanded Vaughn. "Any signs of it?"

The leader of the group shook his head. "No, Chief. We've combed the grounds for a mile around."

"Might have sunk it in the Cove," muttered Vaughn.

"What's that?" demanded Isham.

"Megara's head. Not that it makes a hell of a lot of difference. I don't think we'll even drag."

"I should if I were you," said Ellery. "I was about to ask you if you'd searched for the head."

"Well, maybe you're right. . . . You, there, telephone for the dragging apparatus."

"Do you think it's important?" asked Professor Yardley in a low tone.

Ellery flung his hands out in an unaccustomed gesture of despair. "Damned if I know what's important and what isn't. There's something buzzing about inside my brain. I can't get hold of it. . . . It's something I ought to do—I feel it, know it." He stopped short and jammed a cigarette into his mouth. "I must say," he snapped after a moment, "that as a member of the detective craft, I'm the profession's most pitiable object."

"Know thyself," said the Professor dryly.

Chapter Twenty-Five
THE LIMPING MAN

A DETECTIVE CLIMBED ABOARD with a familiar envelope.

"What's this?" demanded Vaughn.

"Cable. Just got here."

"Cable," repeated Ellery slowly. "From Belgrade, Inspector?"

Vaughn tore open the envelope. "Yes. . . ." He ran his eye over the message, nodded gloomily.

"Just late enough," remarked Isham, "to be of no use. What's it say?"

The Inspector handed the cable to the District Attorney, and Isham read it aloud:

AGENTS HAVE FOUND OLD RECORDS OF TVAR-KROSAC FEUD STEFAN ANDREJA AND TOMISLAV TVAR AMBUSHED AND ASSASSINATED VELJA KROSACS FATHER AND TWO PATERNAL UNCLES THEN ROBBED KROSAC HOUSE OF LARGE SUM OF MONEY THEREAFTER FLEEING MONTENEGRO STOP COMPLAINT OF ELDER KROSACS WIDOW TOO LATE TO APPREHEND TVARS NO TRACE OF TVARS AFTER THIS NOR OF WIDOW KROSAC AND HER YOUNG SON VELJA COMPLETE DETAILS OF FEUD FOR SEVERAL GENERATIONS AVAILABLE TO YOU IF DESIRED

It was signed by the Minister of Police, Belgrade, Yugoslavia.

"So," said Professor Yardley. "You were right after all, Queen. They were nothing but common thieves."

Ellery sighed. "An empty triumph. It merely means that Velja Krosac had an additional motive for the murder of the Tvar brothers. His family wiped out, his money stolen. I can't see that it clears up anything but a minor point. . . . As for Megara's story about having kept track of the young Krosac—it's probably true. Except that instead of sending agents out from Montenegro, they employed men via the mails when they got to this country."

"Poor devil. I can almost find it in my heart to pity him."

"You can't take away the blood and brutality of the crimes, Professor," said Vaughn sharply. "Sure he has motive. There's a motive for every murder. But you don't find murderers getting off scot-free just because they had a reason. . . . Well, what is it?"

Another detective had dropped aboard bearing a sheaf of official-looking papers and telegrams. "Sergeant sent these, Inspector. Last night's reports."

"Hmm." Vaughn rapidly went through the papers. "On the Lynns."

"Any news?" asked Isham.

"Nothing of importance. Naturally people all over the country think they've spotted 'em. Here's one all the way from Arizona—they're following it up. Another from Florida—man and a woman of the general description seen in a car round Tampa way. Maybe, maybe." He stuffed the reports into one of his pockets. "I'll bet they've holed up in New York. Be damned fools to go shooting across country. Canadian and Mexican borders seem to be okay. I don't think they've slipped out of the country. . . . Hullo! Bill seems to have found something!"

The detective was standing up in an outboard waving his hat and yelling something indistinguishable. He scrambled aboard like a monkey, eyes shining.

"Righto, Chief!" he cried, as soon as he had his feet on the deck. "You hit it on the head. Found plenty over there!"

"What?"

"Checked up on the rowboat first; it's the one that belongs to that slip, all right. Rope was cut with a sharp knife; the knot's still hangin' on the slip ring, and the rope on the boat itself shows a cut that matches the other end."

"All right, all right," said Vaughn impatiently. "He used that rowboat; we know that. Did you find anything near the dock there?"

"And how. Footprints." They all echoed the word and leaned forward. Bill nodded. "There's soft earth just behind the slip. In it we found five prints—three lefts and two rights of the same size shoe—man's, about eight and a half, I'd say. And whoever made those prints limped."

"Limped?" repeated Professor Yardley. "How on earth do you know?"

Bill turned a pitying glance on the tall ugly scholar. "What the—Say, that's the first time I ever heard anybody ask a question like that. Don't you read the pulps? Prints of the right shoe were much deeper than the left. A hell of a lot. Right heels dug way in. A bad limp in his left leg, I'd say; left heels hardly show."

"Good work, Bill," said Vaughn; he regarded the antenna masts. "Mr. Megara," he said grimly, "next time—if there's another world and I'm there with, you—you'll listen to me. No protection, hey? You saw where you got *with* protection. . . . Anything else, Bill?"

"No. The path down from the main road, between the Lynn place and Bradwood, is gravel, and the main road is macadam. So there aren't any other prints. The boys are workin' on the limping-man trail anyway; didn't need the prints, although they help."

∽

The boys, it seemed had worked not without success.

A new deputation scudded over the blue water of Ketcham's Cove toward the yacht; several detectives surrounded a middle-aged man with a badly frightened look, who sat on a thwart clutching its edges with both hands.

"Who the devil have they picked up?" growled Vaughn. "Come aboard; who you got there?" he shouted across the narrowing strip of water.

"Great news, Chief!" yelled one of the plainclothesmen faintly. "Got a hot tip!"

He helped his middle-aged captive up the ladder by a gentle boost in the slack of the man's trousers; the man crawled up with a sickly half-grin and took his fedora hat off on deck, quite as if he were in the presence of royalty. They examined him curiously: he was a colorless individual with gold teeth and an air of shabby gentility.

"Who's this, Pickard?" demanded the Inspector.

"Tell your story, Mr. Darling," said the detective. "This is the big chief."

Mr. Darling looked awed. "Pleased to meet you, Captain. Why, it's nothing much. I'm Elias Darling of Huntington, Captain. I own a cigar and stationery store on Main Street there. I was closing up last night at midnight and happened to notice something in the street. There'd been a car parked in front of my store for a few minutes—a Buick, I think it was—Buick sedan. I'd happened to notice the man who parked it—a little fellow with a young girl. Just as I was closing up I saw a man, tall fellow, walk up to the car and sort of look inside—the front window was open, car wasn't locked, you see. Then he opened the door, started the ignition, and drove off in the direction of Centerport."

"Well, what of it?" snarled Vaughn. "Might have been the little guy's father, or brother, or friend, or something. Maybe he was from the finance company taking the car away because the little guy didn't pay up."

Mr. Elias Darling looked panic-stricken. "Goodness," he whispered, "I never thought of that! And here I am practically accusing—You see, Captain . . ."

"Inspector!" shouted Vaughn.

"You see, Inspector, I didn't like the looks of it. I thought of saying something to our Chief of Police, but then I figured it wasn't any of my business. But I remember the man limped on his left foot—"

"Hey!" roared Vaughn. "Wait a minute! Limped, did he? What did he look like?"

They hung on Mr. Darling's words; each man felt that here at last was the turning-point of the investigation—an actual description of the man who called himself Krosac. . . . Detective Pickard was shaking his head sadly; and Ellery sensed that Darling's description would be no more informative than had been Croker's, the Weirton garageman.

"I told the detective here," said the Huntington merchant, "I didn't see his face. But he was tall, kind of broad-shouldered, and he was carrying one of those little valises—overnight bag, my wife calls 'em."

Isham and Vaughn relaxed, and Professor Yardley shook his head. "All right, Mr. Darling," said Vaughn. "Thanks a lot for your trouble. See that Mr. Darling gets back to Huntington in a police car, Pickard." Pickard assisted the storekeeper down the ladder, and returned when the launch glided off toward the mainland.

"How about the stolen car, Pickard?" asked Isham.

"Well," drawled the detective, "it isn't much help. A couple answering the description given by Darling reported the theft of their automobile to the Huntington police at two in the morning. God knows where they'd been—*I* don't. Buick sedan, as Darling says; the little guy was so excited about his broad, I suppose, that he forgot to take his ignition key out of the lock."

"Send out a description of the car?" demanded Vaughn.

"Yes, Chief. Plates and all."

"Fat lot of good it'll do," grumbled Isham. "Naturally, Krosac would want a car last night for his getaway—too risky to take a train at two or three in the morning, where the chances are somebody would remember him."

"In other words," murmured Ellery, "you believe Krosac stole the car, drove it all night, and ditched it somewhere?"

"He'd be a fool to continue driving it," snapped the Inspector. "Sure that's right. What's wrong with it, Mr. Queen?"

Ellery shrugged. "Can't a man ask a simple question without having his head bashed in, Inspector? Nothing's wrong with it, so far as I can see."

"It seems to me," said the Professor thoughtfully, "that Krosac was taking a long chance in depending upon being able to steal a car so close to the time and scene of his projected crime."

"Long chance my eye," said Vaughn curtly. "Trouble is with people, they're generally honest. You could steal a dozen cars in the next hour if you wanted to—especially out here in Long Island."

"A good point, Professor," drawled Ellery, "but I'm afraid the Inspector's right." He paused at the sounds of shuffling feet above. They looked up; the sheet-draped body of Stephen Megara was being lowered from the roof of the radio operator's cabin to the deck. At the rail a few feet away, in a faded old sou'wester under which were his pajamas, stood Captain Swift, gazing with stony eyes at the proceedings. Dr. Temple was at his side, silent, puffing at a dead pipe.

Ellery, Vaughn, Isham, and the Professor descended one by one to the large police launch waiting below. The *Helene,* as they drew off, rode gently in the waters of Ketcham's Cove. The body was on its way over the side to another boat. On shore they could see Jonah Lincoln's tall figure, waiting; the women had vanished.

"What do you think, Mr. Queen?" asked Isham with pathetic eagerness, after a long silence.

Ellery wriggled about and stared back at the yacht. "I think that we're as far from the solution of these crimes as we were three weeks ago. As far as I'm concerned, I confess to complete frustration. The murderer is Velja Krosac—a wraith of a man who might be near-ly anybody. The problem still confronts us: Who is he, really?" He took off his pince-nez and rubbed his eyes impatiently. "He's left his trail—flaunted it, as a matter of fact. . . ." His face hardened, and he fell silent.

"What's the matter?" asked Professor Yardley, anxiously surveying his protégé's bleak expression.

Ellery clenched his fist. "That idea—something! What in the name of six Peruvian devils is it?"

Chapter Twenty-Six
ELLERY TALKS

THEY WALKED QUICKLY THROUGH Bradwood, intent on avoiding the poor victims of bewilderment and nausea moving restlessly about the estate. Jonah Lincoln said not a word; he seemed too stunned for speech and merely followed them up the path as if that were as sensible a course of action as any other. The death of Megara, peculiarly enough, hung far more like a pall over Bradwood than had the death of its owner. A white-faced Fox was sitting on the steps of the porch, his head in his hands. Helene sat in a rocker, staring fixedly at the sky without seeing one wisp of the massing thunder clouds which had sprung up. Mrs. Brad had collapsed; Stallings mumbled that Dr. Temple should see her: she was crying hysterically in her room and no one, not even her daughter, seemed capable of taking care of her. Mrs. Baxter's moans could be heard as they passed the rear of the house.

They hesitated in the driveway, and then forged on by tacit agreement. Lincoln followed them blindly as far as the outer gateway. There he stopped to lean against the stone pillar. The Inspector and Isham had dropped off somewhere, busy about their own affairs.

Old Nanny's wrinkled black face was screwed up with horror; she opened the front door for them, muttering: "Dey's a ha'nt behin' dis, Mistuh Ya'dley, you ma'k mah words."

The Professor did not reply; he went directly to his library, and as if refuge lay there Ellery followed.

They sat down in the same inadequate silence. On the Professor's craggy face, beneath the shock and the distaste, lay challenge. Ellery sank into a chair and began mechanically to search his pockets for a cigarette. Yardley shoved a large ivory box across the table to him.

"What's bothering you?" he asked gently. "Surely the thought couldn't have entirely escaped you."

"It's as if it never was, except for the most ridiculous sensation." Ellery puffed furiously at a cigarette. "You know those intangible feelings? Something leads you a chase through all the back alleys of your brain, and you never once get more than a blurred glimpse of it. That's the way it is with me. If I could catch it . . . It's important. I have the overwhelming feeling that it's important."

The Professor tamped tobacco into his pipe bowl. "A common phenomenon. I've found with myself that concentration on the capture of the idea is futile. A good plan is to erase every thought of it from your mind and talk about other things. It's surprising how often the method works. It's as if, by ignoring it, you tantalize it into popping out at you. Out of nowhere the full, clear picture of what you've been trying to recollect will appear; created, it would seem, out of irrelevancies."

Ellery grunted. A thunder clap shook the walls of the house.

"A moment ago—fifteen minutes ago—" continued the Professor with a sad smile, "you said that you were as far from a solution today as you were three weeks ago. Very well. Then you face failure. At the same time you've made reference on several occasions to conclusions which you've reached, not obvious on the surface, unknown apparently to Isham and Vaughn and myself. Why not go over them now? Perhaps there's something which in the exclusive concentration of your analysis has eluded you, but which will become clear if you express your thoughts in words. You may take my word for it—my whole life has been inextricably tied up with just such experiences—that there is a vital difference between the cold seclusion of independent thinking and the warm personality of a *tête-à-tête* discussion.

"You mentioned checkers, for example. Evidently the Bradwood study, the checker table, the disposition of the pieces, had a significance for you which completely escaped the rest of us. Go over it aloud."

Under the flow of Professor Yardley's deep and soothing voice Ellery's keyed nerves relaxed. He was smoking more quietly now, and the lines of strain on his face had softened. "Not a bad plan, Professor." He shifted to a more comfortable position and half-closed his eyes. "Let me tackle it this way. What story did you piece together from Stallings's testimony and the checker table as we found it?"

The Professor thoughtfully blew smoke toward his fireplace. The room had appreciably darkened; the sun had disappeared behind a barrage of black clouds. "Many theories unsupported by concrete evidence have come to mind, but I see no logical reason for doubting the surface appearance of the data."

"And that is?"

"When Stallings last saw Brad—presumably he was the last person except the murderer who did see Brad—Brad was seated at his checker table playing checkers with himself. There is nothing unusual or incongruous about this; Stallings testified that he often did it, working out moves for both sides—as only an enthusiast and expert will—and I myself can confirm this. Then it would appear that after Stallings's departure, and while Brad was still playing with himself, Krosac gained access to the study, killed Brad, and so on. Brad had in his hand at the time he was killed one of the red checkers, which explains how we found it near the totem post."

Ellery rubbed his head wearily. "You say—'gained access to the study.' Just what do you mean?"

Yardley grinned. "I was coming to that. You remember I said a moment ago that I had many theories unsupported by evidence. One of them is that Krosac—who, as you've repeatedly held, may be someone very close to us—was Brad's expected visitor that night, which explains how he got into the house. Brad, of course, being ignorant of the fact that some one he thought a friend or acquaintance was in reality his blood enemy."

"Unsupported!" Ellery sighed. "You see, I can outline this instant an indestructible case for one theory. Not a stab in the dark, Professor, not a conjecture, but a conclusion reached by clear logical steps. The only trouble with it is—it doesn't thin out the fog in the slightest."

The Professor sucked thoughtfully at his pipe. "Just a moment. I haven't finished. I can offer another theory—again unsupported by evidence, but as far as I can see just as likely to be true as the other. And that is, that Brad had *two* visitors that night: the person whom he expected, and for whose visit he sent his wife, stepdaughter, and household away; and Krosac, his enemy. In this case the legitimate visitor, whether he came before or after Krosac—which is to say, while Brad was still alive or when he was already dead—naturally kept silent about his visit, not wishing to be implicated in any way. I'm surprised no one has thought of this before. I've been expecting you to propound it for the past three weeks."

"So?" Ellery took off his pince-nez glasses and placed them on the table; his eyes were red and bloodshot. A lightning flash momentarily illuminated the room, painting their faces a ghastly blue. "Great expectations."

"Don't tell me you didn't think of it!"

"But I'm not. I never mentioned it because it isn't true."

"Ha," said the Professor. "Now we're getting it. Do you mean to sit here and tell me you can *prove* there was only one visitor to that house on the murder night?"

Ellery smiled feebly. "You place me in an uncomfortable position. Proof is after all dependent not so much upon the prover as upon the approver. . . . It's going to be slightly complicated. And you remember what that French moralist with the improbable name, Luc de Clapier de Vauvenargues, said: *'Lorsqu'une pensée est trop faible pour porter une expression simple, c'est la marque pour la rejeter.** But I'll get to it in due course."

The Professor leaned forward expectantly, and Ellery continued, replacing the pince-nez on the bridge of his nose: "My point depends upon two elements: the disposition of the checkers on Brad's table and the psychology of expert players. Do you understand the game, Professor? I recall you said that you had never played with Brad, or words to that effect."

"That's true, although I understand the game. Rather a dub at it. I haven't played for years."

"If you understand the game, you'll understand my analysis. When Stallings entered the study, before quitting the house, he saw Brad beginning a game with himself, saw two moves of the opening, in fact. It was this testimony which led our friends astray. They assumed that because Brad was playing with himself when Stallings last saw him, he was still playing with himself when he was murdered. You fell into the same error.

"But the pieces on the table told an entirely different story. What was the disposition not only of the checkers in play but of those which had been 'captured' and taken off the playing board? You will recall that Black had captured nine red pieces, which lay in the margin between the board itself and the edge of the table; that Red had captured only three black pieces, which lay in the margin on the opposite side. Obviously, then, to begin with, Black was vastly superior to Red.

"The board itself, remember, held three kings, or double pieces, for Black, plus three single black checkers; and a meager two single pieces for Red."

"What of it?" demanded the Professor. "I still don't see that it means anything except that Brad was playing a game with himself and had worked out a series of moves most disastrous to his hypothetical opponent, Red."

---

* "When a thought is too weak to be expressed simply, that is a sign that it should be rejected."

"An intolerable conclusion," retorted Ellery. "From the standpoint of experiment, an expert gamester is interested only in opening and closing moves. It's as true in checkers as it is in chess, or any other game in which wits are pitted and the outcome depends solely on the skill of the individual player. Why should Brad, playing purely for practice against himself, bother with a game in which one side has the overwhelming advantage of three full kings and a piece? He would never allow an experimental game to reach such a stage. Experts can tell you by a single glance at the board, even when the advantage is considerably less—a single piece, or even an equality of pieces but a strategic advantage of position—what the outcome will be if both sides play without error. For Brad to have seriously played that unequal game with himself would be tantamount to Alekhine playing an experimental chess game with himself in which one side has the advantage of a queen, two bishops, and a knight.

"So we come to this: Whereas Brad was playing an experimental game when Stallings saw him, he nevertheless played a genuinely competitive game later in the evening. For while an expert wouldn't experiment with such a one-sided division of strength, that one-sided division becomes comprehensible when you take the alternative: that he played with some one."

Outside it had begun to pour—sheets of gray water pounded against the windows.

Professor Yardley's teeth showed white above his black beard in a grudging grin. "Granted. Granted. I see that. But you still haven't eliminated the plausible theory that while Brad played checkers with his legitimate *visitor* that night, leaving the game as we found it, he was murder by Krosac later, after the visitor had gone, perhaps."

"Ingenious," chuckled Ellery. "You die hard. And compel me to fire a double barrel—logic and common sense.

"Look at it this way. Can we fix the *time* of the murder in relation to the time period of the game?

"I maintain in all logic that we can. For what did we find? On

Black's first row one of the two red checkers was still in play. But in checkers when you have reached your opponent's first row you are entitled to have your piece crowned, or kinged; which as you know means placing a second checker on top of the first. How, then, does it happen that Red in this game has a man on the king row which is nevertheless uncrowned?"

"I begin to see," muttered Yardley.

"Simply because the game stopped at that point, for it could not have been continued unless the red king were crowned," Ellery went on rapidly. "Is there confirmation that the game stopped at this point? There is! The first question to settle is: Was Brad playing Black in this game, or Red? We have all sorts of testimony to the fact that Brad was an expert checker player. He had once, in fact, entertained the National Checker Champion and held that worthy even. Is it conceivable, then, that Brad should be the Red in this game where Red was obviously the inferior player—so inferior that his opponent had an advantage of three kings and a piece? No, it isn't conceivable, and we can assert at once that Brad was playing Black. . . . Incidentally, to get the record straight, let me interpolate an amendment. Now we know that Black's advantage over Red was not three kings and a piece, but two kings and two pieces, since one of the red pieces is supposed to be a king.

"Still, however, a tremendous advantage.

"But if Brad was playing Black, then he must have been sitting during the game in the chair near the secretary rather than on the other side of the table, away from the secretary. This is so, because all the captured red checkers were on the side near the secretary, and Black captures Red, of course.

"So far, so good. Brad was playing Black, and he sat in the chair near the secretary; his visitor and checker opponent, therefore, sat opposite, facing the secretary while Brad had his back to it."

"But where does that—?"

Ellery closed his eyes. "If you have aspirations to genius, Professor, take Disraeli's advice and cultivate patience. I'm getting in my licks, honored Professor. Many's the time I've sat burning at my desk in your classroom, trying in vain to anticipate your leisurely point about the Ten Thousand, or Philip, or Jesus. . . .

"Where was I? Yes! There was one missing red checker, and we found it outside near the scene of Brad's crucifixion. On the palm of his hand there was a circular red stain. He had been holding the checker when he was killed, then. Why had he picked up the red checker and held it? Theoretically many explanations are possible. But there is only one explanation which has a known fact to support it."

"What's that?" demanded the Professor.

"The fact that a red checker was on Black's king row, and that it was uncrowned. In Brad's hand—in the hand of Black, observe—was the only missing red checker. I don't see," said Ellery crisply, "how you can escape the conclusion that Red, Black's opponent, managed to get one of his pieces on Black's king row; that Black, or Brad, picked up one of the captured red pieces to place it on top of the red piece just arrived on his king row; *that before he could so place the red piece he had picked up, something occurred which effectually terminated the game.* In other words, the fact that Brad had picked up a red piece for the specific purpose of crowning his opponent's man, but never completed the action, shows us by direct inference, not only when the game stopped, but why."

Yardley remained silent and intent.

"The inference? Simply that Brad never completed his action because he could not." Ellery paused, and sighed. "He was attacked at that moment and, to put it mildly, rendered incapable of crowning Red's king."

"And the bloodstain," muttered the Professor.

"Exactly," said Ellery. "And there is the confirmation—the position of the bloodstain on the rug. The bloodstain lay two feet behind the chair in which Black—or Brad—was sitting. We have long ago proved that the murder took place in the study; and that bloodstain is the only one in the study. If Brad had been struck on the head from the front, as he sat at the table, about to crown the red piece, he would have fallen backwards, between his chair and the secretary. And that is precisely where we found the bloodstain. . . . Dr. Rumsen maintained that Brad must have been struck on the head originally, since no other mark of violence showed on his corpse; then it was a free-flowing wound which stained the rug where he fell, before his murderer could lift the body and remove it to the summerhouse. All the details dovetail. But the salient fact stands out: *Brad was attacked as he sat playing checkers with his assailant. In other words, Brad's murderer was also his checker opponent.* . . . Ah, you have objections."

"Certainly I have," retorted Yardley. He relit his pipe, and puffed energetically. "What is there in your argument which invalidates the following? That Brad's checker opponent was either innocent or an accomplice of Krosac's; that while this innocent checker opponent played with Brad, or while the accomplice played with Brad to distract his attention, Krosac sneaked into the study and struck Brad from behind, as I said the day we discovered the bloodstain."

"What? A muchness, Professor." Ellery's eyes twinkled. "We showed long ago that Krosac would not have an *accomplice*. Summarily these are crimes of vengeance, and there is nothing in the crimes to tempt an accomplice from a monetary standpoint.

"The possibility that there were two people all the time, one of them Krosac, the other an innocent visitor who played checkers with Brad? . . . Please consider what this would mean. It would mean that Krosac deliberately attacked Brad in the presence of an innocent witness! Preposterous; surely he would have waited for the witness to leave. But suppose he did attack in the presence of a witness. Wouldn't he then make every effort to silence this witness? A man like Krosac, with so much blood on his conscience, would scarcely balk at the necessity of taking another life. Yet the witness apparently left unharmed. . . . No, Professor, no witness, I'm afraid."

"But how about the witness coming before Krosac, and leaving before—a witness who played checkers with Brad?" persisted the Professor.

Ellery clucked with concern. "Dear, dear, you're becoming groggy, Professor. If he came before or after Krosac, he wouldn't be a witness, would he?" He chuckled. "No, the point is that the game we found was the Brad-Krosac game, and that if there were a previous or later visitor, this would not invalidate the fact that Krosac—the murderer—did play with Brad."

"And your conclusion from all this rigmarole?" muttered Yardley.

"As I said before: That Brad's murderer played checkers with him. And that Krosac was well-known to Brad, although not, of course, as Krosac but as someone else."

"Aha!" exclaimed the Professor, slapping his thin shank. "I've got you, young man. Why well-known? Eh? You mean to say that's logic? That because a man like Brad played checkers with someone, that that someone was necessarily a friend of his? Fiddlesticks! Why, Brad would play with a manure collector. Any stranger was prey, provided he could play the game. It took me three weeks to convince him that I really wasn't interested!"

"My nerves, Professor. If I gave you the impression that it was from the checker game that I deduced Brad's opponent to have been a friend of his, I'm sorry; I didn't mean to. There is a much more potent reason. Did Brad know that Krosac, enemy of the Tvars, was abroad thirsting for that good old Tvar blood?"

"Yes, of course. The note he left shows that, and then Van himself wrote Brad and warned him."

"*Bien assurément!* Would Brad, knowing Krosac to be abroad, make an appointment with a stranger, deliberately sending all possible protectors of his hide from the premises, as he did?"

"Hmm, I suppose not."

"You see," said Ellery with a tired sigh, "you can prove anything if you collate sufficient data. Look here—let me take the most extreme case. Suppose Brad's expected visitor that night did come, did transact his business with Brad, did leave. Then Krosac appeared. An utter stranger, mind. But we've shown that Krosac, Brad's murderer, played checkers with Brad. That would mean that Brad deliberately invited into his defenseless house an utter stranger. . . . Wrong, of course. Then Krosac must have been well-known to Brad, whether he was the visitor expected by Brad or a chance guest of the evening. Actually, I don't care a tittle which. My own belief is that only one person besides Brad was in the study that night—Krosac. But if there were two, or three, or a dozen, it doesn't invalidate the conclusion that Brad knew Krosac well in whatever guise he appeared, and that Brad played checkers with him and was murdered during the game."

"And where does that get you?"

"Nowhere," said Ellery ruefully, "which is why I said before that I'm no better off now than I was three weeks ago. . . . You know, there's another positive fact, now that I come to think of it, which we can fish out of this mess of indecision. I'm an ass not to have thought it out before."

The Professor rose and knocked out his pipe against the fireplace. "You're full of surprises tonight," he said, without turning. "What's that?"

"We can assert with absolute assurance that Krosac does not limp."

"We said that before," retorted Yardley. "No, you're right. We said we couldn't be sure. But how—?"

Ellery got to his feet, stretched his arms, and began to pace up and down. It was humid in the library; the downpour outside redoubled in hissing intensity. "Krosac, whoever he's pretending to be, was well-known to Brad. No one who was well-known to Brad limps. Therefore Krosac actually does not limp; but has utilized his youthful infirmity as a consistent physical characteristic merely to lead the police astray."

"That's why," muttered Yardley, "he's been so apparently careless about leaving a trail to a limping man."

"Exactly. He discards the limp the moment he scents danger. No wonder no trace of him has been found. I should have thought of it before."

Yardley teetered on his big feet, cold pipe jutting from his mouth. "And there we are." He regarded Ellery keenly. "No sign of the fugitive thought, eh?"

Ellery shook his head. "Still hiding behind a convolution somewhere . . . Let's see now. Murder of the first victim, Kling, satisfactorily explained. Krosac, and the pseudo-limp, in the direct vicinity; motive, proximity, peculiar nature of crime—all fit. There is a feud. Krosac thinks he has killed Andreja, one of the brothers. How does he finally get on the track of Van, the most remote of the three Tvars? Query unanswerable; to be answered God knows when . . . Krosac strikes once more. Brad this time; same query, also unanswerable. The plot thickens deliciously: Krosac finds Brad's note which tells him for the first time that he has made a mistake in the introductory murder, that Van is still alive. But where is Van? Must be found, says Krosac to himself, or my vengeance is incomplete. Curtain on second act—very melodramatic . . . Megara returns; Krosac knows he will; enter the sole possessor, according to the note, of the secret of Van's new identity and present whereabouts. . . . Time out. Delay. And then . . . *By God,*" said Ellery.

Professor Yardley stiffened, scarcely breathing. All the signs pointed to the apprehension of the fugitive. Ellery was rooted to the floor, glaring at his host with the ferocious light of discovery in his eyes.

"By God," shouted Ellery, leaping two feet into Professor Yardley's humid air, "what a fool I've been! What an idiot, what an imbecile, moron, mental defective! I've got it!"

"It always works," grinned the Professor, relaxing. "What—Here, my boy; what's the matter?"

He paused in alarm. A remarkable change had come over Ellery's exulting face. His jaw dropped, his eyes clouded, and he winced as people do sometimes at the purely imaginary shock of a fancied blow.

The expression came, and went. Ellery's jaw was outlined on his smooth brown cheek. "Listen," he said rapidly. "I haven't time for anything but the sketchiest analysis. What were we waiting for? What was Krosac waiting for? We were waiting for Krosac to attempt to discover through Megara, the only source of information, *where Van is.* Krosac was waiting to make this discovery. *And then he killed Megara.* It can mean only one thing!"

"He found out," cried Yardley, the gravity of the thought causing his deep voice to crack. "My God, Queen, what fools, what blind fools we've been! It may be too late already!"

Ellery wasted no time in reply. He sprang to the telephone. "Western Union . . . Take a telegram. Fast. Addressed to Constable Luden, Arroyo, West Virginia . . . Yes. Message: 'Form posse immediately and go to hut of Old Pete. Protect Old Pete until my arrival. Notify Crumit Krosac returning. If anything has happened by time you reach hut pick up Krosac trail but leave scene of crime intact.' Sign it Ellery Queen. Repeat, please . . . Krosac—K-r-o-s-a-c. Right . . . Thanks."

He flung the instrument from him, then changed his mind and picked it up again. He put in a call to Bradwood, across the road, asking for Inspector Vaughn. Vaughn, he discovered from Stallings, had left Bradwood hurriedly not long before. Ellery dismissed Stallings peremptorily and asked for one of Vaughn's men. Where was Inspector Vaughn? The man on the other end of the wire was sorry, but he had no idea. The Inspector had received a message, and he and District Attorney Isham had immediately commandeered a car and dashed away.

"Damn it," groaned Ellery, hanging up, "what are we going to do now? We haven't any time to dawdle!" He dashed to a window and looked out. The rain seemed to be steadily increasing in force, coming down in torrents; lightning flashes streaked the sky; the thunder was almost incessant. "Listen," said Ellery, turning back. "You'll have to remain behind, Professor!"

"I really don't like the idea of your going there alone," replied

Yardley reluctantly. "Especially in this storm. How are you going to get there?"

"Never mind. You stay here and try your damnedest to get in touch with Vaughn and Isham." Ellery leaped to the telephone again. "Mineola flying field. Quick!"

The Professor rubbed his beard uncomfortably as Ellery waited. "Oh, I say, now, Queen, you can't be thinking of going up in a sky like this."

Ellery waved one hand. "Hello, hello! Mineola? Can I charter a fast plane for a southwestern flight at once? . . . What?" His face fell, and after a moment he put down the telephone. "Even the elements are conspiring against us. Storm came up from the Atlantic and is traveling west and south. The Mineola man says it will be bad in the Alleghenies. They won't send a plane up. What the devil can I do?"

"Train," suggested Yardley.

"No! I'll trust the old Duesie! Have you a slicker or a raincoat I can borrow, Professor?"

They raced into the Professor's hall and Yardley opened a closet and brought out a long slicker. He helped Ellery into it. "Now, Queen," he panted, "don't go off half-cocked. That's an open car, the roads will be bad, it's a terribly long drive—"

"I shan't take unnecessary chances," said Ellery. "Luden should cover things, anyway." He hopped forward and opened the door, and the Professor followed him into the vestibule. Ellery was silent, and then offered his hand. "Wish me luck, old man. Or rather wish Van luck."

"Go ahead," grunted the Professor, pumping Ellery's hand up and down. "I'll do my best to find Vaughn and Isham. Take care of yourself. You're certain about it now? It isn't an unnecessary trip?"

Ellery said grimly: "There was only one thing that kept Krosac from killing Megara for the past two weeks. That was—he didn't know where Van was. If he killed Megara finally, it must be that he discovered the Old Pete ruse and the mountain hideaway. Extorted the information from Megara, probably, before he killed him. It's my job to prevent a fourth murder; Krosac is undoubtedly on his way to West Virginia at this moment. I'm hoping that he took time out to sleep last night. Otherwise—" He shrugged, smiled at Yardley, who looked longingly after, and then dashed down the steps in the buffeting downpour, under the lightning, toward the driveway at the side where the garage and the old racing car lay.

Mechanically Professor Yardley consulted his watch. It was exactly one o'clock.

Chapter Twenty-Seven
THE SLIP

THE DUESENBERG CLAWED ITS way through New York City, scrambled downtown, darted through the Holland Tunnel, dodged in and out of traffic through Jersey City, slipped through a maze of New Jersey towns, and then straightened out on the road to Harrisburg, shooting ahead like an arrow. Traffic was light; the storm had not abated; and Ellery alternately prayed to the gods of chance and played havoc with the speed laws. His luck held; he shot through town after town in Pennsylvania unpursued by motorcycle police.

The old car, which afforded no protection from the rain, was flooded; and he himself sat with soaked shoes and a dripping hat. Somewhere in the car he had salvaged a pair of racing goggles; and he made a grotesque figure in linen suit covered with a slicker, a light felt hat which sopped about his ears, amber goggles over pince-nez spectacles, and a grim look about him as he sat hunched over the enormous wheel rocketing the car through the storm-lashed Pennsylvania countryside.

At a few minutes to seven that evening, with the rain still driving steadily—he seemed to be traveling in its wake—he slid into Harrisburg.

He had no luncheon and hunger pinched his flat stomach. He parked the Duesenberg in a garage with specific instructions to the mechanic, and strode off in search of a restaurant. Within an hour he was back at the garage, had checked his oil, gasoline, and tires, and made his way out of town. He remembered the route well, sitting there behind the wheel, cold and clammy and uncomfortable. Within six miles he was through Rockville and arrowing straight ahead. He crossed the Susquehanna River, and flashed on. Two hours later he passed the Lincoln Highway, sticking stubbornly to the road he was on. The rain persisted.

At midnight, chilled, exhausted, his eyelids refusing to function, he pulled into Hollidaysburg. Again a garage was his first stop; and after a lively conversation with a grinning mechanic he left on foot for a hotel. The rain lashed against his wet legs.

"Three things I want," he said from stiff lips in the little hotel. "A room, my clothes dried, and a call for seven tomorrow morning. Can you produce?"

"Mr. Queen," said the clerk, after consulting Ellery's signature on the register, "you watch me."

The next morning, considerably refreshed, in dry clothing, stomach full of bacon and eggs, the Duesenberg roaring along, Ellery pressed forward on the last lap of the journey. Evidences of the storm's havoc flashed by him—uprooted trees, swollen streams, wrecked cars abandoned by the roadside. But the storm, which had raged all night, had abated suddenly in the early hours, although the sky still lowered, the color of lead.

At 10:15 Ellery piloted the roaring Duesenberg through Pittsburgh. At 11:30, under a brightening sky, with the sun making valiant efforts to illuminate the peaks of the Alleghenies all about, Ellery brought the Duesenberg to a grinding stop before the Municipal Hall in Arroyo, West Virginia.

A man in blue denim whom Ellery vaguely remembered was sweeping the walk before the entrance to the Municipal Hall.

"Here, mistuh," said this worthy, dropping his broom and clutching at Ellery's arm as he dashed past, "where you goin'? Who you want t'see?"

Ellery did not reply. He ran quickly through the dingy hall to the rear, where Constable Luden's office lay. The constabulary door was closed; and as far as he could see, Arroyo's civic citadel was empty of life. He tried the door; it was unlocked.

The man in denim, a stubborn look on his loutish face, had shuffled after him.

Constable Luden's office was unoccupied.

"Where's the Constable?" demanded Ellery.

"Whut I been tryin' t'tell ye," said the man doggedly. "He ain't here."

"Ah!" said Ellery with a sagacious nod. Luden, then, had gone on to the hills. "When did the Constable leave?"

"Mond'y mornin'."

"What!" Ellery's voice overflowed with astonishment, woe, and a surging realization of catastrophe. "Good heavens, then he didn't get my—" He darted forward to Luden's desk. It was a mess of untidy papers. The man in blue put out his hand in blank protest as Ellery began to toss the Constable's official correspondence—if it was official correspondence—about. And, as he had with dread expected, there it lay. A yellow-enveloped message.

He tore it open, and read:

CONSTABLE LUDEN ARROYO WEST VIRGINIA FORM POSSE IMMEDIATELY AND GO TO HUT OF OLD PETE PROTECT OLD PETE UNTIL MY ARRIVAL NOTIFY CRUMIT KROSAC RETURNING IF ANYTHING HAS HAPPENED BY TIME YOU REACH HUT PICK UP KROSAC TRAIL BUT LEAVE SCENE OF CRIME INTACT

ELLERY QUEEN

A panoramic picture flashed before Ellery's eyes. Through a hideous and mischievous blunder, a turn of the fateful wheel, his telegram to Luden might never have been sent at all for the good it had accomplished. The man in denim patiently explained that the Constable and Mayor Matt Hollis had left two mornings before on their annual fishing trip; they were customarily gone a week, camping out, angling on the Ohio and its tributaries. They would not be back until Sunday. The telegram had arrived a few minutes past three the day before; the man in denim—who announced himself as janitor, caretaker, and man-of-all-work—had received it, signed for it, and in the absence of Luden and Hollis placed it on the Constable's desk, where it might have lain a week but for Ellery's fortuitous visit. The janitor seemed to have something pressing in mind, and began a rambling dissertation, but Ellery brushed him aside and, dim horror in his eyes, scrambled back to Arroyo's main street and leaped into the Duesenberg.

He sent it roaring around the corner and along the route he recalled from his previous expedition with Isham and Constable Luden. There was no time to communicate with District Attorney Crumit of Hancock County or with Colonel Pickett of the county troopers. If what he feared had not yet occurred, he was certain he could handle any situation which might arise; in the pocket of the Duesenberg lay a loaded automatic. If it *had* occurred . . .

He left the car in the old clump of bushes—faint traces of his last visit were still impressed, despite the rain, in the densely brush-covered earth and grass—and, automatic in hand, began the hard ascent up the mountain along the dim trail Constable Luden had followed. He climbed rapidly, and yet with caution; he had no idea of what he might encounter, and he was grimly determined not to be caught unawares by anything or anybody. The lush, dense woods were quiet. He slipped along, praying that he might be in time, conscious through the faint warning bell ringing in his brain that it was too late.

He crouched behind a tree and peered out into the clearing. The fence was intact. Although the front door was shut, Ellery felt encouraged. At the same time he was taking no chances. He slipped the safety catch of the automatic back and emerged noiselessly from behind the tree. Was that the familiar beard-fringed face of Old Pete at the barbed-wired window? No; it had been his imagination. Clumsily he went over the fence, gripping the weapon still. And then he noticed the footprints.

He stood where he was for a full three minutes, studying the story as it was clearly told by the marks on the damp earth. Then, avoiding these tell-tale impressions, he circled widely, setting his own feet down with care until he reached the door.

The door, he now observed, was not entirely closed, as he had thought at first glance. A tiny crack was visible.

Automatic in his right hand, he stooped and placed his ear to the crack. No sound came from the interior of the shack. He straightened, and with his left hand struck the door a smashing blow, so that it swung back quickly, revealing the interior. . . .

For the space of several heartbeats he stood that way, left hand in mid-air, right hand leveling the weapon at the interior of the hut, eyes riveted on the horrible scene before him.

Then he sprang across the threshold and bolted the heavy door securely behind him.

At 12:50 the Duesenberg screeched to a stop before the Municipal Hall again, and deposited Ellery on the sidewalk. A strange young man, the janitor must have thought, for his hair was disheveled, in his eyes burned a maniacal light, and he pounced on the man as if he contemplated, nothing less than mayhem.

"H'lo," said the man in denim uncertainly. He was still sweeping the walk under the hot sun. "So ye're back, hey? Had somethin' t'tell ye, mistuh, but ye wouldn't let me 'fore. Y'r name ain't—?"

"Stow it," snapped Ellery. "You seem to be the sole gentleman of official responsibility left in this energetic bailiwick. You've got to do something for me, Messer Janitor. Some men from New York are going to be here—when, I don't know. But if it takes hours, you've got to wait here, do you understand?"

"We-ell," said the janitor, leaning on his broom, "I don't rightly know. Listen, you ain't a man by th' name o' Queen now, are ye?"

Ellery stared. "Yes. Why?"

The janitor fished in the depths of a roomy denim pocket, and paused to expectorate a stream of brown liquid. Then he brought out a folded scrap of paper. "Tried to tell ye 'fore, when you was here, Mr. Queen, but ye didn't give me no chance. Feller left this here note fer ye—tall ugly sort o' coot. Looked like of Abe Lincoln, by gee."

"Yardley!" ejaculated Ellery, snatching the note. "Heavens, man, why the devil didn't you tell me before?" He almost ripped the sheet in his haste to unfold it.

It was a hurried pencil scrawl signed by the Professor:

DEAR QUEEN:

Explanations in order. Modern magic enabled me to anticipate you. After you left I was worried, and tried vainly to get on the trail of Vaughn and Isham. I discovered enough to find that they had received word of a seemingly authentic trail to the Lynns, from Massachusetts. Left your message with Vaughn's man. Didn't fancy the idea of your trailing a bloodthirsty savage like Krosac alone. Nothing stirring in Bradwood—Dr. T. left for New York. Hester-bound, I'll warrant. Romance?

Up all night during the storm—couldn't sleep. Storm abated and at six A.M. I was in Mineola. Flying conditions better, and I persuaded a private flyer to take me southwest. Landed near Arroyo 10 A.M. this morning. (Most of above written in plane.)

Later: Can't find hut or any one who knows how to get there. Luden gone, town's dead. Your telegram, I suppose, unopened. Fear the worst, of course, especially since I have picked up the trail of *a limping man* [this was heavily underscored] in vicinity.

Limping man carrying a small bag (must be Krosac, for description is vague; man kept face muffled) hired private auto in Yellow Creek, just across Ohio R. from Arroyo, at 11:30 last night. Have talked with owner of car; he took Krosac to Steubenville, O., dropped him at hotel there. . . . Am going to follow K. myself, leaving this message for you with the superintelligent janitor at Arroyo Municipal Hall. Go to Steubenville at once; if I find another trail will leave note at Fort Steuben Hotel for you. Hurriedly,

YARDLEY

Ellery's eyes were wild. "What time did your friend Abraham Lincoln write this note, janitor?"

"'Leven o'clock or there'bout," drawled the janitor. "Not long 'fore ye came yerself."

"Now I know," groaned Ellery, "why men commit murder. . . .When did the rain stop last night?" he asked suddenly, struck by a thought.

"Hour or so 'fore midnight. Rain petered out hyah, though 'twas pourin' like fury 'cross th' river all night. Listen here, Mr. Queen, don't ye think—"

"No," said Ellery firmly. "Give this note to the men from New York when they arrive." He scribbled an additional message on the blank side of the sheet and pressed the paper into the janitor's hand. "Stay out here—sweep, chaw, do anything you like—but stick to this walk until they come. Isham, Vaughn. Police. Do you understand? Isham, Vaughn. Give 'em this note. Here's something for your trouble."

He tossed a bill toward the janitor, jumped into the Duesenberg, and was off down Arroyo's main street in a cloud of dust.

Chapter Twenty-Eight
TWICE DEAD

Inspector Vaughn and District Attorney Isham motored into Bradwood at eight o'clock Wednesday morning, tired but happy. With them was a man from the United States Attorney's office. And seated in the tonneau, sullenly defiant, were Percy and Elizabeth Lynn.

The British thieves were packed off to Mineola under guard, and the Inspector was stretching his arms at luxurious ease when his lieutenant, Bill, ran up waving his arms and talking fast. The expression of triumph faded from Vaughn's face, to be replaced by one of anxiety. Isham heard the full story left by Professor Yardley and swore fretfully.

"What the deuce shall we do?"

Vaughn snapped: "Follow, of course!" and climbed back into the police car. The District Attorney rubbed his bald spot and followed with the weariness of resignation.

In Mineola, at the flying field, they picked up news of Yardley. The Professor had hired an airplane at six that morning, headed for an unnamed destination southwest. Ten minutes later they were in the air, winging toward the same goal in the cabin of a powerful tri-motored machine.

～

It was 1:30 P.M. when they trudged into Arroyo. The plane had set them down in a pasture a quarter-mile out of town. They headed for the Municipal Hall. A man in blue denim sat on the steps of the building, a ragged broom at his feet, snoring peacefully. He scrambled to his feet at the Inspector's growl.

"You from N'Yawk?"

"Yes."

"Name o' Vaughn, er Ish'm, er somethin'?"

"Yes."

"Got a note fer ye." The janitor opened his huge palm; in it, crumpled and dirty and damp but intact, lay Professor Yardley's note.

They read the Professor's message in silence, and then turned the paper over. Ellery had scribbled the addendum:

> Yardley's note self-explanatory. I've been to the shack. Fearful mess there. Follow as soon as you can. Circling footprints before hut mine—other pair . . .
>
> Figure it out for yourself. Be quick if you want to be in at the kill.
>
> Q.

"It's happened," groaned Isham.

"What time did Mr. Queen leave here?" snarled Vaughn.

"'Bout one o'clock," replied the janitor. "Say, whut's goin' on, Cap? Peck o' traipsin' 'bout, seems to me."

"Come on, Isham," muttered the Inspector. "Lead the way. We've got to see that hut first."

They swung off round the corner, leaving the janitor staring and shaking his head.

The hut's door was closed.

Isham and Vaughn with difficulty scaled the barbed-wire fence. "Don't walk over those prints," said the Inspector shortly. "Let's see

. . . These are Queen's, I guess, the ones that make the detour. The other set—"

They stood still and followed with their eyes the line of footprints which Ellery had observed little more than an hour before. There were two complete sets made by the same pair of shoes; and, with the exception of Ellery's, no others. The two sets were plainly defined: one going from the fence to the door of the shack; the other returning on a slightly deviating line. Beyond the wire fence the rocky nature of the ground precluded a visible trail. The prints which approached the cabin were more deeply impressed in the earth than those which left. In all the footprints the impression of the right foot was heavier than the corresponding impression of the left.

"The limping trail, all right," mumbled Vaughn. "That first set—queer." He advanced around the double track of footprints and opened the door, Isham following.

They stared in raw horror at what they saw.

On the wall opposite the door, nailed to the rough-hewn logs like a trophy, was the body of a man. It was headless. The legs had been nailed close together. From the bloody tatters in which it was clad—the tatters of the pseudo-hillman—it was the corpse of the unfortunate schoolmaster.

Blood had dripped to the stone floor. Blood had spattered over the walls. The shack, which had been so neat and cozy when Isham had visited it before, now looked like the inner shrine of an abattoir. The rush mats were mottled with thick red spots. The floor showed red streaks and smears. The top of the sturdy old table, swept clean of its usual objects, had been utilized as a slate; and on this slate, in a gigantic letter of blood, was the familiar symbol of Krosac's vengeance—a capital T.

"Jeeze," muttered Vaughn. "It turns your stomach. I think I'd choke that cannibal with my bare hands, justification or not, if I got hold of him."

"I'm going outside," said Isham hoarsely. "I feel—faint." He staggered through the doorway and leaned against the wall outside, retching with nausea.

Inspector Vaughn blinked, squared his shoulders, and stepped across the room. He avoided the stiffened pools of blood. He touched the body; it was rigid. Little trickles of red emanated from the spikeheads in the palms and feet.

"Dead about fifteen hours," thought Vaughn, clenching his fist. His face was white as he stared up at the crucified corpse. With a raw crimson hole where the head had been, with the arms stiffly outstretched, with the legs together, it was a grotesque and insane travesty on a devil's humor . . . a monstrous and monster T formed of dead human flesh.

Vaughn shook the vertigo out of his head and stepped back. He reflected dully that there must have been something of a struggle; for on the floor near the table lay several objects which told a gruesome story. The first was a heavy ax, its haft and blade painted with dry blood; obviously the weapon which had decapitated Andreja Tvar. The second was a round coil of bandage, like a two-dimensional doughnut; its edges were frayed and dirty, and it was soaked through on one side with a brownish-red liquid, now dry. The Inspector stooped and gingerly picked up the coil; it came apart as he lifted it and, somewhat to his surprise, he saw that it had been sliced through by a sharp implement. A scissors, Vaughn conjectured; and looked about. Yes, a few feet away on the floor, as if it has been flung there in desperate haste, lay a heavy shears.

Vaughn went to the door; Isham, while pale and peaked-looking, had partially recovered. "What's this look like to you?" asked Vaughn, holding up the severed coil of bandage. "Cripes, you picked out a nice place to be sick, Isham!"

The District Attorney crinkled his nose. He looked miserable. "Bandage around a wrist," he faltered. "And a bad wound, too, to judge from the bloodstains and iodine on it."

"You're right," said Vaughn grimly. "From the circumference of the coil it must be a wrist. There isn't another part of the human body exactly that small around, not even the ankle. I'm afraid Mr. Krosac has a little wound stripe on his wrist!"

"Either there was a fight or he cut himself while he was—was butchering the body," ventured Isham with a shiver. "But why did he leave the bandage for us to find?"

"Easy. See how bloody it is. Cut must have been made early in the fight, or whatever it was. So he cut off his first bandage and put on a fresh one. . . . As for why he left it—he was in one sweet hurry, Isham, to get out of the neighborhood of this shack. And he's not really in danger, I suppose. The very fact that he left the bandage tends to show that the wound is in a place which can be kept covered. Cuff probably hides it. Let's go back inside."

Isham gulped and bravely followed the Inspector back into the hut. Vaughn pointed out the ax and shears; and then indicated a large opaque bottle lying on the floor near the spot where he had found the bandage, a bottle of dark blue glass without a label. It was almost empty; most of its contents stained the floor brown where it lay, and its cork had bounced a few feet away. Nearby lay a roll of bandage, partly unwound.

"Iodine," said Vaughn. "That tells the whole story. He got it from that medicine shelf over there when he cut himself. Left the bottle on the table and later upset it by accident, or just threw it on the floor— he should give a damn. It's thick glass, and didn't break."

They went to the wall where the body hung; several feet to the side, in a corner, over the basinlike arrangement and the pump-handle, was the shelf which Isham had noticed on his previous visit to the shack. Except for two spaces the shelf was full; upon it stood a large blue package of cotton, a tube of tooth-paste, a roll of adhesive, a roll of bandage, and one of gauze, a small bottle labeled iodine and a companion bottle labeled mercurochrome and several small bottles and jars—cathartics, aspirin, zinc salve, Vaseline, and the like.

"It's clear enough," said the Inspector gloomily. "He used Van's stuff. The bandage and the big bottle of iodine came from Van's shelf, and he should worry about putting 'em back."

"Just a minute," said Isham, frowning. "You're jumping to the conclusion that it was Krosac who was cut. Suppose it was this poor chump hanging on the wall. Don't you see, Vaughn? If it wasn't Krosac who got the wound, and it was Van, then we'd be on a false trail if we looked for a man with a cut wrist, thinking it was Krosac."

"You're not so dumb," exclaimed Vaughn. "Never thought of that. Well!" He threw back his chunky shoulders. "Only one thing to do—take a look at the body." He advanced toward the wall with set lips.

"Oh; say," groaned Isham, wincing, "I—I'd rather not, Vaughn."

"Listen," snarled Vaughn, "I don't like this job any more than you do. But it's got to be done. Come on."

Ten minutes later the headless body lay on the floor. They had extracted the spikes from the palms and feet. The rags Vaughn had shorn away from the corpse and it lay nude and white, a mockery of God's image. Isham leaned against the wall with his hands pressed to his stomach. It was the Inspector who, with an effort, went over the bare flesh for wounds; turned the hideous thing over, and repeated his examination on the back.

"No," he said, rising, "no wounds except the nail holes in the palms and feet. That wrist cut is Krosac's, all right."

"Let's get out of here, Vaughn. Please."

They returned to Arroyo in thick silence, breathing deeply of the untainted air. In town Inspector Vaughn sought out a telephone, and called Weirton, the county seat. He spoke to District Attorney Crumit for five minutes. Then he hung up and rejoined Isham.

"Crumit'll keep quiet," he said grimly. "Was he surprised! But it won't leak out and that's all I'm interested in. He's bringing Colonel Pickett down here, and the Coroner. I told him we took a few liberties with Hancock County's newest stiff." He chuckled humorlessly as they emerged into Arroyo's main street and hurried toward the tiny garage. "Second time they'll have to hold an inquest into the death of Andrew Van!"

Isham said nothing; he was still in the clutch of nausea. They hired a fast car and set out—an hour and a half behind Ellery—raising an identical cloud of dust. They headed for the Ohio River, the bridge, and Steubenville.

CHALLENGE TO
THE READER

Who is the murderer?

It has been my custom to challenge the reader's wits at such point in my novels at which the reader is in possession of all facts necessary to a correct solution of the crime or crimes. The Egyptian Cross Mystery *is no exception: by the exercise of strict logic and deductions from given data you should now be able, not merely to guess, but to prove the identity of the culprit.*

There are no ifs and buts in the only proper solution, as you will find upon reading the explanatory chapter. And although logic requires no helping hand from fortune—good reasoning and good luck!

—Ellery Queen

Chapter Twenty-Nine
A MATTER OF GEOGRAPHY

THAT WAS AN HISTORIC Wednesday, the beginning of as odd and exciting a manhunt as the records of four states contained. It covered some five hundred and fifty miles of zigzag territory. It involved the use of all forms of modern rapid transit—automobile, express train, and airplane. Five men took part in it—and a sixth whose participation came as a complete surprise. And it covered, from the time Ellery set foot in Steubenville, Ohio, nine hard hours which to all except the leader seemed nine centuries.

A triple pursuit . . . It was remarkable how they chased one another—a long strung-out hunt in which the quarry was always just out of reach; in which there was no time for rest, for food, for consultation.

At 1:30 Wednesday afternoon—just as District Attorney Isham and Inspector Vaughn trudged up to the Municipal Hall in Arroyo—Ellery Queen raced his Duesenberg into Steubenville, a busy town, and after a short delaying during which he questioned a traffic officer, pulled up before the Fort Steuben Hotel.

His pince-nez glasses were awry on his nose and his hat was pushed far back on his head. He looked the motion-picture conception of a reporter, and perhaps that is what the clerk at the hotel desk took him for; for he grinned and neglected to push the register forward.

"You're Mr. Ellery Queen, aren't you?" he asked, before Ellery could catch his breath.

"Yes! How did you know?"

"Mr. Yardley described you," said the clerk, "and said you'd be along this afternoon. He left this note for you."

"Good man!" cried Ellery. "Let's have it."

The note had been written in great haste, in a most unprofessorial scrawl:

QUEEN: Don't stop to question clerk. Have all information necessary. Man of K's description stopped this hotel arriving about midnight last night. Left 7:30 this A.M. in hired car. Limp discarded on leaving hotel, but sports bandaged wrist which puzzles me. Broad trail shows no fear of pursuit; actually said he was going to Zanesville. Going after him by car. Have vague description from clerk. Will leave further instructions for you with clerk Clarendon Hotel, Zanesville.

YARDLEY

Ellery's eyes were gleaming as he tucked the note into his pocket. "At what time did Mr. Yardley leave Steubenville?"

"Noon, sir, in a hired car."

"Zanesville, eh?" Ellery was thoughtful. Then he picked up a telephone and said: "Let me have the Chief of Police of Zanesville, please. . . . Hello. Police department? Let me speak to the Chief. . . . Hurry! Never mind who I am. . . . Hello! This is Ellery Queen of New York City speaking. Son of Inspector Richard Queen of the New York homicide squad. . . . Yes! I'm in Steubenville, Chief, and I'm on the trail of a tall dark man with a bandaged wrist in a hired automobile, followed by a tall man with a beard in another hired car. . . . The first man's a killer. . . . Yes! He left Steubenville at half-past seven this morning. . . . Hmm. I suppose you're right; he must have passed through long ago. Pick up what trail you can, please. The second man can't have reached Zanesville yet. . . . Keep in touch with the clerk at the Clarendon Hotel. I'll stop by as soon as I can."

He hung up and dashed out of the Fort Steuben Hotel. The Duesenberg, like the Pony Express, clattered off toward the west.

In Zanesville Ellery quickly found the Clarendon Hotel, the Clarendon Hotel clerk, and a short tubby man in police uniform who met him with outstretched hand and a wide Rotarian smile.

"Well?" demanded Ellery.

"I'm Hardy, the chief here," said the fat man. "Your man with the chin whiskers telephoned a message to the clerk not long ago. At least, he identified himself as such. Seems that the first man changed his route and instead of coming to Zanesville took the road to Columbus."

"Oh, heavens!" cried Ellery. "I might have known Yardley would bungle it, poor old bookworm. Have you notified Columbus?"

"Sure have. Important arrest, Mr. Queen?"

"Important enough," said Ellery shortly. "Thank you, Chief. I'm on—"

"Excuse me," said the clerk timidly. "But the gentleman who called said he would leave a message for you at the Seneca Hotel in Columbus. The clerk there is a friend of mine."

Ellery retreated with celerity, leaving the short gentleman in uniform slightly bewildered.

At 7:00—while Vaughn and Isham were blundering along the muddled trail between Steubenville and Columbus—Ellery was threading his way through East Broad Street in Columbus looking for the Seneca Hotel, after a hair-raising drive from Zanesville.

He met with no obstacle this time. From the clerk behind the desk he got Yardley's scribbled message:

QUEEN: Fooled me that time, but I quickly picked up the scent again. Don't think it was intentional on his part—just changed his mind and went on to Columbus. Have wasted a little time, but discover that K. took train out of here at 1 o'clock for Indianapolis. Am taking plane here to make up lost time. What fun! Shoot along, young man. May catch the fox in Indianapolis, and will your face be red!

Y.

"When he gets colloquial," muttered Ellery to himself, "he's almost insufferable. . . . What time did this gentleman write the note?" He swabbed the perspiration from his grimy brow.

"Five-thirty, sir."

Ellery snatched a telephone and put in a call for Indianapolis. In a few moments he was talking with Police Headquarters. He introduced himself and discovered that word had already been passed along by the Columbus police. Indianapolis was extremely sorry, but identification had been difficult from the unsatisfactory description, and they had found no trace of the hunted man.

Ellery hung up with a toss of his head. "Any other message for me from Mr. Yardley?"

"Yes, sir. He said he'd leave word at the airport in Indianapolis."

Ellery produced his wallet. "A fat largess, old man, for rapid service. Can you get me an airplane at once?"

The clerk smiled. "Mr. Yardley said you might want one. So I've taken the liberty of chartering one for you, sir. It's waiting at the field."

"Damn Yardley!" muttered Ellery, tossing a bill on the desk. "He's stealing my thunder. Whose chase is this, anyway?" Then he grinned and said: "Great work. I didn't think I'd find such intelligence in the hinterland. My car is outside—an ancient Duesenberg. Take care of it for me, will you? I'll be back—God knows when."

And he was out in the street hailing a taxicab. "Flying field!" he shouted. "Fast!"

It was a little past eight o'clock—an hour after Ellery had left Columbus in the chartered airplane, nearly three hours behind Yardley, and seven hours after their quarry had left Columbus by train—when Vaughn and Isham, two sorely fatigued travelers, raced into Columbus. Vaughn's official position had lent their trip wings. Messages had flashed ahead from Zanesville. An airplane waited for them at the Columbus port. They were in the air, bound for Indianapolis, before District Attorney Isham could groan three times.

The chase would have been humorous had it not had such grim purpose behind it. Ellery relaxed in his plane and thought of many things. His eyes were abstracted. So much that had been unclear and indecisive for seven months was clear now! He went over the entire case in his mind, and when he came to the murder of Andrew Van he regarded the result of his mental labor and found it good.

The plane sailed on, quite as if it hung in the cloud-strewn air, and only the crawling of the town-dotted terrain far below destroyed the illusion of a body at rest. Indianapolis . . . Would Yardley pounce on the fox there? It was, Ellery knew after a rapid calculation, temporally possible. The man who hid beneath the cloak of Krosac had left Columbus by railroad train; he could not reach Indianapolis before approximately six o'clock, perhaps a few minutes later—a trip of some five hours by rail. Whereas Yardley, leaving Columbus by plane at 5:30, should cover the comparatively short air-distance by seven o'clock. Flying conditions were favorable, as Ellery could see and feel. Should Krosac's train be the least bit late, or should he be delayed in leaving Indianapolis for the next stop on his itinerary, there was every possibility that the Professor would catch up with him. Ellery sighed and half wished that Krosac would evade the Professor's unpracticed clutches. Not that Yardley had done badly, for a novice, so far!

They drifted down on the field of the Indianapolis airport like a scudding leaf in the rosy afterglow of dusk. Ellery consulted his watch. It was 8:30.

As three mechanics grabbed the wings of the plane and rammed chock-blocks under the heels, a young man in uniform came running up to the door of the cabin. Ellery stepped out and looked around.

"Mr. Queen?"

He nodded. "A message for me?" he asked eagerly.

"Yes, sir. A gentleman named Yardley left it for you a little less than an hour and a half ago. He said it was important."

"A mild word," muttered Ellery, grabbing the note. This affair, he reflected as he opened it, was becoming a saga of wild rides and alternate messages.

Yardley's scrawl merely said:

Q.: Looks like the last lap. Thought I might catch up with him, but missed him by the skin of my teeth. Arrived here just as man of K's description took off in plane for Chicago. That was at 7. Cannot get plane until 7:15. K's craft due in Chi between 8:45 and 9:00. Suggest if you arrive before 8:45 notify Chi police to nab our flitting gent, on flying field there. I'm off!

Y.

"Mr. Yardley caught a plane at seven-fifteen?" demanded Ellery.

"That's right, sir."

"Then he should get to Chicago between 9:00 and 9:15?"

"Yes, sir."

Ellery slipped a small bill into the young man's hand. "Lead me to a telephone and you're my benefactor for life."

The young man grinned and broke into a run, Ellery loping after.

At the airport terminal building Ellery frantically put in a call to Chicago. "Police Headquarters? Give me the Commissioner. . . . Yes, the Commissioner of Police! . . . Hurry, you fool, this is a matter of life and death. . . . Commissioner? What? . . . Look here, this is Ellery Queen of New York City and I have a personal message for the

Commissioner. Important!" He stamped his feet in impatience as his cautious *tête-à-tête* at the other end of the wire asked questions. Five minutes of mingled abuse and pleading elapsed before the voice of the august gentleman who controlled Chicago's police affairs boomed into his receiver. "Commissioner! You remember me—Inspector Richard Queen's son. . . . Cleaning up the Long Island murders. Yes! . . . Tall dark man with a bandaged wrist is arriving between 8:45 and 9:00 at Chicago tonight in an Indianapolis plane. . . . No! Don't nab him on the field. . . . Matter of personal satisfaction. Will you have him trailed to wherever he goes, and then surround the place? . . . Yes. Arrest him only if he tries to leave Chicago. It's possible he's heading for Canada . . . or the Pacific coast, yes . . . He doesn't know he's being followed. . . . Incidentally, look out for a tall man with a beard like Abe Lincoln's on the same field flying from Indianapolis—Professor Yardley. Tell your people to grant him every courtesy. . . . Thanks and good-by.

"And now," shouted Ellery, to the grinning young man outside the booth, "lead me to a plane!"

"Where are you going?" asked the young man.

"Chicago."

At 10:25 the monoplane circled the Chicago field, brilliantly illuminated throughout its length and breadth. Ellery, craning before the glass window, could make out the sprawled buildings, the hangars, the landing field, a line of machines, and the scurrying figures of people. These details blurred in the swoop of the landing—his pilot had been energized by the offer of a premium for speed—and by the time he regained his breath and the proper stomachic balance they were very near the ground, hurtling toward the line. He closed his eyes, and felt the wheels of the monoplane bump on the ground; the nature of the sensation changed, and he opened his eyes to see that they were taxiing along the cement in a swift glide.

He rose rather uncertainly and fumbled with his tie. The end . . . The motor uttered a final triumphant roar, and the machine's motion stopped. The pilot twisted his head and yelled: "Here we are, Mr. Queen! Did the best I could."

"Excellent," said Ellery with a grimace, and staggered to the door. There was such a thing as obeying orders too well. . . . Someone opened the door from the outside, and he dropped onto the field. For a moment he blinked in the strong glare at a group of men ten feet away, watching him.

He blinked again. There was the tall, pseudo-saturnine figure of Professor Yardley, his beard almost horizontal in a grin; the strong beefy figure of Chicago's police commissioner, whom Ellery recalled from that initial trip to the Windy City which he had taken with his father seven months before, and which had resulted in his investigation of the Arroyo murder; several indeterminate figures, whom he took to be detectives; and . . . who was that? That small man in the neat gray suit, with the neat gray fedora, and the neat gray gloves—that little chap with the old face and the cocked head . . . ?

"Dad!" he cried, springing forward and seizing Inspector Richard Queen's gloved hands. "How in the name of all that's holy did you get here?"

"'Lo, son," said Inspector Queen dryly. He grinned. "You're one hell of a detective if you can't figure it out. Your friend Hardy, of the Zanesville police, telephoned me in New York after you called him, and I told him you were my son. Just wanted to check up on you, he said. I put two and two together, decided it was the end of your case, figured your man would head either for Chicago or St. Louis, left New York by plane at two, landed fifteen minutes ago, and here I am."

Ellery threw his arm about his father's spare shoulders. "You're the eternal wonder, the modern Colossus of Rhodes. By the good Lord, Dad, I *am* glad to see you. It's a caution how you old fellows get around. . . . Hullo, Professor!"

Yardley's eyes twinkled as they shook hands. "I suppose I'm included in the septuagenarian classification? Your father and I have had a hearty talk about you, young man, and he thinks you've got something up your sleeve."

"Ah," said Ellery, sobering. "He does, does he? How d'ye do, Commissioner? Thanks a thousand times for your quick acceptance of my nasty telephone manner. I was in the devil of a hurry. . . . Well, sir, what's the situation?"

They walked slowly across the field to the terminal. The Commissioner said: "It looks great, Mr. Queen. Your man arrived by plane at five minutes to nine—we barely got our detectives here in time. He doesn't suspect a thing."

"I was just twenty minutes late," sighed the Professor. "I was never so frightened in my life as when I hauled my creaking old bones out of the ship and a detective grasped my arm. 'Yardley?' he said in a stern voice. Well, my boy, I—"

"Hmm, yes," said Ellery. "Where is—er—Krosac now, Commissioner?"

"He took his sweet time getting off the field, and at five after nine he got into a taxi and was driven to a third-rate hotel in the Loop— the Rockford. He didn't know it," added the Commissioner grimly, "but he had an escort of four police cars all the way. He's there now, in his room."

"He can't get away?" asked Ellery anxiously.

"Mr. Queen!" said the Commissioner in an offended voice.

The Inspector chuckled. "Incidentally, I understand that Vaughn and Isham of Nassau County are trailing you, son. Aren't you going to wait for them?"

Ellery stopped short. "Heavens, I forgot about them! Commissioner, will you be kind enough to detail some one as an escort for Inspector Vaughn and District Attorney Isham as soon as they arrive? They're only an hour or so behind me. Have them taken to the Rockford Hotel. It would be a shame to cut them out of the last act!"

But District Attorney Isham and Inspector Vaughn were considerably less than an hour behind Ellery. They descended out of the dark sky upon the Chicago airport at precisely eleven o'clock, were met by several detectives, and were escorted to the Loop in police cars.

The reunion of the pilgrims was slightly hilarious. They met in a private suite at the Rockford which was thick with detectives. Ellery was stretched out on the bed, coat off, blissfully resting. Inspector Queen and the Commissioner were conversing in a corner of the room. Professor Yardley was washing the accumulated grime of several states off his face and hands in the lavatory. . . . They looked around, two journey-battered gentlemen with bleary eyes.

"Well?" growled Vaughn. "Is this the end, or do we keep on chasing our tails to Alaska? What is this guy—a marathon runner?"

"This," chuckled Ellery, "is truly the end, Inspector. Sit down, and you too, Mr. Isham. Rest your weary bones. We have all night. Mr. Krosac can't get away. How about a snack?"

There were introductions, steaming food, remarkably hot coffee, laughter and speculation. Through it all Ellery remained quiet, his thoughts on something far distant. Occasionally a detective would report. Once word came that the gentleman in Room 643—he had registered as John Chase, Indianapolis—had just telephoned the clerk to make a reservation for him on the morning transcontinental to San Francisco. This was delicately discussed; it was evident that Mr. Chase, or Mr. Krosac, was planning to leave American shores for an extended tour through the Orient, for it was not reasonable that he would stop in San Francisco.

"By the way," said Ellery lazily, at a few minutes to midnight, "just whom do you think, Professor, we'll turn up when we burst in on Mr. John Chase of Indianapolis, Room 643?"

The old Inspector regarded his son quizzically. Yardley stared. "Why, Velja Krosac, of course."

"Indeed," said Ellery, blowing a smoke ring.

The Professor started. "What do you mean? By Krosac I refer, naturally, to the man born with that name, but who's probably known to us by a different one."

"Indeed," said Ellery again. He rose and stretched his arms. "I do think, gentlemen, it's time we brought Mr.—Krosac, shall I say?—to earth. Is everything ready, Commissioner?"

"Just waiting for the word, Mr. Queen."

"One minute," said Inspector Vaughn. He looked wrathfully at Ellery. "Do you mean to say you *know* the real identity of the man in 643?"

"Of course! I'm really astonished, Inspector, at your lack of perspicacity. Wasn't it plain enough?"

"Plain? What was plain?"

Ellery sighed. "Never mind. But I daresay you're in for a whopping surprise. Shall we go? *En avant!*"

Five minutes later the corridors on the sixth floor of the Rockford Hotel resembled the parade ground of an army encampment. There were police and plainclothesmen everywhere. The floor above and the floor below were impassable. The elevators had been shut down, very quietly indeed. Room 643 had only one exit—the corridor door.

A small and frightened bellboy had been pressed into service. He stood before the door, encircled by the group—Ellery, his father, Vaughn, Isham, the Commissioner, Yardley—awaiting the word of command. Ellery looked around; there was no sound except the sound of breathing. Then he nodded grimly to the boy.

The boy gulped and advanced to the door. Two detectives with drawn revolvers stood flat against the panels. One of them knocked briskly. There was no reply; the room, as they could tell from the transom, was in darkness and its occupant probably asleep.

The detective knocked again. This time there was a faint sound from behind the door, and the creaking of bedsprings. A man's deep voice called out sharply: "Who's there?"

The bellboy gulped again and cried: "Service, Mr. Chase!"

"What—" They heard the man snort, and the bed creaked again. "I didn't call for service. What do you want, anyway?" The door opened and a man's tousled head stuck out. . . .

Of all the incidents that followed—the instant pounce of the two plainclothesmen, the scrambling away of the bellboy, the struggle on the floor, halfway across the threshold—Ellery remembered only one picture. It was in that split second during which no one moved, during which the man took in the scene in the corridor—the waiting officials, the detectives, the uniforms, the faces of Ellery Queen and District Attorney Isham and Inspector Vaughn. The expression of utter stupefaction that was stamped on that white face. The flared nostrils. The distended eyes. The bandage on the wrist of the hand which gripped the jamb. . . .

"Why, it's—it's—" Professor Yardley wet his lips twice, and could not find the words.

"It's as I knew it would be," drawled Ellery, as he watched the fierce struggle on the floor. "I knew it as soon as I had examined the shack in the hills."

They managed to subdue Mr. John Chase, of Room 643. A slight dribble of saliva ran from a corner of his mouth. His eyes were wholly mad now.

They were the eyes of the schoolmaster of Arroyo—Andrew Van.

Chapter Thirty
ELLERY TALKS AGAIN

"I'M STUMPED. I'M ABSOLUTELY stumped," snapped Inspector Vaughn. "I can't get it through my head how a solution was possible from the facts. I'm stumped, Mr. Queen, and you'll have to convince me that it wasn't just guesswork."

"A Queen," said Ellery severely, "never guesses."

It was Thursday, and they were seated in a drawing room compartment of the Twentieth Century Limited en route to New York. Yardley and Ellery and Inspector Queen and Isham and Vaughn. A tired but not unhappy party. Their faces betrayed the strain of the nerve-racking experience they had been through—all except, of course, Inspector Queen, who seemed to be enjoying himself in his quiet way.

"You're not the first," chuckled the old man to Vaughn. "I've never known it to fail. Every time he solves a humdinger somebody wants to know how it was done and says it was guesswork. I'll be damned if I know myself how he does it most of the time, even after he explains."

"It's pure mystery to me," confessed Isham.

Professor Yardley seemed nettled at the challenge to his intellect. "I'm not an untutored individual," he growled, as Ellery grinned, "but I'll hang as high as Haman if I can see how logic applied in this case.

It's been a welter of inconsistencies and contradictions from beginning to end."

"Wrong," drawled Ellery. "It was a welter of inconsistencies and contradictions from the beginning to the fourth murder. At that point it became clear as crystal, all the mud decanting off. You see," he said, knitting his brows, "all along I felt that if I could grasp just one tiny piece and place it in the key position, all the other pieces—so scrambled and illogical in appearance—would take comprehensible shape. That piece was supplied in the West Virginia shack."

"So you said last night," grunted the Professor. "And I still can't see how—"

"Naturally not. You never examined the hut."

"I did," snarled Vaughn, "and if you can show me what solved the damned thing—"

"Ah, a challenge. Certainly." Ellery blew smoke at the low ceiling of the compartment. "Let me go back a bit. Up to the murder in Arroyo Tuesday night, I knew little enough. The first murder in Arroyo was altogether a mystery until Andrew Van himself appeared. He said at that time that his servant Kling had been killed by mistake, that a man named Velja Krosac with blood-motive had been the murderer of this Kling. Thomas Brad, Van's brother, was murdered. Stephen Megara, Van's brother, was murdered. Megara had confirmed the story of Krosac, as had the official investigators in Yugoslavia. It all seemed clear enough in its general purport—a monomaniac whose brain had been addled by a lifelong unsatisfied vengeance was running amok among the killers of his father and uncles. When we discovered that the Tvars had also robbed Krosac of his inheritance, an additional motive bolstered the theory.

"I've explained to Professor Yardley that there were two definite conclusions to be drawn from the circumstances surrounding the death of Brad. One was that Brad's murderer was well-known to him; the other that Brad's murderer did not limp. Is that correct, Professor?" Yardley nodded, and Ellery quickly summarized his reasoning based on the disposition of the checkers and the other facts known to Vaughn and Isham.

"But these conclusions got me nowhere. We had already assumed the possibility of both without conclusive reasoning. The fact that I proved them was therefore of little value. So until I found the body in the shack my only explanation for the queer details of the first three murders was Krosac's insanity and obsession with a peculiar T phobia—the severing of the heads, the scrawling of the T's, the very odd T significances surrounding all three crimes."

Ellery smiled reminiscently and regarded his cigarette with affection. "The astonishing part of it was that very early in the investigation—in fact, seven months ago when I looked upon the first horrible corpse in the Weirton courthouse—a thought struck me which, had I followed it through, might well have terminated the case then and there. It was an alternative explanation for the scattered T's. It was just a groping thought, the result of my discipline in logic. But it seemed so remote a possibility that I discarded it; and continued to discard it when nothing occurred thereafter to give it the slightest factual support. But it kept persisting . . ."

"What was that?" asked the Professor with interest. "You recall when we discussed the Egyptian—"

"Ah, let that go," said Ellery hastily. "I'll come to it in a moment. Let me first go over the details of the fourth murder." Rapidly he drew a word-picture of the physical scene that had met his eye when he stepped over the threshold of the barricaded hut just the day before. Yardley and Inspector Queen listened with drawn brows, concentrating on the problem; but when Ellery had finished they regarded each other blankly.

"A perfect vacuum as far as I'm concerned," confessed the Professor.

"Count me out, too," said the Inspector.

Vaughn and Isham were looking at Ellery suspiciously.

"Good lord," cried Ellery, flinging his butt out of the window, "it's so clear! There's an epic story written in and around that hut, gentlemen. What's that motto hanging in the classroom of the School for Scientific Police at the Palais de Justice, Dad? 'The eye sees in things only what it looks for, and it looks only for what is already in mind.' Our American police might take that to heart, Inspector Vaughn.

"Outside the hut, the footprints. You examined them carefully?"

Vaughn and Isham nodded.

"Then you must have seen at once the patent fact that only *two* people were involved in that murder. There were two sets of prints—one ingoing, the other outgoing; from the shape and size of the tracks both sets had been made by the same shoes. It was possible to fix roughly the time the tracks had been made. The rain had stopped in Arroyo at about eleven o'clock the previous night. It had been a heavy rain. Had the prints been made before the rain stopped they would, in their exposed position, have been completely washed out and obliterated. Then they were made certainly at eleven or later. The condition of the body crucified to the wall of the hut at the time I saw it showed me that the victim was dead about fourteen hours—had died, in other words, at about eleven o'clock the night before. The prints—the only prints, incidentally—were made therefore at approximately the time of the murder."

Ellery stuck a fresh cigarette into his mouth. "What did the prints reveal? That only one person had walked into and out of the hut during the approximate period of the murder. There was only one entrance or exit—the door; the single window being effectively barred with barbed wire."

Ellery applied a match to his cigarette and puffed thoughtfully. "It was elementary, then. There was a victim and there was a murderer. We had found the victim. Then it was the murderer whose tracks were impressed on the wet earth before the shack. The tracks showed a limping man—so far, so good.

"Now, on the stone floor of the hut there were several most illuminating objects. Exhibit Number One was a bloody and iodine-stained coil of bandage which from its shape and circumference could only have been wound about a wrist. Nearby lay a partially used roll of bandage."

Again Isham and Vaughn nodded, and the Professor said: "So that's it! I wondered about the wrist."

"Exhibit Number Two: a large blue-glass bottle of iodine, its cork a few feet away on the floor. The bottle was opaque, and it had no label.

"The question immediately confronted me: On whose wrist had that bandage been wound? There were two people involved: victim and murderer. Then it came from one or the other. If the victim had worn the bandage, then one of his wrists would show a wound. I examined the wrists of the corpse—both unmarked. Conclusion: the murderer had cut one of his own wrists. By inference when he had wielded the ax on the victim's body, or possibly during a struggle before the victim was killed.

"If the murderer had cut his wrist, it was he then who had used iodine and bandage. The fact that he had cut off the bandage later was irrelevant—the wound must have bled profusely, as the bandage indicated, and he merely changed dressings before leaving the hut."

Ellery brandished the smoking cigarette. "But observe what a significant fact has been brought out! For if the murderer used the iodine, what have we? It should be child's play now. Don't you see it yet, any of you?"

They tried very hard, from their scowls and finger-gnawings and looks of deep concentration; but in the end they shook their heads.

Ellery sank back. "I suppose it's one of those things. To me it seems extraordinarily clear. What were the two characteristics of the iodine-bottle, peculiar to that bottle itself, which the murderer had left on the floor? First: it was of opaque blue glass. Second: it bore no label.

"Then how did the murderer know it contained iodine?"

~

Professor Yardley's jaw dropped, and he smote his forehead in a manner amusingly reminiscent of District Attorney Sampson, that admirable prosecutor associated with Ellery and Inspector Queen in so many of their metropolitan cases. "Oh, what an idiot I am!" he groaned. "Of course, of course!"

Vaughn wore a look of immense surprise. "It's so damned simple," he said in a wondering tone, as if he could not understand how it had escaped his observation.

Ellery shrugged. "These things generally are. You see, therefore, the line of reasoning. The murderer couldn't have known it was iodine from the bottle itself, since there was no label and the blue color and opacity of the glass disguised the hue of its contents. Then he could have known its contents only in one of two alternative ways: either by being familiar with the contents of the bottle from previous experience, or by uncorking it and investigating.

"Now you will recall that there were two blank spaces on the medicine-supply shelf above 'Old Pete's' homely little lavatory. It was apparent at once that those two blank spaces had held the two objects on the floor—the bottle of iodine and the roll of bandage—both of which would normally stand on a medicine shelf. In other words the murderer, having wounded himself, was constrained to apply to the medicine shelf for bandage and iodine."

Ellery grinned. "But how odd! What else was on the shelf? Surely you recollect that, among miscellaneous and innocuous articles, there were two bottles which the murderer might have taken down for use in his extremity—one of iodine and one of mercurochrome, *both plainly labeled?* Why, then, should he uncork the unlabeled, opaque bottle in a search for an antiseptic when there were two clearly marked bottles of antiseptic in full view? Actually, there can be no reason; no man, a stranger to that hut, with time at a premium, would explore a bottle whose contents were unpredictable when what he wanted was right before his eyes all the time.

"Then the first of my two possibilities must apply: the murderer must have been familiar with the large opaque unlabeled bottle, must have known *in advance* that it contained iodine! But who could have such knowledge?" Ellery sighed. "And there it was. From the circumstances and Van's own story of the isolation of his hideaway, only one person could have had such knowledge—the owner of the hut."

"I told you so," said Inspector Queen excitedly, as he reached for his ancient brown snuff box.

"We have shown that only two people were involved—murderer and victim—and that it was the murderer who cut his wrist and used the iodine. So if the owner of the hut, Andreja Tvar, alias Andrew Van, alias Old Pete, was the only one who could have known in advance that the mysterious bottle contained iodine, then it was Andrew Van whose wrist was cut, and the poor fellow crucified to the wall was not Andrew Van, but had been murdered by Andrew Van."

He lapsed into silence. Inspector Vaughn stirred uneasily, and District Attorney Isham said: "Yes, but how about the preceding murders? You said last night after we took Van in custody that the whole thing was clear to you from beginning to end as soon as you investigated the last murder. I can't see, even granting the argument about Van as the culprit in the last murder, how you can logically prove him to have been the murderer in the preceding crimes."

"My dear Isham," said Ellery, raising his eyebrows, "surely from here it's an open-and-shut case? Just a matter of analysis and common sense. Where did I stand at that point? I knew then that the missing man, the man who had left the limp-footprints, the murderer, was Andrew Van himself. But that he was the murderer was not sufficient. I could visualize a situation in which Van might have murdered a marauding Krosac, for example, purely in self-defense; in which case he could not under any circumstance be considered the murderer of the other three. But one fact stood out: Andrew Van had killed somebody and left the corpse of that somebody in his hut *dressed in the rags of Old Pete;* which is to say, dressed as himself. Then here was deception!

I knew then that the problem would be relatively simple. Who had been murdered in this last butchery?

"The body was not Van's, as I've already shown. The incongruous possibility that it might be Brad's I considered and discarded: Brad's body had been positively identified by his widow through the strawberry birthmark on his thigh. Purely for logical purposes I asked myself in the same vein if this last corpse was Megara's. No, it could not be; Dr. Temple had diagnosed Megara's ailment as a specific form of hernia, and Dr. Rumsen had found in the body strung up on the *Helene's* antenna-mast an identical hernia. Then the bodies taken to be Brad's and Megara's had been genuinely theirs. Only two other figures were involved in the case—discarding the remote possibility of a total stranger: they were Velja Krosac and Kling, Van's manservant."

Ellery paused for breath, then continued: "Could the body have been Krosac's? This would be the superficial conclusion. Yet if this was Krosac and Van had killed him, Van would have had a perfect plea of self-defense! All he would have had to do was call in the police, point to the body, and with the background of the case known and accepted, would have been freed without question. From Van's viewpoint, if he were an innocent man, such a procedure would be inevitable. The fact that he didn't do this proves that he *couldn't*. Why? Because the body was not Krosac's!

"If it wasn't Krosac, it must have been Kling, the only remaining possibility. But Kling was supposed to have been killed in the first crime, that murder in Arroyo at the crossroads seven months ago! Ah, but how did we know that first body was Kling's? Only through Van's own story, and Van is now proved a murderer, and a deceiver to boot. We have a perfect right to hold that any unsupported testimony given by Van is open to doubt, and that under the circumstances, since the facts point to it as the sole possibility left, the last corpse must have been Kling's."

Ellery went on rapidly. "See how everything fell neatly into place. With the last body Kling's, where the devil was Krosac? Brad's body and Megara's body are accounted for in their respective murders. Then the only person who logically could have been done to death in Arroyo seven months ago was Krosac himself? The 'devil' who for seven months has been sought by the police of forty-eight states and three nations. . . . No wonder no trace of him was found. He was dead all the time."

"Amazing beyond belief," said the Professor.

"Oh, you listen to him," chuckled Inspector Queen. "He's full of surprises like that."

A Negro porter appeared with a tray of iced drinks. They sipped in silence and stared out of the windows at the chameleon landscape. When the porter had gone, Ellery said: "Who killed Krosac in Arroyo? We lay down the fundamental qualification at once that, whoever committed that first murder, knew and utilized the history of the Tvars by leaving those T signs. Who had knowledge of the Tvar history? Van, Megara, Brad, and Krosac; for both Van and Megara told us that only the Tvar brothers and Krosac knew this back-history. Could Megara, then, have murdered Krosac in Arroyo and left the T signs? No; Megara is ruled out for purely geographical reasons—he was on the other side of the world. Brad? Impossible; Mrs. Brad had testified in the presence of persons who could deny it if it were untrue, that Brad had entertained the National Checker Champion *on Christmas Eve* and had played with him incessantly that night Krosac, the victim, is out, of course. Kling, the only other physical possibility? No, for besides being ignorant of the fatal T significances he has been repeatedly characterized as a weak-witted, moronic individual, who would be mentally incapable of executing such an intelligent crime. Then Krosac must have been murdered by Van, the only factor remaining who fills all the qualifications of the Krosac killer.

"And there it was. Van had murdered Krosac. How, under what circumstances? The story can be pieced together. He knew Krosac was after him and his brothers. In some way he discovered where Krosac was—traveling with the old lunatic, Stryker. He himself must have baited Krosac into coming to Arroyo by an anonymous letter. Krosac, seeing that his dream of vengeance was actually on the brink of fulfillment, swallowed the bait—not questioning the source of his information in his eagerness—and maneuvered the movements of his dupe, Stryker, so that the caravan came to the neighborhood of Arroyo. Then Krosac—Krosac himself, for the one and only time he actually appeared in the case as an active participant—hired the car from Croker, the Weirton garage-man, and had himself driven to the crossroads. Krosac carried no valise, you recall, in Weirton—significant when you consider that the murderer did carry a valise in the subsequent crimes. Why didn't Krosac carry a valise that first time—that only time, for him? Because he had no intention of making chop-meat out of his victim; he was probably a sane, if determined, avenger who would have been satisfied by the mere death, not the butchery, of his enemies. If Krosac's plan had succeeded, we should have found the body of the Arroyo schoolmaster, quite unmutilated, probably shot to death.

"But Van, the instigator of the entire chain of events, was lying in wait for the unsuspecting avenger, and killed him. Having already bound up and hidden the *living* body of the unfortunate Kling, Van proceeded to dress the dead Krosac in his own clothes, then decapitated the corpse, and so on and so on.

"It's evident that this was the plot of Van, or Andreja Tvar, from the beginning. A crime of years in the making. He planned the series of murders in such a way that they appeared to be the vengeance of a man, Krosac, who might very well have become crazed by years of brooding. He hid Kling away for the express purpose of using his body at the end to appear his own. Then his plot made it seem that Krosac, after killing an innocent man first, murdered two of the Tvar brothers and finally the third—a correction of the apparent error seven months before. As for Van, this last deceptive murder made it seem as if he, too, had been caught by the monomaniac's revenge; while he himself actually made an escape with his life's savings and the tidy sum which he had craftily managed to worm out of his brother Stephen. Meanwhile the police would search eternally for the phantasmal, long-dead Krosac. . . . The deceptions in the bodies were easily contrived; remember that Van himself hired Kling in the Pittsburgh orphan asylum, and so could select a servant whose physical appearance was similar to his own. As for the first deception—making Krosac's body seem to be his own—it was probably the similarity in physique between himself and Krosac—a similarity he discovered when he first located the Montenegrin, before sending the anonymous letter—that helped inspire the entire plot."

"You said something before," remarked the Inspector thoughtfully as he dipped again into his snuff box, "about having been on the right trail in the beginning but going off it. What did you mean?"

"And not only in the beginning," said Ellery mournfully. "It kept recurring throughout the case, and I kept throwing it aside. It wasn't sufficiently exclusive. . . . For, observe. Even in the very first murder one point stood out: the head of the corpse had been severed and taken away. Why? There seemed to be no answer then except the one of the killer's mania. Later we discovered the business of the Tvars and the surface meaning of the T's as the symbol of Krosac's vengeance. So, of course, we said the heads were lopped off to give the dead bodies the physical appearance of a capital T. But that old doubt . . .

"For after all there was an alternative explanation for the severing of the heads—a remarkable theory. That the body was made to resemble a T, that the other T elements—the crossroads, signpost, and scrawled T in the first crime; the totem post in the second; the antenna mast in the third (the scrawled T kept recurring, of course—in the fourth crime as well)—that all these conglomerate T elements had been strewn about the scenes of the crimes for only one purpose: *to cover up the fact that the heads had been cut off.* Other means of identification being unknown, the head, or face, is the most marked means of identifying a corpse. So, I said to myself, it is logically possible that these are the crimes not of a monomaniac with a T obsession, but of a perfectly lucid (if unbalanced) plotter *who cut off heads for the purpose of falsifying identification.* There seemed to be a confirmation of this: none of the heads were found. Why didn't the murderer leave the heads at the scenes of his crimes, or nearby, getting rid of them as soon as possible—which would be the natural impulse of a murderer, insane or not? The bodies would still form T's, still satisfying his T complex. But the heads were irretrievably gone. It seemed possible to me that all was not exactly as it should have been; yet because this was only a theory, and because all the other facts pointed so damningly to a crazed vendettist as the murderer, I kept discarding what was in reality the truth.

"But when, at the investigation of the fourth murder, I knew Andreja Tvar to be *deus ex machina,* the whole motif was plain. In his first murder—the killing of Krosac—he was forced to decapitate Krosac to prevent identification of the body and to permit an acceptance of the initial idea that the body was Van's, and the subsequent idea that the same body was Kling's. Yet merely to sever the heads would have been to invite suspicion and disaster; any investigator would have swung into the right track. So Van manufactured the brilliant and objectively irrational conception of maniac-conceived T's—T shapes of every description and with no possible interrelationship. These so confused the main issue that he was sure no one would grasp the real significance of the missing heads; which was, of course, to permit false identifications of the first and last bodies.

"Once started, naturally, he was forced to continue the vagaries of the nightmarish T's. He had to cut off Brad's head and Megara's head to maintain the continuity of a Krosac-T-phobia interpretation. At the last murder, of course, the head-severing served a genuine purpose again. It was a damnably clever plot, both psychologically and in execution."

"About the last murder," said Isham, swallowing. "Er—was it just my imagination, or was the set of footprints leading into the hut deeper than the set coming out?"

"Excellent, Mr. Isham!" cried Ellery. "I'm glad you brought that up—a good point. It served as a prime confirmation of the entire recapitulation of the case. I noticed, as you say, that the murderer's footprints approaching the shack were deeper than those departing from it. Explanation? A simple enough syllogism in logic. Why should the identical footprints in the identical earth be heavier in one case than the other? Because in one case the murderer was carrying something heavy; in the other he was not—the only argument which will logically explain the strange difference in weight of the same individual in approximately the same period. This fitted admirably. I knew that Kling's was the last body found. Where had Van kept Kling? Not in the hut; then it must have been somewhere in the vicinity. Constable Luden once said that the hills in West Virginia are riddled with natural caves; Van himself at one point said that he had found the abandoned hut while he was on a little *cave-exploring* expedition! (Probably with this very thought in mind!) So Van went to the cave where he had kept Kling a prisoner for long months, got Kling, and *carried* him into the hut. The rain must have stopped after Van left the hut to get Kling, but before he returned carrying Kling; it wiped out his outgoing footprints, but took the impression of his returning footprints. So the deep prints were made when he lugged Kling into the shack; and the shallower ones when he left the hut after the murder, for the last time."

"Why didn't he make Kling *walk* into the hut?" demanded Isham.

"Obviously because he intended from the first to leave a trail to a *limping* man, Krosac. By carrying Kling and limping he achieved the double end of getting the victim into the house and also making it appear that one man—Krosac—had entered. By limping away he clinched the illusion of Krosac's escape. He made only one mistake: he forgot that, weighted down, the impressions in soft earth would be deeper."

"I can't get it through my thick skull," muttered the Professor.

"The man must have been—must be—a genius. Perverted, and all that; but that plot of his required a brilliant brain."

"Why not?" asked Ellery dryly. "An educated man, with years in which to plan. But brilliant nevertheless. For example: Van was faced throughout with this problem: he had to arrange matters so that there was always a legitimate reason for Krosac to have done the very things that he himself, Van, had to do. That business of the pipe, for instance, and the turned-about rug with the bloodstain on it, and the deliberate leaving of Brad's note. I've already related to you *Krosac's* reason for wanting a delay in the discovery of the real scene of the crime—which was to have it discovered only when Megara arrived on the scene, so that Megara could seemingly lead Krosac to Van, who from the note Krosac supposedly learned was still alive.

"But Van, while he provided us with this ingenious *Krosac* reason, as the real murderer had even better reasons for causing the delay. If the police searched the library at once they would have found Brad's note—undoubtedly suggested to Brad by Van himself—long before Megara's return. They would know at once, then, that Van was still alive. If any slip-ups in Van's activities caused the police to suspect that Old Pete was Van, then Van's position became precarious. Suppose Megara never returned, died on shipboard somewhere. Then there would be no one left alive to confirm for the police the fact that Old Pete, or Van, was actually a brother of Brad and Megara. By causing the delay he insured a confirmation of his brotherhood at precisely the time Megara returned. On his unsupported word he might come under suspicion; with Megara to corroborate every statement he made, he looked like an innocent man.

"But why should he want to reappear on the scene at all? Ah, but here we see the real end achieved by his complicated arrangement of a delay until Megara returned. By contriving beforehand that Brad leave the note that instituted the whole chain of events which ended with the return to the scene of Andrew Van as an accredited brother of the Tvars, *Van clinched his inheritance.* By that I mean: Van could have made the police believe he actually had been murdered in the first crime, and could have remained legally dead thereafter, while he continued his plot of killing his brothers from the dark of the Krosac guise. But if he had remained legally dead, how was he to collect the money which Brad was leaving him by will? So he had to come back—*alive*. And at a time when Megara could confirm the fact that Van *was* a brother. In this way he collected the five thousand dollars due him with perfect safety. Incidentally, his constraint was commendable. Do you recall that Megara, touched by his 'frightened' brother's plight and his own conscience, actually offered Van an additional five thousand—and Van refused? He wanted only what was coming to him, he said. . . . Yes, a clever rogue. He knew that refusal would cement the illusion of the eremetic character he had so carefully built up.

"And finally, by means of the note and the story he told on his return to the scene, he prepared the police for an acceptance of his own second murder, since now they knew that a vendettist was on the trail of the Tvars and had discovered that he had made a mistake in the first murder. Devilish, really."

"Too deep for me," said Vaughn, shaking his head.

"That's what I've been up against ever since I became a father," murmured Inspector Queen. He sighed, and looked happily out of a window.

But Professor Yardley had no paternity to feed his ego, and he did not look even remotely happy. He was pulling at his short beard with powerful if abstracted fingers. "Granted all that," he said. "I'm an old hand at puzzles—chiefly ancient, I confess—so another example of man's ingenuity doesn't precisely amaze me. But one thing does. . . . You say Andreja Tvar, blood-brother to Stefan and Tomislav Tvar, partner in their family and personal iniquities, planned for years the extermination of these same brothers. Why? In the name of a merciless God, why?"

"I can see what's troubling you," said Ellery thoughtfully. "It's the horrible complexion of the crimes. Aside from motive, there's an explanation for *that*. You will grant two things? For the whole plan to be successful, it was necessary that Andreja Tvar do various unpleasant things—cut people's heads off (including his brothers'), nail dead hands and feet to makeshift crosses, spill an uncommon quantity of blood. . . . And second, that Andreja Tvar is a madman. He must be. If he was sane when he conceived this grotesque plan, he was insane when he began to carry it out. Then the whole thing clarifies—a madman spills oceans of the divine ichor, part of which comes from the bodies of his own brothers." Ellery stared at Yardley. "Wherein essentially does the difference lie? You were ready to accept Krosac as a madman—why not Van? The only distinction is the fine one of mutilating strangers as against mutilating brothers. But surely even your unprofessional knowledge of crime includes the sordid stories of husbands incinerating wives, of sisters chopping sisters into little bloody pieces, of sons battering out the brains of their mothers, of incest and degeneracy and every form of intra-familial crime. It's hard for a normal human being to understand; but you ask my father, or Inspector Vaughn—you'll hear true stories of atrocities that would make that beard of yours curl up in horror."

"True," said Yardley, "I can understand such things even on a basis of repressed sadism. But the motive, my boy, the motive? How the devil could you have known Van's motive if up to the fourth crime you yourself considered Velja Krosac the culprit?"

"The answer to which," smiled Ellery, "is that I didn't know Van's motive, and that I don't know it this minute. Actually, what difference does it make? A madman's motive—it may be as evanescent as air, as hard to crystallize as a pervert's. When I say madman, of course, I don't necessarily mean a raving maniac. Van, as you yourself saw, is apparently in full possession of his sanity. His mania is a quirk, a twist in his brain—in everything but one he is sane. My father or Inspector

Vaughn can quote you scores of cases in which murderers are apparently as normal as you or I, but actually are the most vicious psychopathic cases."

"I can tell you the motive," said Inspector Queen, sighing. "Too bad you weren't present last night, son, or you, Professor, while the Commissioner and Vaughn, here, had Van on the griddle. Most interesting examination I've ever attended. He almost had an epileptic fit, but finally he calmed down and told it—between the curses on the heads of his two brothers."

"Which, incidentally," remarked Isham, "he said he had sunk in the Sound with weights. The other heads he buried in the hills."

"His motive against his brother Tomis—Tomis—Tom," continued the old man, "was the usual thing—a woman. It seems that in the old country Van had loved a girl, but his brother Tom stole her away from him—the old story. That was Brad's first wife who, says Van, died through Brad's ill-treatment. Whether that's true or not we'll probably never know; but that's what he says."

"And against Megara?" asked Ellery. "He seemed a decent, if saturnine, sort of chap."

"Well, it's a little foggy," replied Vaughn, scowling at his cigar-tip. "It seems that Van was the youngest of the three brothers, and as such wasn't entitled to any of the old man Tvar's estate. Seems that Megara and Brad did Van out of his dough, or something. Megara was the eldest, and he controlled the old exchequer. And then they didn't give Van a cent of the money they stole from the Krosacs—told him he was too young, or something. Did he show them!" Vaughn grinned sardonically. "He couldn't squeal, of course, because he was in on it. But all this explains why, when the three brothers came to this country, Van broke away from the other two and kept by himself. Brad must have felt a little conscience-stricken, because he left Van that five grand. Fat lot of good it did both of 'em!"

They were all silent for a long time. The Twentieth Century thundered across New York State.

But Professor Yardley was a bulldog. He refused to loosen his grip on his perplexities. He sucked at his pipe for many minutes, turning something over in his mind. Then he said to Ellery: "Tell me this, O Omniscience. Do you believe in coincidence?"

Ellery sprawled on his spine and blew smoke-rings. "The Professor's in trouble. . . . No, I do not—not in murder, old chap."

"Then how do you explain the tormenting fact," demanded Yardley, his pipe waggling in rhythm, "that friend Stryker—another lunatic; heavens! there's a coincidence in itself!—appeared both on the scene of the Arroyo crime and on the scene of the subsequent crimes so far away? For, since Van is the culprit, poor old Ra-Harakht the sun-god must be innocent. . . . Isn't his presence in the second murder an appalling coincidence?"

"You're a valuable companion, Professor. I'm glad you brought that up," said Ellery briskly, sitting erect. "Of course it wasn't coincidence, as I explained inferentially the day we had our first talk in your friend's *selamlik*—how I love that word! Can't you see the logical inferences from the facts? Krosac was not a myth, he was reality. He learned that one of the Tvars was in Arroyo, West Virginia; it isn't fanciful to say, therefore, that the same 'anonymous' letter which Van wrote also told Krosac where the other Tvars were— Brad in Long Island, Megara living with Brad. There could be no hitch in Van's own plot; Van knew that Krosac was traveling about with Stryker in Illinois, or even farther west, and that since he had to pass through West Virginia on his way East, he would tackle the schoolmaster first.

"Very well. Krosac, we must believe, is himself, not altogether the fool. He is going to kill first the Tvar calling himself Andrew Van, and then the Tvars calling themselves Brad and Megara. He knows, too, that the murder of the poor 'unsuspecting' schoolmaster, Van, will raise a hullabaloo, and that it will be necessary for him to hide out. Conclusion: why not hide out in the vicinity of his second and third victims' dwelling? So he looks in the New York papers, finds old Ketcham's ad for the rental of Oyster Island, gets poor Stryker to agree to go there and start a sun cult, leases the Island by mail long in advance. . . . You see what happens? Krosac is himself murdered. Stryker, *le pauvre innocent*, aware of none of the nuances, hooks up with equally innocent Romaine, shows Romaine the lease to Oyster Island, and out they go. Which explains the presence of the sun worshipers and nudists on Oyster Island."

"By God," exclaimed the Inspector, "Van couldn't have arranged things better if he wanted Stryker a suspect!"

"And that reminds me," said the Professor thoughtfully. "That Egyptian business, Queen. You don't suggest that there was any preconceived plan in Van's mind to tie up old Stryker's Egyptology with the murders?"

"Thanks to you," said Ellery with a grin, "I suggest nothing of the sort. Come to think of it, I made something of an ass of myself on that 'Egyptian cross' peroration of mine, didn't I, Professor?" He sat up suddenly and slapped his thigh. "Dad, a perfectly cataclysmic thought!"

"Listen," snapped the Inspector, his good humor quite deserting him, "now that *I* come to think of it, you must have spent half the Queen bank account hiring airplanes and whatnot on that wild and woolly chase of yours up, down, and across country. Do I have to foot the bill?"

Ellery chuckled. "Let me apply logic to the problem. I have one of three courses open. The first is to charge my expenses to Nassau County." He looked at District Attorney Isham, who, started, began to speak, and finally sank back with an uncomfortable and rather silly grin on his stout face. "No, I see that—to say the least—is impracticable. The second: to stand the loss myself." He shook his head and pursed his lips. "No, that's much too philanthropic. . . . I told you I had a cataclysmic thought."

"Well," grumbled Inspector Vaughn, "if you can't put it down on a swindle sheet, and you won't stand it yourself, I'll be damned if I see how—"

"My dear Inspector," drawled Ellery, "I'll write a book about it, call it as a memento of my sometimes impulsive erudition *The Egyptian Cross Mystery,* and let the public pay for it!"

> *Si finis bonus est,*
> *Totum bonum erit.*
> —GESTA ROMANORUM

DISCUSSION QUESTIONS

- At the moment of the "Challenge to the Reader," were you able to predict any part of the solution to the case?

- After learning the solution, were there any clues you realized you had missed?

- Did any aspects of the plot date the story? If so, which ones?

- Would the story be different if it were set in the present day? If so, how?

- What role did the setting play in the narrative?

- If you were one of the main characters, would you have acted differently at any point in the story?

- Did you identify with any of the characters? If so, who?

- Did this novel remind you of anything else you've read? If so, what?

- If you've read other Ellery Queen novels, how does this compare with what you've read?

AMERICAN MYSTERY CLASSICS *from*

PENZLER PUBLISHERS

Available now
in hardcover and paperback: